Charlene Sands is a *USA TODAY* bestselling author of more than forty romance novels. She writes sensual contemporary romances and stories of the Old West. When not writing, Charlene enjoys sunny Pacific beaches, great coffee, reading books from her favourite authors and spending time with her family. You can find her on Facebook and Twitter, write to her at PO Box 4883, West Hills, CA 91308, or sign up for her newsletter for fun blogs and ongoing contests at charlenesands.com

Karen Booth is a Midwestern girl transplanted to the South, raised on eighties music and repeated readings of *Forever...* by Judy Blume. When she takes a break from the art of romance, she's listening to music with her nearly grown kids or sweet-talking her husband into making her a cocktail. Learn more about Karen at karenbooth.net

TEXAN FOR THE TAKING

CHARLENE SANDS

TEMPTED BY SCANDAL

KAREN BOOTH

FSC

Paper from
responsible sources

FSC C007454

This book is produced from independently certified FSC™
paper to ensure responsible forest management.

For more information visit: www.harpercollins.co.uk/green

Printed and bound in Spain
by CPI, Barcelona

MILLS & BOON

First Published in Great Britain 2019
by Mills & Boon, an imprint of HarperCollinsPublishers,
1 London Bridge Street, London, SE1 9GF

Texan for the The Taking © 2019 Charlene Swink
Tempted by Scandal © 2019 Harlequin Books S.A.

Special thanks and acknowledgement are given to Karen Booth for her contribution to the Dynasties: Secrets of the A-List series.

ISBN: 978-0-263-27180-5

0519

MIX

TEXAN FOR THE TAKING

CHARLENE SANDS

To my sister, Carol, and her hubby, Bill,
two of the nicest people on earth.
Thanks for your love and support
and always being there for us!

And to Eric, Whitney, Reese and Quinn,
and Angi and Zane, my nieces and nephews
who make our family even more special!

One

Of course *he* had to be here.

Mason Boone.

Drea MacDonald had avoided him all these years, but there was no hope for it now. She had to deal with him on a strictly professional level. She liked to think she'd moved beyond what had happened, had moved way beyond *him*, but how could that be? Something that profound in her life, something that had scarred her so permanently, wasn't easily forgotten.

Mason pressed his tall frame against the back wall of the hospital conference room, arms folded, watching her through intense coal-black eyes. She couldn't ignore him. He was a presence in the room; a tall, dreadfully handsome man, dressed impeccably in a dark suit, who commanded respect and exuded confidence.

As a young girl, all those traits had lured her in. But he'd rejected her without a second thought.

Her best bet would be to treat him with indifference, to give him a nod and get on with her business. He didn't have to know the pain he'd caused her. He didn't have to see the hurt look in her eyes or the flush of her skin. It would take an award-winning performance, but she was up to the task. After all, she'd imagined this moment in her head fifty times, if not more.

Her heart sat heavy in her chest because she wasn't the only one who had lost something precious. She wasn't the only one who'd been deeply scarred. Mason had, too. He'd lost his wife and unborn child nearly two years ago. His loss and grief only contributed to the tremendous guilt she felt for disliking him so. He had the town's support. Everyone was sympathetic to his loss. It was hard to hate a guy everyone else rallied around. Guilt ate away at her even though she had every right to hold a grudge.

She stood at the head of the conference table, just finishing up her presentation. "And thanks to the generosity of Mason Boone and his family," she said, grinding her teeth as she gave him praise, "we'll hold our multifaceted weekend fund-raiser at Rising Springs Ranch. Our goal, two million dollars."

The doctors, hospital administrators and committee members overseeing the fund-raiser gazed at each other, raising skeptical brows. It was a tall order, true, but she had always banked her reputation on fulfilling her goals. And this part of Texas was rich with donors of cold hard cash.

"It's doable," said an assured voice from the back of the room.

All heads swiveled to Mason Boone. His family had founded the Texas town of Boone Springs decades ago, and the hospital had recently changed names from County Memorial to Boone County Memorial. The Boone family and their kin practically owned the entire town. Well, they owned the best parts, so when a Boone spoke, people listened.

"It's very doable, if we're smart," Drea persisted, again avoiding Mason's dark eyes. "And I intend to be…very smart."

"Thatta girl," gray-haired Dr. Keystone said. "We trust you, Andrea. You're one of our own."

"Thank you, Doctor. I appreciate your support. Together, we'll make this work."

She smiled, feeling powerful in her black suit and three-inch cherry-red heels. She wore her long, dark cocoa hair up in a sleek, practical style. She meant business.

Landing this job at the hospital served many purposes. Nailing it would all but guarantee her promotion to vice president at Solutions Inc., the consulting and events planning firm she worked for in New York. But more importantly, she wanted to help the community where she'd grown up by raising funds for a much-needed cardiac wing, to honor her mother, who'd died of heart failure. And she also wanted to reconnect with her ailing father. Unfortunately, that meant living in the cottage the Boones had gifted Drew MacDonald after practically stealing Thundering Hills Ranch out from under him. Her father's acceptance of the living arrangements irritated her to this day. How could he be okay with their charity, while Drea's life had been snatched right out from under her as a young girl when the Boones took over Thundering Hills? She'd lost her home, too, but her father hadn't seemed to notice how much that had disrupted her life.

After the meeting, as Drea collected her papers, carefully placing them in her briefcase, she heard footsteps approaching and held her breath.

"Nice job, Drea."

That deep confident voice unsettled her. The timbre,

the tone, the way Mason said her name—memories came rushing back, tilting her world upside down. *God.* Why was he heading this committee? Deep in her belly, she knew. He'd lost his pregnant wife to heart disease. Drea couldn't really fault him for wanting to be involved; she had similar reasons for being here. Yet, even knowing the pain he'd recently endured, seeing him in the flesh for the first time in years curdled her stomach. She resented the Boones, but him most of all.

Mason stood facing her, his eyes boring in, and finally, because she felt defiant and fearless, she stared back and gave him her best aloof smile. "Thank you."

Twelve years had only given his good looks a more rugged edge. She took in the sharp angle of his jaw, the facial scruff that hadn't been there before, the length of his hair, whipped back and shining like black ink. None of it mattered. She was merely observing. She'd turned off all her buttons, leaving him none to push anymore.

"You look good," he said.

The compliment slid off her back.

"Drew will be glad to have you home."

"It's temporary," she said, closing the clasp on her briefcase.

"Still, it'll be good for him."

She looked away. What about what was good for her? What about all those days and nights when she'd had to be the adult because her father was passed out drunk on the floor? What about the dinners he'd never cooked, the clothes he'd never washed? What about a twelve-year-old kid having to baby her own father? And what about the heartsick motherless girl who'd desperately needed…love?

"We'll see."

"You haven't been home yet?"

She shook her head. "No, I came here straight from the airport."

"Drea?"

She couldn't look at him, even though there was something pleading in the way he'd said her name. Instead, she continued fiddling with the closure on her case.

"It's good to have you home," he said finally.

Chin down, she nodded. "I have a job to do."

"Yeah, about that. We should probably coordinate on the events you have planned. We could look at them over dinner one night or—"

"No." Her voice was sharper than she'd intended. So much for being professional. He was staring at her like she'd lost her mind. Maybe she had, thinking she could come home in hopes of doing something good for the community, something to honor her deceased mother, even if it meant working alongside Mason. Were her emotions so tangled up that she couldn't separate her professional life from her private one?

Goodness, but she had to. She'd committed to this fundraising campaign. She was being paid to see it through. And she had to remind herself over and over that she was doing this to honor her mother. It was time she came home. At least temporarily.

"No?" Mason narrowed his eyes.

"I mean, I'll email you. I really am very busy, Mason. I have a lot on my mind today."

She gave him a plastic smile, one he immediately picked up on as bullshit. He nodded. "Yeah, I get it." His mouth curled in a frown and there was an edge of annoyance in his voice now. *Ha!* He had no right being annoyed with her. Not when the last time she'd been with him, he'd treated her like dirt.

He slipped a business card into her hand, his long lean

fingers skimming over her knuckles. Immediately her heart beat faster, her nerves jumped. The shock of his brief, warm touch strummed through her body. "Email me when you find time. We have exactly one month to pull this off."

His urgency wasn't lost on her. This was as important to him as it was to her. They had that in common. Both wanted a special cardiac wing of the hospital built in Boone Springs. But all of a sudden one month in Texas seemed like an eternity.

Not to mention she'd be living at the cottage on Rising Springs Ranch again.

On Mason's home turf.

"Yum, this is just as delish as I remembered." Drea swallowed a big hunk of her Chocolate Explosion cupcake. Unladylike, but Katie Rodgers, her bestie from childhood and owner of the bakery, would expect no less.

Her friend laughed and removed her apron. She put the Katie's Kupcakes is Klosed sign on the door and joined Drea at the café table.

"You do not disappoint," Drea said. "And you remembered my favorite."

"Of course I did. Can't forget all those times you'd come over and we'd bake up a batch. We were what, ten at the time?"

"Yeah, but ours never came close to these marvels you crank out at four in the morning. Gosh, you always knew what you wanted to do with your life. I'm so proud of everything you've accomplished, Katie. I bet you've got all of Boone Springs wrapped around your sugary fingers, with lines out the door in the morning."

"I have no complaints," she replied. "Business is good." She sighed sweetly. "It's great to have you back in town. I've missed you."

Drea grabbed Katie's hand and squeezed. "I've missed you, too. I couldn't drive out to Rising Springs without seeing you first."

"I'm glad you did. Only I wish it wasn't temporary. I kinda like seeing you in person instead of on Facetime."

"Well, let's try to make the most of my stay here. We're gonna both be busy, but we have to make a pact to see each other a few times a week," Drea said.

"Pinkie promise?" Katie curled her last digit, and they linked fingers just like they had when they were kids.

"Pinkie promise."

"Good, then it's settled." Katie began to rise. "Would you like a cup of coffee to wash down the cupcake? I could brew up a fresh pot."

"When did your cupcakes ever need washing down?" She smiled. "No thanks. Any more coffee today and I swear I'll float away. Let's just talk."

Katie smiled and plunked back into her seat. "Okay. So, you're working on the hospital fund-raiser."

She nodded.

"With Mason?"

"Yeah, which is the major drawback to my coming home. I have to make the fund-raiser my high priority, so I'm enduring the Boones for as long as it takes."

"I get that it's hard for you, Drea. I really do. It was hard on Mason, too, losing Larissa and the baby. From what I hear, he's only just starting to come out of his grief."

"It's a tragedy. But let's not talk about the Boones. Because if we do, then I'll have to ask you about Lucas."

Katie's eyes rounded. "Lucas? We're just friends. If that anymore."

"Uh-huh. So you say."

"For heaven's sake, he was engaged to my sister. And

he broke Shelly's heart when he went off and joined the Marines."

"But I hear he's back now." Drea took another bite of cupcake, certain she'd die from an overdose of decadence.

"Don't remind me. Shelly still hasn't healed from him running out on her like that. It was such a shock. Luke seemed true blue. After the breakup, Shelly hit some rough patches. Mom's convinced it's all Luke's fault. I mean, it sounded more like something Risk would do. Not Luke."

River "Risk" Boone, heartthrob and one-time famous rodeo rider, was the player in the Boone family.

"Yeah, well, we can't forget he's a Boone. It's part of his DNA," Drea said.

Katie's right brow rose and she shook her head. "So, after all these years you haven't gotten over it, either?"

"Over what? The fact that the Boones preyed on my father's grief and then stole Thundering Hills out from under him? Our families had been friends for years, but as soon as my dad hit a rough patch, the Boones swooped in, stole our ranch and we were reduced to living at the cottage on Boone property. They gave Dad a pity job as caretaker. Then there's Mason and all that he put me through... Oh, never mind. I don't want to rehash it." She waved her hand, ending her rant.

Katie gave her a serious knowing look. But Katie didn't know everything. Drea hadn't told her best friend what had happened after her debacle with Mason. How she ran into the arms of the first willing man and gave up her virginity. How she'd gotten pregnant and lost her baby. It had been the worst time of her life.

"I guess we need to put the past behind us, Drea. That's what I keep telling my sister."

"Yeah, easier said than done sometimes."

She was through talking about the Boones. She polished off the cupcake and licked the frosting from her fingers, closing her eyes as she relished every last morsel of goodness. "Mmm."

"So, I hear your dad is struggling a bit. The fall he took last week was pretty bad. When I heard about it, I stopped by his place with a batch of apricot thumbprints and half a dozen cupcakes."

"Ahh, you're the best. He loves your thumbprint cookies. Thanks for checking in on him."

"He's very excited to have you home."

"I know." She couldn't say too much; her emotions were curled up in a knot about going home to Drew MacDonald. Maybe that's why she was procrastinating. She'd missed her father, and she loved him. But she was a realist. Her dad would never win a Father of the Year award. Hard fact, but true.

"He's changed, Drea. He's trying very hard."

She sighed. "I'll believe it when I see it." She glanced at her watch. "Which is what I should do just about now. I hate to go, but I've really gotta get on the road."

"Will you text me later?"

"Of course."

They both stood and then Katie went behind the counter. "Just a sec. I'm not sending you home empty-handed." She packed up a white box with goodies and sealed it with a pastel pink Katie's Kupcakes sticker. "Here you go," she said, handing over the box. "Welcome home."

"Thanks, friend. My hips will never be the same."

"Your hips and my thighs. We're all doomed."

Drea chuckled and kissed Katie on the cheek. "At least we'll both go down together."

After she excited the shop, a sense of real doom flashed through her system.

She couldn't procrastinate any longer.

It was time to go to the place she'd never considered home.

Drea parked her car in front of her father's house just as the autumn sun was setting. Splashes of deep pink and purple painted the sky overhead. She'd forgotten the stunning sunsets in this part of Texas. How many years had it been since she'd seen a horizon so rich and vibrant? These wide-open spaces were tailor-made for such amazing spectacles. Texas was known for doing things large and the sight brought a little peace to her jittery heart.

Lordy be.

She chuckled at the slang that had come back to her after crossing state lines.

But she wasn't that Texas girl any longer.

She gazed toward the cornflower-blue cottage trimmed in white, and saw her father sitting in a rocking chair on the front deck. As soon as he spotted her, he made an attempt to rise. His face turned a shade of red, not from pain, she assumed, but from frustration as he faltered and slid back down onto the seat. On his next try, he pulled himself up and leaned against a post. His hair was lighter gray than she remembered, his body chunkier, but he was still a handsome man, and there was a spark in his green eyes as he waved to her.

She waved back, holding her breath. She reminded herself this wasn't the same drunken man who'd given up on life after her mother died. He was trying to be a good father. He'd honed his skills on a smartphone so he could send her text messages. He called her every week to talk. He never once made her feel guilty for not coming to visit. He never once asked her to give up her adult life to be with him. But she'd felt bad anyway.

She got out of the car and retrieved her luggage from the trunk. As she approached, wheeling her suitcase behind her, a big smile surfaced on his ruddy face, making him look ten years younger than his sixty-five years.

"Hi, Daddy," she said. *Wow.* Whatever possessed her to call him that? She hadn't referred to him that way since she was a kid.

"Hey there, my girl. Welcome home."

As far as she was concerned, Thundering Hills, a large parcel of land to the west that was now incorporated into Rising Springs, had been her true home. Before the Boones got their hands on it. "Thank you."

She climbed the steps to come face-to-face with her father. He was pale and moving slowly but the light in his eyes was bright with excitement.

He opened his arms and took a step toward her, a shadow of fear crossing his face for a moment. He didn't trust that she'd embrace him. There'd been so many times in her young life when she'd needed a hug from him or a kind word, and he hadn't been there. For right now, she put that behind her. Well, as much as she could hope to. That kind of rejection was hard to forget.

She stepped into his arms and gave him a brief hug before backing away.

"It's good to see you, Drea. You look so pretty, just like your mama. You've been well?"

"Yes, I've been well. How about you, Dad?"

"Ah, I'm doing just fine."

She didn't believe him. He'd taken a fall and had downplayed it to her when she'd questioned him over the phone. He'd blamed it on a bad case of arthritis, but according to Katie he'd refused to go to the doctor for a health screening.

Back in the day, her father would lose his balance and crumble in a drunken stupor a few times a day. Now he probably feared she wouldn't believe he was clean and sober if he admitted to falling down the steps.

God, she hoped he wasn't backsliding. Not after all this time.

"We have a lot to catch up on, girl."

"Yes, we do. Let's go inside. I'll make us some dinner."

Her father's eyes brightened. "It's already done. I made your favorite, pot roast and red potatoes. I even attempted your mama's special biscuits."

"You did?" Nobody made homemade biscuits like her mother. Maybe Katie was right. Maybe her father was really trying. She could count on her fingers and toes how many meals her father had actually cooked for her as a child.

"Well, let's go inside and try them out," she said. "I'm starving."

"Sounds good to me. My stomach's been growling. But mostly I'm just pleased to have my little girl back home."

She was twenty-nine years old, hardly a little girl anymore, but she was here now and she'd have to deal with old memories and the pain those reminders evoked.

She forged into the house, wheeling her suitcase easily as her father followed behind her.

The next evening, Drea breathed a sigh of relief as she arrived back at the cottage after a very productive Mason-free day at the hospital. All day long she'd held her breath, thinking she'd run into him and have to make nice for appearance's sake, but he was a no-show and she was glad of the things she'd accomplished without having to deal with him. She'd gone over some important aspects of the fund-raiser with the supervisors of various departments and had called to confirm donors for the art sale. The rest of the event details involved the Boones and she had no other option than to deal with Mason on that.

She walked into her bedroom, left untouched since she'd lived here, and shed her business suit and high heels for a comfy pair of washed out jeans and an I ♥ New York T-shirt she'd received for running a 5K race. After pulling her hair up in a ponytail, she washed her face and brushed her teeth. Man oh man, she thought, glancing in the mirror. There was no denying she looked like a schoolgirl again. It was amazing how a little makeup and a sleek hairstyle could transform her appearance. But inside, she was still that unsure, guarded little girl.

At least it wasn't horrible living here, and her father was making a gold-star effort on her behalf. She was trying like hell to keep an open mind, trying to put the past behind her, but her scars ran deep and it wasn't easy to forgive and forget all she'd gone through here in Boone Springs. Not a day went by that she didn't think about the baby she'd lost, about the child she would never know. It wasn't Mason's baby, yet she'd blamed him for rejecting her, destroying her confidence and causing her to run into the arms of the first man who'd showed interest in her.

A knock at her bedroom door shook her out of her thoughts. "Drea, can I speak to you?"

She opened the door and glanced at her father. Beyond him, down the hall, she saw four men standing in the parlor. What were Mason and Risk Boone doing here? The ranch foreman, Joe Buckley, and Dwayne, one of the crew, were also there. "Sure. What's going on?"

Her father shook his head, his expression contrite. "I forgot about the poker game. We, uh, the boys usually come here on Tuesday nights. I'm sorry, Drea. I guess I've been so wrapped up in you being home, it slipped my mind. Should I send them away?"

"No, Dad. Of course not. I don't want my being here disrupting your routine." The irony was that as a kid, she'd always felt like a disruption in his life. She got in the way of his drinking.

"They brought dinner. Pizza from Villa Antonio. Will you come out and eat with us?"

What could she say? She liked Joe; he'd always been decent to her, and Dwayne was her age. They'd gone to school together. She didn't like breaking bread with the Boones, but she was hungry and she couldn't hide out in her room all night. "I suppose I can do that."

She walked into the parlor with her father and the men took off their hats. Everyone said hello but Mason. Hat in hand, he gave her a long stare and nodded.

"You still breaking hearts in New York, Drea?" Risk asked, his wide smile almost infectious. Risk was a charmer and she'd always been a little wary of him. He was too smooth for her liking.

"I don't know about that, but I like to think I'm killing it in other ways."

"I bet you are."

"Good to see you, Drea. You're looking well," Joe said. "It's been a while."

"Yeah, it has," she said. "How's Mary Lou?"

"Doing fine."

"Please tell her hello for me."

"Will do," he said, smiling.

"Hey, Drea," Dwayne said. "Missed you at the ten-year reunion."

"I know. I just couldn't get away, but Katie caught me up to speed on everyone. Congrats, I heard you just had a baby."

"We did. Heather and I named him Benjamin, after my father." He took out his phone and showed her a picture of his son.

"He's precious."

"We think so, too. Thanks."

"So you and Mason are gonna work together on the fund-raiser." Risk shifted his glance from her to his brother, a twinkle in his eye. Was he trying to cause trouble, or just being Risk? She didn't know how much his family knew about her history with Mason. True, it was old news. But not for her.

"That's the plan," Mason said, eyeballing her. "After the game tonight, I'd like to talk to you about it."

"We don't usually finish up too late," her father interjected. "It's a workday for everyone tomorrow."

"Okay, fine." She'd just have to put on her big girl panties. She couldn't postpone it any longer. She'd gotten herself into this and she had a job to do.

Mason gave her a nod and they all sat down at the dining room table. As she chewed her pizza and drank iced tea, every so often she'd steal a glance Mason's way, and each time, his coal-black eyes were on her, as if she was the only person in the room. He made her jumpy. She didn't like it one bit, and she fought the feeling.

But there'd always been *something* between her and Mason. Well, maybe it was all one-sided. At age seventeen her feelings had started out as hero worship for a guy six years older than her and had grown from there. Until he'd shot her down and humiliated her.

After dinner, the men got serious about poker, and Drea busied herself cleaning the kitchen, collecting and trashing pizza boxes and setting the coffeemaker timer to brew a dark rich roast in two hours. The guys had brought beer, something Drea knew her father had insisted upon. He wasn't going to spoil their night because he had a drinking problem. A tall glass of iced tea sat in front of her dad and he seemed fine with it.

Three years clean and sober.

God, she hoped the worst was behind him now. But there was always doubt in her mind, and maybe her father was trying to make a point by showing her he was a changed man.

During the game, she disappeared into her room and flipped open her laptop. She stared at the screensaver, a golden Hawaiian sunrise, wishing she could jump right into the picture.

But no, that wasn't going to ever happen. Was that kind of serenity even real?

She clicked open her spreadsheet and calendar and got busy working on items for the fund-raiser. There were dozens of moving parts for the big push and she was beginning to make headway.

After twenty minutes or so, she was totally engrossed in her work. A knock at her door broke her concentration and she jumped.

It wasn't her father's light rapping. No, she knew who it was. *Ugh.* She got up and yanked open the door, ready to face Mason.

Immediately the woodsy scent of his cologne wafted to her as she looked into his dark eyes. It was hard to miss the broad expanse of his chest as he braced his arms against her doorjamb, making her feel slightly trapped. "Hi," he said.

She'd expected him to be demanding, to insist they get to work, to pressure her. But that one word, spoken softly, surprised her and her defenses went up. "Mason."

"I, uh, I know it's late, but we should probably talk. If that's okay with you?"

It wasn't late. It was barely nine thirty. On really busy days, she'd often work until midnight. But things in Boone Springs were different than the big city. The pace was slower, the nights shorter, and the mornings came earlier. "It's fine."

"It's a nice night. Why don't you grab a jacket and meet me out back?"

She blinked. She didn't want to be alone with Mason on a moonlit night, but she wasn't about to show fear.

"Your dad's probably tired. I wouldn't want to keep him up with our chatter," he explained.

"Right," she said. "Give me a minute and I'll meet you outside."

Mason nodded and took his leave.

Drea shut the door and leaned against it, her pulse pounding in her ears.

Memories flashed through her mind, but she halted them in their tracks. She had a job to do. She was vying for a vice president position at Solutions Inc. A lot was riding on her communication and marketing skills with this fund-raiser.

And she couldn't allow Mason Boone to get in her way.

The screen door opened and Drea stepped outside. Mason shot up from his seat the second he glimpsed her. Her boots clicked on the deck as she approached. She was wearing jeans and a pretty pink blouse underneath a black leather jacket. Her hair was pulled back in a ponytail, with a few wavy strands falling loose, caressing her cheeks. She looked soft and pretty, so different than the uptight, buttoned-to-the-neck woman he'd met in the committee room yesterday.

Years ago, he'd been attracted to her for a short time, until rational sense had kicked in and he'd backed off from the hell storm it would create. At seventeen, Andrea Mac-Donald had looked at him with adoring eyes and his ego had taken flight. But she was Drew's daughter, a mixed-up girl yearning for affection. Affection that couldn't come from Mason. He'd been twenty-three, six years older than her, and supposedly wiser. He would've only screwed her up more.

Now, he wanted to tell her she had nothing to fear from him, that he was dead inside and had been for a couple years, ever since Larissa died. But that was assuming too much. Maybe her coolness wasn't necessarily aimed at him. Maybe she'd changed from that sweet, caring, innocent girl she'd been to someone he didn't know, didn't recognize. Lord knew, he'd changed over the years as well, and he was simply here to work alongside her. The past was the past and maybe it was better to let it alone.

"Brought you some coffee," he said, grabbing for the cup on the wicker table beside him.

She smiled, apparently surprised at the gesture. "Thanks."

"I didn't know how you like it."

"Black is fine."

He handed it to her, their fingers brushing in the transfer, and he gazed into her pretty eyes. She lowered her lids and looked away. Those sage-green eyes were the same as Drew's, and her long, lustrous dark hair and olive skin were all her mother, Maria. Drea was a striking mix of Irish and Latina.

"You want to have a seat?" He gestured toward the bench he'd been sitting on. He could feel her reluctance, sensing she'd rather have a root canal than sit with him, but she finally perched on one end. He sat as far away from her as possible, which was all of twenty-four inches, if that.

"So, you still resent all the Boones?" he asked on impulse. The question had been bugging him since he'd laid eyes on her yesterday.

Her head snapped up and coffee sloshed in her cup. Luckily, it didn't spill onto her hand. He would've never forgiven himself for that.

"Some more than others." Her eyes narrowed on him and suddenly she wasn't looking quite so pretty anymore.

"We tried to help your father, Drea. He was in desperate need and—"

"I know the story your family tells. I don't need to hear it from you."

"Maybe you do. Maybe that's the only way this is going to work between me and you."

"So, I'm supposed to forget all about the fact that when my father came to yours, asking for help with Thundering Hills, asking for a loan to tide us over for a few months, he was flat-out refused. Our families had been friends for years. And then, the next thing I know our land was bought out from under us and all we got were crumbs. Dad had to swallow his pride and take a job on Rising Springs. I had to move off our land to come live in this little cottage. We lost everything."

"That's not the way it happened, Drea."

"That's the way I see it, Mason. Total betrayal."

"Your dad…"

"What? What about my dad? He took to drinking heavily after mom died and…he's never been the same."

Mason didn't have the heart to tell Drea the truth. If Drew hadn't after all these years, then it wasn't his place to tell her that her little girl's perception of what happened had been all wrong. Drew had made Mason's father promise not to reveal details of the deal. Since both of Mason's folks were gone now, victims of a small plane crash years ago, he felt it was up to him to see that vow was upheld. If Drew wasn't willing to set his daughter straight, Mason surely wasn't going to do it.

"Drew's doing real good now." It was all he would say on the matter.

"So everyone in Boone Springs is telling me."

Mason didn't understand her. He was just barely coming out of his own grief, and related to how Drew MacDonald had been in the same situation, losing his wife the way he had, so unexpectedly. Mason hadn't taken to drinking the way Drew had, but everyone coped with heartache differently. He wasn't excusing Drew's bad behavior, but he knew what the man had been feeling.

Mason shook his head. "Aren't you glad he's getting better?"

"Of course I am. If it's the real thing this time." Her voice lowered to a whisper. "I've been disappointed before."

Mason ran his hand down his face. "I know it wasn't easy on you, Drea."

She shook her head, and he took in how her long hair flowed in natural waves down her back. "You know nothing about me, Mason."

He met her sad green eyes and something shifted in his heart. She tried to talk tough, but she wore her pain on her sleeve and her vulnerability grabbed him. "I know more than you think."

"That's a Boone for you, claiming to know every—"

He pressed two fingers to her lips, quieting her tirade. "Shh, Drea."

Her eyes snapped to his.

He couldn't believe he'd done it, touched her this way. But grazing her soft lips, looking into those defiant eyes was like a live wire sparking and jolting inside the dead parts of him. He felt alive for the first time in years. It was heady and he wanted more. He wanted to hold on to that spark that told him he was a living, breathing man.

Sliding his fingers off her mouth, he cradled her face, his thumb circling her cheek, strands of her hair caressing the back of his hand.

"Mason, are you crazy?" she whispered, yet the look in her eyes told him she was thinking something different.

"Maybe."

"You're not going to—"

"Yes, I think I am."

He put his mouth to hers and tasted her sweetness, the plump ripe lips that were meant to be kissed. Sensation flooded him. He remembered her. As a teen. A girl who'd needed affection, and he'd given it to her without question, until the night that she'd bared her soul to him and offered her body.

He'd had to turn her away.

Any decent man would have.

But she wasn't a kid anymore. And it was good, so damn good that instant guilt flooded him. His heart belonged to another and always would. That jolt of life he felt worried him and scared him silly. It was as if he was losing his wife all over again. He hadn't done anything this impulsive in years, much less with Drea, the very last woman on earth he should be kissing.

Two

Drea's mouth trembled as Mason brushed his lips over hers. She couldn't believe this was happening. She didn't want this. She didn't want him, even though his lips were firm and delicious, scented by coffee and the fresh night air.

He grabbed her upper arms, demanding more of the kiss. Her heartbeats raced, her body warmed and a sudden realization dawned. Whatever she and Mason had between them hadn't completely disappeared. It was real and hot and almost too out of control, but no, she couldn't do this. In the past, he'd caused her to do crazy, impulsive things. Her infatuation with him had almost ruined her life and she couldn't forget that. Ever. She squeezed her eyes tight, laid her hand flat on his chest and pushed as hard as she could.

He reared back, startled. "Damn, Drea."

"Mason, I don't know what you think you were doing—"

"The same thing you were. Kissing."

"I didn't w*ant* to kiss you." She'd wanted to slap his face, but…she wasn't a drama queen. The push sent the same message.

"I didn't want to kiss you, either. Okay, I did, but only in the moment."

"I thought you were a grieving widower." Her hand flew to her mouth, but the damage was done. She couldn't take it back.

He stared at her, his eyes losing their brightness. "I am," he said quietly.

Then why kiss her? "I'm…confused, trying to make sense of this. It was…unexpected."

"I know. For me, too."

She folded her arms over her chest, her lips slightly bruised from his kiss. "You had no right."

"I know that, too."

"Why did you?" She searched his eyes, saw raw emotion there.

"I, uh… You want honesty?"

"Always."

He ran his hand down his face again, stroked his chin. "I felt something. Something that wasn't dead inside me. Something that came to life the second I touched you, and I wanted to continue feeling it, even for a few more seconds."

"Oh, wow." She understood. Sort of. He'd been happily married with a baby on the way. And suddenly, it had all been taken away. She'd known that kind of loss, too, impetuously running into the arms of the first man she'd met after Mason rejected her, and getting pregnant. She'd lost that child in a miscarriage and walked away from Brad Williamson, the man who'd loved her. That year had been the hardest in her life.

And now what shocked her the most about all this was

that *she'd* been the one to make Mason feel something. How was that possible? "Why…me?"

He smiled crookedly and shook his head. "I have no idea."

"Well, that's honest."

"Why did you kiss me back?"

She wasn't going there. She wouldn't tell him how much he'd once meant to her. How painful it had been when she was seventeen. And how much she resented him now because he'd made her feel something, too. "You're a good kisser."

"That's it?"

"Of course that's it. I haven't dated in a while and…"

"Okay, I get it." He blew out a breath and jammed his fingers into his hair. He seemed frustrated and a little bit angry. "Listen, let's forget this ever happened."

"Amen to that. So what now?"

"Now we do what we came out here to do. Talk about the fund-raiser."

"Okay, I guess we have no choice."

Mason frowned and she felt a little triumphant. At least he wouldn't try to kiss her again. That would be a big mistake on his part, and an even a bigger mistake for her. As long as he kept his hands off her, she'd be fine. She took a big breath, willing her racing heart to calm down.

"So, where do we begin?" he asked.

"With me telling you my ideas and you thinking they're all incredible."

Half an hour later, Mason said good-night to Drea in the kitchen and waited until she headed off to her room, before grabbing another cup of coffee.

"You having more?" Drew said, coming in from the parlor.

"Yeah, if that's okay. We didn't disturb you. Did we?"

"Nah, not tired enough to sleep. Thought I'd get some coffee and sit for a while. I think I'll join you."

Mason knew how the older man liked his coffee. He poured him a cup, stirred in two lumps of sugar and handed it to him. Drew had a sweet tooth but it was harmless enough, a substitute for alcohol perhaps. "Actually, I was hoping to talk to you for a bit," Mason said. "If you're up to it."

"Winning always perks me right up. I figure I'm good for a few more minutes while I drink this mud. You and Drea were out there awhile. Everything good between you two?" he asked.

Mason had kissed Drea. He wasn't sure if he'd ever forget the spark that had lit him up inside like fireworks on the Fourth of July. So no, everything was not good. Drea didn't like him much, and he, well, he was feeling a hefty dose of guilt now, like he'd cheated on his wife. That gnawing ache wasn't going away and he doubted he'd get much sleep tonight. "Yeah, everything's fine. She's a smart woman. She's focused on the fund-raiser."

"She tell you all her ideas then?"

"She did. They're right on target. She seems to know how put on an event and build momentum."

They'd kick off the weekend on Friday evening with the HeART Auction of Boone Springs, garnering donations from local and not so local artists to sell on-site. For Saturday, she was planning a Family FUNd-raiser Festival, full of games and pony rides and raffles for children. Saturday night was reserved for a dinner-dance and she was in negotiations with a Grammy-nominated young country band to provide the entertainment. She'd managed to enlist a talented designer to create a website and was in the process of soliciting volunteers for the event.

Mason would be in charge of logistics and overseeing the big picture, while Drea and her committees would work on the details.

Their thirty-minute talk after they'd locked lips had managed to get his mind off her pretty green eyes and sweet body, and back on track.

"I'm sure proud of her, but I wish she'd let up a little bit."

"She only has a short time to make it all happen, Drew."

"I know, but is it selfish of me to want her to myself? I mean, I know I don't deserve it, and Lord knows, I'll spend the rest of my days trying to make up for being a lousy father to her when she needed me the most."

"She'll come around. She loves you, Drew."

"Yeah, but she doesn't always like me so very much."

Mason rubbed his jaw. Drea didn't like him, either, and maybe that was a good thing. It would keep him from making the mistake of kissing her again. But he wasn't one to give advice to Drew or anyone on matters of the heart, so he kept his mouth shut. "Aunt Lottie's back home. She arrived last night from her trip to Africa and she's thrilled that Drea's here. I think you can expect her to come for a visit."

"Lottie, huh? What the hell was she doing in Africa for all those months?"

Mason grinned. He suspected Drew was sweet on his aunt, but the two were like oil and water. And they had history: Lottie and Drew's late wife, Maria, had been best friends until the day she'd died. "Don't know. Maybe you should ask her when she stops by."

Drew looked away and grumbled something about her not wanting to see him.

"What?"

"Nothin'."

"Aunt Lottie wants to surprise Drea, so don't say anything to her, okay?"

"I won't say a thing. My lips are sealed."

"Dad, are you talking to yourself?" Drea wandered into the kitchen and stopped short when she spotted Mason. "You're still here?"

He nodded, speechless. Drea was in her pajamas, a pair of soft pink cotton pants and a matching top that clung to her breasts, hiding little. His mouth was suddenly dry, but Mason kept his composure, even while that *alive feeling* bombarded him. "I was just going."

She folded her arms around her middle. If she thought that shielded her, she was mistaken. The material only pulled tighter across her chest.

Mason turned and brought his coffee mug to the sink. He couldn't look at her another second without showing her—and her *father*—how much she affected him.

He could hardly believe it. Drea had poked the sleeping bear and he needed to get out of here, pronto. He headed for the front door, keeping his back to the MacDonalds. "Thanks for the game tonight, Drew. Good night, Drea." Then he exited the cottage without giving either of them a parting glance.

The next day, Drea must've put a good one hundred miles on the car making stops all over the county, checking items off the to-do list on her cell phone. She'd be lost without her list. It was sort of scary thinking how if anything happened to her phone or tablet, her entire life would be erased. Lately, for this project, she'd been taking pen to paper, jotting notes as a backup, too. But her mind was crowded just the same with all the details for the event.

As she parked the car in the driveway of her father's cottage, she closed her eyes, thoughts running rampant through her head.

Check in with the caterers.

Make the rounds at local art galleries.

Double-check with Katie regarding the children's cup-cake-decorating booth.

Plead with The Band Blue to donate an evening of entertainment.

Stop thinking about Mason.

Darn it. The more she tried, the harder it was. She'd be right in the middle of planning her next move with the fund-raiser when her mind would flash to Mason. His fingers softly touching her, the immediate red-hot spark that baffled them both and then the determination in his eyes when he'd finally bent his head and made exquisite contact with her lips. He'd stirred something deep inside her, more than curiosity, more than bravado, and she'd had to see the kiss through.

He'd said she made him feel alive. Now if that wasn't an ego boost. And she hadn't lied; it had been the best kiss she'd had in a long time. That was where it got confusing. She resented Mason. For how he'd humiliated her. For how he'd dismissed her so easily and broken her heart. She'd lost so much of herself then and had run into the arms of the first man who'd paid her attention, giving him her body, but not her heart.

A knock on the car window snapped her out of her thoughts. She opened her eyes and focused on the woman smiling in at her.

"Drea, sweetheart. I couldn't wait another second to see you. I hope I didn't startle you."

"Lottie?"

"It's me. I'm back and I'm dying to talk to you."

Drea couldn't get out fast enough to give her "aunt" a long, lingering hug. "Oh, Lottie. It's so good to see you!" Because Drea's mom and Lottie had been BFF all their lives, she'd been in Drea's life, too. After her mother died,

Lottie had given her the love and attention Maria couldn't any longer.

Drea pulled back to look into Lottie's eyes. They still held sparkle and spunk. At sixty, Lottie was no wilting flower. She'd kept up her appearance, wearing trendy clothes, staying slender and coloring her gray a honey-blond shade, her silky locks reaching her shoulders. "You look beautiful, Lottie. I swear you never age."

"Age is just a number, sweetie. And that's so kind of you to say." Lottie smiled again, giving her the once-over. "You're the one who's beautiful, Drea. You're all grown up. I know I say that every time I see you, but it's true. You look more and more like your mama every day."

"I'll take that as a compliment."

"As well you should. Gosh, what has it been? Two years since I've seen you?"

"Yeah, two years. You came to visit me in New York."

"We had a great time, going to shows, shopping."

"It means a lot to me that we stay in touch." They'd made an effort to call or text every month or so whenever Lottie wasn't traipsing around the globe.

"I promised I would."

"Hey, what's all the fuss about?" Drew came ambling out of the house.

Lottie rolled her eyes and whispered, "Your father has turned into an old man."

"I heard that, Lottie," Drew said with a scowl.

"I don't care if you did, Drew. It's true. You're not ready for the grave yet. Lose a few of those extra pounds you're carrying and see if you don't feel like a new man."

"Well, now you're my doctor, too. Did you learn all that in Africa?"

Lottie grinned. "Actually, I learned a lot of things on

my trip. I spent a good deal of time on the tour bus with a homeopathic doctor, as it happens."

"Oh, yeah? Did he cure your ailments?"

"If I had any," Lottie said softly, "I'm sure Jonathan would've cured them."

Drew's eye twitched and just for a second his face grew pale. "Well, come in. You girls can jabber all you want inside the house."

Drew held the front door open for Lottie and Drea and they marched into the parlor. Lottie had brought them all a home-cooked dinner, Cajun chicken and shrimp pasta, her signature dish and one of Drea's favorites. It was warming on the stove.

Drew took a seat and listened to his daughter and Lottie chat about Broadway plays, clothes and music. Whenever Lottie was around, Drew felt old. Her vibrancy and zest for life looked darn good on her. She was a pain in his rear end, but she was also a lifelong friend. One who never ceased to speak her mind. Whenever she was gone, he missed her. And whenever she was home, he wished she'd keep her opinions of him to herself. He was tired, his bones ached, but listening to his daughter and Lottie chat lightened his mood.

"Dad, did Lottie tell you she went on safari?"

"She did."

"Sounds exciting, doesn't it?"

"Well… I suppose."

"It was a grand adventure," Lottie said, her soft brown eyes gleaming. "I loved every minute of it."

"But now you're home for a while, right?" Drea asked.

"Lord above, yes. I'm home for a good long time. Texas is in my blood. I missed it and my nephews."

The relief Drew felt gave him pause. Why was he so

darn happy to have her home? Hell, whenever Lottie was around, his head became jumbled up with all sorts of mixed emotions.

"And I'm especially glad I'm back in time to see you." She took Drea's hand. She'd been more a mother to Drea than he'd been a father.

"How long are you here, honey?"

"I'll be staying for several weeks, putting together the fund-raiser for the hospital."

"Mason told me about it. You two are working together, so I know it'll be successful."

"I think dinner's just about ready," Drew announced.

"Gosh, I smell something delicious cooking," Drea said.

"It's Lottie's Cajun supper."

"Your favorite, Dad." Drea gave him a big smile, her eyes twinkling.

"As I recall, it's your favorite, too. And Lord knows, she wouldn't be fixin' anything so delicious if it was just me."

Lottie whipped her head his way. "Drew MacDonald, why are you always so disagreeable?"

"You saying you fixed that special meal on my account?"

Lottie rolled her eyes. She did that a lot and he found it annoyingly cute. "I'm saying we all like the dish, so why not dig in."

"Sounds great to me. I missed lunch and I'm starving." Drea stood and gave them both a quick glance.

"I've got the table set," Drew said. Well, Lottie had helped. She'd arrived just a few minutes before Drea got home and they'd worked quickly together. His heart flipped over the second he'd laid eyes on Lottie, after her being gone for so long, and he'd been a bit flustered ever since.

"Sounds good to me. I only hope the meal's as good as you two remember it."

"If you made it, Lottie, we're gonna love it." Drea eyed him, sending him a message to give Lottie his assurances, as well. But she didn't need any more encouragement, he decided. She was the strongest woman he knew.

As Lottie walked past him, arm in arm with his daughter, the woman's sweet, fruity scent teased his nostrils, reminding him of freshly picked strawberries. Oh man, it was going to be a long night.

The autumn sun arced over the horizon, shedding light and warmth on the morning. Drea squatted in the dirt and gave a good hard pull on one of the many weeds, gripping the base near the root with her gloved hands. The darn thing wouldn't budge. She'd be damned if it would get the better of her. She stared at it, as if hoping it would wilt under her intense scrutiny.

No such luck.

While she was here in Boone Springs she'd vowed to tidy up her father's neglected yard. Since her meetings didn't begin until eleven, today was a good day to get started.

"Okay, you monster, you're not getting the better of me." On her knees now, she tightened her grip and pulled with all her might. "You're going…down."

The weed popped from the earth and the momentum sent her flying back. She landed on her butt in a pile of wilted petunias. "Ow."

"Looks like the weed wasn't the only one going down."

She stared up, straight into Mason's face, and saw a smirk twitching the corners of his mouth. "Are you kidding me? Where did you come from?"

He put out his hand to help her up.

She ignored it, bracing her hands on the ground and shooting to her feet, then dusting the dirt off her jeans.

Why was this man always catching her in embarrassing situations?

"I usually run this way in the morning."

She took in his black jogging pants and snug white T-shirt. His arms were two blocks of muscle straining against the cotton material. It was sigh-worthy how good he looked this early in the morning. The whole package smacked of good health and vitality and…sexy man.

The truth was the truth. Mason was still handsome, but that one kiss the other night meant nothing to her. She clung to her resentment, because the alternative—getting hurt again—wasn't an option.

"I'll remember that," she said. She would make sure not to bump into him again at this hour.

"You're up early."

"Gardening, as you can see. My dad's been neglecting the grounds and I'm hoping to make a dent in all this."

"If I know you, you'll fix up this garden and make it shine." His words came with an approving gleam in his dark eyes.

"You sound so sure of yourself."

"I am."

"And you know that about me how?"

"I can see how hard you're working on the fund-raiser. You won't stop until you reach your goal."

He was right. She was a woman on a mission. She'd never had much approval in her life, having to fight for everything she'd attained, without much recognition. Not that she'd needed constant glory, but a compliment now and then was always welcome. "Thank you."

He pushed his hand through his hair and gave her a solemn look. "Listen, we've sort of hit a snag with The Band Blue. I spoke with their agent last night and it doesn't look like it's going to happen for us."

"What? How can that be? They seemed interested last time we spoke."

"Yeah, about that. You spoke with Sean Manfred, the lead singer, and apparently the kid has a soft spot for our cause. His mother is a heart attack survivor and he wants to help, but their agent isn't onboard. He says the band couldn't possibly come until his demands are met."

"What are his demands?"

"He wouldn't say. He wants a sit-down to go over everything."

"That's fine. I can do that. I think when he hears how much good—"

"The thing is they've got a gig at the Hollywood Bowl in LA this weekend and their manager will only agree to a face-to-face meeting. I suppose he's trying to appease Sean, while making it harder on us. Frankly, we can't afford to waste any more time on this. If we can't get them to agree, we're dead in the water as far as entertainment goes on such short notice."

"We?"

"Yeah, we."

"I can handle it on my own, Mason."

"Showing up as a team will help persuade him. We can take my company plane, and besides, it'd give me a chance to check out a piece of property I've had my eye on."

"In Los Angeles?"

"Yeah, on the beach."

"I didn't know you were a beach kind of guy," she said matter-of-factly, while her heart pumped overtime. She'd have to spend a lot of time with Mason on the trip. It was business, but still…

"I'm not really, but maybe it's time for me to branch out a little. I mean, Larissa always loved the beach. Claimed it soothed her, gave her peace."

"And you can use a little of that?"

He shrugged. "Yeah, I guess."

He gazed down at Drea as if puzzling something out. Perhaps he was looking for inner peace, while his body craved vitality. She could understand that.

"So it's settled? We'll leave Saturday morning."

"Uh, sure. We'll be home Saturday night, right?"

Mason eyed her and she saw him calculating what they needed to accomplish in one day. It was a three-hour trip to Los Angeles. That meant six hours of flying in one day. "If the agent isn't being an asshole, we should be able to make it back in time." His eyes twinkled. "Do you have a hot date on Saturday?"

"Me? I have no time for dating. I'm concentrating all my efforts on the fund-raiser."

"Okay, then. I'll make the arrangements and let you get back to fighting weeds."

"Sounds…good." It didn't. She nibbled on her lip, battling emotions. On the one hand, she really needed to nail down the entertainment for the night. She'd hit a brick wall on getting a band to agree, until she'd spoken with Sean. He'd made it seem as if there wouldn't be a problem; all they had to do was iron out a few details. But she should've gotten the okay from their agent first. Her mistake. Now she had to do some fast talking to secure their commitment. But on the other hand, traveling with Mason meant they'd be spending a full day together. She vowed not to let her ill feelings about him get in her way. "And I wish you'd stop doing that."

His brows pulled together. "Doing what?"

"Catching me in embarrassing situations." First the pajama thing and today her ungraceful battle with a weed.

His smirk spread into a wide smile. "Just lucky I guess." He took off jogging down the road and she stood there watching him slice through the wind with those long strides. An unwanted thrill ran through her body and she chewed on her lip, silently cursing the warmth filling her up inside.

Three

Saturday morning, Drea rose and double-checked her luggage making sure she packed her usual change of clothes just in case of an accidental spill or a delay, along with the necessary paperwork for the deal with The Band Blue.

Almost as important, she brought along her notes on her top five reasons it would be advantageous for the band to join in their fund-raising event. No one would ever call her lazy or doubt her determination. She'd done extensive research on the group and was prepared to use all the tools in her arsenal to get them to sign on the dotted line.

She showered and dressed in black slacks and a white bell-sleeve blouse, all the while going over her business strategy in her head. She'd wear her blazer during the meeting, but for now, a comfy cardigan would do for the plane ride. A pair of short beige boots completed the outfit.

She tiptoed into the kitchen and found her father up

and dressed already. "Dad, you're up early." It was barely seven o'clock.

"That I am."

He tied the laces on a pair of walking shoes that looked brand-new.

"What's going on?"

"Lottie wants me to walk with her. Claims I need to get in shape."

"Oh, uh…"

He glanced at her and frowned. "I'm not so old I can't still get around, you know."

"But…you haven't been exercising. Maybe you should take it slow."

"If I don't go, Lottie's gonna keep pestering me."

"Dad, I think you're darn glad Lottie's here to pester you."

"I don't know. Maybe." He shrugged. "I'm meeting her at the main house in half an hour."

"Is it like a date?"

Her dad groaned as if she was insane. "It's a walk, period."

"Dad, I'm going out of town. What if…" She bit her tongue. She knew what he was going to say and couldn't very well stop him.

Her father finished tying his shoes and looked up at her. "I've been on my own a long time, Drea. Don't worry about me. I've gotten along all this time without you."

Bingo. It was true, so she couldn't argue with him on that.

"Okay, well, I'll probably be home late tonight. I'm going to California with Mason. We have hospital business."

"You need a suitcase for that?" Drew eyed her momentarily and she mentally cringed. She didn't want to think about spending the night with Mason, yet it was a possibility. But that didn't mean she had to pack her prettiest lingerie, a light sage nightie that barely covered her thighs. Why had she done that?

"I have papers in there, mostly. And a change of clothes, just in case, Dad."

Her father's pale green eyes lit up. "I bet Mason's hoping for *just in case*."

"What? Don't be silly, Dad. He's the last man on earth…"

"He's hurting and you two go way back, Drea."

"It's business, Dad. You know I don't like the Boones, Mason most of all."

"All right, honey. If you say so."

She felt like she was ten years old again. "I say so. I'll text you before we take off."

"To make sure I survived the walk around the ranch?"

She smiled. "Making sure you survived Lottie's well-intentioned nagging."

That made her father grin. "That woman is a pain in my rear end."

"She's a sweetheart and you know it. You just give her grief."

"Turn that around, and it'd be true." But there was a lightness in his voice she hadn't heard in a long time.

There was a knock at the front door. "Sounds like Mason's here," her father said.

"I'll get it." Drea headed there through the parlor.

She found Mason dressed in a pair of crisp jeans and a snap-down shirt under a black jacket. Business casual. At least they were in tune in the apparel department. "Mornin'," he said in his sexy Texas drawl.

"Mason, I'll be right with you. Unless," she began, her manners getting the best of her, "you'd like to come in?"

"Come in, boy," her father called from the kitchen. "I've got a fresh pot of coffee going."

Mason eyed her outfit and hairdo. Maybe she should've put it up, instead of leaving her hair free to drape down her back. "Man, right about now, I'd kill for a cup." He glanced at his watch. "I think there's time. Our flight leaves at eight."

"Thank goodness," she said. "I'd kill for a cup, too." She let him in.

"A quick one. We'll have breakfast on the plane, so no worries there."

Drea bit back a snide comment. His company plane was just another classic reminder of losing Thundering Hills to the Boones. Mason spoke of it casually, as if normal every-day people could fly around in their own airplanes. The Boone empire had flourished, while her legacy, the land she'd loved, had been swept away.

Hastily, she poured them each a cup and listened while Mason and her father spoke about the weather, cattle prices and Lottie. "I'm afraid she's on a crusade," Mason said, grinning. "She spent some time with that doctor and now she thinks she can cure the world."

"Well, I'm gonna give it a go."

"Exercise never hurts. But be warned, next she might tackle your diet."

"That'd be the day."

"Mason," Drea said, slurping the last sip of her coffee. "We should probably go."

"Yeah, I've gotta get a move on, too," her dad said. "You be sure to take good care of my girl while you're gone. Okay, son?"

"Dad!" She sucked in a quick breath. "I don't need Mason or anyone else taking care of me. I'm perfectly cap—"

"Yes, sir," Mason interrupted. "I'll be sure to keep her safe."

Drea shook her head and kissed her father on the cheek. "Don't strain yourself today."

"I'll be just fine. You have a good trip now."

Mason grabbed her luggage in the parlor and then held the door for her. "All set?"

As much as she was going to be. "Yes."

He put his hand to her lower back and guided her to a shiny black limousine in the driveway. The warm contact felt too good. She stiffened up and focused her gaze on the uniformed driver standing at attention beside the car.

"I've got this," Mason said to him. He put her luggage in the back and then gestured to the open door. "After you."

She slid inside and he followed. His presence seemed to fill the lush leather interior, and she was surprised at how little physical space there was on the seat between them.

She'd seen the inside of a limousine exactly four times. The first had been during her mother's funeral. That had tainted her perception of limos for life. The ride had been the hardest she'd ever taken. She hadn't been able to look at her father's ashen face another second, so during the drive she'd stared out the window in utter silence, her young heart breaking.

Who ever said limos were fun?

"Let's head to the airport," Mason told the driver.

She glanced over at him, noting how he seemed to be in total control of his environment. She could really respect the business side of Mason. He was focused and driven. She'd dwell on that aspect during her time with him and not think about his pleasing musky scent. Or how the sunlight seemed to catch the inky strands of his hair in just the right way. Or how intense his dark brown eyes were. No, she'd concentrate on her newly thought up theme, *Business with Mason*.

"Just so you know, I can keep myself safe. I don't need you protecting me."

He grinned. "I know that. I was humoring your father."

"Oh." She sank back in her seat. Should she believe him? It didn't matter. She knew the truth. She'd been taking care of herself for a very long time now.

She spared him another glance. His eyes were twinkling, as if he found her amusing.

She tried to drum up anger or resentment, but neither emotion surfaced. She hated to admit it, but he'd been sweet to consider her father's feelings.

And who would've thought she'd ever associate the word *sweet* with Mason's name?

"Comfortable?" Mason asked, sitting down across from her on the plane.

The white leather seats were wide and luxurious. A small table separated them. She was aware of the stocked liquor bar behind her and a television screen on the opposite wall. The flight attendant had just taken her order for breakfast.

"Yes."

"Okay, we'll be taking off soon."

"At your command," she said.

He stared at her and put a finger to his eye, struggling not to frown. "Drea, what?"

"Nothing."

She smiled. She was a master at hiding her demons, but somehow being with Mason made them all come out again. "I'm fine."

"Fear of flying?"

Fear of Boone. "No, nothing like that. I think I'm just hungry."

"Breakfast is coming right up."

The pilot's voice came over the speaker. He explained the flight route and weather conditions and asked them to put on their seat belts. Shortly after, the plane began to taxi on the runway.

She and Mason were quiet until they were airborne.

"Here you go. I hope you enjoy this. It's one of Mr. Boone's favorites." The flight attendant presented her with a vegetable egg white scramble and a cup of coffee. Mason had the same.

"Looks wonderful, thank you," Drea said.

The stewardess walked off and Mason began digging in.

"So, you really think we can get The Band Blue to sign on the dotted line?" he asked her.

"With my people skills, yeah, I do."

"You have people skills? You mean the way you charmed me?"

He was teasing, but he'd caught her red-handed. "I'm not a phony."

"You mean if you liked me a little more, I'd know it? Never mind," he said, dropping the subject. "So how did you come upon fund-raising as a career?"

"It was accidental, actually. My college roommate came down with a rare type of lung disease in our senior year. It was pretty serious and she needed treatments that required hundreds of thousands of dollars, treatments that her insurance didn't cover. I knew I had to help her. I gathered up a bunch of her friends and fellow students and started a fund-raising page on social media. I wrote articles for the local newspapers and even did a morning show with Sandra's parents to bring awareness and raise funds. Within a matter of weeks, we had more than enough money for her procedures."

"Impressive. How is your friend now?"

"She's doing well. There's no cure for her condition,

but she has a good quality of life and I was just invited to her wedding."

"Nice. You saved her life."

"Not me, the doctors."

"You're being modest."

"I wish there was something I could've done for my mother, though. I know I was just a kid, but I always think that maybe my father and I missed something. Her heart attack came on so suddenly and we never had a clue she had heart disease. She had no symptoms and, well, after that first attack there was so much damage…"

Drea lowered her head as emotions whipped through her system. Her mother had lasted only three days after the attack. And Drea wished she'd said more to her, wished she'd realized that she was losing her, wished she'd told her how much she loved her. Instead, everyone had tried to protect her, to make it seem that Maria MacDonald was going to be fine, when they'd probably all known differently.

Drea didn't know why she'd exposed herself to Mason this way. She never talked about her mother's illness, much less confided in a man she thought of as the enemy. She lifted her eyes and found pain in Mason's expression.

"Yeah, I know what you mean," he replied.

"Mason, I'm sorry." His pain had to be more raw. More fresh. He'd lost his wife and unborn child to heart failure just two years ago.

Drea reached out to him, put her hand over his. It was instinctive, a move she'd afford anyone in pain. The connection flowed between them, strong, powerful, sorrowful. She resented the hell out of him, hated what his family had done to hers, but in a moment of shared grief, she'd forgotten all that. And then she pulled her hand away. *Business with Mason.*

"All through here?" The stewardess appeared, ready to remove the plates.

"Yes, all through," she said.

"Would either of you like more coffee?"

"No," they answered simultaneously.

"Okay, if I can get you anything else, Mr. Boone, please let me know."

He nodded. "Thank you."

The flight attendant went back to her station and Drea was left alone with Mason once again. "You know, I think I'll stretch my legs."

Why not? The plane was roomy enough to move around in and she needed space.

When she stood, Mason stood, too, his Southern manners on full display. As she started to walk past him, the plane lurched and she was tossed against his chest. Immediately, he wrapped his arms around her. Even after the quick bout of turbulence was over, Mason didn't let go.

"You okay?" he whispered in her ear.

"Uh-huh."

From where she was nestled in his arms, the slightest hint of his masculine cologne teased her nose. She closed her eyes, enjoying a few seconds of comfort. "Thanks for the catch."

"My baseball days come in handy."

"Tee-ball?"

"College. All Star."

"Of course. You wouldn't be anything else."

Her snarky remark brought a chuckle. "You make me laugh, Drea."

He skimmed his hands over her back, stroking her ever so gently, bringing her closer. His legs pressed against hers. She didn't want to know what a brush against his groin would bring. She didn't want this. But her heart was pounding and the strength of him, his *maleness*, sent thrills careening through her body.

The plane lurched again, this time breaking them apart. Mason reached for her, but she was too far from his grasp. It seemed the stratosphere had more sense than either of them.

"Sorry about that, folks," the pilot said over the loudspeaker. "There shouldn't be any further turbulence. You can relax and enjoy the rest of the flight."

"Good news," Mason said, but his words belied the dangerous gleam in his eyes.

Drea grabbed her bag from where she'd been sitting and pointed to a sofa a few feet away. "I think I'll just sit over there for a while. I…have some work to go over."

While Mason watched, she moved as gracefully as she could down the aisle and then plopped onto the sofa and avoided him for the rest of the trip.

A few hours later, as she and Mason were driving down the highway in a rented Cadillac SUV, breathing California air and enjoying West Coast sunshine, his cell phone rang. He tossed her the device. "Can you get that for me, please?"

Drea picked it up and glanced at the screen. "It's the agent," she said to Mason before answering. "Hello, this is Drea MacDonald."

"Hello, Drea. Alan Nesbitt here."

"Yes, Mr. Nesbitt. We've just landed and we're on our way."

"That's why I'm calling. I'm afraid I can't do lunch today. Something's come up that I have to deal with. I hate to do this to you, but it can't be helped."

"But we've flown in from Texas. And we need to speak with you."

"Yes, yes. That's fine. I don't have a spare minute until after the show."

"You mean tonight?"

"Yes, the band goes on right before the headliner. We can talk then. I'm afraid that's all that I can do. I'm swamped today."

"Okay, we'll come to the show."

"I'll leave VIP tickets and backstage passes for you. We'll have a good hour to talk then."

"I guess that will have to do. We'll be there. This is important."

"I understand. I'll see you tonight."

Drea pushed the off button and faced Mason. "He's canceled lunch."

"I heard."

"He claims he has time to see us tonight at the show."

Mason frowned. "We have to give it a try. What else can we do? We're here already."

"I agree. But now we have a lot of time to kill. What are we going to do for eight hours?" Drea was not happy about this. She and Mason would be spending the entire day together. And after what almost happened between them on the plane, she had to be on guard.

"I can think of a few things," he said cryptically. Yet there was no villainous arch of his brows or twitch of his lips. When she didn't respond, he asked, "Are you hungry?"

"I'm not starving, but I could eat."

He nodded. "Me, too. Do you like seafood?"

"Who doesn't?" She actually loved it. When she was in college, she'd go for Friday night fish frys with her friends. It was always something she'd looked forward to.

"Great." At the next signal, Mason whipped the car around. "I know this little place on the beach I think you'd like."

And soon they were on Pacific Coast Highway, the ocean to her left and the cliffs to her right. The homes on both sides of the road had amazing views of the sea. "Have you have been to LA before?" Mason asked.

"Yes, once, but I never saw the outside of my hotel."

His brows arched and he glanced at her.

"I was attending a conference," she explained. Not that it was any of his business how she'd spent her time here. "So yes, technically I've been here, but not enough to get a West Coast vibe."

"I think I can remedy that."

It didn't sound awful so she nodded. "Okay."

A few minutes later, Mason pulled into the parking lot of an outdoor café. Big Fish was a small take-out restaurant with picnic tables and café chairs facing the water. "Not fancy," he said, "but the fish are fresh and everything is delicious."

After being on the plane for three hours and then in the car this past hour, sitting outside in the autumn sunshine sounded pretty good. "I'm game."

They got out of the car, Drea stepping down before Mason could open the door for her. She wasn't a feminist really, and understood he was just displaying his ingrained Southern manners, but she was perfectly capable of getting out of a vehicle without his assistance. Still, he put his hand to her back and guided her through the parking lot to the take-out window. She glanced at the chalkboard menu on the wall. "What do you recommend?"

"If you love shrimp and scallops, their Big Fish Special is pretty good. Everything comes with fries and coleslaw."

There wasn't a salad on the menu. Or a fruit plate. She decided to throw caution to the wind today and go for broke. "I'll have the Big Fish Special then, thank you."

"Make that two," Mason said to the lady behind the window.

When the food was ready, they walked over to a picnic table near the water. Drea took a seat and Mason slid in next to her. Both wore their sunglasses and silly bibs around their necks while they enjoyed the food. She had to admit Mason didn't look intimidating now; his body was relaxed, his hair swept back by the slight breeze, his usual glower gone.

"This was a good idea," she said, plucking up the last of her French fries.

"You mean I did something right for a change?"

She caught the twinkle in his eye. "All I mean is you have good taste in food, period."

"I figured."

"So, what's the plan now?"

Mason glanced at his watch. "It's a little after one." They still had several hours before the meeting. "How do you feel about carnivals?"

"Carnivals?"

"Santa Monica-style. We'll hit the pier next. It's not far from here. If you've never been, it's worth seeing. And I promise you, they have the best ice cream on the beach."

"It's your nickel," she said. "I'm going along for the ride."

A short time later, Drea had settled on a cup of strawberry ice cream and was spooning small bites into her mouth as they relaxed on the Santa Monica pier.

Mason shook his head at her choice of dessert. "You're no fun."

"I'm a lot of fun," she said, "when I want to be."

He held a mouthwatering double-fudge-brownie ice cream waffle cone in his hand. They stood against the guardrail overlooking the ocean, listening to the lapping waves hitting the shore. It was something they didn't get in their part of Texas.

"Oh yeah? When do you want to be?"

His eyes were on her, watching her lick the cream from her spoon. It unsettled her, the gleam in his eyes, the sudden flirty tone in his voice. "When I…"

"When you what?"

He seemed intent on her answer. "Well, not now. Today is all about business." At least it should be.

"We're taking a business break…out of necessity."

She blinked.

"This is a no-business zone," he continued. "Look at the people here. Think they're worried about numbers, spreadsheets, their boss's latest tirade? No, ma'am. I don't think so."

He did have a point. "So if this is a no-business zone, do you mind sharing some of your double-fudge-brownie ice cream?"

"It depends," he said. "What do I get in return?"

"What do you…uh, what do you want?" A memory flashed of being nearly naked in his bedroom, craving his kisses, wanting his touch. She didn't allow those recollections often, but today they came easily, and for a second she was reminded of the good parts of that memory. How it felt when he'd released her hair from her braid. He'd weaved his fingers through it, as if the strands mesmerized him. And how it felt to be in his arms, his lips on hers, his body hot and demanding. She'd never known a greater desire in her young life than anticipating making love with him. But it had ended there. Mason had put a stop to it, and she was left with only rejection and humiliation.

"A ride."

She blinked, pulling herself back to the present. "What kind of ride?" Back then, there was only one she'd wanted from Mason.

"Take your pick." He nodded toward the amusement park attractions behind them. The hum of laughter, mechanical noises and screams merged in her head. It was the sound of good, honest fun.

"But I get my ice cream first?"

"Fine."

She went in with her spoon and he backed away. "You can't eat a cone with a spoon. Take a big bite and enjoy it."

He offered her the side he hadn't licked yet. But still, wasn't it too intimate to be sharing ice cream this way?

The I-dare-you look in Mason's eyes sparked a desire to prove something to him. She grabbed the cone out of his hand and dug in, taking a bite of the waffle and the dreamy chocolate ice cream in one big mouthful. She'd literally bitten off more than she could chew and Mason's eyes were on her, watching her deal with it, watching her mouth move inelegantly. Then he laughed and his well-hidden dimples appeared. There was a brightness in his expression she hadn't seen since they were much younger. He lifted a napkin to her lips, catching a drop of ice cream.

Their eyes connected then, and there was a moment of intense awareness.

He was touching her face again, standing close enough for her to see the coal-black rim around his deep dark eyes. Close enough to see his jaw tighten suddenly, to see his expression change. She felt it, too. Every time he touched her, she felt desire. Here, with dozens of people milling about on the pier, it was as if they were the only two people on the beach. If he bent his head and leaned in, would she allow him to kiss her again?

"Excuse me, miss. Would you mind taking our picture?" A woman stepped up, unaware that her interruption had just prevented them from making another mistake. Drea should have been relieved. Instead she didn't know how she felt. Let down, maybe. The woman waited patiently, holding a cell phone in her hand. Adorable twin boys stood beside her.

"Of course. I'd be happy to," Drea answered, handing Mason back his cone.

With the beach at her back, the woman ushered her two boys in front of her and Drea snapped the picture.

"Thank you," she told Drea, then took off with the children.

Mason stepped up. "Let's take that ride now."

Getting chummy with Mason put her nerves on edge. She didn't want to enjoy the day so much, and in the back of her mind she was second-guessing all her decisions. While she wanted to stick to her *Business with Mason resolution*, he was trying his hardest to change it into a no-business zone.

"Well?" he asked, watching her closely. "Have you decided?"

She turned around to peer at the rides and made a decision. "I'd like to try the Pacific Wheel. I overheard someone saying it's the only solar-powered Ferris wheel in the world."

He shook his head. "Boring."

"Boring? But you said it was my choice?"

"That's before you slurped up half my ice cream cone. I figure you owe me."

Of course Mason wouldn't play fair. She knew that about him. "I do, do I? Why don't I like the sound of that?"

He led the way. "C'mon. Let's see what the Pacific Plunge is all about."

Mason drove down Pacific Coast Highway with Drea beside him in the passenger seat. Her hand was braced on her midsection, which she rubbed every so often. She hadn't wanted to go on that ride; he'd seen it on her face, the fear, the doubt. Yet she'd been a trouper, bravely getting on the contraption that lifted them up ninety feet over the water.

He'd wanted her to see the view from the highest point of the pier, and it had been amazing. But then, as promised, once they'd reached the top, they'd plunged. Other people had screamed and laughed as they went down. But not Drea. She'd turned the same shade of green as her pretty eyes. Once they'd touched ground he'd helped her off the ride as she'd clutched her queasy stomach.

"Feeling any better?" he asked, taking his eyes off the road to look her way.

"A little." She adjusted herself in her seat. "I'll be fine. The fresh air is helping. Even if it didn't end well, I'm okay with taking the plunge."

"I'm glad. It was fun."

"For you, maybe."

He sighed. Drea wasn't giving an inch, but he knew darn well she had enjoyed getting a little taste of the beach town. "I meant, I'd hoped it was fun for you, too. I'm glad you're feeling better."

"Thanks," she said simply.

Hell, Mason couldn't remember the last time he'd felt so carefree, but he focused on the drive now, since Drea seemed to be lost in thought.

Ten minutes later, she asked, "So, are you meeting a Realtor at the beach house?"

He shook his head. "No. I have the keys."

"Is that a privilege of the rich and famous? You get keys to homes you're thinking of buying?"

"I'm not famous."

"Gee, I don't know too many people who have whole towns named after them."

"My family settled Boone Springs decades ago," he told her. "*They* built the town, not me. I'm not going to apologize for them." He couldn't hide the pride in his voice or miss the pout forming on Drea's mouth.

Right now that pouty mouth looked very kissable. Ever since he'd kissed her that night, he'd had mental flashes of how wonderful it had been to touch his lips to hers, to taste her sweetness.

Yet, every night, his heart ached for his wife. He missed her like crazy and so these unexpected thoughts of Drea were confusing the hell out of him. Part of him wanted to hold on to the guilt and sadness, but another part was trying to break free. It was all so new to him and he could only go with what felt right in the moment.

She remained silent. He knew what she thought about his family. She had no warm feelings for any of them, with the exception of Aunt Lottie. Drea had misconceptions and so much hurt buried deep inside, he didn't know if she'd ever find resolution or peace. So he let the subject drop. Today wasn't the day to be on a Boone family soapbox.

"Actually, the beach house belongs to a business associate of mine. She was nice enough to overnight me the keys so I could look the place over at my leisure."

"Have you been here before?"

He almost heard the "with her" in her question.

"Yeah, I have been. Once. Missy coaxed me to come out and stay here shortly after Larissa passed."

"Missy? I see. So you stayed with her?"

"I did."

He glanced at Drea and she immediately looked away, concealing her expression from him. But her face had turned that green shade again. Was it disapproval? Disappointment? Jealousy?

Thinking of her being jealous made him smile inside. Maybe she'd been fantasizing about him a little bit, too.

"For a few days, yeah. Missy needed me almost as much as I needed her."

Slowly, Drea nodded, as she fiddled with straightening her blouse. She wouldn't look him in the eye.

"Missy's husband had passed, just about the same time my wife… Uh, anyway, after her grandchildren showed up to the beach house, I went home."

"Grandchildren?"

Mason grinned. "Yeah, she has five of them, as I recall. Did I mention Missy's in her seventies?"

"No," Drea said, then cleared her throat. "You left that part out."

"Well, she's an incredible woman."

Drea's eyes narrowed on him. Had he deliberately led her down a merry path? Maybe. He sort of liked thinking she'd been jealous.

"You know, you're a—"

He gave his head a shake. "Uh-uh, Drea. Don't say it."

Her shoulders slumped. "You're right. I won't."

Mason kept a straight face, but inside he was actually grinning.

Four

The beach house, two stories of gorgeous space, smart styling and incredible views, was set on a shelf of land just above the ocean. Drea looked out on the waves as the fall sun began to lower to the horizon. Ten steps led down to the sandy shore, where the water foamed only thirty feet away.

"It's perfect," Drea mumbled.

Mason placed a glass of white wine in her hand as he came up behind her. "Now it's perfect," he said.

Both of them watched the waves hit the shore, and quietly sipped wine.

After several minutes, Mason asked, "I take it you like this place?"

She turned to look into his eyes. He seemed genuinely interested in her opinion. "What's not to like?"

He shrugged. "It's different than Texas."

"Isn't that the point? You'd use it as a getaway, right?"

He shrugged again. "I'm…not sure."

"Then why are we here? I mean, why are you considering buying this house, if you don't think you'll be comfortable here?"

Mason finished his wine and set his glass down on the white wooden railing. Both floors had a wraparound veranda.

"It's hard to explain. I feel as if I need to do something to move forward with my life. I thought a change of pace, something new, might help me figure it out."

He stared at her, as if wondering why he'd told her something so intimate. Most of the men she'd known weren't forthright in sharing their innermost thoughts. Was he sorry he'd confessed this to her?

"It's weird, right?" he asked, doubt evident in his eyes.

"No. Not weird at all." She didn't want to sympathize with Mason. It was crucial to hold on to her anger and indignation and never let it go. Because her life hadn't been peachy, either. Not only had she lost her home, her mother, and her father to alcohol, she'd lost something even more precious.

A baby.

"Hey, are you okay?" Mason tipped her chin up so he could meet her eyes.

Sincere concern washed over his features, frightening her. She didn't want to be friends with Mason. She didn't want his concern. Quickly, she snapped out of her musings. "Sure, I'm fine."

She faked a smile and turned to walk into the house, but he grabbed her hand, halting her retreat. "Would you look at that." He pointed to the ocean. Following his gaze, she glanced at the water and saw a frolicking school of dolphins close to the shore, their smooth, silvery forms rising up from the water and then diving back down, making perfectly shaped arches. Up and down, up and down.

"Wow, I've never seen this in person."

Mason tugged on her hand. "Let's go get a better look. You game?"

"I'm game."

Once they were both barefoot, Mason led the way down to the beach, where sand squished between her toes. The air was cooler by the ocean and beaming sunlight cast a beautiful sheen on the water. Breezes kicked up as she kept her eyes trained on the dolphins swimming by. She stood stock-still, watching them until they faded from sight. "That was something."

"It's pretty incredible." Mason glanced along the empty beach. "I'd like to take a walk before we have to leave. Care to join me?"

She wanted to say no, to put some time and space between them, but when would she ever get another chance to stroll a Pacific beach? "I think I'll tag along."

They walked along the shore, with the foamy waves inching up the sand and teasing their feet. She'd never been a beachgoer, but this little game of keep-away was fun.

Until she stepped on something sharp. It jabbed at her right foot, catching her off guard. "Ow!"

She stumbled, and Mason rescued her midway before she fell, grabbing her waist and righting her. "You okay?"

"I think so. I stepped on a seashell or something buried in the sand."

Mason looked around. "You're right. It was a seashell."

He held her still, his hands clamped around her waist. Ocean breezes swept his hair back and ruffled his shirt. As they stood facing each other for a moment, a monumental thrill scurried down her spine. He was incredibly handsome like this, appealing in a way she didn't really want to admit.

She was about to tell him that maybe the cowboy was also a beachcomber, but her lips parted and nothing came out. When Mason's gaze slid to her mouth, a little gasp escaped her throat. Before she could utter a word, he pulled her closer, bent his head and delivered a gift to her lips. It was so pure, so natural a gesture, with them standing on the deserted beach, the sun lowering on the horizon and all the planets aligning, that she didn't think to stop the kiss. Or him.

He pressed his mouth more firmly now, and she parted her lips in a gasp of pure pleasure. He wasted no time inserting his tongue and tasting her, shocking her senses in the very best way. His kiss shot hot beams of pleasure straight through her, and if that wasn't enough, his arm snaked around to bring her even closer. Her legs were touching his, with her hips against his groin and her breasts pressed to his chest, She was willing and at his mercy.

Yes, Mason knew how to kiss.

He knew where to touch her to elicit a needy response, too.

He wove his free hand through her hair.

His other hand dropped from her waist, his long fingers inching down to graze her rear end. *Oh God.* She craved his touch, wanted more, wanted to stay like this a good long time.

His masterful kiss did that to her.

They were molded together, lip-locked and fully engaged. She felt his shaft, thick and hard, pressing against her. It didn't surprise her to feel it, but what did surprise her was her total acceptance of the situation.

She sighed deeply, majorly turned on but confused all the same.

"Don't think," Mason whispered, as if reading her thoughts. "I'm not."

He nipped at her lower lip and then drove his tongue into her mouth again.

I'm not thinking. I'm not thinking.

When the kiss finally ended, Mason's dark eyes probed hers. He reached out to touch the side of her face, his fingers a gentle caress on her cheek. "Thank you," he said softly.

She blinked. Instead of saying *that was amazing*, or *you're beautiful* or *wow*, Mason was thanking her?

And then it hit her like a ton of bricks. She made him feel "alive." He'd already admitted she'd been the only woman to make him feel that way. *So far.*

She could turn him on. Make him hard. Get his juices flowing.

Yet she couldn't help feeling used. Slightly. It pissed her off a bit.

She didn't want to be Mason's *test kitchen*.

She didn't want to be Mason's anything.

His phone alarm buzzed and he reached into his pocket and pushed a button on his cell to shut it off. "It's time to go. There could be traffic."

She nodded, speechless, and when he grabbed for her hand, she pretended not to see it and jogged up to the house. Once she was on the veranda, she turned to him as he approached the steps.

"Just so you know, thanking me wasn't necessary. You're a good kisser, Mason. And like I've said before, it's been a long time since I've been kissed."

His eyes narrowed. She whirled around before she had to acknowledge the deep frown surfacing on his face.

It was definitely safer to harbor resentment for Mason.

But it sure wasn't as easy as it had once been.

Electricity charged the air at the Hollywood Bowl that night. The iconic outdoor stadium in the Hollywood Hills held a huge crowd of country music fans. A person might think she was back in Texas for all the cowboy hats, silver belt buckles and snakeskin boots filling the arena. Drea's sour mood lifted the second she entered the place and they were shown to their center stage seats. She had to hand it to Mr. Nesbitt.

They'd arrived just in time to see The Band Blue walk onstage amid a roar of cheers. To be the opening act at the Hollywood Bowl was huge. Landing a commitment from the band would almost surely guarantee the fund-raiser's success. She understood that Nesbitt was just doing his job; she understood his hesitation. From this point on, their careers depended on visibility. Drea just had to make sure Nesbitt would see it her way. At least she had Sean Manfred, the lead vocalist, in her corner. The kid had an amazing voice.

During the performance, she found Mason's eyes on her. Too often. It was as if he was puzzling her out. But her puzzle pieces didn't fit with his and it was time she made that clear to him.

No more hand holding. No more kisses. No more intimate conversations.

Business with Mason.

She sat with her hands in her lap, swaying to the music and applauding when the songs ended. The Band Blue drew a noisy crowd bordering on rowdy. But it was all in good fun and she found herself really enjoying the music.

Thirty minutes in, Sean angled his guitar to his side and spoke into the mic. "Thank y'all for coming. The band and I, well, we sure do appreciate your support."

"We love you," a woman shouted from behind Drea.

Sean chuckled. "We love you guys, too. And now, if you're ready, we're gonna end our night with a song I think you'll recognize. Recently, my mama took sick with her heart, but she's one of the lucky ones. She survived."

Drea drew a deep breath. Mason glanced at her, his eyes

soft, and for a second—okay maybe more than a second— she connected with him emotionally.

Sean went on. "So tonight I'm dedicating this here song to my mama. Love you, Bethy Manfred," he said. The crowd shouted words of support and adoration, and then quieted as the band began to play.

When the sweet love ballad called "Your Heart Is Mine" was over, Sean thanked the crowd again before the lights dimmed and the band walked off.

"Time to get backstage," Mason said.

Drea rose and Mason ushered her down the aisle and over to the backstage door. They showed their VIP passes and were immediately let into a special room. A buffet table lined one wall and they were told to help themselves. Drea grabbed a bottle of water and took occasional sips.

Finally, the band entered the room, led by a guy who couldn't have been more than thirty years old. He actually looked like he belonged in the band, with his wispy blond hair and casual dress. He took a look at Drea and Mason, then immediately walked over, while the band members hit the refreshment table. "I'm Alan Nesbitt," he said, no smile, all business.

"I'm Drea Macdonald."

"Mason Boone." The two men shook hands.

"The show was spectacular," she said.

Alan shook his head. "It's always a challenge with outdoor acoustics, but yeah, the boys did real good. Would you like to sit down?" He gestured to a group of tables. "We have a bit of time before they go on for an encore performance with Rusty Bonner."

The conversation was stilted and one-sided, and Alan didn't seem to want to make any allowances. He called the band a hot property and said that right now they needed to keep their options open.

"I understand all that," Drea said. "But what if we promised you they'd get a ton of exposure? And don't forget the goodwill this charity would invoke."

"Listen, I'm not hard-hearted, but there are costs involved. We'd need a place to stay, since traveling with a band is expensive. These boys have played for pennies, and now's their big chance. We're just gaining momentum."

"Okay, so you'd need a place to stay and travel expenses." She glanced at Mason and he nodded. "Got that covered. What else?"

"We need maximum exposure. This is a small-ass town, right? Who's gonna see them perform?"

"We can accommodate about five hundred people on the grounds."

"Did you see the size of the Bowl? Try five thousand for starters."

"Yeah, but Boone County is full of larger-than-life Texas donors. These are people who have connections all over the globe. Isn't it all about networking?"

Alan's brows lifted. "Keep talking."

"This fund-raiser is a big deal for the community. There'd be a lot of local news coverage."

"Understood."

"So what if we auctioned off one of the band members for a date with a fan? We could start promoting it now, and by the time the event rolled around, you'd have a ton of exposure, and the fund-raiser would get an added boost, as well."

"I'm volunteering to do it," Sean said, walking over to the table. "I think it's a great idea. And… I'm single at the moment." A crooked grin spread across his face. He was probably twenty at best.

He put out his hand to Mason first. "Hi, I'm Sean." They

shook and then he turned to her. "You must be Drea Mac-Donald. Nice meeting you in person, ma'am."

Drea smiled. "Same here."

"Yeah, uh, I'm sorry about what happened to your mom, Miss MacDonald. Losing her like you did must've been very hard."

"It was. Still is," she said honestly.

"I like the date idea," Alan said quietly, considering it. "It's a good marketing ploy."

"If you agree, I promise no one will work harder to get the coverage you want than I will," Drea declared. "I'll write up a press release tomorrow."

"I'd like to help your cause." Sean looked at his agent. "I've been telling Alan that we should do this. It's important. Chances are my mother wouldn't be here today if she hadn't had excellent cardiac care. I spent a lot of time in the hospital chapel praying for her recovery. I think this is a way I can give back and make good on the promises I made that day."

If Drea had liked this young man before, now she adored him. "Thank you, Sean. And it *is* important." She glanced at Mason. "Many of us have lost loved ones."

Mason's expression softened, his gaze touching hers. She hated the effect he had on her. Tonight she wanted no distractions.

"My family owns a hotel in Boone Springs," Mason said to Alan. "We'd be happy to put you all up. And I can make sure the company plane is available to fly the band in."

Alan Nesbitt's expression changed, his skepticism replaced with consideration. She'd done all she could to address his main concerns, and luckily, the group had that weekend free. This might work out, after all.

The rest of the band members walked over and stood

around the table. "It's a good gig," the drummer said. "I'm in."

The others nodded.

"We've got the details covered," Drea said. "Now we just need an agreement. And I happen to have something written up here in my briefcase."

Drea felt as if she was floating on air, spreading her arms like wings and gliding through the parking lot. She'd signed the deal with the band. "Can you believe it?"

Mason grinned. "You were amazing in there. You had a comeback for every single one of Nesbitt's demands. I'm impressed."

"Now we can go back to Texas with clear heads."

"Yeah, we can." Mason glanced at his watch. "But not tonight."

"What?" Drea stopped in her tracks.

"I told my pilot if we didn't need him by 10:00 p.m. to go to bed and rest up. It's only fair. We'll have to take off in the morning."

"What time is it?"

"Eleven thirty."

"Oh, wow. I didn't realize how late it was." Sean had asked them to stay for the final song of the night, when the band joined the headliner, Rusty Bonner, and Drea had been happy to agree. "Can we get a hotel at this hour?"

"We could try. But the beach house is twenty minutes from here. We could be there faster than trying to find rooms on a Saturday night."

Drea eyed him carefully.

"There's five bedrooms, Drea. You can sleep downstairs and I'll—"

"I get it." She wasn't worried. The house was enormous, and all she wanted to do was plop her head on a pillow and get some sleep. It had been a long day. "It would be cool to wake up in the morning at the beach."

Mason nodded and they took off immediately. The drive to the house was traffic free. When they got there, he parked the car and grabbed their bags. They entered the house quietly; the gentle roar of the ocean was the only sound in Drea's ears. She welcomed the peace and quiet.

"Pick a room down here," he said. "I'll check things out before turning in upstairs." Their eyes met. Mason hesitated briefly, as if he wanted to say something, but then thought better of it. "Good night, Drea."

"Night," she said. "See you in the morning."

Drea entered a bedroom decorated in dove blues and grays, the furniture sleek and modern with sharp lines. The contemporary feel of the place was so different from anything Mason Boone was accustomed to in Texas. She had a hard time picturing him being happy here. There was too much Texan in his bones.

She unpacked her bag, taking out fresh underwear and her nightie, and walked into the bathroom. What had she been thinking, bringing her finest lingerie on this business trip? She chuckled at the absurdity. After that kiss today on this very beach, Drea knew better. The kiss had only reinforced her resolve to steer clear of Mason. As soon as she was back on Texas soil, her focus would be on the fund-raiser, and not on Mason's swoon-worthy body and masterful kisses.

After undressing, she showered quickly. Then she dabbed herself dry with an ultrasoft towel, donned her sage nightie and crawled into bed.

Pure heaven.

Closing her eyes, she sank down into the comfy mattress and settled in.

Minutes later, a piercing alarm brought her head up from

a sound sleep. She glanced at her surroundings, disoriented, until she finally remembered where she was. The alarm rang louder, more urgently.

"It's okay, Drea," she heard Mason call over the deafening noise.

She rose and opened her door just as she heard a crash in the other room. "Ow! Damn it."

"Mason?" She ran into the living room and found a shadowy form pushing up from the floor, then hopping on one foot. "What on earth?"

"Hang on a second," he shouted above the blaring alarm. He limped over to the hallway wall and punched a code into the security system. The harsh ringing immediately stopped. Turning, he explained. "Sorry. I, uh, couldn't sleep and decided to get some air. I forgot I'd set the alarm and when I ran inside to shut it off, I knocked over a lamp."

"Are you hurt?" she whispered.

"Just my pride," he said.

In the darkness she could barely make him out.

"Let me take a look." She found a light switch and clicked it on. When she turned back to Mason, the expression on his face faltered as he looked her up and down. His mouth dropped open and a fiery heat filled his eyes.

"Holy hell, Drea," he rasped.

Oh yeah, her slinky nightie.

He cleared his throat. "Is that what you wear to bed?"

His chest was bare, his pants dipping well below his waist. She swallowed, her heart racing, his hard body disturbing her sanity.

"No, I, uh…yes. Sometimes."

"Sometimes, meaning when you're on a business trip with me?"

"Don't flatter yourself."

"I'm not. I'm…*grateful*."

"I just grabbed the first thing I found." What a lie. "Let's just forget about this."

"Don't think I'll ever forget it."

She closed her eyes. She was drawn to him in inexplicable ways, and right now her body was calling the shots. Seeing that look in his eyes wrecked her good sense. She spun around. She couldn't submit to him. She hated him. She... she didn't want him or anything to do with the Boones.

"Don't go, Drea."

She squeezed her eyes tighter. Her feet wouldn't move. "This isn't going to work," she murmured. She couldn't possibly cave, not after all that had happened—or rather, hadn't happened—between them years ago, all that had changed the path of her life.

"We have the night. One night, Drea. Here. You and me."

"There is no you and me."

"There could be."

"Mason, we can't do this. There are things you don't know. Things that make this impossible." Why was he being so persistent? Why wouldn't he just let her go? Maybe for the same reason she'd packed her sexiest nightie for this trip. Maybe there was something that needed finishing.

"All I see are possibilities tonight."

He was pleading his case, countering every one of her refusals. It was hard saying no to him. Not when her body cried out for him. To know Mason that way one time. Would that be a punishable crime?

She pivoted around slowly and Mason was there, in front of her, his eyes raking her in as if he'd already touched her. As if he was making love to her with his deep dark gaze.

Just once. Just once. Maybe she needed to finish this.

Yet she wanted to scream at the injustice. She hated him more because she *wanted* him.

* * *

Mason knew the exact moment Drea decided their destiny tonight. It was in the sudden release of tension in her shoulders, the parting of her sweet lips, the tiny, almost imperceptible nod of her head.

He reached for her hand. "Come with me."

"Where?" she whispered.

"Upstairs."

Without another word, she took his hand and he led her up the staircase to the room he'd chosen to sleep in. The bed was massive, but that wasn't why this space spoke to him. He'd slept in big beds before, but never one with a wall-to-wall window looking out to the ocean and a big beautiful moon. It was as exquisite as a painting. And to have Drea here, set against this stunning backdrop, only heightened the moment, heightened his arousal, made him ache for her. "You're beautiful, Drea."

She looked away, out the window to the seascape. She was still unsure.

"Just one night," he promised. He couldn't take anything more. His heart wasn't healed yet and he didn't know if it would ever be. But Drea woke something in him and he couldn't let it go. He couldn't stop what was about to happen between them.

Taking her hand, he placed it flat on his chest, right over his heart. Her body trembled and her lips quivered.

Was she remembering the last time they'd been like this? Ready to make love, until his brain finally clicked in. It seemed like a lifetime ago. He'd wanted her then, but she'd been young and pure, a virgin, and Drew's daughter.

Tonight was different. She was no longer that young, insecure girl who'd needed affection, who'd needed to feel loved. Drea was all woman, decisive, someone who knew what she wanted. Even though she was reluctant, she would have walked out the door if she truly didn't want to be here with him.

Right now her sweet palm was on his skin and he burned for her touch. He had been empty for so long, but Drea was filling him up, making him overflow with need.

No other woman had done that to him. Not since Larissa.

Tomorrow he might regret this encounter. Tomorrow they'd have to forget all about this and go back to working on the fund-raiser. But not now. Tonight was about the two of them finally coming together.

Just once.

Her fingers glided over his chest. He sucked in oxygen and moved closer to her, giving her better access to his body. "Oh man, Drea."

She put her lips to his chest and her lustrous black hair fell forward. He spread his fingers through the strands as Drea's mouth skimmed over him, licking, kissing, gently, timidly.

She was driving him insane.

He tipped her chin up and brought his mouth down, tasting her sweetness. Her lips were soft and plump, and deserved to be ravaged.

A tiny moan escaped her throat, proof that she wanted things to move faster. His body was on fire and each kiss brought them closer and closer to…more.

All he could think about was getting her naked and touching every single part of her. "I'm glad you wore this," he murmured, slipping a finger under one strap of her sexy gown.

"Why?" she asked, sounding innocent.

"Because I'm dying to take it off you."

"Mason?"

He lowered the strap all the way down her arm, then did the same to the other, allowing her gorgeous, perfectly rounded breasts to pop free. It was suddenly hard for him to breathe. "Wow."

She smiled and wrapped her arms around his neck, causing all that beautiful softness to crash into his chest. His skin burned hot where her nipples pressed against him, and he struggled for control. He kissed her once more, then moved her back against the window and undressed her, removing the flimsy garment carefully.

"You've got it off me," she whispered. "Now what are you going to do with me?"

"Are you kidding me, sweetheart? What am I not gonna do with you?"

"Hmm. I like the sound of—"

He brushed his mouth over hers again, impatient and yearning to touch her. Then he whipped her around so that she faced the window, her back to him, and cupped her breasts in his palms, stroking her again and again. He kissed the nape of her neck and watched her reflection in the window as she opened her mouth to gasp, to smile, then squeezed her eyes shut at the pleasure. His thumb flicked one rosy peak, then the other, and she squirmed in his tight hold. "Drea, open your eyes and look out. It's—"

"Stunning." She gazed out at the glistening water, and then her eyes met his in the reflection from the window. "You're a devil," she whispered, fully aware now that he'd been watching her. "I've never…" She didn't finish her thought, but she wasn't backing off, wasn't angry. Instead, there was awe in her voice.

"Don't close your eyes, Drea. Try to keep them open."

She nodded, the back of her head gently knocking into him.

He rained kisses along her shoulder blade and then slid his palm down her torso, leaving the comfort of her beautiful breasts, seeking another comfort below her waist.

She jumped when he touched her there. "You okay?" he asked.

"Oh, I'm perfect," she murmured, meeting his gaze again in the window, her eyes smoky.

"I can't disagree, darlin'."

And then he began a slow deliberate stroking, eliciting whimpering moans from her. She was so ready, so willing, and he wanted to go on making love to her this way.

In just a matter of minutes, she came apart, and he witnessed the pleasure on her face, knowing full well he'd given that to her.

She turned around and fell into his arms. He clasped her to him and held on tight. It seemed so natural with her, like it was meant to be.

Then he lifted her up and carried her to the bed.

The night was just beginning.

Five

Drea lay on the bed, not quite believing what had just happened with Mason. It was so much more than she'd expected. Now she had to face her new reality: she'd just given in to the enemy and liked it. How monumental was that? And how did she feel about Mason now?

He stood by the bed, his eyes dark, bold and dangerous, totally wiping out her long-ago fantasies of him. He was better than anything her young mind could've conjured up. But back then, it had been about more than sex. Then, it had been about love.

Mason unzipped his pants and pulled them down, never once looking away from her.

A lump formed in her throat. Her body immediately revved up again when she saw him fully unclothed for the first time. All that bronzed skin and muscle. Below the waist, he was pretty awesome, too. He caught her eyeballing him and smiled, but she didn't care. She wasn't a kid anymore. She knew lust and desire, and if this was her only night with Mason Boone, she wasn't going to hold back. "Come to bed," she demanded.

"Bossy," he said with a wide, gorgeous grin. "Are you always like this in bed?"

She chewed on her lower lip and went for the truth. "I'm never this way…in bed."

"Then I think I like it."

He placed one knee on the bed and the mattress dipped. The reality of what was happening hit her, but she focused her attention on him, his masculine beauty, this drop-dead handsome guy covering her body with his.

Every touch, every caress was thought out, meant to bring them both the greatest amount of pleasure. He played the boss game with her, asking her what next, what did she want from him, and he obliged, but deep down she knew Mason wasn't a pushover. He was in full control at all times. And secretly, it turned her on even more.

She wanted to think of this as an impulsive, quick encounter, one they'd both probably come to regret later on, but there was nothing impulsive about the way Mason made love to her. He was slow and deliberate and knew exactly how to make her cry out, how to make her want more, how to make her forget everything but what was happening right now.

"Tell me when you're ready," he murmured against her throat.

"I'm ready," she blurted.

He pressed a kiss to her mouth. His face was a picture of sheer lust and promise.

"Hang on, darlin'," he said, leaning over the bed. He rummaged through his pants pocket and came up with protection.

"Do you always bring those with you?" she teased, watching him rip open the packet.

"I grabbed them at the last minute," he said. "Sorta like how you brought along that slinky piece of fluff you were wearing tonight."

She smiled. Wasn't he clever. "How many *did* you bring?"

"Three." And then he was settling over her body, laying claim, joining them together in a hot flurry of lust and craving.

Drea lay in the crook of Mason's arm, her head resting on his shoulder, her body drained, all her energy spent. She didn't know how long she'd been resting against him. She must've dozed off for a time. Clouds partially covered the moon now and through light and shadows she saw the steady rise and fall of his chest.

She considered going downstairs to sleep in her designated bed, because somehow, sleeping like this with him seemed far too intimate. Yes, they'd taken liberties with each other tonight, but that was about sex. And this was about intimacy and closeness.

She still didn't know Mason any better than she had before.

Except to say he was better than good in the sack.

Her decision made, she slowly backed off, slinking away from the warmth of his arms.

But he pulled her closer. "Drea, where are you going?"

"To…to my own bed."

He sat up then, and urged her to do the same. She kept a sheet around her nude body, covering her to the neck. His eyes dipped there and he frowned slightly.

"Why?"

"Because…it's for the best."

"You know what's best? Getting something to eat. I'm starving," he said. "You must be hungry, too."

Now that she thought about it, they really hadn't had much of anything to eat since having lunch at Big Fish. "I am a little bit hungry."

"Missy keeps the fridge semistocked."

"We can't just eat her food."

"Sure we can. I'll replace everything. I owe her for the busted lamp, too."

Mason swung his legs over the bed and stood up. He wasn't shy, that was for sure. She had a great view of his backside as he slipped on his pants. He grabbed his shirt and stepped around her side of the bed to hand it to her. "Come on, Drea. The night's not over yet. Let's raid the fridge."

According to the digital clock on the nightstand, it was 2:15, the middle of the night, for heaven's sake. But Mason bent his head and kissed her softly on the lips, and her arguments dissolved. There was still some time left before this magical night would end. "Turn around."

His brows shot up. "You're kidding, right?"

He had a point. There wasn't any part of her body he hadn't caressed or kissed, so she shouldn't be shy with him. "I'm not kidding."

He didn't argue as he turned away from her, which gained him a brownie point. She rose and slipped on his shirt; it almost reached her knees. Her fingers quickly worked the buttons all the way up to her throat. "Okay."

He turned and nodded. "Cute." He took her hand in his and they went down the stairs together, bumping bodies in the dark and chuckling about it.

Once in the kitchen, they set the dimmer switch to soft lighting. Mason opened the fridge and she peeked around him to see inside.

"Eggs, bacon, bread, milk," he said.

"Do you like French toast?"

He looked back at her. "You willing to make it?"

"I am. I might cook up some bacon, too."

"I didn't think this night could get any better," he said. He sounded serious and his tone sent shivers through her body. He wasn't teasing. He wasn't making a joke. So far it had been a pretty spectacular day *and* night, yet everything about it scared her silly.

She reached past him and grabbed the bacon. "I'll get this started."

When she turned, he was there, smiling. "Drea, you're an amazing woman."

"Tell me that after you try my French toast."

He curled his hand around her neck and kissed her, hard. When he finally let her go, she rocked back on her heels, her heart hammering.

"You could burn the damn toast and you'd still be amazing."

She felt a blush coming on. Was she that good in bed, or was it that she was the first woman he'd been with since his wife? Could that be true?

Had he been celibate for two years?

She was getting too deep inside her head. That wasn't good. This was a one-time thing and in the morning she'd go back to being cranky Drea from New York and he'd be the man she loved to hate.

Things would get back to normal.

"Uh, thanks," she said, then set about searching for a pan to fry the bacon.

Ten minutes later, she flipped the French toast on the griddle while the bacon cooled on a plate. Mason came up behind her, lifted her long hair and planted tiny kisses behind her ear and along her neckline. Ever since they'd come downstairs, he'd found ways to touch and kiss her while she cooked. And each time, her heart raced and her mind flashed on how he'd made her feel upstairs in the bedroom.

"Did you set the table?" she asked softly.

"All done," he said.

She dished up a platter of brioche French toast halves and bacon, and turned toward the table. "You're only half-way done, Mason. You only set out one plate."

He took the platter out of her hand, set it down and then sat in front of that one place setting. "One plate is all we're gonna need, darlin'."

"What are you—"

"Come here." He grabbed her hand and guided her down onto his lap.

Her body nestled into his easily and he placed a hand on her thighs. "Comfy?"

She laughed. "Are you serious? You want me to feed you?"

"My stomach's growling, but you get the first bite." He lifted a strip of bacon to her mouth.

She hesitated half a second, looking into his eager eyes, then took a small bite. After chewing and swallowing, she offered a piece to him. He gobbled a big mouthful chewing with gusto like a little boy getting his first taste of candy. "Mmm."

"You like my bacon?" she asked.

His mouth twitched, a wicked gleam entering his eyes. "Very much."

She caught his meaning and shook her head.

They took turns feeding each other in the dimly lit kitchen, munching on French toast and bacon in between sweet kisses until most of the food was gone. Mason's body reacted every time she moved on his lap. His large hand held her in place as he stroked her thighs with the flat of his other palm. Her skin prickled and moisture pooled at the apex of her legs. Beneath her, Mason's body was hard, his shaft nudging her side. Her breaths came faster now, and he caught her mouth and kissed her thoroughly until they were both breathless.

"Drea, sweetheart," he whispered hastily, lifting her body and turning her so she straddled him on the chair.

His hands worked underneath her shirt and he tormented her unmercifully.

There was no hope for it. She gave him everything she had, and when he joined their bodies again, her release was instantaneous and damn near glorious.

And when they were through in the kitchen, Mason carried her upstairs to the bed. "The night's not over yet," he promised.

They still had two hours before the dawn of a new day.

Drea doodled on a pad, drawing irregular circles and juvenile-looking flowers, her mind a million miles away from her fund-raising update that would begin in ten minutes in the hospital boardroom. Her lists were all prepared, but it hadn't been easy concentrating on the task. She had Mason Boone on the brain and she kept reliving the magical night they'd shared in California. She would probably never top those twenty-four hours. She and Mason had allowed themselves a brief interlude and made the most of it.

One night.

That's what they'd agreed on.

She'd reminded Mason of that as they'd left the beach house two days ago. Two days of not seeing Mason by her request. She'd insisted on delegating duties and carrying them out separately. He hadn't argued, but her gut told her Mason didn't like it much.

It had made for a long, tense plane ride home. No touching, no teasing, no easy conversation.

And now her body ached, yearning for what was forbidden.

"Good morning, Miss MacDonald. Am I too early for the meeting?"

Her head snapped up at the sound of the female voice. She faced a pretty blonde woman dressed impeccably in a pencil skirt similar to the one she was wearing. "No, not at all. Please call me Drea. We're all working toward the same goal here."

"All right, Drea. Nice to meet you. I'm Linda Sullivan. I missed the initial meeting, but I've been briefed. I'll be your go-to publicity person."

"Great, we're gonna need you. Our financial goal is lofty, but I think we can do it. Are you on the hospital staff?"

"Oh no. I don't have a medical background. I work for Boone Inc. Mason Boone sent me over to help out."

"Oh, so he's not coming?" A dose of relief washed over her.

"That I don't know. He told me about your incredible idea to raffle off a date with the singer from The Band Blue. I've been working behind the scenes and have already contacted their agent. We're putting our heads together on some ideas."

"Okay, great. Sean is a great kid and so are the other band members. We're lucky to have them. So I'm hoping we can make this happen seamlessly."

"I'll do my best," she said.

"Is Mason your boss?"

"I work for all three of the Boones, but mostly for Mason. Risk does some traveling for the company and Lucas was just recently discharged from the military. He's working his way back into the family business, I guess. Mason is pretty awesome to work for."

Drea tilted her head. "How so?"

Linda shrugged. "He's…nice. Not just to me, but to everyone in the office. You know, he seems to really care about his employees."

"Does he?" She sounded skeptical and Linda gave her a funny look.

"Sure he does. When my mama took ill, he gave me all the time off I needed and then called me once a week to make sure I was okay."

Drea didn't want to hear this. She didn't want Linda's hero-worship of her boss to sway her opinion of the Boones. Especially Mason. "I'm sorry to hear your mom was ill."

"She's recovered now and living a good life again."

"I'm glad."

The committee members and volunteers began filing into the conference room, greeting Drea as they took their seats. Once they were settled, she rose to address them.

"Hello, ladies and gentlemen. Thank you for coming. I'm pleased to say that because of all of your hard work, the fund-raising event is shaping up nicely. We're right on target and things are really coming together. I'm thrilled that The Band Blue has agreed to be a part of the festivities, with an added bonus. We'll be raffling off a dream date with Sean Manfred, the lead singer of the band, to one lucky fan. We're hoping this will spark more interest and bring in more revenue for the hospital."

She spoke to the volunteers in charge of the game booths and the art auction, and introduced Linda Sullivan to everyone. Linda stood up and spoke about her ideas, all of which were right on target, and then Drea took the floor again. She went over her to-do lists and was just finishing up when Mason walked through the door, holding a poster board.

Their eyes met, and she froze inside. He smiled at her, a dazzler that revealed his dimples, then apologized to everyone for being late and interrupting. Mason took a place beside her at the front of the room, and the slight hint of his cologne immediately filled her personal space. Breathing it in jarred a memory of being naked with him, losing her inhibitions and giving herself so freely. My goodness, she'd never done anything as wildly erotic as making love to a man on a kitchen chair before. It had been thrilling. Her body heated at the memory and she reined herself in from the rampant thoughts totally unfit for the boardroom.

"It appears Mr. Boone has something to share with us, so I'll let him have the floor now."

Mason turned to her, but she couldn't bring herself to meet his eyes again for fear the entire boardroom would see something she was dead set on concealing. She immediately took her seat.

"Thank you, Miss MacDonald."

She only half listened as he showed the volunteers a detailed mock-up of the grounds at Rising Springs, where everything would take place, from the pony rides and game booths to the art auction and dinner. He was impressive, but she already knew that firsthand.

When he was done with his presentation, he answered questions about the ranch and how it would all work. The dream date raffle also drew enthusiastic praise from the group.

Once the meeting concluded, Drea made quick work of gathering up her notes. When she heard laughter coming from the other side of the room, she looked up. Mason and Linda were chuckling about something they thought dreadfully funny, and sudden sharp pangs stole into her heart. It wasn't easy seeing the two of them smiling at each other, seeing Linda's gleaming eyes fixed on Mason. It was obvious she thought the world of him.

Drea grabbed her briefcase and moved toward the door.

"Drea, hang on a sec. I need to discuss something with you," Mason called out in his deep baritone.

She turned to find both of them looking at her. "I'll be in touch, Drea. Bye for now," Linda said, giving her a little wave.

"Goodbye, Linda."

When the woman exited and closed the door behind her, Drea was left alone in the room with Mason. He walked over to her. "Where are you running off to?" he asked.

"I'm a little busy today," she said.

"Too busy to say hello?"

"Hello," she said softly.

He didn't find her joke funny. His eyes were on her, that dreamy, deep dark gaze latching on. He smelled delicious and looked even more so. She backed up a step.

"I've been thinking about you," he said. "How are you?"

"Fine. Busy, like I said," she blurted.

"Actually, I can't stop thinking about you. Have you been thinking about me, Drea?"

"No."

He gave her a crooked smile. "Liar."

Mason was so confident; he would never believe he hadn't left an impression. And she would have a difficult time denying it. "This isn't the place," she said, as forcefully as she could.

"Name the place, Drea. And I'll be there."

Oh God. No. No. "We can't, Mason. We said one night."

"Maybe we were wrong. Maybe we need more than one night."

His hand came up to her face and he stroked her cheek. His touch warmed everything cold inside and now she couldn't look away, couldn't stop staring at him. "Go away," she whispered.

"I can't," he said, stepping closer, cupping her face in his palm.

"I don't like you," she said, so quietly she could barely hear herself.

"I know. But you like the way I make you feel."

And he liked how she made him feel alive and vital again. Though he hadn't mentioned it since the very first kiss, she understood his attraction to her. He'd been dead inside, deeply grieving the loss of his family, a heartbroken man in pain. She'd been the one to wake him up to pleasure again, and of course he wanted more. His body was obviously craving life and lust again.

But could the same be true of her? Was having a satisfying sexual relationship good for her, too?

It sure felt that way when she was with him.

"Drea, you're thinking about it."

"I'm…not. I need to go."

He dropped his hand from her face and immediate disappointment set in. What was wrong with her? Deep down she understood this wouldn't end well, so shouldn't she be relieved that he let her go?

He was messing with her head, confusing her.

"You can't avoid me forever," he said.

"I know that. We've got a common work goal. It's important to remember that."

"I haven't forgotten the good we can do for the community." He focused on her mouth and then quickly swept his gaze over the rest of her body. It was enough to send shivers along her spine and quicken her pulse. "We're capable of separating the two, Drea."

"I'm not so sure of that." He had no idea what he was asking of her. He had no idea of her pain and suffering. She had too much pride to tell him what she'd gone through. She hadn't trusted anyone with her secret, and Mason was the last person on earth she'd tell.

"Maybe I'm sure enough for both of us."

She glanced at his mouth, recalling what those lips had done to her, how expertly he'd kissed her, and the memory caught her off guard. Her mask of indifference crumbled and she felt completely exposed.

"Drea, sweetheart." He took her hand and pulled gently until she was encircled in his arms, pressed against his chest. Then he kissed her thoroughly, devouring her lips as if he were starving. The kiss ended too quickly, yet both of them were completely breathless. Mason smiled at her, satisfaction in his expression as if to say he'd been right. They needed more time, more nights.

Maybe they did. Maybe Mason *was* right but it scared her and she had to end it now. "I'd better go." This was not what she'd expected when she'd come home to Boone Springs. Mason was changing all the rules and confusing her. It wasn't fair.

"I'll see you soon, Drea," Mason said confidently.

Oh no, he wouldn't. Not if she could help it.

"Dad, next time please ask me before you accept a dinner invitation from the Boones. I was planning on working late tonight." And the last person she wanted to see socially was Mason. They'd had their day and night, and now it was over, but she couldn't tell her father that.

Drea muttered under her breath as she and her father walked up the path to the Boone mansion. When she'd seen Mason as the hospital earlier, he didn't say a word about dinner, yet he must've known.

"I thought you'd want to spend more time with Lottie. Lord above, Drea. Can't I do anything right?"

Drea's shoulders fell. She had been hard on her dad for years, and she'd never accepted his *acceptance* of losing Thundering Hills to the Boones. Why hadn't he fought harder to save their home? "Yeah, Dad, you can. You do." He'd made a supreme effort to win her over since she'd been home. She shouldn't take out her bad mood on him. He had no idea what Mason had put her through, back then and…now.

She couldn't fault Mason for *now;* she took full responsibility for spending the night with him. It had been her own once-in-a-lifetime guilty pleasure, and now she was trying desperately, and without much success, to put that all behind her. "I'm just… Never mind."

"For what it's worth, I'm sorry…about everything," her dad said.

His tone was heart-wrenching.

She didn't mean to sound like a scrooge. And none of this was really his fault. It was hers, for caving in and letting Mason upend her life the way he had. "No, I'm sorry, Dad. I guess I'm stressed about the job. And yes, of course I want to spend time with Lottie. Let's just go and have a nice time tonight." She slipped her arm through his and smiled. "Okay?"

He hesitated a moment, then gave her a nod and a smile back. He seemed relieved and that was all she could ask for at the moment. "Sounds good to me."

Her father looked really nice tonight. He'd never had a smoother shave, his silvery hair was newly cut and tidy, and he'd put on a crisp button-down shirt and pair of slacks for the occasion. On his head was his ever present tan Stetson.

He rang the doorbell and a few moments later Lottie appeared, wearing an apron tied around her waist over a lovely rose silk blouse and skirt, her blond hair touching her shoulders. Drea heard a sudden noise: a quiet intake of breath from her father as he removed his hat.

"Welcome, you two," Lottie said, opening her arms to Drea. "You come here and let me give you a big hug."

Drea laughed and stepped forward, immediately cocooned in Lottie's brand of motherly love. She closed her eyes and hugged back. Only Lottie could make her feel this way, as if she was loved unconditionally. "So good to see you again, Lottie. You look wonderful."

"Thank you. Same here, sweetheart."

Her father remained stonily quiet.

"Hello, Drew."

"Lottie."

Drea wanted to roll her eyes at the two of them, but whatever it was between them they'd have to work out on their own.

"Please come in. Everyone is here."

Lottie led them into the main drawing room, where all three Boone brothers were conversing. Lucas and Risk leaned against the river rock fireplace mantel, and Mason immediately stood up from his chair as they walked in.

His gaze latched on to her and she felt the burn from across the room. Suddenly all the intimate things they'd done to each other were up front and center in her mind. It was as if Mason owned her, at least a little bit, because of what they'd shared. How they'd been with each other.

But she'd had too many years of crushing on him as a young girl and then too many years of hating him as an adult. She was tired of being owned by Mason. Tired of letting him have that much power over her.

She aimed her greeting at Mason's brothers, the other culprits of the Boone clan.

"Hey, Drea," Lucas said, giving her a smile. He'd grown

into a handsome man, with his military haircut and piercing eyes. Risk gave her a wave.

"Lucas. Risk." She wasn't exactly on friendly terms with them, but had to be cordial since she'd been invited to dine with them, and they'd be helping with the fund-raiser.

Lottie made a good effort to engage them all in conversation, the topic being fund-raising. It was a good ice-breaker; Drea could speak for hours on the subject. Mason chimed in, too, adding his insights as Lottie poured wine for everyone but Drew. She handed him a tall glass of iced tea.

Five minutes into their discussion, the doorbell rang. "We've given Jessica the night off, so please excuse me while I get the door," Lottie said.

A short time later, Lottie led Katie into the room. She held a big pastry box in her hands. "Look who was kind enough to deliver our dessert to us. I've invited her to stay for dinner, but I think Katie needs some arm-twisting."

Katie scanned the room, her gaze stopping for a heartbeat on Lucas. He put down his wineglass and faced her squarely, giving her a look that smoldered, before catching himself. Everyone else spoke up. Drea especially wanted her friend to stay. With Mason here, she could really use reinforcements. "Please join us, Katie."

She glanced at Drea's form-fitting black dress, silver jewelry and high heels. "I'm, ah, I don't think so," she said. Clearly, Katie thought she was out of place in her work clothes. "Thank you, though."

Katie had shoulder-length blond hair and the softest blue eyes, and she could wear a pair of jeans like nobody's business. More importantly, she was a good person, through and through.

Mason stepped up. "Why not stay and have a bite with us? We have a new foal in the stable you'd just about fall in love with. I'm sure Luke would love to show it to you."

Katie was a horse lover from way back and this sparked a light in her gaze, though she avoided eye contact with Luke, staring at Mason instead.

"He's a beauty, too," Risk chimed in.

"Looks like the decision's made, Katie," Lottie said. "You're staying."

Katie forced a smile and nodded. "Okay, thank you. I would...love to."

Lottie took the box out of her hands and replaced it with a glass of wine. "Here you go. You all talk while I put these away and check on dinner."

"Want some help?" Drea's father asked Lottie.

Lottie's brows rose. She couldn't recall the last time Drew had offered her any help with anything. "Well now, that would be nice."

Lottie entered the kitchen, Drew a few steps behind her as she mulled over her confusing feelings. She'd known him forever, it seemed, but he'd always been Maria's guy. He'd started off being a good provider for his family, a good father to young Drea and a pretty good husband to her best friend. But after tragedy struck, he'd simply given up... on everything. He'd let his ranch go to ruin, he'd stopped fathering Drea, and worst of all, he'd sought comfort in a bottle. How many years had he wasted? Lottie had promised Maria that she'd watch out for Drew and Drea when the time came. And she had, as much as she could without being a thorn in their sides. But Drew had been so dang hard to deal with. There was no reasoning with an alcoholic. Drew had had to come out of it on his own. He had, but not before causing a lot of damage.

Lottie put the cupcakes on the kitchen counter and turned to find Drew's soft green eyes on her.

"You look real nice tonight, Lottie."

"I bet it killed you to say that," she said, giving him a brief smile. There was truth to her words, but Lottie also had trouble accepting compliments from him. They were rare and made her uncomfortable.

"Well, no. It didn't, actually. That shade of pink suits you."

He looked good tonight, too, better than she'd seen him in a long while. "So do you. Look nice, I mean."

He cleared his throat and stared at her. When they weren't bickering, as they were prone to do, Lottie didn't know how to react. "Here, make yourself useful." She handed him a bowl of fresh greens.

"What's this?" He gave the dish a horrified look, as if weeds were growing inside it.

"Quinoa and kale salad."

Drew's face wrinkled up, but even that couldn't detract from his good looks. "Why?"

She laughed. He was so predictable. She knew he'd rebel against her nourishing meal. "So you can get used to eating healthy foods."

"Oh, the devil. Mason said you might try to change my eating habits. What else do you have planned for supper?"

"All good things, I assure you."

"That's what I'm afraid of. You got dressing for this *salad*?"

"Yep, right here. Lemon vinaigrette."

She handed him the carafe and their fingers brushed.

His gaze shot to hers and she paused for a second, taken by unfamiliar sensations of warmth. She didn't know where to stash those feelings. And Drew wouldn't stop staring at her, the moment seemingly suspended in time. Finally, she snapped out of it. "You go on, bring in the salad. I'll get the rolls."

"Rolls? Now we're talking," he said eagerly.

"Don't get too excited. They're gluten free."

As he marched out of the kitchen, Drew muttered something about how a man could starve to death from good intentions. Lottie braced her hands on the edge of the counter and smiled. She was trying to do right by Drea and Maria, and Drew giving her grief about it wasn't unexpected.

What was unexpected was how much she enjoyed ringing his bell.

Six

Drea finished her meal. She had to admit the dinner hadn't been uncomfortable at all. Lottie had made sure of it. She could talk endlessly about her adventures. She'd traveled the world, and had led a really intriguing life. The woman wasn't the least bit shy about telling everyone about the ups and downs of living large. The one thing she didn't have was a husband and children of her own. Oddly, she'd never married. Drea had always thought the Boones were Lottie's fill-in family. Whenever she decided to stop and rest up a spell before heading out again, she'd spend time with her nephews. Lord knew, the boys loved and respected her to pieces.

"Mason, you haven't touched your broccoli." Lottie narrowed her eyes at him.

"You know I'm not a fan, Aunt."

"And Risk, that poached chicken isn't going to eat itself."

"Yes, ma'am," Risk said, eyeing his brothers for mercy.

"And—"

"I had a late lunch, Aunt Lottie." Lucas rubbed his stomach. "I'm about to bust."

Lottie pursed her lips. The boys were not helping her cause in the least and Drea wasn't going to let her go down without a fight, especially since her father had a big smug smile on his face. All the woman was trying to do was to get her dad to eat a healthier diet. Apparently, none of her nephews were in her corner.

"Lottie, this is a wonderful meal. I think I'll have seconds," Drea said, and right away Mason lifted the dish of chicken and passed it to her. His smirk was nothing short of daring. "Thank you," she said, tipping up her chin as she helped herself to another piece.

"Me, too," Katie said. "I love how you made the salad, Lottie. It's light and delicious."

Lottie nodded at Drew before passing over the salad bowl. "Here you go, Katie. I can tell you girls have a good palate."

Drea's father put his head down, concealing his amusement. Well, at least Lottie could make him smile. It was a good distraction from having to deal with Mason.

His eyes were forever on her and it rattled her nerves. As much as she was at ease during dinner, thanks to Lottie, every time she stole a glance at Mason he was watching her. Not only did his eyes burn straight through to her unguarded heart, he looked devastatingly handsome tonight in a pair of dark pants and a caramel-brown snap-down shirt. What was under that shirt made her head spin; she was reminded of the ripped chest with just enough wisps of hair to weave her fingers through as she'd kissed the hot skin there. His face was chiseled perfection, made even sexier by the dark stubble on his jaw.

Why did he have to appeal to her so much? Why couldn't

she forget about the night they'd shared? She'd promised herself it would be only that. *One night.* She wasn't foolish enough to think that she could totally forgive Mason and his family, or to believe that he was over the loss of his wife.

They'd agreed on one night and now Mason wasn't playing fair. He wasn't letting it be. He was pursuing her, and Lord, if all he had to do was aim some scorching looks her way to get her to rethink her resolve, she was in deep trouble.

"How about you all take a look at that adorable new colt in the stable," Lottie said. "I'll get some coffee brewing and set out Katie's scrumptious cupcakes."

Katie rose. "I'll help you, Lottie."

"Don't be silly. You need to see that colt. Luke, take Katie on up to the stable, will you?"

Luke tossed his napkin onto the table and rose. "Okay, sure. Katie?"

Her friend's tight smile only confirmed to Drea that she didn't want to be alone with Luke. He'd been engaged to Shelly, Katie's older sister, and had walked out on her right before their wedding. He'd joined the Marines and had been gone a while, but Katie's family still hadn't forgiven him. "Will the rest of you be joining us?" Katie asked.

"I'd like to see it," Drea said, coming to her friend's aid. Katie and Luke had once been easy friends. Now things were strained between them.

"I'll stay behind," Risk said. "I've already seen the colt."

"I think I'll just sit a spell on the porch, if you all don't mind," her father said.

Mason didn't say a word, but as Luke ushered Katie out the door, Mason waited for Drea on the threshold. "Haven't you seen the colt?" she asked him.

"Not since Trinket gave birth."

He gestured for her to exit, and when she did, he followed. She did her best to catch up with Luke and Katie, and she was making ground until Mason took her hand from behind, slowing her down.

"Let the two of them talk," he said quietly. "I think Luke needs to repair some of the damage."

She stopped and looked at him. "You think Lucas can do that?"

"He can try. They were pretty close friends."

"Yeah, well. Things change. People change. I'm not sure Katie wants to be alone with Luke."

"What you really mean is you don't want to be alone with me. Isn't that right?"

She sighed and all the fight went out of her. "Maybe."

"Why?"

"You know why! We made a deal and now you're going back on it."

Once Luke and Katie were way up ahead, Drea and Mason began slowly walking toward the stable. "I just think the deal was a mistake."

"Taking that trip to Los Angeles together was the mistake," she said.

"It's killing you that you're starting to like me."

"I don't…like you."

Mason grinned. Oh, he was infuriating. He had enough confidence to fill up a football stadium. Normally, she liked that trait in a man. She'd never been attracted to weak-kneed men who were wishy-washy about themselves. Mason seemed so sure of everything, except when it came to his own heart. He'd been broken, and he was just coming out of that. He was starting to rebuild himself again, but she had no place in his life. Correction: she wanted no place in his life.

When they were in LA, it had all seemed so easy. They were far away from Texas, away from family and friends, away from reality, sharing the night on a beautiful beach. It had almost been as if she were a different woman and Mason a different man. She'd fully expected things to get back to normal once they'd touched down on Texas soil again.

"You don't like me, even a little?"

"Well, maybe I see some redeeming qualities in you." She was being honest.

"Like what? I'm curious."

"You're decisive. You get things done. I admire that."

He nodded. "Anything else?"

"Well…" She stared at him for a long moment. The sun was setting, and only a glimmer of light touched his face now. "You're good—"

"In bed?" He was smiling, and those hidden dimples popped out underneath his sexy day-old beard.

She shook her head. "You have a tremendous…"

His brows lifted wickedly.

"Ego."

"I thought you were going to say—"

"Mason," she warned. "Don't."

"We had a good time in LA."

"It's going nowhere."

"Do you want it to go somewhere?" he asked.

"Of course not. But I can't forget certain things."

"I can't forget certain things, either. Like the way you tremble when I touch you. Or the way your body responds to mine, or the feel of your silky hair or—"

"Mason, please…that's not what I meant."

They reached the stable and Mason glanced inside. "Let's give the two of them some privacy." He took her hand and tugged her toward the back of the structure. She followed his lead, not putting up any resistance. Why didn't she? She had no answer to that question. She could've just as easily held her ground and walked inside the building to meet up with Katie and Lucas.

Now her back was to the wall, literally, and Mason's big body blocked her vision of anything else. All she saw was one gorgeous man, staring at her like she held the answers to the universe in the palm of her hand. "What are you doing?" *To me?* she really wanted to ask.

"I'm spending time with you. I've thought about little else these past few days."

She had to admit that Mason was getting to her. What she liked about him was his determination to never give up. But that trait could also be her downfall.

"I'm leaving when the fund-raiser is over."

He lifted a strand of her long hair and twirled it around his finger. "It's not like we both don't know that, sweetheart."

Sweetheart. There it was again. She wasn't his sweet anything. She really wasn't, but his soft tone made her think otherwise. And it confused her to no end. "This isn't good."

"You're right. It isn't good. It's pretty great."

He leaned in, his face coming inches from hers, his mouth, that delectable expert mouth, so close.

"I—I make you...feel things," she stuttered.

His lips lifted in a smile. "So true."

"That's all this is."

"I make you feel things, too," he whispered, cradling her face in his hands. "Tell me it's not so and I'll back off, Drea."

She opened her mouth to deny it. To deny him. But the words wouldn't come. What was wrong with her? Why couldn't she say no to him and mean it? The look on his face, the hunger in his eyes spoke to her. He smelled of lime and musk, something expensive and rare that was drawing her to him, making her want, making her crave.

All she could do was feel his approach, leaning closer until his hips touched hers and her breasts were crushed against his chest.

Memories flooded in. Of unparalleled kisses. Of being naked with him. Of their two bodies completely in sync with each other. A whimper escaped her mouth as she surrendered totally.

And then his lips were on hers, his mouth taking claim, his kiss a beautiful reminder of how much she'd missed… this. Not *him*. She wasn't missing him so much as she missed the womanly way he made her feel. Desirable and attractive. She had his total approval and that was something she hadn't often felt while growing up. To be honest, her adult life hadn't been all that glorious, either. So naturally, she would take what Mason offered. That had to be it. That had to be the reason his kisses made her legs weak and her heart flutter wildly.

At least that's what she told herself as Mason's mouth demanded more of her, as his body went rigid. It was heady knowing she made him come alive. A true boost to her morale, she had to admit.

As he pressed his hard body home, her lips parted in a moan of pure delight. Everything tingled. Every sensation was heightened.

Voices and then footsteps reached her ears. "Oh no," she whispered.

"Shush." Mason kissed her quiet.

Lucas and Katie were leaving the stable and heading back to the house. It was dark now. Drea and Mason stood still and waited until the sound of their footsteps receded.

"We need to go back," she whispered. An owl hooted and leaves of surrounding trees rustled in the night breeze. The fall air grew crisp but Drea's body was still heated, her heart still raced.

Mason released a deep sigh. A houseful of people waited for them and they couldn't do this any longer. He took her hand. "Let's go see the foal for a minute," he said.

"Okay, yes. We should." So that they could say they had. So that no one would get suspicious.

Once in the stable, they watched mama with her new babe. It was a thing of beauty and grace, and Drea was struck by deep yearning. Remembering her loss, the child she would never know, only compounded the feeling.

Mason stared into the paddock filled with a layer of straw to cushion the horses from the wooden walls and hard ground. Drea had grown up on a ranch, too, and welcomed the pungent scents, the smell of leather and earth.

"Meet me later tonight," he said, his voice firm, determined.

She squeezed her eyes closed. Not because it was a ridiculous idea, but because it was an enticing one. "I…can't."

Mason turned to her and his eyes spoke of promises he would fulfill.

Her body still hummed from his kisses. He wanted more. So did she. But it was impossible.

"Why can't you?" he asked. "And I'd like the truth."

She drew breath into her lungs. "Aside from the obvious reasons—"

"Like you hate me for hurting you, for taking away your family land? You blame me for all the woes of the world?"

"Mason."

He pressed closer to her. Wrapping his hand around her neck, he pulled her in and kissed her thoroughly, without pause, softening up all her hard, unsettled edges.

"Now tell me the truth," he whispered over her lips.

"Where would we meet? I mean, you live here, and it's not exactly private. And my dad's place is off-limits."

Perhaps she'd revealed too much of her thoughts. She

should be denying him this, outright refusing his suggestion. But she couldn't. Maybe she wanted to see what he had in mind. Maybe she was more than a little bit intrigued by a secret rendezvous.

Mason stroked a finger across her cheek, his tender touch creating tingles down to her toes. "At The Baron. I keep a room there, for when I work in town."

"Your hotel?"

He nodded. "I'll be there at eleven. Waiting for you."

A dozen questions filled her head. She wasn't a teenager, sneaking out for a date. She wasn't a woman who liked lying. But she'd have to do one or the other in order to meet Mason.

"I don't know."

"Think about it, sweetheart. And you do know. You just can't face it yet."

Face what? That she wanted him? That after their time in LA she'd been thinking about Mason in a purely unbusinesslike way.

So much for *Business with Mason.* That had lasted as long as a snowball in hell.

He kissed her again, then took her hand and led her out of the stable.

Already she felt like a fraud, entering the Boone home pretending that nothing monumental was happening between them. Pretending that they weren't crazily attracted to each other.

Back at the house, Katie pulled her into the kitchen as the others were drinking coffee. Her friend whispered, "What happened to you two out there?"

"You mean, when we didn't show in the stable?"

"Yes, that's what I mean. You were supposed to be my cover. I didn't want to be alone with Lucas."

"I know. Sorry. I let you down. Was it horrible?"

"What? No, not really. We're just distant friends now, is all."

"Okay, good. That's what I was hoping. But he was sort of ogling you at dinner tonight."

Katie giggled. "I was just going to say the same thing about Mason. He wasn't letting up. His eyes were all for you. So, what happened out behind the stable tonight?"

Drea gasped, partly in shock. Not about Katie knowing something was going on, but the idea that maybe the others were piecing things together, as well. "You know?"

"I don't think Luke gave it a thought, but I figured something was up."

"It's complicated," Drea said, keeping her voice down. "I can't go into detail, but something happened between me and Mason when we were in LA and now he wants to see me again. Like, later tonight."

"Go."

Drea blinked. "What do you mean, go?"

"Drea, you haven't been with a man in a long while. And maybe…well, maybe you just need to get Mason out of your system. Geesh, I sound like a guy, don't I? But it's true. How can you move on with your life until this part of it is satisfied? See what happens with Mason. I mean, if you didn't want to meet him, if you thought it ridiculous, you wouldn't have told me. You would've shot him down immediately. But you didn't do that. You want to go."

"I don't like sneaking around."

"Sounds kind of exciting, if you ask me." Katie's voice got animated, making Drea smile and shake her head.

Her decision now made, she gave Katie her best stern look. "If this goes south, I'll come after you, Katie girl."

Her friend kissed her cheek. "Go, and have a good time on my behalf. Heaven knows, I've been a safe little mouse all my life, so at least let me enjoy a bit of intrigue through my bestie."

"So glad I'm a source of your entertainment."

Katie shoved a bunch of extra napkins into Drea's hands while she grabbed the plate of cupcakes, "Come on, let's get back out there before someone comes looking for us."

"Yeah, Luke might come searching for you."

"That would be a no-can-ever-do," Katie said.

"Yeah, and that's what I thought about Mason Boone for all of my grown-up life. Just goes to show, never say never."

Drea stood outside the door of The Baron Hotel's top floor suite, ready to knock. That she was here at all still shocked the stuffing out of her. But Katie had been right. Drea had unfinished business to settle with Mason and so his proposed midnight interlude might not go exactly as he'd planned.

Getting away hadn't been hard at all. She'd waited until her father was sawing logs, before quietly stepping out of the house. She'd left him a note saying that she had trouble sleeping and had gone for a drive, just in case he woke and didn't find her home. All that was true, so she hadn't really lied. At least that was what she told herself.

She knocked on the door softly and heard footsteps approach.

Swallowing hard, she braced herself. When Mason opened the door, his shoulders relaxed, a small smile surfaced and she read great relief in his expression. This wasn't the confident man she'd expected to find. Instead, Mason's vulnerability had shone through, touching something deep and precious in her heart. He hadn't been sure she'd show up. And he'd been worried, perhaps even saddened, to think she'd let him down.

It wasn't fair. She had Mason pegged as an arrogant pain in her side, and he was proving her wrong.

"Drea." There was a wistful tone in his voice. So different than the man who ran an empire, the man who commanded respect at all times. Mason Boone was full of surprises.

"I'm…here." She lifted her shoulders, then let them fall.

He took her hand and gently pulled her into the room. "I'm happy to see that."

He let her hand go and she walked into the suite taking in the living area, with its fireplace and twin sofas facing each other, the dining area and the hallway that led to the other rooms. It was luxurious and grand, something she'd expect from a Boone. But it was also homey in a way that said Mason spent a lot of time here, from the scattering of square, embroidered pillows on the floor, to the sports magazines on the coffee table to a giant screen TV on the wall. She recognized the pillows as being Lottie's handiwork. Peaches, oranges and apples filled a bowl on the kitchen counter and photos of Rising Springs Ranch graced the hallway walls. Soft classical music played in the background, perhaps the biggest surprise of all.

"Is this your Zen place?" she asked turning to find him watching her from the middle of the living room.

"Or my man cave."

His gaze was forever on her, as if to say he couldn't believe she was really here.

"No, it's definitely Zen." She walked to the window and stared out at the town Mason's ancestors had established. How must that feel? To know your family had built this town from the ground up. To have streets, a hospital, an entire town named after the Boones. To have that entitlement.

She looked at Mason, standing there, curiosity on his beautiful face. "You didn't think I'd come, did you?"

He sighed and walked over to her. "I'm...a little surprised."

"No one is more surprised than me, Mason."

He stood at arm's length from her and his presence consumed her. He was that type of man, one who could overpower with just one glance. Usually he loomed large, but tonight she was seeing a different side of him. "Do you still resent me and all the Boones?"

"My feelings about you are...complicated."

He stepped closer and entwined his fingers with hers. "Can we try to uncomplicate things? Can we just talk about it, Drea? About that night so long ago?"

His question made her jittery. She wanted to yank her hand away, to turn her back on him, to walk out the door if necessary. She'd lost her baby and a big part of herself, after all. How could she possibly explain the damage that was done after that night? She'd struggled for years with all of it.

But as Katie had said, she needed to be able to get on with her life. To move past this. And maybe there was no better way than to talk it through. "At one point in my life, you were my everything, Mason." God, it was hard to admit that.

"Come here," he said, leading her to the sofa. She sank down and he sat beside her. They faced each other, still holding hands. "You were saying?"

"You heard what I said. I was halfway in love with you, Mason."

"And I shouldn't have let it go that far. I was attracted to you. I'd always liked you. We used to play together, if you remember."

"Of course I remember. We were friends once."

"And then, when you were bucked from your horse and took a hard fall, I found you in the meadow. Your ankle was bruised and you couldn't put any pressure on it."

"You were wonderful that day," she said, remembering how gallant he'd been. He'd stayed with her, helping remove her shoe and using a cold can of soda pop he'd been drinking to keep the swelling down on her ankle. He'd missed a baseball game with his friends to stay with her. And then, when she was able to stand up, he'd lifted her and carried her to an old carriage house on their property. The chemistry between them had been off the charts. She'd never looked at Mason that way before, but having him tend her, having his dark concerned eyes on her, having him touch and care for her, had made her dizzy. From that moment on, she'd set her sights on him.

"And you were seventeen."

"A month away from my eighteenth birthday, Mason. I wasn't a kid."

"I didn't think so, either. But you were a virgin and I was going for my final semester at Texas A&M."

"I was willing, Mason. That night, up in your bedroom. We were all alone."

He heaved a big sigh. "I know. It was so hard to say no to you. But I had to. You were Drew's daughter, for one. And he was a family friend, even if you didn't want to think so at the time."

"But we'd been seeing each other every day for a full month and I knew my heart. I told you I was ready."

"Look at me, Drea," he commanded, and she lifted her chin to meet his gaze. "You also said one other thing to me. Do you remember what that was?"

She thought back and couldn't really recall what else she'd said. For all these years, she'd blocked out the hurtful memory of that night, the exact words spoken, but the humiliation had lingered on. She shook her head. "No."

He squeezed her hand gently. "You said...you needed me. Not wanted, not loved, but needed me."

She pulled back, wrenching her hand from his in utter shock. "Oh, so you thought I was this needy kid, starving for affection. You thought you'd get stuck with me, the pathetic daughter of a widower drunk, a girl so confused about her feelings that she'd give up her virginity to you. What you did to me that night was cruel."

Tears stung her eyes. This was horrific. She didn't think she could ever be more humiliated than when she'd bared her body to Mason and he'd rejected her. But this was just as bad, if not worse.

"No, that's not what I'm saying." Mason's voice sharpened immediately. "I wanted you, Drea. But there were too many obstacles blocking us and I had to be the grown-up. I had to deny you and myself. It was for the best. And I'm sorry that I hurt you, but I had to be firm. I had to make sure not to leave any doubt in your mind, because…because there was doubt in mine. So yes, I spoke harshly to you and I've regretted it every day since. But we did the right thing, Drea. We did."

She got up and walked to the window, staring at the lights of the town. "You wanted me to hate you. Well, you succeeded. You have no idea what your rejection did to me."

Mason came up behind her. "I did what I thought best for you at the time. I cared about you too much to use you, to have you for one night and then take off. My conscience wouldn't allow it, but no, I didn't want you to hate me."

"But I did. Especially after what your family had already done to mine. I thought you heartless and mean, and wondered if I'd ever meant anything to you."

"Drea, listen to me. The Boones aren't as bad as you seem to think. We're not greedy robber barons after people's land. My family tried to help yours."

He wasn't convincing her.

Mason clasped her shoulders, his hands gentle, as if testing to see if she'd flinch. But his touch, like always, comforted her instead, giving her solace and peace. She'd spent so much time hating him that now there wasn't much hatred left. Only regret. She had so many regrets.

"If it's any consolation to you, I didn't date for nearly a year after that. Every time I looked at a woman, I thought of you. I swear it, Drea. It's hard to admit, but I have second-guessed that night in my head many times."

If she could believe him, it helped knowing that he'd suffered a little bit, too. That he'd had doubts about letting her go. It helped her ego and her pride and also helped put things in perspective. She'd never heard his side of the story before. She'd never known his motivation for breaking things off and breaking her heart.

Yet there was more to her story, but she couldn't reveal it to him. It would only serve to prove he'd been right. She had been needy, a girl craving love and affection.

She'd done a stupid thing and maybe now she could put the past behind her. Her hatred depleted, maybe now she could move on with her life, just like Katie had said. For the first time in a long time, she would be free of that burden. Her feelings about the Boones in general were a different story. Her resentment about Thundering Hills was still there, but no longer was she driven by contempt and anger. "It does help knowing that."

Mason kissed the back of her neck, then nibbled along her collarbone. She arched her head, giving him more access. The skin where he kissed her burned.

"If you want to leave, I'd understand. But I don't want you to, sweetheart. I want you to stay."

She turned around and he immediately wrapped her in his arms. His head came down and his lips brushed hers gently, sweetly. Mason pulled back and smiled at her, and there was that vulnerability in his eyes again. When he was like that, she was even more attracted to him. The look on his face as he waited for her answer had her melting inside.

"I want to stay."

A wide grin spread across his face. He squeezed her tightly and kissed her again, but briefly. "Would you like something to drink? Eat?"

"After eating Katie's Molten Ganache cupcake, I don't think I'll ever eat again. But I would like a drink."

"A drink it is. What can I get you?"

"White wine?"

He nodded and headed toward the kitchen. "Have a seat. I'll get it for you."

She settled on the sofa, and while she waited, made note of the fact that Mason didn't have one photo of his wife in any of the rooms she'd been in. No wedding pictures, no pictures of the two of them lounging around, riding horses or sitting on a fence at Rising Springs Ranch.

Were the memories too hard for him?

She'd heard people say Larissa was the love of his life. He'd been crushed when she died.

Yet Mason almost never brought her up.

And so now here Drea was, hardly a replacement for his dead wife. No, she was a brief interlude, and she had to remember that. After the fund-raiser, she'd head home to her pretty, cool apartment and life in New York, and Mason would move on, too.

"Here you go," he said, handing her a glass of wine. He sat down beside her with his own drink, something golden-brown, bourbon probably.

"Thank you." She sipped her drink and breathed in Mason. She should never mix alcohol and the scent of a gorgeous man. Or maybe she should. She smiled.

"What's going on in your head?"

"Nothing."

She took another sip.

"You smiled. What were you thinking?"

"Okay," she said. "I'm thinking that I'm here with you without…"

"Without hating me?"

She nodded.

"So you like me now?"

"Well," she said, bringing the glass to her mouth. "Let's not go that far."

There was a gleam in Mason's eyes. He wasn't vulnerable anymore, far from it. His expression meant danger and pleasure and promise.

He took the glass out of her hand and set it down. "Actually, let's go as far as we can tonight," he whispered. He took a last gulp of alcohol and then kissed her hard on the lips.

Her body reacted to the potent taste of whiskey, to the scent, the kiss, the man.

"You look amazing. I wanted to tell you earlier. That dress is—"

"Coming off?" She loved the look the surprise on his face.

He chuckled deep in his throat. "That, too, but it's gorgeous on you."

And five minutes later, after skillfully undressing each other, piece by piece, kiss after kiss, Mason lifted her up in his arms and carried her to the bedroom.

The bedroom was low-key but luxurious, with large dark furnishings. The windows looked out over the other side of town, toward the quiet suburbs of Boone Springs. The drapes were pulled back, and the light of the half-moon filtered in through nearly sheer curtains, splashing over

Mason's body as he lowered her onto the bed. She felt the cool, silky sheets on her back.

Mason stared at her a moment, something dark flickering in his eyes before he joined her on the bed. That look frightened her. Was it guilt? Or doubt? Was he second-guessing all this? Had he lost his desire for her? "What?" she asked softly.

He didn't hesitate. "I'm thinking how beautiful you are."

His words sent a thrill through her body. Yet she had never wanted this. To be his experiment, to have him want her solely due to a crazy chemical attraction he had for her. But here she was, also lured by that undeniable chemistry, waiting and wanting to be dazzled by him again. It would all be okay as long as she recognized this for what it was. As long as she didn't let him in, the way she had as a teen.

"But are you okay with all of this?" he asked her.

"He asks as I'm naked in bed with him."

"Just making sure, sweetheart."

His next kiss wiped away any doubt.

Mason was a thorough lover, from his mind-numbing kisses to his attention to her body. He caressed her lovingly, gently massaging her breasts until her nipples ripened to tiny hard pebbles. His tongue did wonderful things, making her whimper in a way that couldn't be mistaken for anything other than pure sexual pleasure.

Her skin prickled as sizzling, sweeping heat poured into every crevice, and when he paid deep attention to the sweet spot below her navel, she cried out. His mouth was relentless, his hands were masterful. Her back arched off the bed as an earth-shattering release tore through her. She panted his name.

"I'm right here, darlin'."

And he *was* right there, now sheathed with protection

and rolling onto his back so he lay next to her. She was still coming down from her high and Mason waited for her patiently.

Then he whispered, "Come to me, Drea."

He guided her so that she was on top, her legs straddling him. He circled her waist with his big hands and helped her, fitting her body to his. She sank onto him and her eyes shuttered closed. It was a beautiful joining.

"You are incredible like this." His voice was a husky mixture of awe and gratitude. "Your hair, your skin. You feel like heaven, Drea."

His words brought her joy. And her skin prickled again, the heat from before magnified. She didn't wait for him to move, but began a slow, steady gyration, sinking farther down, giving Mason a reason to grit his teeth and groan.

He touched her all over, his thumbs flicking across her breasts, his hand working magic below her waist. She sped up her pace, cementing that look of awe on his face. Her second release was intense, stronger than before, her voice at a higher pitch as she called out Mason's name.

Her completion couldn't be compared to anything she'd experienced before. Not that she was an expert. She'd had exactly three relationships in her life, and yes, Mason topped them all. But if she'd had a hundred, he would still come out the winner. She knew that for a fact.

She fell into his arms and he kissed her silly. And then he rolled them both over, so that he towered above her on the bed. She gazed up into his handsome face filled with hunger and lust.

"I want you, Mason," she said softly.

"You've got me," he said.

Then he drove his point home, telling her yes, indeed, she had him.

* * *

Mason's phone alarm woke him from a deep sleep. Normally, he liked waking up to Larissa's favorite song, Faith Hill's "Breathe." It was a humbling reminder of his wife, and the child he'd never know, and somehow it made him feel closer to them. He'd never thought to change it. If he did, it would be like losing another piece of Larissa. Another soul-emptying piece of her.

But today, he shut off the alarm quickly and hinged up to a sitting position.

"Hell." He ran his hand down his face. He didn't have to see the empty place beside him on the bed or look around the suite to know that Drea was gone. He should've been more considerate. He shouldn't have fallen asleep. At the very least he wanted to make sure she'd gotten home safely last night.

He would have gladly driven her home. He would've kissed her goodbye in the wee hours of the night and watched as she entered the cottage.

He rose and dressed then wandered over to the window. Boone Springs was just rising, too, and the autumn sun was warming everything up.

He craved a cup of coffee to clear his head. Right now, his thoughts were on two women.

His wife, for one. Dead and buried two years ago next week. He didn't need a calendar under his nose to remember the date. He still saw her pretty face and the silky cinnamon hair that bounced off her shoulders when she walked. And those light blue eyes that lit like fireworks every time he smiled at her.

She'd moved to Boone Springs seven years ago, and he'd met her at his friend Trace Burrows's wedding. She'd been a college friend of the bride, just visiting town and looking for work. Mason had fallen hard for her immediately and was desperate for her to stay on in Boone Springs. Without her knowing it, he'd pulled some strings and she'd been hired as a television anchor for the local news station, WBN. She'd been great on camera and off.

After they were married, he'd fessed up about his desperation to keep her in town, hoping she wouldn't go ballistic. She'd only smiled. "I would've gotten the job without your help. I nailed that audition." That was Larissa. She'd been fierce and smart and wonderful.

Mason grabbed his phone and walked into the kitchen. He set up the coffeemaker to brew. Later, at the ranch, he'd get breakfast. For now, the steady drip, drip, drip of dark roast was enough to satisfy him.

That's when something shimmery on the hardwood floor caught his eye. He walked over and bent to pick it up. It was a long strand of looped silver, the necklace Drea had worn last night. As he stared at it, memories rushed in, of him removing her black dress, taking off her shoes and every other pretty little thing she wore. Man, he'd wanted her so badly last night.

He'd been struck that she'd shown up at all. And that they'd finally cleared the air about their past.

That's when his doubts had rushed in. He'd had a moment, a panic attack of emotion. Drea's resentment about him and his family had always been misguided, yet it had provided protection he could count on, a barrier she wouldn't allow to be broken. Because he was never going to fall in love again. He'd never have another permanent relationship. His wife was still in his heart.

"So now what, idiot?" he murmured, holding Drea's necklace in his hand. It was warm, like her. And sleek and beautiful. Also like her.

Mason picked up his phone and texted Drea. I have something of yours.

He waited a minute, poured his coffee and then received her answer. Did I lose my panties?

He laughed so hard coffee sloshed from his cup, just missing his hand. If you had, I wouldn't be giving them back.

Ha! What then?

Wait and see. I'll bring it by your place this morning.

I'll be at Katie's Kupcakes.

Great, save one for me. I'll see you there.

Mason put away his phone before she could text him not to come over. He was going to see her. To tell her he'd wanted to take her home last night. Any man of honor would do the same.

And that's where it got confusing. Because he had a sinking feeling that even if she hadn't lost her necklace and slipped out of his place quietly last night, he would've found a reason to see her again today.

Seven

Drea didn't have to try another cupcake. She'd chosen her favorite and that was that. When she set her sights on something, usually there was no changing her mind. "This one, Katie. This has got to be one of them."

In the back work area of the bakery, Drea leaned over the stainless-steel countertop and took another big lick of raspberry cream cheese frosting. The cupcake was so pretty, a lemon rosemary cake infused with raspberry filling and covered with delicious icing. "I love your idea, by the way."

Katie had offered to come up with two signature cupcakes for the fund-raiser, one that appealed to adults and one for the kids. Of course, her other cupcakes would be for sale, too, and Katie was donating all the proceeds she earned to the cause. She was also overseeing the cupcake decorating booth.

"Thanks. And I agree. I love the combination of flavors in this one. So now we've got one for the adults. What about the kids?"

"Kids love all cupcakes." Drea continued to devour hers.

Great sex had a way of making her hungry. Her heart sped as she thought about the incredible night she'd shared with Mason. After he'd fallen asleep, she'd quickly dressed and driven home, making as little noise as possible as she entered the cottage. Luckily, her father had been sound asleep. She'd tiptoed to her room, undressed quietly and gotten into bed.

Sleep hadn't come easily. She'd missed Mason, missed waking up with him like she had at the beach house, breathing in his after-sex scent and snuggling up tight. But it was best this way. At least she didn't have to answer questions from her dad. That would've been awkward for sure.

"I want to make it special for the kids—a cupcake they can't pass up," Katie said.

Drea tapped a finger to her lips. "Well, what do kids love more than anything?"

"Christmas?"

She laughed. "So true, but not Christmas this time. I know…they love parties. Can you conjure up a party cupcake?"

"Confetti cake isn't new."

"No, but what about…a rainbow cupcake?"

Katie's eyes widened, and Drea could just see the wheels of invention turning in her head. "I think I can do that. We'll have three flavors on the inside, and then I'll do a rainbow frosting on top. I don't know a single child who doesn't like rainbows."

"That sounds wonderful," Drea admitted, but then as an afterthought said, "But isn't it a lot of work?"

Katie grinned. "Not if you're helping me."

"Are you serious? I can't…bake. I'm so not a baker, and definitely not one of your caliber."

"You are a baker. It's not that hard. But I was teasing. I'll get extra help from Lori, my assistant, and it'll all work out. Besides, you'll be running the entire show at Rising Springs. You're gonna have your hands full that weekend."

"I know. It's hard to believe it's less than two weeks away."

"I'm looking forward to having the kids learn how to frost a cupcake. I've got all these ideas for decorating. Some moms and dads from Park Avenue Elementary School are going to run the booth with me."

"I think that's going to be a hit. Kids love that sort of thing."

The overhead bell on the shop door chimed. Katie took a peek out front. "Speaking of having your hands full. There's a gorgeous hunk of a guy out there, and I don't think he wants a cupcake."

"Mason?"

Katie nodded. "He looks impatient. He must be dying to see you."

"Don't be silly. He's only returning something of mine."

"That you left at his place last night?"

Drea opened her mouth, but nothing came out. She straightened out her dress, slipped her feet back into her heels and fluffed her hair a bit.

"You look great. Go. And remember, I want deets later. You owe me."

"Okay," she answered breathlessly.

She walked into the café, coming around the corner of the glass display case to face Mason. "Hi."

His eyes filled with warmth. She tried not to notice, not to make a big deal of the way he was looking at her. But her heart swelled and she was absolutely certain she was eyeing him with that very same look.

"Hi." His voice was husky and deep. He wore a tan shirt under an ink-black suit, no tie, his collar open at the throat. He removed his hat, smiled and then gave her a kiss on the cheek. "You ran out on me last night."

"Shh," she said, glancing out the window. It was mid-morning and the bakery café was empty yet someone could walk in at any moment. "I didn't run out. You knew I had to get home before I turned into a pumpkin."

"Well then, Cinderella, I came to see if this fits." He dug into his pocket and came up with her silver loop necklace.

She smiled. "Not exactly a glass slipper."

"And I'm hardly a prince. But let's see if it fits."

Mason walked behind her, his body so close, his memorable scent teasing her nostrils. He lifted her ponytail out of the way, and his warm breath caressed the back of her neck. "You're trembling," he said as he secured the clasp.

"It's a little cold in here." It wasn't.

He nibbled on her nape, planting delicious kisses behind her ear. Her breathing hitched and she felt a hot tingling in her belly. "I can keep you warm."

"I know." Heat flushed her cheeks. She didn't often blush, but Mason was capable of bringing out new sides of her personality.

When he came around to face her, he noticed her pink cheeks, which should've embarrassed her. But there was an incredible softness in his eyes. Then he glanced at the necklace and his brows furrowed, his expression turning serious. "I would've driven you home last night."

"I had my car."

"Still, I should've made sure you got safely home."

"Thank you. But I didn't want to wake you."

"I missed you when I woke up."

Her breath caught in her throat. She didn't have a response for him. He was too devastatingly handsome and honest for her peace of mind. She'd felt the same way; leaving him asleep in his bed had made her feel terribly lonely. She hadn't felt that way in a long time.

When she didn't reply, he sighed. "What are you doing for lunch?"

"Lunch? I'm working through lunch. In case you don't realize it, the fund-raiser is less than two weeks away."

"And look at all the progress we've made. It's all gonna come together. Linda is working her buns off on promo for The Band Bluc and the date with Sean. You've got a handle on the art auction. I heard you managed to get donations from several art galleries. That's huge."

"Yes, I'm excited about that. More than twenty-five paintings and five bronze sculptures, and some wood sculptures, as well. It should bring in a good deal of revenue. Is everything going well at the ranch?"

"Yeah, but I need your advice. There's things we need to go over."

"I'm happy to. When?"

"We can discuss it over lunch." His eyes twinkled. He'd caught her and all she could do was smile.

"You are persistent."

"It's for the cause, Drea. We both have to eat. Can't afford to run our bodies down."

As if the man had ever been sick a day in his life. He was fit and she knew that firsthand. "So *survival* is your new pickup line?"

"Do I need a pickup line?"

No. Never. But she wasn't going to admit that to him. "Where should I meet you?"

"At the ranch...in about an hour and a half?"

"Okay, I'll finish up here with Katie and meet you."

He nodded and turned to leave, then pivoted around, strode over to her and landed a kiss on her mouth that literally rocked her back on her heels. *Wow.*

He grinned, plopped his hat back on his head and then took his leave.

"Bye, Katie," Drea said, giving her friend a peck on the cheek. "I'm off now. Got a few errands to run before I head back to the ranch."

Katie shook her head. "To meet Mason. Boy, oh boy. You sure do lead an exciting life."

Drea slung her handbag over her shoulder. "We're discussing business over lunch, is all."

"Didn't sound like the two of you discussed much business last night. Don't get me wrong, I'm glad you two hooked up. It's about time."

Drea stood on the threshold of the bakery kitchen, grateful Lori was busy serving customers and no one was within earshot of their conversation. Katie had pried some deets, as she called them, out of her about last night's trip to The Baron as Drea helped bake an experimental batch of rainbow cupcakes. Katie sure knew her stuff; the cupcakes had turned out perfect. And now she was matchmaking, which wasn't allowed between close friends. Or at least it shouldn't be.

"I bet you two don't get much work done this afternoon, either. I bet he takes you somewhere really nice."

"You do have a crazy imagination."

"Just go. You don't want to leave his hunkiness waiting."

"I'm going, I'm going."

Drea left Katie in the bakery kitchen and had reached the front door when it opened suddenly and she bumped into the man walking in.

"Excuse me. Sorry," he said.

"No, no. It was my fault, too. I wasn't looking where I was…" She glanced up and found the man's eyes on her. It wasn't just any man, it was Brad. Dr. Brad Williamson, the taker of her virginity, the man who'd offered to marry her. The man she'd had to walk away from because it wouldn't be fair, since she didn't love him.

"Drea, is that you?"

She bit her lip and nodded. Too many emotions stirred inside, pain and regret being at the top. She hadn't seen Brad in ten years. But he looked the same, if a bit fuller in the face, more solid all the way around. He was in his early thirties, an age when men flourished, showing a certain mature confidence and grace. He had intelligent blue eyes, a nice tan, and his longish hair was the same sandy-blond color she remembered.

"W-what are you doing here, Brad?" she blurted. He was a blast from her past and not necessarily a welcome one. Immediately, her nerves jumped. It wasn't him, but the memory of the entire ordeal that rattled her. "I mean, I never thought I'd see you in Boone Springs."

"You and me both," he said, smiling at her as if he was really glad to see her. "But I had the opportunity to give a few interviews and lectures on my book tour not far from here, and well, when I read about the hospital fund-raiser and your part in it, I thought I'd come by and see for myself."

"You've written a book?" After college, Brad had gone on to med school and had become a pediatrician. She knew this only because he'd texted her occasionally after the breakup, updating her, though she'd never replied. She'd just wanted that part of her life to be over. After a time, he'd stopped texting her.

"Yes, on the trials of raising a toddler."

"Do you…" She swallowed hard. "Do you have children?"

His blue eyes softened immediately and he nodded. "Two. Meggie is three, Charlie is five. Living with their mother now, but we have joint custody."

"Must be hard," Drea said.

"The kids are well-adjusted. My ex and I try our best to make sure of that. That's one reason I wrote the book. It's called *The See-Saw Effect of Parenting*."

She nodded. Brad had been destined to be a leader in his field. He was superintelligent, determined and, well, very handsome. Not that it had anything to do with anything, but she couldn't help noticing that about the man she'd singled out and seduced her first week of college, just to get back at Mason, just to prove that she was desirable. Mason's rejection that summer had her running into a stranger's arms, and lucky for her, Brad had turned out to be a decent guy. A guy who'd fallen for her, a guy who'd planned on marrying her to give their child security.

God, she'd been so confused, so scared and so damn naive.

The door chimed again and a few customers walked in and. Drea and Brad had to move over to continue the conversation. "Guess we're in the way," he said. "Do you have a few minutes…for an old friend? Just to catch up?"

She glanced at her watch. "I have a few minutes before my meeting." With Mason.

"Here?"

No, not here. Not where people might overhear their conversation. "There's a park just a few streets down. We could walk there. Did you want coffee? Or a cupcake?" she asked, figuring it was the reason he'd come.

"No, I'm good. How about you?"

She shook her head. "Katie's a friend and I've been tasting cupcakes all morning, so no. I'm definitely good."

"Well, then. Let's go." He opened the door for her and

she walked out onto the busy sunny street. Donning her sunglasses, she waited for Brad. Once he caught up, after holding the door for a few more customers walking in, they headed south toward the park.

The tree-lined street looked so smalltown compared to New York, with its skyscrapers blocking the sun so that some streets were in shadow most of the time.

"How have you been?" he asked, keeping stride with her.

"I've been really good. This project is very special to me, since it'll fund a cardiac wing at the hospital in my hometown. I'm here for a few more weeks."

"Are you okay with me looking you up?"

"Sure. It's…good to see you, Brad."

"Same here. I, uh, think about you and what you've taken on here. Because of your mom?"

She stopped and stared into his blue eyes. "You remember?"

"Of course I remember, Drea. When we met, your mother's death and your helplessness over it were a big part of who you were. And now you're doing something to make a difference. I remember you'd always wanted that."

She looked away for a second, tears misting her eyes. She was touched that he remembered what made her tick, how vulnerable she'd been when they'd met. "You're right. It was."

When he smiled at her, her spirits lifted a bit. She hadn't been thrilled to bump into him, but now, after talking with him a few minutes, she began to relax.

When they reached the park, they took a seat on a bench facing the playground. A few toddlers were giving their moms a merry chase around the slide.

"How about you?" he asked. "Did you ever marry? Do you have a family?"

"No and no. I'm married to my job right now."

"I hear that." He didn't criticize her for not settling down, like so many others had. If a woman closing in on thirty wasn't married, well then, either there was something wrong with her or she was too ambitious for her own good.

They spent the next hour catching up on news, keeping the conversation light without mentioning the heartache they'd both endured. Brad seemed to hold no grudge toward her. Even though he'd been in love with her and would've married her, baby or not, she'd broken up with him after she'd miscarried. She'd made one mistake after another, but marrying Brad when she didn't love him would've been cruel.

Drea had learned a valuable lesson. Love is only right when it's two-sided and equal. There could be no imbalance.

Brad told her about himself, his years in med school and how he'd opened a pediatric practice in Manhattan and gotten married shortly after that. When she asked about his children, his face lit up and he spent a good deal of time on his little Meg and Charlie.

"I'll be in town until your fund-raiser," he said. "I plan on making a donation."

She smiled. "That's wonderful. We have lofty goals, so it will really be appreciated."

"Drea, do you mind if I ask you a personal question?"

Her heart stopped. *Oh no. Here it comes.* She braced herself. "What would you like to know?"

"Are you seeing anyone right now?"

That was totally unexpected. She fidgeted with her blouse, her head down. So he wasn't going to dredge up the past, or excoriate her for breaking his heart. "No, not really." It wasn't as if she was dating Mason or anything. *Just sleeping with him.*

Brad's face broke out in a big smile. It was almost laughable how obvious he was. "Well then, I'd like to ask you to dinner one night."

Why? She wanted to know, but she held her tongue.

"As a friend," he added. "I'm staying close by and have the book signing in a few days, but I'd love to catch up more over a nice relaxing dinner."

She hadn't expected a dinner invitation. Sure, she could tell him she was too busy, but he was looking at her earnestly and what would it hurt? Maybe it would actually be therapeutic to spend time with him. How odd, but just being with him this past hour had helped relieve some of the remorse she felt over the whole situation.

"I think, maybe…" She tilted her head. "Yes."

"Great, I'll give you a call. Are you at the same number?"

"Let me give you my new one."

After they traded phone numbers, she stood up and he rose, too, though a bit reluctantly. "I really should get on with my errands," she said, excusing herself.

"Okay. Thanks for today," he replied, taking her hand in what was definitely not a shake but a touch of reconnection. "I should be going, too."

And that's when she realized…

Holy crap! She was late for her meeting with Mason.

Mason glanced at his watch for the third time as he paced up and down along the wraparound veranda at his house. He got out his phone, debating whether to text Drea. She was late, but only by fifteen minutes, and though he was anxious to see her again, to spend time with her, he didn't want to come off as…what? Pushy? Needy? Worried?

Because he was worried about her. She wasn't one to be late. She was usually professional and prompt. He didn't know where it was coming from, but it gave him hives thinking something might've happened to her.

Risk stepped onto the porch, a beer in his hand. He lifted the bottle to his lips and took a swig before turning to Mason. "You're pacing? Bro, that's not like you. You must be waiting on someone." His brother had a penchant for stating the obvious.

Mason gave him a look.

Risk grinned. "You're waiting on Drea. Well, isn't that something."

"We have an appointment, about work."

"Right..." Risk smirked before taking another swig. "I wouldn't worry overly much, Mase. She's fine. When I was in town, I drove right past her. She was sitting on a park bench with some guy. The two looked pretty cozy, if you ask me. She probably lost track of time is all."

Mason eyed him. "Some guy? Who was he?"

"I have no idea. Never saw the man before. But he was all buttoned up in a suit and tie, and looked like he wasn't from around here. Just my observation."

Mason cleared his throat. "Okay, thanks."

Just then Mason's phone buzzed. It was an incoming text from Drea.

Sorry, my errands ran long. I'll be there soon.

Mason stared at the message a few seconds, relieved and curious.

"That her?" Risk asked.

"Yeah, she's running late."

Risk put a hand on his shoulder. "You care about her? And give me the truth, because lying to your brother is punishable by a swift kick in the ass."

"Like to see you try." It was an old joke between them.

Risk had always stood his ground, no matter that Mason was older and stronger. But that was Risk, always snarky, always trying to defy the odds. He was the last one to give relationship advice. He went through women like a cat licking up bowls of sweet milk: quick and none too pretty.

"I'm serious," he said.

"Of course I care about Drea. She's Drew's daughter and I've known her most of my life. That's all there is to it."

"Okay, bro. Just thinking it would be pretty cool if you did. You've sorta been *not living* these past two years, you know what I mean?"

He knew. He just didn't like the idea that his whole family was worried about him. They didn't understand how grief had to work its way out of you, and there was no speeding the process. "Yeah, I do know."

And now, just the thought of Drea on her way to meet him sent a jolt of adrenaline speeding through his system. She'd been the only woman to break through the wall of his grief, and he would welcome that relief for the time she had left in Texas.

Thirty minutes later, Drea pulled up to the house and dashed up the steps. He was waiting on the porch for her, reading local news on his phone. It had been hard to focus, and as soon as he laid eyes on her, his body jerked to attention as if Drea had defibrillated him with paddles to his chest.

"So sorry I'm late," she said, her face flushed.

"It's okay. What happened?"

"I lost track of time running errands. I have a lot on my mind these days. I hope I didn't mess up your schedule for the day."

So she wasn't going to tell him about the guy. It was probably nothing, maybe a meeting with someone related to the project. And little did she know he'd cleared his schedule this afternoon to be with her. "Not at all. But I am hungry. How about you?"

"Yes."

"Okay, let's get going."

"Where?"

"You'll see."

Mason led her to his truck, opened the door for her and watched as she slid onto the seat. Her dress hiked up her thighs, giving him a clear view of her long tanned legs. Legs that had driven him insane wrapped around him last night.

When he was with Drea the world seemed right, but he was taking this one day at a time and living in the moment. Because it would end. It had to end. He was counting on it ending. That was the only way he could justify this brief interlude with her. He wasn't ready for anything permanent, anything that could go awry and scar him deeply. He hadn't healed from his first heartache. He didn't need another. Drea was leaving soon, and they would part ways. But for now, he wanted to spend as much time with her as he could.

A few minutes later, he parked the truck and helped Drea climb out. Holding her in his arms, he bent his head and kissed her lightly.

Her eyelids fluttered and he wanted more, but he held back, straining his willpower. "Close your eyes and come with me."

"What?"

He put his fingertip to her nose. "Just do it."

She closed her eyes, a big smile on her face. "I don't like surprises, just so you know."

"Trust me, you'll like this one."

He took her hand and guided her down a grassy pathway that led to the spot he'd picked out just for her. "Okay, open your eyes."

* * *

The sound of ducks quacking reached Drea's ears first, and then came a noisy flutter of wings. But when she popped her eyes open, the first thing she spotted was a café table dressed with a white tablecloth and two chairs set up on the bank of a small, secluded lake she'd never been to. A cut-crystal vase filled with pearl-white roses served as the centerpiece and wine was chilling in a bucket. The whole scene looked too good to be true.

A family of ducks glided across the water just at the right moment, as if it their swim was choreographed. She smiled at the sight they made. "Wow. What's going on?" She hadn't expected anything like this.

"Lunch."

"I know, silly." She turned to Mason, noting a gleam of satisfaction in his eyes. "But why?"

He shrugged, a myriad of emotions flowing through his expression. She didn't know if she'd get the truth out of him by the look on his face.

"You've been working hard. I thought you'd like a quiet lunch out here where it's open and peaceful."

"You went to a lot of trouble," she said, truly touched. Her heart warmed every time Mason did something nice for her like this. And to think she'd nearly canceled lunch with him today. But she knew she was treading dangerous ground. "Thank you."

He smiled. "You're welcome."

"Are we still on Boone land?" she asked, although she was pretty sure of the answer.

"Yep. This is Hidden Lake. I named it myself."

"You did? When?"

"Just now." He laughed and so did she. "Seems appropriate, doesn't it?"

"You have a knack," she said. "But I never knew this lake existed."

"It's been here the entire time, but through years of drought it had nearly dried up, the water level too low for it to be considered anything but a big puddle. We've had some good rainfall the past few years. And now Hidden Lake is once more."

"It's beautiful."

"Yeah, it's a nice spot." He held out a chair for her. "Ready?"

"I am." She took a seat and Mason served her one dish after another. The food was catered by Bountiful, the best restaurant in town.

She feasted on lemon chicken, shrimp risotto and roasted vegetables. There were three kinds of bread and a nice bottle of white wine. She nibbled on her meal, enjoying the ambience, but the best thing of all about the scenery was the tall, handsome man in front of her.

Mason's gaze never strayed from hers. He chewed his food and looked at her. He sipped his wine and watched her sip hers. The conversation was light and fun, and he smiled a lot, which made her smile a lot, too.

Peace surrounded her and she squeezed her eyes closed, soaking it all in. It was truly what she'd needed today. "Thank you," she said. "I almost don't want to spoil this by talking about work."

"Work?" he asked.

"You said you needed advice. What was that all about?"

"I do need advice, but it's not about work."

She chewed on her lower lip a moment. "Then what is it about?"

"The beach house in Los Angeles. Missy has a potential buyer for it, but she wanted to give me the first option to purchase. I really don't know what I want to do."

"And you think I can help with your decision?"

He nodded. But she wasn't sure she wanted to be included in such a major decision in his life.

"You've seen it. What do you think?" he asked.

"I love it. I mean, what's not to love? But it's not up to me. Would you actually use it as a second home? It's definitely a big change from Boone Springs. Do you think you'd be comfortable there?"

Mason shrugged. "I was, when I was with you."

Oh... Her heart did a little flip at his unguarded reply. She'd had a great time while she'd been there, too, but she couldn't make a big deal about it. Mason was talking past history. He had to think about the future, and that didn't include her. "That was a one-time thing," she said softly.

Mason stared at her for several seconds and nodded slowly, conceding the point. "Yeah."

Then he rose from his seat. "Take a walk with me along the lake."

"That sounds nice," she said, rising in turn.

He took her hand and led her down to the lake's grassy edge. He pointed at the cute duck family still swimming nearby, and they laughed together as Mason took her into his arms. Her heart nearly stopped when he kissed her fully, thoroughly, as only he could do. "Meet me tonight, Drea. Be with me."

Drea murmured her agreement.

Because she just couldn't help herself.

Eight

Drea didn't know where the time had gone. There were only six days left before the big event. In the days since their lunch by Hidden Lake, she'd mostly been holed up with Mason, working. But when they weren't working, they were playing. Mason had retaught her the art of horseback riding and they'd gone riding several times on Rising Springs land. It *was* just like riding a bike. She'd never really forgotten. Once the reins were in her hands, it had all clicked again. She was thankful to him for making her take that first ride, and for the long walks, the meals they shared and especially for their secret nights at The Baron.

Tonight, she had dinner plans with her father. It would be just the two of them. As she walked up the steps of the cottage, she realized how full her life was right now. Family, friends and the attention of her fantasy man all put a smile on her face.

She no longer counted the days before she would return

to New York and resume her life there. She was falling in love with Boone Springs again, something she thought would never happen. She questioned it every day, tried to find fault in her thought patterns, but that was just it. It wasn't so much what she was thinking, but more what she was feeling. And those emotions were getting stronger every day.

"Daddy, I'm home." She entered the house and found her father at the kitchen table, going through a big wooden box she'd never seen before.

"Hi, dear girl." He quickly closed the box and latched it.

"What do you have there?" she asked, more than mildly curious now that he'd seemed so secretive about it.

"Just some things from the past."

"Mom's things?"

He nodded and shrugged. "Yeah, there's some of your mama's stuff in here."

"Can I see?"

She sat down next to him, watching him carefully. Fear entered his eyes, followed by a look of resignation. Or was she mistaken? Maybe the box just held mementos. When her mother died, her father had given her keepsakes of her mom that she would always treasure, including a birthstone ring, her wedding ring, a favorite silver locket and a pair of diamond earrings.

"It's just some old stuff. I haven't gone through this box in a long time."

"Why now?"

"Maybe because you're here visiting." Her father opened it and revealed a treasure trove of clippings and old ticket stubs to concerts, movies and dances. "I saved all this. I don't know why."

"I do, Dad. It's a testament to your life with Mom. It's like your history together." She picked up a photo she'd never seen before, of a very young couple standing in front of a diner, obviously crazy about each other. "When's this from?"

"Oh, sweet girl. That's one of our first dates. I took your mama to some fancy restaurant and she took one look at the prices and said she'd rather have burgers and fries. Back then, I was working for my daddy and he was harder on me than on his crew. Said I had to work my way up the ladder if I wanted a piece of Thundering Hills one day, so money was tight and your mama, even then, had my back. She wasn't going to have me break the bank to impress her. I think I fell in love with her that night, Drea. She was something."

Tears welled in Drea's eyes. But she wasn't sad, not at all. She was truly amazed at the beautiful love the two of them had for each other. Clearly, her father had adored his Maria.

Drew shared several more memories with her and showed her a couple trinkets that made her smile. And then he brought out an unsealed envelope. He tapped it against his other hand a few times and turned to her. "Tell me, Drea," he said, his gravelly voice sharper than usual. "You and Mason are getting close, right? I see the way he looks at you."

What? Goodness, she wasn't prepared for a question like that. "Dad, we're working on the fund-raiser together. We both have a vested interest. And no, I could never get seriously involved with a Boone. You know why. I can never forgive them for what they did to our family."

"Drea, my brain hasn't gone to seed yet. I know you're going out at night. I'm assuming you're meeting with Mason. You're a grown woman and it's none of my business, but I got a reason to be asking."

She felt heat rising to her face; she was probably turning the shade of a ripe tomato. "Dad, you know?"

"I do now," he said without sarcasm.

"It's… Mason and I…we're just casual."

Her father's bushy brows rose. "Doesn't matter. I've been talking to Lottie and she thinks I've been doing you an injustice. Maybe I have. Maybe I was just making myself look better in your eyes by putting the blame on the Boones all these years. I'm sorry, Drea."

"For what, Dad? What are you talking about?" Her heart began to pound as dread overtook her. She'd never heard such remorse in her father's tone.

"All those years ago, after your mama died, I let the ranch go to ruin. I couldn't deal with the loss, the pressure and raising you. I was a terrible father, Drea. I know that, and I'm making amends now, by telling you the truth. I didn't go to the Boones for a loan like I told you. They didn't deny me. The fact is, I didn't ask them to help me save my ranch. I practically begged them to take it off my hands. I knew they'd give me a fair price. I made the deal with them, specifically stipulating that the money would go into a fund for your college education. I didn't trust myself with the money. I knew I'd drink it away. That's at least one good thing I did. I wanted to protect you, from myself."

Bile rose in her throat and she felt dizzy. "Dad…are you saying that they didn't steal Thundering Hills out from under you? Are you saying the Boones paid for my education?"

He ran a hand down his face. "Yeah, darlin' girl. That's the truth. It's all here in this personal agreement I made with Henry Boone."

Drea snatched the envelope out of his hands, opened it and took out the written agreement. She scanned the contents quickly, her eyes keying in on words that verified her father's claims until there was no doubt. "Oh my God. Why? Why didn't you just tell me the truth?"

"And admit yet another failure to my only daughter?

I was a coward. It was easier to let the Boones take the blame. To let you think they'd robbed you of your birthright, when actually, I was guilty of that myself. It's eaten at me all these years. And now, Drea, I see you and Mason together, and if there's a chance for the two of you, well, I couldn't let that get in the way of your happiness. I couldn't bear it, not again. Lottie said it's about time."

"Lottie?" It was the second time he'd mentioned her. "So everyone knew the truth but me?"

Her father shook his head. "Not everyone. We kept the terms of the agreement private. Let people come to their own conclusions. But the Boone brothers know, yes."

"And you let me berate them, hate them, think the very worst of the people who actually saved your hide?"

"I'm sorry, Drea. Truly sorry."

"Sorry's not enough, Dad. Not nearly...enough."

Limbs shaking, tears spilling down her cheeks, she dashed out of the room. When she got to her bedroom, she slammed the door and then slumped against it, slowly sinking into a heap on the floor. She'd been betrayed and lied to one too many times. Everything she thought she knew about her life had just been whisked away. Was she overreacting? Maybe, but why did she always have to be the grownup? Why couldn't she be the kid, the one who needed tending, the one who needed comfort? She wanted to fall apart. She needed to. It was her right, something she'd been deprived of for too many years. She didn't care if this episode would send her father back to the bottle. She'd lived with that fear for too long.

This was her time to grieve and she wasn't holding back.

"Drea, please. I'm sorry," her father said from the other side of the door.

"Go away, Dad. Leave me alone."

It was a while before she heard him sigh heavily and walk away, his footfalls receding until there was no sound.

No sound but the deep, stabbing sobs racking her body.

It was after eleven when Mason got the text from Drea.

I need to see you tonight. Can we meet?

Mason was at home at Rising Springs, already in bed, going over the final details of the fund-raiser. It was hard to believe the event was coming up so quickly and he'd wanted to make sure he had everything covered. He didn't like leaving things to chance. That's what he and Drea had in common: they paid attention to details. She was having dinner with her dad tonight and they hadn't planned on seeing each other, so getting this text message from her this late surprised him.

What's going on? he typed.

Please, I need to see you.

At The Baron?

Yes, in thirty minutes?

I'll be there.

Mason wasn't going to pass up an opportunity to see Drea. The nights when they weren't together felt strange to him and he didn't much like analyzing why that was, especially after the conversation he'd had with Larissa's mother earlier in the day. She'd let him know she and Larissa's father were driving to town, coming all the way from Arizona, and they wanted to see him. He knew why. They were coming to lay flowers on Larissa's grave on the second anniversary of her death. Two years had gone by. Two. In one respect, the time had seemed to crawl by as he relived his wife's final days and the singeing loss he felt even before she'd taken her last breaths. But it also seemed as if the past two years had flown by. How could it be both? And how could he have lived two full years without Larissa by his side?

Now, as he headed to the hotel to meet Drea, he was conflicted and guilt-ridden. His in-laws were coming to town. They were coming to help him grieve, to honor their daughter's memory, to feel closer to her. But all he could think about was Drea.

Yet her ominous text message made him nervous. She'd never been cryptic before. She'd never initiated their meeting. So he pressed his foot down on the gas pedal and sped through the relatively empty roads leading to town. He made it in quick time and entered his suite before Drea got there.

He was just removing his jacket when he heard her knock.

He opened the door and she flew into his arms. He stood there stunned for a second, until her warm breath caressed his face and she planted a kiss on him that had him forgetting his first name. Hell, she didn't come up for air, just kept kissing him, tearing at the buttons of his shirt, splaying her soft palms on his skin, making him sizzle, making him want.

He slammed the door shut behind her. He didn't know where the hell this was coming from, but he wasn't about to question it. Or her. His body reacted, as it always did from Drea's touch, and he was immediately caught up in the urgency, the intensity. He tore away at her clothes, too, pulling her blouse out of her jeans, unbuttoning it between kisses. She removed her bra without his help and her beautiful breasts sprang free.

He was hard and ready. This aggressive, wild Drea was a big, big turn-on.

He held her long hair away from her chest and bent his head, moistening one rosy areola with his mouth, his tongue, causing the tip to perk up. She was gorgeous, too damn beautiful for his sanity. She whimpered, a cry of need that pierced his soul. She was on fire, hot and frenzied, and he wasn't far behind. He removed the rest of her clothes, then his. But when he stopped kissing her to lead her into the bedroom, she shook her head and kept him right there, as if even the slightest separation would be too much for her.

After pressing her against the door, he had just enough time to grab a condom and sheath himself before lifting her back into his arms. Instinctively, she wrapped her legs around his waist and her kisses became softer, slower, as if she were savoring him, as if she were committing this to memory. Her soft mewling nearly killed him. He was too far gone to play games. His need to join their bodies was intense, ferocious. He picked up the pace, taking charge now, kissing her thoroughly, nipping at her swollen lips, tasting her hot skin and trailing a path down her throat.

He positioned her over him, his hands cupping her butt, and then guided her down onto his shaft. She was warm and wet and the look of pure pleasure on her face was so damn perfect.

It was fast, fiery, frenzied and about the most incredible thing he'd ever done with a woman. When she cried out, her throaty sounds of pure bliss sent him over the edge.

He tightened his hold on her, feverishly moving, his body desperately seeking the ultimate prize. Then, making one deep, long, final thrust with his hips, he let out a groan of contentment that shattered him.

He was done.

Totally destroyed.

He held on to Drea and carried her to the bedroom.

That was when he got a good look at her face. Her pretty green eyes were rimmed with red.

She'd been crying.

Mason lay with Drea nestled in his arms, her head resting on his shoulder. He stroked her arm, absorbing the softness of her skin. She was quiet now, seemingly drained of energy. Why had she been crying? He had no clue. She'd come here like a woman on a mission, and it was only afterward that he took note of her distress. "Are you okay?" he asked quietly.

"No," she replied. "I'm not okay. I haven't been okay for a long time, Mason."

The sadness in her voice nearly broke him. "Why?"

She sighed deeply, her voice brittle. "I found out the truth about Thundering Hills tonight. My father told me... everything." She nibbled on her lip a moment and then continued. "At first I didn't believe it. My entire life I was led to believe one thing, only to learn that none of it was true."

She lifted her head from his chest and those sad, sad eyes touched something deep inside him. "I've misjudged you, Mason. I've been awful to you."

He rubbed her shoulder and smiled. "What are you talking about, sweetheart?"

"I hated and resented you for years."

"I know."

"Why didn't you tell me the truth? Why did you let me go on hating you? Why did you lie to me all those times? It wasn't fair, Mason. It wasn't fair to let me go on believing the worst about your family."

"It was the way your father wanted it. He made a pact with my dad to keep the terms of their agreement a secret. He must've had his reasons for keeping you in the dark. And as far as we're concerned, I always thought you'd figure out on your own that you didn't hate me."

She frowned. "Because you're so darn irresistible?"

"Because you're a smart woman and eventually you would see me for the man I really am."

"To think I've blamed your entire family, I've had terrible thoughts of them all this time. I thought you were all greedy and now I find that it wasn't anything but kindness and generosity. The Boones are responsible for me getting my college degree, for heaven's sake."

"Your father did right by you, Drea. At least in that way, he put your needs above his own."

"He didn't want me to see him as a complete failure. He told me so tonight, how he put the blame for our loss on the Boones. It wasn't right or fair of him and I let him know it. I was really hard on him tonight."

"Is that why you're so upset?"

"Yes, it's a lot to take in." She ran her hand down her face, then gently tapped her cheek. "Do I look terrible?"

"You look beautiful, Drea."

He sat up on the bed, drawing her with him, and wrapped his arms around her. "Did he say why he chose tonight to tell you?"

"It was your aunt Lottie. She told him it was time for me to know the truth. Gosh, I wish one of you would've told me before now. I'm feeling betrayed…by everyone. But I also think the two of them were conspiring about…"

"About?"

"About us… They think—no, my father knows I've been seeing you. He said he didn't want my feelings about the Boones to stand in our way."

"Our way?" Mason wasn't sure what she was getting at. She was leaving after this weekend. She had a life to go back to.

"I think he meant just in case we fall for each other," she said, so softly he could barely hear her.

Mason bit down, keeping his mouth clamped shut. Drea had to know going in he wasn't available. Not emotionally. Not in any way. Just the thought of a permanent relationship made him shudder. He wasn't ready for anything like that. He didn't know if he ever would be. The thought of loving someone again, and losing her, scared the hell out of him. Yes, if it was going to be any woman, he'd want it to be Drea. But he just couldn't…go there again. Call him a coward, but his head and his gut told him no, no, no.

"I mean," she said quietly, "we aren't falling for each other, are we?"

There was such hope in her voice, such tenderness, as if the answer could break her.

He shifted away from her on the bed. Here they were, stark naked after a blistering night of wild sex. He felt closer to Drea than any woman he'd met in the past two years. He liked her, admired her and cared deeply for her. Yet he didn't have an answer for her. He didn't know what to say. She'd already been hurt enough.

All he could do was speak the truth. He stared into the distance, keeping his back to her. "You're leaving in a few days, Drea."

He hoped like hell the words came off gentle, kind. It was a statement of fact. Not a yes, not a no. Well, maybe a no. He'd made it clear he wasn't committing to anything.

He turned to her finally and stared into her eyes, hoping to see understanding, a note of agreement. But all he saw was her attempt to mask pain.

It hurt like hell seeing the emotions pass over her face, one after another, as she tried to conceal what she was really feeling. At this moment, she didn't have to hate him; he was doing a pretty good job of hating himself.

"Right," she said quietly. "I… This has been great. But it's…nothing."

The *nothing* stung. She hadn't meant it to, she'd merely been searching for words, and he hated that he'd put her in that position.

She rose then and headed for the living room, where she'd left her clothes. "I'd better get home. It's very late and we have a big day tomorrow. Sean and the band are coming."

"Drea?" Mason got up and followed her. "Let me drive you home."

"Really, Mason. I have to go. Just know I don't h-hate you anymore."

With her clothes thrown on haphazardly, she picked up her bag, slung it over her shoulder and took her leave.

Last night, after learning the truth, Drea had finally been free to open her heart and let her emotions fly. Now what she felt for Mason was love. She *loved* him. She loved him so much the burn of his rejection seared her heart. After the last time he'd rejected her, she should've learned her lesson. She should have known it would never work out between the two of them. She'd been a fool, a silly fool for falling in love with a man who was still painfully in love with his dead wife.

He wasn't a bad man. He wasn't horrible. He was loyal and true blue. For some reason, she'd been the woman to wake his sexual senses after two years of hibernation. She'd made him come alive and sparked something in him he thought long dead. She would always have that. She'd gotten over Mason once before, and would just have to find a way to do it again.

While her heart bled for a love that would go nowhere, she had to forge on. She had a job to do and that meant dealing with Mason. Her wounds were raw and open, but this project was too important to her. She couldn't fall apart. She had to maintain, to keep up, appearances.

Drea poured tea into her mother's favorite hand-painted floral teapot and walked into the dining room to rejoin Lottie. She'd invited the older woman over after Drew left to visit a friend earlier this morning.

Drea's relationship with her father was still on rocky ground. She hadn't had a chance to speak to him yet, to clear the air and perhaps try to forgive him. She'd put that on the very long list of things she needed to do.

"Lottie, would you care for more tea?"

"Sure, thank you. It's delicious. I'm so glad you invited me over. We don't see enough of each other."

"I know. I'm sorry. I've been superbusy."

"Mason tells me you've been doing a fantastic job."

At the mention of Mason's name, she frowned. It was automatic, and she righted herself, but she didn't fool Lottie. Her eyes softened and she gave Drea a knowing look. "Something tells me this is more than a social visit. You need to talk to me, don't you, sweetheart?"

Drea nodded, sinking down in the chair. Tears welled in her eyes. "I do."

"Is it your dad or Mason?"

She smiled halfheartedly. "Both."

"What is it?"

"I need some direction, Lottie, and I need to tell someone the whole truth. I thought I could tell Mason last night when we were together. Instead we ended up…well, breaking up. Which is so dumb because you actually have to be a couple in order to break up. But we never were, not really."

"Oh, sweetheart…you love him."

She nodded. "I do. But he isn't over Larissa, and maybe he never will be."

Drea spent the next half hour pouring her heart out. She explained how she knew the truth about Thundering Hills now, and the Boones' part in all of it. She told Lottie how she'd fought with her father, unable to see the logic in what he'd done, the lies he'd told.

She told Lottie everything, from her infatuation with Mason and his abrupt rejection years ago to how she'd run into the arms of Brad Williamson, conceived a child with him and miscarried. Her scars were finally exposed, and it was brutal revealing all the secrets she'd held inside. All the pain and injury she'd suffered through the years.

Lottie held her hand through most of it, and wiped Drea's cheeks when tears flooded her face. "I've loved Mason, hated him, and now I'm so terribly out of my element I don't know what to do. Brad is a doctor now and he's here in Boone Springs for a short time. I've spoken to him. He's a really good guy. I hate that I hurt him. He was ready to marry me, and that would've been a big mistake. I didn't love him. So how can I fault Mason for not loving me, and easing out of our relationship, when I did the same thing to Brad?"

"You know what I think?" Lottie said. "My nephew has been living in the past for far too long. He's got to get over it."

Drea sucked in a sob to steady her breath. "No one can make him do that, Lottie."

"Don't be so sure about that." Lottie's voice took on a mischievous tone. "Will you be joining us for dinner tonight, sweetheart?"

"I have to be there," she said. She wouldn't let her queasy stomach stop her from doing her job. The Boones were hosting a dinner for The Band Blue. "It's the band's first night in town."

"Good."

Drea dabbed at her face with a napkin. She was too busy for any more crying jags. And shedding her burden to Lottie had been the best therapy. At least now someone knew the entire truth. At least Drea had someone to confide in.

Lottie finished her tea and rose. "Don't you worry about a thing."

Drea wished she had her confidence. Her life was a total mess. And perhaps most of it was her own fault. That's what stung the worst.

When Lottie put out her arms, Drea got up and flowed into them. Lottie was warm and soft and welcoming, all the things Drea's life had been missing. She closed her eyes and absorbed the comfort, missing her mother so very much, but grateful for this woman who had loved them both.

They hugged a good long time, and then Lottie spoke softly. "You're an amazing woman, Drea. I love you with all of my heart."

It was the best thing she could've said to her. "I love you too, Lottie."

Lottie pulled away and looked into Drea's eyes. "Thanks for the tea, sweetheart. I'll see you tonight."

"Yes, I'll be there." Suddenly Drea felt stronger, a bit more like herself. She had a job to do, and she'd focus on that for the next three days.

As Lottie exited the cottage, she heard noises coming from the back woodshed. In the past, when Drew had been up to it, he'd built things there. Of course, those days had been few and far between. Now, letting her curiosity get the better of her, Lottie went behind the house to investigate.

She found Drew at a worktable, his jacket slung over an old chair. He must've just been dropped off by his friend. She thought it odd that he hadn't come right into the cottage.

Then she saw him lift a bottle of Jack Daniels from the table, the amber liquid swishing around inside. She had only a moment to react. Only a moment to stop the foolish man from doing something he'd regret later on. "Drew, don't you dare take a swig of that bottle."

He jumped and turned around quickly, still clutching the bottle in his hand. "Geesh, woman. You nearly scared me half to death. What are you—" Then he blinked and his eyes darkened as her words finally sank in. He looked from her to the bottle. Then back at her again.

His shoulders slumped and his eyes hardened. "Why in hell would I take a swig of shellac, Lottie Sue Brown?"

Lottie took a better look at the bottle. It said Jack Daniels on the label, but there was a thin strip of masking tape around the center spelling out SHELLAC. "I, uh, it's just that I know you and Drea had some issues to deal with and I, uh…couldn't see too well with the morning shadows and all."

"You think a spat with my daughter would've turned me to drink again?" His voice was quiet. "You have no faith in me, Lottie. None at all, and that's not about to change, is it? Don't answer. I won't believe anything you say right now. You want to know what I'm doing with this bottle, which I borrowed, by the way, from my friend Rusty? I'm trying to shine up Drea's softball trophies to give to her. I never made it to many of the games back then, and these things mean a lot to me now. I'm always looking for ways to make amends with my daughter."

Lottie had stepped in it now. She'd been quite effectively told off. Oh boy, she'd let preconceived notions about Drew influence her judgment. If only she'd kept her trap shut. If only she'd had more faith in him. He'd been trying to prove to her he was a changed man, but now she feared she'd destroyed any trust they had between them. "Oh, Drew. Forgive me. I'm sorry, very sorry."

He turned away from her. "Lottie, just let me get back to this."

"But Drew—"

"Go, Lottie. You've said enough this morning."

And suddenly, her heart ached and her stomach burned.

Had one incident of mistrust ruined things with him forever?

Nine

Drea straightened her snow-white, curve-hugging dress and knocked on the front door of the Boone mansion. She was flying solo tonight, her father opting to stay home. They'd had a good long talk this afternoon and had agreed to put the past behind them. She could forgive him for past mistakes, but it would be a long time before she would truly be over it. She loved her dad and he loved her. All they could do was go from there.

She wore red high heel pumps and the silver jewelry she loved so much. The Boones' housekeeper, Jessica, opened the door and greeted her. It appeared the entire staff was on call tonight. Drea had no idea of the scope of the dinner, but apparently the Boones had invited more than family. The sheriff of Boone County and several hospital administrators were in attendance, as well as the mayor. Mason's cousins, Rafe, Nash and Cord, were also in attendance. They were part-time cattle ranchers, among other things, and obviously big country and western fans. So of course they were invited to meet the band.

"Drea, you look drop-dead gorgeous," Risk said, being the first to grab her hand and lead her into the fray. The house was hopping with laughter and music.

"Thank you. Are Sean and the band here yet?"

"Yep, they're out back. Come with me." Risk kept a tight hold of her hand as he led her to the poolside area. It was quieter out here and cooler.

"Wow, this is quite a welcome for the band."

She shivered a bit and Risk took note. "You need a drink to warm you up."

"I won't refuse. Just one."

They wandered over to a bar set up under a pillared deck. "What'll it be?"

"White wine, please."

Risk shook his head. "Make that two whiskey sours," he told the bartender.

"Risk!" She laughed, finally able to let loose with the Boones, finally able to see them for the good men they were. "Why'd you bother to ask me?"

He shrugged. "White wine won't warm you up, sweetheart. Take it from me. You need something stronger."

"I do, do I? And why is that?"

He was charming and quite a player.

"Baby, that dress you're wearing exposes more skin than it covers. Don't get me wrong, I'm digging it, and I would offer to keep you snuggled tight tonight, but I think my brother would have me hung from the highest rafter."

She tilted her head and stared at him. Risk handed her the drink, and took his own as he pointed toward Mason, who was standing alone by the side of the house, watching her. She shivered again and glanced away. She couldn't give in to Mason's penetrating stares. He'd made up his mind and that was that.

"What's going on between you two?" Risk asked.

"As of tonight, not a thing," she answered, drinking deep from her glass.

"Well, in that case," he said, bending his head and kissing her cheek, "do I get a chance at keeping you warm tonight?"

She smiled at him. "I think the drink you fixed me up with is doing the job."

"Damn. Should've gotten you the white wine, after all," he replied, and both of them laughed.

After finishing her drink, she walked over to a group conversing with the band. Sean spotted her and broke away from the others. "Hey, Drea. Good to see you."

"Sean, it's good to see you, too."

He hugged her, a shy kind of hug that tickled her to death. She gave him a hug back.

"This is great. The Boones sure know how to do it up, don't they?"

"Yes, they sure do. I take it you got in okay today? All set up in your hotel?"

"Yep, the hotel is really cool. Alan has no complaints and we're all happy to be doing this gig."

"I'm happy, too. Listen, about the Dream Date event, we have it all set. Do you have any questions or concerns? I hope you'll let me know, since I was the one who kinda got you involved with it."

"Nope. I have no concerns."

"That's fantastic."

Mason approached, eyeing her before greeting Sean. It was *Business with Mason* all over again. It didn't matter that he looked fine, in a form-fitting charcoal suit with no tie, or that his hair was just as she liked it, brushed back with the very tips curling up at the collar. She could do this. She could. She entered into the conversation, smiling, and enjoyed getting to know Sean a little better.

A few minutes later, Sean was pulled away and she was left standing with Mason. "I think everything is ready for the big day," she said brightly. "I'm confident that, as long as the weather holds, we'll be able to pull it off."

Mason eyes were dark and serious, and when he opened his mouth to speak she shook her head immediately. If it wasn't going to be work talk, she wanted no part of it. "Don't, Mason. There's nothing more to say."

Lottie approached then, looking dazzling in a blue floral chiffon dress, on the arm of… Brad Williamson. Drea was too stunned to utter a word. Brad was smiling at her, looking a little sheepish, as well.

"Hello, you two," Lottie said. "Mason, I'd like you to meet Dr. Brad Williamson. Brad's visiting here from the East Coast. He's a dear friend of Drea's and so I thought it fitting that he join us tonight. They've known each other since college, right, Drea?"

She nodded. "Yes, that's right." Wasn't it just a few hours ago she'd been pouring out her heart to Lottie about Brad, Mason, her father? Goodness, Lottie didn't let up.

While the two men shook hands, Lottie's eyes met hers.

"Nice to meet you," Brad said to Mason. "Drea's told me all about the fund-raiser. I'm on board. It's an important thing you're doing."

"Thank you. We think so, too," Mason said. Then he clamped his mouth shut, glancing at her with a question in his eyes.

"Lottie, may I have a word with you?" Drea didn't know what exactly Lottie had hoped would happen by inviting Brad to the dinner party.

"Oh, uh, I can't right now. Chef needs me in the kitchen. You three have a nice talk and I'll see you all later."

An awkward moment passed. Mason remained tight-lipped.

"Brad, how did you meet Lottie?" Drea asked. It was the question of the day.

Brad looked handsome tonight, dressed in a casual gray suit. His eyes were mesmerizing, almost a transparent blue. "Well, we met at the local bookstore. I was signing copies of my book and we got to talking about the fund-raiser. So when she found out I was a country fan and that I knew you, she invited me. I'm sorry I didn't run it by you first. You're okay with this, aren't you? Since we never did get to have dinner together, I was hoping—"

"It's perfectly fine, Brad. I'm glad you're here."

"Then I'm glad I am, too." He smiled. "You look...*amazing*."

She didn't dare glance at Mason, but she sensed him stiffening up. "Thank you."

Drea's nerves were shot. She was standing between the two men who'd had a major impact in her life and she had no idea what was going on in either of their minds.

Lucky for her, one of the hospital administrators joined the conversation and she was able to slip away leaving the men behind. She walked out the front door and kept on walking. She was on the path to her father's house, her mind all mixed up. She wasn't sure where she belonged. Or whom she belonged with. It was dark and the path she traveled was lit only by moonlight, so when she heard footsteps behind her, she sucked in a breath and turned around. "What are you doing here?" she asked, seeing it was Mason.

"Walking you home," he said casually, as if he hadn't just broken her heart last night. As if he had a right to walk her anywhere.

"Not necessary. I'm capable of seeing myself home."

"You left early."

"Go away, Mason." She turned her back on him and resumed walking.

He caught up with her. "Why'd you leave?"

"Maybe because you didn't." Oh, that was cruel. She was better than that. She didn't want to lash out at him. She just wanted some peace.

"Who is he to you?"

So that was it. His ego was bruised. "A friend."

"Not just a friend. I get the feeling it's more than that."

"It's none of your business, Mason."

"I say it is."

She stopped and shook her head, looking into his troubled eyes. It hurt to still feel something for him, to care that he was as frustrated as she was. "You can't have it both ways."

He looked puzzled. "Is that what I'm doing?"

"I have no idea what you're doing. It doesn't matter anymore. Once the fund-raiser is over, I'll be leaving, as you already mentioned."

She pivoted and continued walking. She'd gotten as far as three steps when he looped his arm around her waist, stopping her. He stood behind her, his body inches from hers, his breath at the nape of her neck, and for a minute she allowed herself to remember him, his touch, his kiss, the way he could make her feel unglued, yet whole at the same time. It wasn't to be. She had to accept it. She untangled herself from his grasp and turned to stare at him.

His arms dropped to his sides, a defeated look on his face. "Drea."

"I know you still love Larissa. I know you can't commit, so why don't we just move on and not torture ourselves this way?"

"Are you moving on with the doctor?"

She rolled her eyes. Then a fissure of anger opened up quickly becoming one giant sinkhole of incensed emotion. "No. I'm not, but not because Brad isn't wonderful. I just can't get involved with him again. I did that last time after you scarred me with your brutal rejection. I ran into the arms of the first man who'd have me. It was Brad. I shamelessly seduced him the first week of college and gave him my virginity. I gave him what I'd wanted to give you. I gave him my body, because you didn't want me and because I'd been unwanted since my mother died. And weeks later, when I turned up pregnant, the clichéd virgin too stupid to use protection, Brad was there for me. He loved me and offered to marry me."

Mason's throat was working, as though he was taking a big gulp. He stood there in stony silence.

"I almost went through with it, almost married him. But then I lost the baby, Mason. I lost my child and I was devastated. I broke up with Brad. I couldn't marry a man I didn't love. I hurt him badly, when all he wanted to do was take care of me. But you see, I couldn't love Brad. Not when I was still in love with you."

"Drea, I didn't know. I'm sorry." And she believed he was truly sorry—the emotion in his eyes was inescapable. "I never wanted to hurt you. Ever. You have to believe that."

Mason reached for her. Trembling, she moved out of his grasp, her heart breaking again. Yet it felt good to finally get the truth out, to lighten her heavy load.

"I loved you, even though I hated you, too. It doesn't make any sense, but it's true. I've never stopped loving you, Mason Boone. And all I want from you now is to leave me alone. Please. Let's get through the weekend, do our jobs, honor the people we've loved the most and then be done with it. Can you do that for me, Mason? Can you leave me alone?"

Mason's eyes grew wide; she could almost swear he was tearing up. His expression was raw, full of sympathy.

He reached out for her again and once again she backed away. She didn't want to be his friend. She didn't want to see him after this weekend. It was too hard.

"Please."

Mason finally relented, giving the smallest nod of agreement.

This time when Drea walked away, he didn't follow.

But she knew that Mason was probably still standing there, unable to move. Unable to register all that she'd confessed. She'd shocked him and worried him and made him ache with the pain he'd put her through. He probably thought she hated him again.

But that wasn't true.

She couldn't hate him.

She would probably go to her grave loving him.

Mason woke with an intense headache. He'd drunk half a bottle of bourbon last night, but even with all that mind-numbing alcohol, he couldn't forget the pain on Drea's face, the words spoken straight from her heart. He couldn't believe what she'd gone through at seventeen years of age. He'd been responsible for that. He knew that now. He thought he'd been doing right by her by turning her away, but the honest truth was he should've never let his fascination with the olive-skinned beauty mar his judgment. He'd known she was a mixed-up kid, missing her mother, having to deal with an alcoholic father. If Mason hadn't gotten involved with her in the first place, none of it would've happened.

He pushed his hand through his hair. Just thinking about

how alone Drea must've felt when she'd learned of her preg-
nancy, how scared she must've been, filled him with guilt.
And then to lose her child…well, he knew something about
that. The pain never really went away. It lingered under
the surface and every time you saw a child on the street,
whether laughing or crying, happy or sad, you wondered.
What would your child be like had he or she lived?

It deadened a part of you and you hurt quietly, without
anyone ever knowing.

A sudden knock at his door sounded more like a fire
alarm going off. "What?"

"It's Aunt Lottie, Mason. Are you all right? We thought
you'd be down by now."

"Who's we?" he asked, trying to sort through the cob-
webs in his head.

"Larissa's parents are here."

"Holy hell." He jolted up from the bed. What time was
it?

Within ten minutes, he was showered and dressed, his
head still hurting like a son of a bitch as he walked into the
parlor to greet his in-laws. He was in a fog, but there was
one thing he was crystal-clear about this morning.

Drea had said she loved him.

And he couldn't get that out of his head.

"Paul and Wendy, good to see you." Mason shook hands
with Paul Landon and then gave Wendy an embrace. She
was a petite woman, much smaller than Larissa had been,
but her hug was fierce and affectionate. He hugged her back
with equal intensity. They'd all been through hell, and that
tended to bring people closer.

They drank coffee and ate pastries, catching up on news.
The Landons would stay in town for the all-important fund-
raiser, which started tonight with the HeART auction.

Mason had a thousand things to oversee today, but this

morning was reserved for Larissa and her parents. The time had finally come for him to drive them all to the site of Larissa's grave.

Mason visited monthly, taking a bouquet of flowers for his wife and unborn child. He grieved silently, and today, on the anniversary of Larissa's death, he'd grieve along with her parents.

They paid their respects on grounds that were impeccably groomed. It was a serene resting place. There were wrought-iron-and-wood benches under old mesquite trees; bold, beautiful statues; water stations and two chapels on the property. Mason had donated the benches; Larissa's name was engraved on the one closest to her grave.

They all stood together, laying down flowers, saying prayers, and then he walked away to give the Landons a bit of privacy.

A short time later, he felt a hand on his arm and turned to find Wendy's soft, caring eyes on him. "Mason, this is a hard day for you."

He nodded. "For you, too."

"Yes, it is. But what you're doing this weekend is a good thing. It's something that will make a difference. Paul and I feel that it takes some of the pain away. I think it's time to move forward, hard as it is. Building a cardiac wing at the hospital is a great testament to Larissa's memory. And to so many others. We can't look back anymore, Mason. We have to look ahead."

He nodded, though he felt pulled in two directions. He'd clung to his grief for so long, he almost didn't know himself without it.

"You should give yourself a break. You've mourned a long time. Maybe it's time to start a new life," she said. "Guilt-free. You deserve that, Mason. No one has honored a love more than you have."

"Thank you, Wendy."

She slipped an envelope into his hand. He thought it was a donation for the fund-raiser until he recognized the handwriting as Larissa's. "What's this?"

"I don't know. It's sealed. But when Larissa was sick she gave it to me, trusting me to give it to you. She said specifically to give it to you in two years."

Two years? "You've had it all this time."

She nodded. "It was her wish."

"Okay, thank you," he said, not knowing what to make of it. But he wouldn't open the letter now. No, he needed privacy...and *courage*. It had taken him an entire year before he could dream about her at night without breaking down, eighteen months before he could watch videos of the two of them together. But to read words written by her when she'd been alive... That would require something he didn't know he had. Just holding the letter in his hand unsettled him. He slipped it into his jacket pocket.

Wendy seemed to understand his need to read it alone, to keep this last moment between them private.

An hour later, with the Landons promising to return this evening for the auction, Mason climbed the steps of his home. But he turned when he heard Drea's sweet laughter. She was walking with Sean Manfred, and they were obviously enjoying each other's company.

After the way they'd left off last night, he didn't think she'd want to see him. But the sound of her voice beckoned him and he turned and walked toward them.

"Hey, Mason." Sean's tone was friendly. "We were just going over the plans for the concert and dance tomorrow. The stage looks great. Drea's got everything under control."

"She always does," Mason said, meaning it.

Drea didn't hesitate to smile, and that smile reached

down deep and battered the heck out of him. Apparently, she was still the grown-up of the two of them, forging ahead for the sake of the event.

"Thank you. I think we're all set for the art auction tonight. The tent is up and the committee is busting their buns to have everything in place. The art has all come in, and it's impressive."

"Can't wait to see it," Mason told Drea.

"It's just a precursor to tomorrow. That's our big, big day," she stated, more to Sean than to him. "We have a dozen wheels turning, and hopefully, there will be no glitches. I'm happy to say the tickets for both the Fun Day and the Dinner-Dance and Dream Date are sold out. Thanks to you, Sean. I think all the high school girls in three counties bought up every raffle ticket."

"Somebody save me," he joked, his eyes wide.

"Not to fear, your date will be chaperoned."

"By you?" he asked in a hopeful tone of voice.

"No, sorry. I'll be gone by then. But I promise you'll have a good time."

"Are you leaving right after the event?" Sean asked. Mason wanted to know, too.

"My flight leaves on Sunday night."

Mason's throat tightened up. His chest hurt like hell.

"Hey, Drea, can I have a word with you?" It was Brad Williamson. He'd walked up from the festival area, his eyes only on Drea. Mason clenched his teeth. Sure, he'd tied one on last night, but his sour stomach had nothing to do with bourbon right now. Why wouldn't wonderful Brad Williamson, the guy who'd loved Drea and probably still did, get lost?

"Hi, Brad," Drea said. "I didn't expect to see you until tonight."

He scratched his head, looking too conveniently perplexed. "Lottie had a good idea, something that would help the cause, and I wanted to run it by you."

"What is it?"

"I could give away free signed copies of my book during the festival tomorrow, if you can squeeze me in at the last minute. I have author copies I'd like to donate."

Drea's face lit up. "That's a great idea. Excuse us a minute," she said, looking at Sean.

She walked off with Brad, practically rubbing shoulders with the guy.

Sean watched her go. "She's really amazing," he said to Mason. The kid had a bad case of hero worship.

Mason nodded. "Yeah."

"Are you two…a couple?"

Mason looked at Sean. "No, we're not a couple. Why do you ask?"

He shrugged. "Back in LA, I thought you were. You seemed kinda flawless together."

Flawless… That word struck him. They *had* been flawless together, two parts of a whole. But that was back at the beach, when everything seemed surreal.

"We just work well together." Mason said, feeling the lie down to his snakeskin boots.

"Yeah… I guess," Sean said.

He wasn't sure the kid believed him.

He wasn't sure of anything anymore.

Ten

Standing inside Katie's Kupcakes' decorating booth, Drea nibbled at the raspberry cream cheese frosting, then took a giant bite of Katie's signature cupcake. "Mmm, this is the best, my friend." She licked frosting off her finger and dabbed at her mouth with a napkin. "You have outdone yourself."

Katie shook her head, her eyes bright. "You're the one who's outdone herself. Look around. This was your brainchild. Whatever money is raised, you're the one behind it."

"I had help. The volunteers have really come through," she said, thinking about Mason and how on board he'd been from the get-go. He'd been instrumental in donating his property, his time and his support to get this project off the ground in a month.

She was putting on a good show for everyone, hoping to keep the spirit of the event alive, while inside, her heart was broken. Totally, sadly broken. Tomorrow afternoon would be here before she knew it and she'd be leaving behind people she loved. Her father, her friends and… Mason. Her pain was very real, very frustrating.

The festival was in full swing and she was thankful to see the vendors' booths crowded with paying customers. Almost all the businesses in town had either made donations or offered to sell their goods at no cost to raise money for the cause. Children were taking pony rides, food and beverages were being sold, and pretty soon Katie would be swamped with young cupcake makers.

Last night's auction had been successful. Every item had been purchased. Drea wouldn't know the final weekend tally for some time, but all in all, things were going smoothly.

Her father walked up and kissed her cheek, wrapping his arm around her waist. "Hi, sweetheart," he said.

"Hi, Daddy. Glad you made it out today."

"You're looking good, Mr. M," Katie said. "Want a cupcake?"

"Ah, thank you, Katie. But actually, I came to see if I can help you girls today."

Katie glanced at Drea and then back at him. "Sure. I could use a hand in here. Gonna need to keep the cupcakes and frosting flowing when the booth opens for decorating."

"Glad to help," he said.

Drea and her father had come to terms with the past, and ever since then, their relationship had flourished. He was back to being her dad, the man she'd known before her mother died, the man who was a loving father and sound businessman. She'd have days and days in New York to get over it, but now was a time for healing between them. She wanted to leave on a good note.

She glanced across the field to where Brad was setting

up his booth. Luckily, they'd had extra room for him. "If you two have it covered, I need to check on something."

Katie gave her a nod. "Go. Your dad and I will handle the kids."

"Thanks. I won't be long."

Drea walked through the crowds of people having a great time. When she arrived at Brad's booth, she said hello.

"Hi, yourself, pretty lady. This festival is really something."

"It is. Thanks. And thanks for donating your time and books. There are a lot of families here, and I'm sure many parents are in need of advice about their toddlers."

"Uh, Drea? May I have a word with you?"

"Of course," she said, curious about what Brad wanted to discuss.

He took her hand and walked her to the back of the booth. "I know you're leaving tomorrow, and I'll be back in New York in a month. I was wondering if you…and me. Well, if I can call you sometime."

Drea paused, trying to hide her indecision, and not doing a very good job, judging by the wary expression on Brad's face.

"We've been through a lot together, Drea. I know there's painful history between us, but I care very much about you. I never stopped."

If he had anything but friendship in mind, she'd have to come clean. She didn't want to use Brad, to run to him just because things got rough and lonely when she got back home. And she didn't want to hurt him again.

"I know you do. And I care very much about you," she said, as sincerely as she knew how. "But the truth is, I'm in love with someone."

Brad let a beat go by. "It's Mason, isn't it?"

She gave him a long look and nodded. "Is it that obvious?"

Brad smiled. "Ever since you walked over here, Mason's had his eyes on you. He's like a hawk, that guy. And I think he'd like to kill me where I stand for talking to you."

She rolled her eyes. "Please."

They laughed, but when she turned around she found Mason's deep, smoky eyes on her, and her heart skittered to a halt. He was leaning against a tree, his hat tipped low, cowboy-style, his jeans and black boots dusty. He'd been helping out with the ponies making sure the riders were safely on their mounts.

It wasn't fair that he had the ability to turn her life upside down like this. Their eyes connected for a moment and it was as if his heat traveled across the twenty feet of space between them. He was all she saw through the crowd and her insides immediately warmed up.

She dropped her head and sighed. "It's impossible." Then she brushed a chaste kiss on Brad's cheek. "I'd better go. Good luck today. I'll be sure to talk to you later."

Drea walked away, getting as far from Mason as possible, heading toward the Boone kitchen, where the caterers were prepping for tonight's dinner and dance.

Hours later, the sun set in a brilliant orange blaze. All the festival goers who'd filled up on fun, cupcakes, rides and games, were gone. On another part of the grounds, a stage was ready for The Band Blue. Fifty round tables with elegant white tablecloths and short pillar candles surrounded the parquet dance floor.

People were arriving for the dinner and concert. Women were dressed in classic Western wear, jean skirts and leather boots or elegant gowns or somewhere in between. Drea, being the co-master of ceremonies had put her best foot forward, treating herself to a form-fitting gold gown. Shimmering sequins covered the crisscross back straps. Her hair was held away from her face with two rhinestone clips, allowing it to flow softly down her back.

Mason walked up behind her, putting a hand on her shoulder. "Are you ready for this?"

She glanced at him, felt his familiar mind-numbing touch, and for a moment her breath stuck in her throat. He wore his suit well, a dark three-piece with a gold brocade vest. In another lifetime she would've grabbed him by his bolo tie and dragged him behind the stage to have her way with him.

What a dream that would be. "I think so."

He leaned in close and whispered, "You look like a goddess."

"Th-thank you." She absorbed the compliment and they stood there together, in the background, watching the donors taking their seats.

When everything was in place, Mason took her hand. "Let's do this," he said.

They walked up on the stage together. Mason gave her the floor first. She went to the podium and spoke from the heart, thanking everyone for coming, thanking all the volunteers and thanking The Band Blue for donating their time. "This is a project near and dear to so many of us, but as you know, both my family and the Boones have lost someone to heart disease. We hope, with all of your generous donations, we will make our ambitious goal of raising two million dollars for the cardiac wing. I hear we've come close, as donations have been pouring in from citizens who couldn't attend the festivities this weekend." Drea put her fist over her heart, tears welling in her eyes. "This means so much to me, personally. Thank you all."

She turned to find Mason's eyes on her, filled with pride.

There was a moment between them, something sacred, something that went beyond their personal relationship issues, something that connected them. Nothing could ever take that away. "And now Mason Boone will say a few words."

As he sidled up to the podium she began to walk away, but he discreetly curled his hand around her waist, drawing her close. They stood beside each other, and Mason took over the microphone. "Once again let me thank everyone who helped put this fund-raiser together. All of you have done a great job and we can't thank you enough. I have to give most of the credit to the woman standing beside me, Andrea MacDonald. She has been absolutely dedicated to the cause.

"Our goal was to break ground on the new wing in two years, but the Boone family hopes to make that a reality even sooner. To that end, our family is pledging an additional one million dollars to the cause."

Applause broke out. Drea opened her mouth to speak, but words wouldn't come. She stared at Mason as he continued. "The only stipulation I have is to be able to name the new cardiac wing. It will be called the Maria MacDonald Heart Center."

He turned to Drea then, his dark eyes full of emotion, and she'd never loved him more.

"Th-thank you," she mouthed, still unable to speak aloud.

"And there'll be a garden on the grounds named for my late wife. It'll be called Larissa's Blooms."

Mason paused a second, struggling a bit. Then he went on. "Miss MacDonald and I hope you have a wonderful evening, starting off with a concert from Grammy nominees The Band Blue. Feel free to come up onto the dance floor and swing your partner around. Oh, and after dinner, be warned, we'll be raffling off a Dream Date with Sean Manfred. You girls on the back lawn there will just have to be patient."

There were hundreds of girls sitting beyond the tables, under the twinkling lights strung from the trees. Their raffle tickets had also admitted them to the concert.

Drea and Mason walked off the stage just as the band stepped up to take their places.

Her mind swirling, she heard Sean give the guests a warm welcome. But just as she turned to speak to Mason about his generosity, a local news reporter with a film crew nabbed him.

"Mr. Boone, do you have time for that interview now?"

Mason sighed. "Sure thing. Give me one second, okay?"

Of course they'd want to speak with Mason. After his announcement and personal donation to the cause, he was newsworthy.

He looked into her eyes. "Save some time for me later. Maybe a dance?"

She didn't want to dance with him. She didn't want to suffer any more than necessary. Her scars were too raw right now. Mason had impacted her life in too many ways to name, and she would never forget him. But the sad fact remained, that he'd had many opportunities this month to sort out his feelings for her. To allow himself a fresh start and get over his guilt and pain. To allow someone else in. He, too, was scarred. He, too, had endured great loss. And it was extremely hard for him. It was hard for her, as well, but at least she was willing to take the chance.

It was obvious he wasn't.

"I…c-can't, Mason. I'll always remember you and this." She spread her arms out to encompass the festival. "We did a wonderful thing here. And…well, naming the wing in my mother's honor was…"

Once again stung by his generosity, she felt her eyes begin to burn. She didn't want to cry in front of him. "Thank you." It was all she could say. "You'd better get on with that interview."

She turned away from him then and headed for her dad who was standing off to one side looking a bit overwhelmed and misty-eyed after the announcement honoring her mother Maria. He needed her as much as she needed him right now.

Her heartache aside, she and Mason pulled this weekend off, and with the Boone's charitable donation, they may have far exceeded their goals. She had to feel good about that.

Evening turned into night as the band played, wowing the guests. Dinner was served when the band took their first break, and then as they began to play their second set, Sean encouraged everyone to get up on the dance floor.

Drea found Lottie sitting at the Boone table off to the side, and took a seat next to her. Lottie gave her a big hug. "Drea, this has been a fantastic evening. I'm so proud of what you have accomplished."

"Thanks. I'm really thrilled with the outcome."

"Thrilled?" Lottie's eyes narrowed a bit and she took both Drea's hands in hers. "I don't see thrill on your face, sweetheart. I see sadness and regret."

"I'm leaving tomorrow afternoon. I didn't think I'd say this, but I'm going to miss Boone Springs. And my dad."

Lottie stiffened at the mention of Drew. "I understand. This place is your true home, Drea. You've got roots here. And friends."

"I do. I promised Dad I'll come visit often. We're doing pretty well now and I've forgiven him for what he did. But

Lottie, what's up between the two of you? I've noticed you haven't spent a minute together this entire weekend."

"Oh, um…" Lottie shook her head and glanced away. "I'm afraid he's very angry with me. He's been avoiding me for days. You know us. We've always had a rocky relationship."

"Yes, but… I thought this time things were different."

They were interrupted by the sound of Mason's voice coming from the microphone onstage. "And now it's time to announce the winner of the Dream Date with Sean raffle. To do the honors, our own publicity pro, Linda Sullivan, will come up here and pull the winning ticket. As you know, Linda was instrumental in putting this part of the event together."

When Linda reached the stage, Mason turned the mic over to her. She made a few jokes about the girls languishing on the back lawn, waiting for this moment. Then she had Sean come up to a big Plexiglass cube filled with raffle tickets. "It's only fitting that Sean pick the winner. Don't you think so, girls?"

Shouts and giddy laughter broke out as Linda gestured for Sean to dig deep into the cube and grab a ticket. Everyone at the tables and on the lawn quieted.

"And the dream date with Sean goes to… Regina Clayborne!"

Lofty sighs of disappointment filled the back lawn, except for where the winner was standing, surrounded by her friends. She began jumping for joy, her blond hair bouncing in the breeze. Linda brought her up onstage to meet Sean and the girl couldn't stop crying happy tears.

"Well, I guess my part is officially over," Drea said to Lottie. "I think the committee can finish up tomorrow."

"What are your plans then?"

"I want to spend the entire morning with my father. My flight leaves in the late afternoon."

Lottie folded her arms around her middle, looking none too pleased. "And here I was hoping that you and Mason would have worked it out by now."

"I can't fight a ghost, Lottie. I can't make Mason feel things he doesn't."

"You're hurting."

"Love hurts sometimes."

Lottie's eyes glistened with moisture. "Yeah, sweetheart, sometimes it does."

As the guests filed out of the concert area and the band packed up to go back to their hotel, Mason walked over to the Boone family table and found Lottie sitting with Risk and Lucas.

"Well done, brother," Risk said.

Luke nodded in agreement.

"Thanks, guys." Mason should be flying high. After this past month of hard work, their fund-raiser had achieved its goals. The new cardiac wing of the hospital was destined to break ground, but one important thing was missing. Or one person, rather. "Didn't I see Drea sitting here a few minutes ago?"

"You did," Luke said. "But she's gone now. I grabbed a dance with her earlier this evening."

"Yeah. Me, too," Risk said. "She's pretty light on her feet."

Mason gave his brothers a good-natured frown. They liked busting his chops. "So where did she go?"

"Home, I think," Lottie said.

Mason swallowed hard. "Already?"

"She said she was tired and had some packing to do."

Risk sipped from his glass of wine. "She promised to

come back to Boone Springs soon, though. I made a date to take her to dinner."

"Yeah. Me, too," Lucas added.

"All right, boys," Aunt Lottie said to Mason's pain-in-the-ass brothers. "You've made your point. Let me have a chat with Mason."

The guys got up, and both gave him a conciliatory pat on the back before walking off.

"Mason, what's going on?" Aunt Lottie asked.

He slumped into the seat next to her. "I just need to talk to Drea."

"No, you don't. The time for talking is over between you two. You have to act. And if you can't, then it's best you leave that girl alone."

"Are you saying I've been taking advantage of her, Aunt Lottie?"

"That's not what I'm saying, my thickheaded nephew. What I am saying is that you have less than twenty-four hours to figure out what you truly want. If it's not her, then let her leave town. And you should resume your life."

Resume his dreary life? Go back to all that emptiness? Go back to dwelling on his loss, dwelling on the pain? Go back to life before Drea? What in hell was wrong with him? He couldn't do that.

Aunt Lottie was right.

He needed to act.

Wearing daisy-yellow gardening gloves, Drea inserted the last vinca plant in the landscaped border surrounding the cottage and then gave the soil a loving pat. The garden was finished, returned to its former glory. That had been her goal.

Her father watched from the front porch. "Drea, don't you tire yourself out now."

"I'm not. It feels good to finish this. Doesn't it look great?" She stood up to gaze at her handiwork. Flowers and shrubs adorned the land once overrun by weeds.

Drew came down the steps, his eyes sharper than she'd seen them in a long time. "Yeah, it's beautiful."

"You have to promise to keep the weeds at bay and water the plants."

"After all your hard work, you know I will." He looked at his watch. She had only a few hours left at home with him.

"You ready for breakfast now, sweetheart? I made you pancakes with chocolate chips and apple bacon and—"

"Whoa, Dad. You had me at chocolate chip pancakes."

He laughed and hugged her shoulders. "Go shower and I'll get the meal on the table."

She kissed his cheek. "You're on."

Half an hour later, Drea patted her stomach and pushed her plate away. She'd dressed in the clothes she'd wear later when she boarded her plane, a soft pink, lightweight sweater and a pair of designer jeans that were feeling a little snug about now. "I ate too much."

Her dad grinned. "Me, too. How about we take a little walk, burn off some of those pancakes."

Whatever he wanted to do, she was game. This was their last morning together for a while and she was happy just being with him. Walking in the morning air would help keep her mind off leaving town. "That's a great idea."

"I'm ready." Her father glanced at his watch again. "Let's go."

They walked down the road a bit, taking sure but slow steps, just enjoying the scenery and weather this autumn morning. Drew MacDonald was healthier than when she'd come. He'd been eating better and had lost some weight, and his daily walking rituals were really helping build his strength.

About a quarter mile into the walk, after rounding a turn, she spotted a black SUV parked on the side of the road just a few feet away. A man climbed out, long legs in fitted black jeans, silver belt buckle gleaming, with a familiar Stetson atop his head. Mason. Her heart began to pound. "Dad, what's going on?"

Her father's eyes grew soft and he smiled. "Hear him out, darlin' girl."

"What?"

"Mason needs to speak with you."

Her mind clicked away. "But I don't want… Is this a trap?"

Her father grinned. "God, I hope so." He kissed her cheek and gave her a big hug. "Don't be mad, and listen to your heart." With that, he turned around and began walking back toward the cottage, leaving her dumbfounded in the middle of the road.

It took only four long strides for Mason to reach her. He gave her a warm smile, as if he hadn't just hijacked her. "Mornin'."

She clamped her mouth closed. She didn't like surprises. At least not like this, especially when Mason was looking all casual and gorgeous. But his eyes, those dark, dark eyes, weren't filled with his usual confidence. He had that vulnerable look on his face that always got to her.

"Good to see you." His gaze flowed over her intently as if…as if he was… No. She wasn't going to think it. She wasn't going to hope. Mason had made his choice and it wasn't her.

"What's this all about, Mason?"

"It's about me and you. I want to show you something."

"I don't think so. I'm supposed to—"

"Please," he said. "It won't take long and I'll bring you back to Drew's quickly." He extended his hand, palm up, and waited.

She gestured to the car. "Are you driving me somewhere?"

"That's the plan. It's not far."

Listen to your heart. Listen to your heart. Her father's advice helped her make the choice.

She began slowly walking to the SUV, ignoring Mason's outstretched hand. She wasn't going to make this easy on him, whatever it was. But her reluctance didn't faze him. Instead, he raced to open the car door for her and she climbed in.

Mason got in and didn't look at her, didn't say anything. They drove in silence down the road and then Mason took a cutoff that led to the west end of the property that was once Thundering Hills.

He stopped the car and they both got out, her heart hammering in her chest. At one time, this had been MacDonald land, her home. She hadn't come here in a long, long time.

Mason leaned against the grill of his car and grabbed her hand so she landed next to him.

"Sean said something to me the other day that made a lot of sense," he said softly, his eyes touching hers. "He said you and I were flawless together."

She blinked. "Sean said that?"

"Yeah. The kid's pretty damn smart."

"Unlike you."

He laughed and it was so hearty, she had to smile, too. "When you're right, you're right."

"Excuse me, did I hear correctly?"

"You did. You heard me right. And I got to thinking that when we were first together, some weeks back, I thought you were good for me. There was something about you that jump-started my life again. You were the catalyst I needed, the fire under my ass, whatever you want to call it. I don't know, maybe it was because we had history together, but you came to Rising Springs and saved me from drowning in my own grief. After that one kiss, I was suddenly filled with light and energy and I wanted more. I wanted to feel again. But I was afraid, too, because I'd clung to Larissa's memory for so long and I didn't know if I could go through something like that again. I didn't know if my emotions were all screwed up."

"What are you saying, Mason?"

"I'm saying that after I learned about what happened to you in college, I freaked out a little bit. I blamed myself for getting involved with you, for taking advantage of a much younger woman."

"But you didn't. I wanted you, Mason. It was your rejection that hurt me. I wasn't a very secure girl back then, and I guess I understand now why you did what you did."

He squeezed her hands and looked solemnly into her eyes. "We've both been hurt in the past, and it's time to put that behind us, Drea. Sweetheart, I realize now that all those sparks you ignited in me weren't just sexual. It was love, Drea. I love you. You're the only woman for me. We are meant for each other and I can't stand the thought of you leaving. We belong together."

It was a stunning declaration that left her breathless. But she wasn't sure she could truly trust it. "Mason, are you sure you're ready? I know you care about me, but love?"

"Believe me when I say I am ready. Granted, I'm a late bloomer, but last night, after you left the event, it finally hit me how much I love you. I'm never afraid when I'm with you, Drea. Just the opposite. When I'm with you, I am the man I'm supposed to be. I was so sure of myself last night at our event that I asked your father for his blessing, and he gave it to me. Drea, I want to do it again, I want to marry you. I want a family with as many kids as you'd like. I want it all, as long as it's with you."

She smiled at the notion. It was a precious thought. She wanted babies with Mason. Lots and lots of them. All week long, she'd been dreading going back to New York, dreading leaving this place that now felt so much like home, her true home. In her heart of hearts, here with Mason was where she really wanted to be.

Mason got down on one knee and presented her with a brilliant square-cut diamond ring. It was so beautiful her breath caught in a big gasp.

"Andrea MacDonald, I promise to love and honor you for the rest of our lives. Will you marry me?"

She took his upturned face in her hands, gazing into those dark, sincere, beautiful eyes. "Yes, Mason. My dream, my heart. I'll marry you."

He grinned widely and placed the ring on her finger. "My grandmother would have been happy to see her ring on your finger, Drea. She would've welcomed you and loved you almost as much as I do."

He stood then and claimed her lips in a kiss that sealed their love. A kiss that meant forever. And they stayed cradled in each other's arms for long, sweet moments, Mason stroking her hair as she gazed out onto the hills.

"When you brought me out here, you said you wanted to show me something?" she finally asked, looking at him curiously.

"I wanted to propose to you here, on the land you've always loved. We can build a place of our own here, if you'd like. We can design a house you'll love overlooking the hills."

"I'd like that. I guess I'm moving back to Rising Springs."

Mason pulled away slightly. "I know your career is important to you and I'll support whatever you want to do about it. You don't have to decide now, sweetheart."

Her job had once been the only thing she'd actually had in her life. And since coming home, she realized that there was so much more she wanted. She loved Boone Springs. She loved her father and her friends. And she loved Mason Boone, more than she'd thought possible. "Actually, I think I'd like to do volunteer work in Boone Springs. I can donate my time and hope to continue to make a difference here."

"That sounds like a good plan."

"It's the best plan as long as we're together," she said.

"It is," he agreed, placing a light kiss on her forehead. "Missy isn't selling the beach house, after all. She decided to keep it for family and friends. And I was thinking it's a good place for our honeymoon. Shall I book it, say, for the spring?"

"You want to get married that quickly?" Drea asked, liking the idea of being Mason's wife.

"I do. As soon as we can plan the wedding."

She leaned against him, looking out at the place she'd once called home, the place she would finally return to. It was uncanny, something she never would have believed possible.

"And there's one more thing," he said quietly. "Larissa's parents gave me a letter she wrote to me two years ago, right before she passed. It's her last words to me. I haven't opened it yet."

"Why not?"

Mason drew a deep breath and pulled an envelope out of his pocket. "I didn't realize the reason I've been holding on to this letter until last night. It's because I wanted you by my side when I read it. Larissa was my past, and I loved her deeply, but you…you are my future. And I needed you to know that no matter what's inside this letter, it won't change my love for you. You need to know how much I love you."

"I think I do now," she said, her eyes filling with tears. "I love you very much, Mason. If you're ready, go ahead, read the letter privately." She squeezed his forearm, holding on to him. "I'm right here and I always will be."

Mason unsealed the envelope and pulled out the piece of paper. He took a few moments to read Larissa's words and then faced Drea. He swallowed hard, his eyes glistening. "Larissa knew me so well. She knew I'd grieve a long time. She said she wanted me to be happy, to find someone to share my life with. She wanted me to move on."

He sighed and then kissed Drea's lips gently, sweetly, and she felt his love all the way down to her toes. "And I have, Drea. I am moving on. I've found happiness with you. I promise you'll never doubt my love. We'll have a good life."

"Yes we will, Mason. I believe it, too. After all, together the two of us are absolutely *flawless*."

* * * * *

TEMPTED BY SCANDAL

KAREN BOOTH

For Cat Schield, Reese Ryan and Joss Wood,
my incredible Desire sisters.

One

Nadia Gonzalez didn't believe in regrets. She simply did her damnedest to never make a mistake. Being careful but determined always paid off—that approach got her into the college she wanted to attend and a scholarship for the tuition she couldn't afford. When she was younger, her resoluteness had helped her win several beauty pageants—not her proudest achievements but ones that had meant a great deal to her mother. More recently, her perseverance had helped her land her job as executive admin for Matt Richmond, one of the wealthiest and most powerful men in the world. That was the real feather in her cap and she wasn't about to do anything to put that at risk.

But there was a very good chance that Nadia had made a mistake that put her job in jeopardy. She'd done the unthinkable. She'd fallen into bed with her ridiculously hot boss. As a woman who prided herself on meticulous organization and great attention to detail, as someone who didn't want to be judged first by her physical appearance, this might have been a gaffe for the ages.

But the minute she saw Matt in a perfectly tailored, sleek black tux at the hospital fund-raiser last night, looking unfairly handsome, she knew she was in trouble. He almost never put on a tie. He'd joke with people that he wasn't big on formality, but that wasn't entirely true. He loved champagne, extravagant parties and expensive cars. He simply didn't want to get dressed up to enjoy it. But as difficult as it was to get Matt into a suit, it turned out that Nadia had a talent for getting him out of it.

This was no small development in Nadia's life. She'd spent the past fourteen months, virtually every moment she'd been employed by Matt, secretly pining for him. He was everything Nadia could ever want in a man—the embodiment of sexy confidence, high IQ and seemingly endless brilliance wrapped up in six feet two inches of the most appealing package Nadia could imagine, topped off with thick sandy blond hair. When he walked into a room, men and women alike turned their heads. The air crackled with electricity. His mere arrival trumpeted his greatness, and was punctuated by his bracing blue eyes. Just thinking about him made her fingers and lips tingle.

Now, driving up a steep and winding hillside an hour east of Seattle, her foot gunning the gas, these thoughts of Matt were ill-timed at best. It felt like her thighs were about to burst into full flame. Thankfully she finally crested the hill, took a deep breath and flipped on her blinker, zipping into the main drive for The Opulence resort, managed by one of the many divisions of Matt's massive company, Richmond Industries. A sprawling, luxurious property tucked away on a thickly wooded and rocky mountaintop, the setting for The Opulence exemplified the Pacific Northwest at its most beautiful, as towering trees nearly scraped the pale blue sky. On a bright October day like today, the air was so crisp you wanted to breathe it in forever. In five short weeks, Richmond Industries' fifth-anniversary retreat would be held here. Nadia really hoped she'd still have her job by then.

"Checking in, miss?" the young man at the valet stand asked.

Nadia climbed out of her car and handed over her keys. "Just for one night. I'm Nadia Gonzalez. I work for Matt Richmond."

The valet nodded. "Yes. Ms. Gonzalez. Mr. Richmond arrived about an hour ago."

Nadia hadn't spoken to Matt since she'd left his magnificent house at four thirty that morning, slinking off under cover of night, still wearing the evening gown she'd donned for the hospital fund-raiser. Leaving that early had been Matt's suggestion and Nadia agreed. He was an incredibly powerful man and men like him drew attention. Neither of them could afford the optics of a boss-assistant tryst, but especially not Matt. There were too many people eager to tear him down. That's what happens when you have success mere mortals can't begin to comprehend.

"Great," Nadia said. "I'm heading in to meet with him right now." The thought of seeing Matt was making the thighs-on-fire situation that much more intense. "Be sure to take good care of my car. It's my baby."

"Of course, Ms. Gonzalez." The valet hopped into her month-old silver Audi, a bonus from Matt for a job well done on the still-secret Sasha project, a joint partnership between Matt and Liam Christopher, his best friend from college. Nadia had worked hard for that car. She'd earned it.

But thinking about crossing the line with Matt while watching her prized car disappear into a parking garage made her question her priorities. Yes, she'd wanted Matt for a long time and they'd shared an unbelievable night of passion. But so what? Was she really willing to throw away her career and quite possibly the most primo admin job in the US? No. Was she willing to discount the years she'd scraped by so she could make a better life for herself and her family? Absolutely not. A guy like Matt was not the settling-down type. There would be no happy ending with him. Which meant that her first priority when speaking to him today would be to make sure he understood that last night was a one-time thing. They would both be better off if they forgot about it and returned to their strictly professional dynamic, even though that was going to break her heart.

Nadia made her way up the flagstone promenade to the massive double doors of the main lodge. Two doormen in smart black jackets opened them in unison, and she swept into the grand but warm lobby. Every detail was perfect—mahogany wood moldings, high ceilings and elegant chandeliers. She'd spent a lot of time in surroundings like this since she'd started working with Matt, far removed from her modest upbringing in Chino, California, outside Los Angeles. It felt good to be in this world. She liked being able to help pay her younger sister's college tuition, and chip away at her mother's medical bills so her parents could sleep easier at night. All the more reason to hold on to her job tightly and put Matt back in a box with a note saying, "He's your boss. Don't be stupid."

Nadia arrived at the front desk and gave her name. As the clerk checked the computer, Nadia's phone beeped with a text from Matt.

Come up when you arrive. 310. Meeting with Teresa St. Claire at 2:00.

"Yes," the clerk said. "Ms. Gonzalez, we have you in room three-twelve. Right next to Mr. Richmond."

Nadia smiled and swallowed hard, swiping the keycard from the gleaming wood counter. Nothing like staying next door to the man you can't resist. "Fantastic."

"Elevators are at the far side of the lobby. I'll have a bellhop bring up your bag."

"Thank you." Nadia hustled over and jabbed the button then typed out a quick response to Matt on her phone. On my way.

Good. A single word was his only response, a stark reminder that he was an impossibly busy man who always put business first.

The trip up three floors was just long enough to sort out what she had to say to Matt. Today would mark the end of their personal involvement. They had to put a stop to it before it went too far.

At the very end of the long hall, she passed by her door and knocked on his, staring down at her feet, choking back the anticipation of seeing him again. She would not falter. She would be the picture of capable and confident, even when she was feeling nothing more than weak. She would shrug off their tryst, let Matt off the hook and move on. She was too smart and had worked too hard to give herself anything less.

Matt Richmond looked out the windows of his hotel suite, allowing himself to be momentarily entranced by the sight of Centennial Falls. This was one of the calling cards of The Opulence—the main building was precariously perched at the edge of the stories-high drop. He watched as ice-cold water rushed, churned and poured over the rocky ledge, leaving behind only mist and spray. Mother Nature was one of the only things that amazed him anymore. Everything man-made could be explained. He liked the mystery. He liked that he couldn't control it.

Honestly, that was part of the appeal of Nadia. On the outside, she was unflappable. A beautiful closed book. But he'd sensed that on the inside was a woman untamed. That inkling had made him play with fire. The thought of having her in his bed sent a ripple of heat right through him. It was as if the fire was still here.

He jumped when the knock came at the door. *Nadia.* He'd spent hours trying to decide how to handle their working relationship now. He'd determined his only course was to let her lead the way. He bounded across the room and opened the door. She regularly knocked the breath out of him, but today her effect on him was even stronger.

"Mr. Richmond." Without making eye contact, Nadia swept into the room and set her purse and laptop bag down on the coffee table, then strode over to the desk. She immediately began straightening the papers he'd left strewn about. "You've been busy."

He followed her, walking through the heavenly wake of her perfume. Her wavy blond hair was up in a twist and he caught himself wanting to pull it out. Instead he stuffed his hands into his pockets. "You don't have to do that."

"You have a very busy day and you work better when you're organized."

He couldn't help but smile. "You know me better than I know myself."

"It's my job to know you." She turned and finally looked at him, but her eyes weren't warm and inviting like they'd been last night. Now they were full of worry. "Which makes me wonder what you were thinking when you had the hotel put me in the room next to yours. That doesn't seem like a good idea."

"What? I had no idea. You made the reservation."

"And the Richmond Hotel Group manages the hotel." She took in a deep breath. "Look, Mr. Richmond…"

He reached out and placed his hand on her arm. The connection to her was immediate. He craved her the way he needed to breathe. "You're going to call me Mr. Richmond now? After the things we did together? We're alone, Nadia. Please, call me Matt."

"Fine. Matt. Last night was a mistake."

That word sliced through him. The only mistakes he ever made were in trusting the wrong people. Had he slipped up by trusting her?

"We both need to forget it ever happened," she continued.

That didn't sit well with him, either. "That's going to be a difficult task when I go home tomorrow and climb into bed and realize my sheets smell like you."

"So have one of your ten housekeepers change them."

Matt didn't enjoy having his success thrown in his face. It wasn't his fault he was successful or rich. From the desk, his phone rang. Nadia turned and picked it up, glancing at the screen.

"It's Shayla." Shayla Jerome was Richmond Industries' head of Public Relations.

"Is this important?" Matt answered. "I'm in the middle of something."

"Yes, it's important. We have a situation on our hands."

Matt hated the way Shayla couched every bit of news she had to deliver. "Please spit it out. I don't have time for this. If there's a fire, get out the extinguishers."

She cleared her throat. "Fine. *TBG* just posted pictures of your beauty-queen admin leaving your house in the middle of the night wearing the gown she'd been photographed wearing hours earlier at the hospital benefit."

Matt's stomach sank. *The Big Gossip*, or *TBG*, was a tabloid website with an unsavory reputation and a massive following. He ran his hands through his hair. Nadia glanced over at him and her eyes narrowed. Nadia had an uncanny ability to read him and he wasn't ready to share this bit of news with her. He turned and walked away. "How did this happen?"

"That's not really a question for me now, is it? I'm guessing that somebody on your security detail fell down on the job. Or more likely, fell asleep."

A low rumble escaped Matt's throat. "Fine. I'll talk to Phil."

"That only helps with preventing this from happening again. For now we have a story trending about you sleeping with an employee. It does not look good."

"So kill it."

"*TBG* has new ownership and a whole new editorial team. They're not about to bend to the whim of a publicist."

"Then offer them something better."

That was enough to get Nadia to walk over to where he was standing by the windows, her flawless face full of worry. He did enjoy the way her full lips went slack. "What's going on?" she whispered.

Matt merely shook his head.

"Access to the Saturday night gala during the retreat?" Shayla asked.

Matt had refused *TBG*'s request for access. That retreat was meant to be an exclusive weekend-long getaway for the business elite and Matt's closest celebrity friends. People came to a party like that to have fun outside the public eye. "Is there another way?"

"I can deny the story and make something up. Say there was a work emergency and you had to go straight to your house from the fund-raiser. You needed Nadia's help and it was closer than the office."

Matt thought it through for a second. "That could work."

"Oh, my God," Nadia said, looking at her phone. She showed him the screen. There was the story. And that horrible headline, plain as day: "Beauty and the Boss?" Whoever had taken the picture of her tiptoeing her way out of his house had used a camera with night-vision technology.

"I need Nadia to sign a nondisclosure agreement before I do this, though," Shayla said. "Richmond Industries can't afford to have her turn around and decide to sell her story to the highest bidder."

Matt's stomach was done dropping and was now angrily churning. "I don't think that's necessary."

"Do you trust her implicitly? Because I don't."

"You don't trust anyone."

"A man in your position shouldn't, either. For all we know, Nadia tipped off that photographer."

Matt refused to believe Nadia was capable of that. "Just take care of it. Please." With that, Matt ended the call.

Nadia's wide eyes were pleading. "Is this why Shayla called?" She glanced down at her phone in disgust and handed it to him. "We have to do something. I don't want my coworkers knowing that I slept with you."

Matt hated that the memory of his amazing night with Nadia had now been eclipsed by a pulpy story, but at least he knew that Nadia had not played a role in the photographer's presence. If she had, she wouldn't be so upset right now. "I told Shayla to kill it. Don't worry about it. It will go away."

"It's so easy for you to say that. You have all the power here. I'm nobody." Nadia wrapped her arms around her waist and turned to the window overlooking the falls.

He hated hearing her refer to herself that way. She wasn't nobody to him. And looking at her right now, all he could think about was how badly he wanted her. It made it nearly impossible to think straight. "Nadia." He put his hand on her shoulder and watched as she turned and looked back at him, her warm brown eyes inviting him in. "I don't want you to regret the things we did together. We're two consenting adults." Matt knew it wasn't as simple as that. People would talk. All the more reason for Shayla to get rid of the story as soon as possible.

She sighed and her shoulders dropped in defeat. "I

know that, but it doesn't matter. We can't let this happen again. There are too many prying eyes. It could destroy us both."

Nadia was right. Matt only wished he wasn't so disappointed by the truth. If he could have anything he wanted right now, it would be her. "I won't let that happen."

"See? Power. You can control this. I can't."

He brushed her cheek with the back of his hand. He knew he shouldn't, but the way she subtly pressed against his touch sent the blood coursing through his body. "If you understood how badly I want you right now, you would know that the power is all yours."

Two

Teresa St. Claire's heart hammered at the thought of what was only ten or fifteen minutes away, but she took several deep breaths and reminded herself that this was exactly what she'd worked so hard for. Meeting with billionaire businessman Matt Richmond would be intimidating for anyone—few people in the world had as much money and influence as he did—but he was also her client. *Her client.* Her dreams were coming true. She was here to plan Richmond Industries' fifth-anniversary extravaganza. She was here to make Matt Richmond happy, and she would rock it so hard he'd never hire another event planner in his entire life.

The young man running the valet stand rushed to Teresa's door and opened it. He flashed a warm smile, and her nerves settled. "Checking in, miss?" he asked.

She left the keys in the ignition and eased out of the

car. "I am. Just for the night right now, but you'll see a lot of me over the next five weeks." She held out her hand. "Teresa St. Claire. Limitless Events. I'm planning the Richmond retreat."

"I'm Michael." He cocked his head to the side, face full of surprise. Perhaps he wasn't accustomed to guests introducing themselves, but Teresa made a habit of knowing everyone by name. That's how you got things done. Plus, he reminded Teresa of her younger brother, Joshua, whom she missed terribly and hadn't seen in months. "I'll have the bellman take your suitcase up to your room. Let me know if you need anything at all, Ms. St. Claire."

"Nice to meet you, Michael. I'm sure I'll see you around." Teresa hooked her navy leather Fendi bag on her arm, straightened her black peplum jacket and marched into The Opulence. The lobby was stunning, but Teresa was already brainstorming ideas to make it better for the retreat. It was an automatic shift in thinking. Her training with Mariella Santiago-Marshall at MSM Event Planning in Santa Barbara had served her well. Mr. Richmond and his guests would be taking over the entire resort and Teresa wanted them to step into an event they would talk about for years. That was how she'd cement Limitless Events' spot on the map. Billionaires, business moguls and celebrities from all over the world would know her name.

Teresa stopped at the front desk, and the clerk led her through the lobby, past the bar and down a hall to a meeting room. The space was modest but stately, with a gleaming wood conference table for six and a seating area with beautifully upholstered chairs poised in front of a wide picture window. She wandered over to admire the view of Centennial Falls. Sitting in a front-row seat was the ideal place to meet with Mr. Richmond so she could paint the picture of his perfect event. Mariella Santiago-Marshall had taught her that—tell the client a story, let them imagine their guests stepping into a world unlike anything they've ever experienced. That's how you made memories, and memories were how you made lifelong clients.

She was about to sit in one of the chairs when her cellphone rang with a call from her assistant, Corinne Donovan. "Hey," Teresa answered. "I only have a minute. Matt Richmond should be here soon."

"Did you not get my messages?"

"No. What messages?"

"I left you three voice mails."

"There's a dead zone between Seattle and The Opulence. I'm sure I lost cell service. What's wrong? You sound frazzled."

"A man has been calling the office for you. He won't tell me his name. He kept asking for your cell number and I didn't want to give it to him, but then he said it was urgent so I finally just did. He said it's life or death."

Goose bumps raced over Teresa's skin. "Is he going to call me?" Before Corinne could answer, Teresa heard the beep telling her that she had a call on the other line. "This must be him. I'd better take this."

"Call me when you get a chance. I'm worried."

So am I. "I'll fill you in when I can." Teresa ended the call and answered again. "Hello?"

"Ms. St. Claire." Despite Corinne's report of this being a life-or-death situation, the man's voice was careful and measured, as if he had all the time in the world.

"This is Teresa. Who's calling?"

"I'm a messenger. I'm calling about Joshua."

Teresa's blood ran cold. By design, very few people knew about her younger brother. "What about him?" She hated that defensive tone in her voice, but it came out by pure instinct. She would do anything to protect Joshua.

"Your brother has a habit of getting into trouble, doesn't he?"

Teresa wasn't going to answer that question. Yes, Joshua had gotten himself into quite a mess a few years ago in Las Vegas, but she'd gotten all of that cleared up via The Fixer, a longtime associate of Mariella Santiago-Marshall's husband, Harrison. The Fixer did exactly what his moniker suggested—he made problems go away. "What do you want?"

"Joshua owes some very important people and he's not going to be able to weasel his way out of it."

"Owes what?"

"With interest, seven million dollars. Payable now."

Teresa's heart nearly stopped. What could Joshua have done that would get him into that deep a hole? "Joshua doesn't have that kind of money."

"Which is why I went to the person who cares most about keeping him alive."

Teresa's stomach lurched. "That's preposterous. I don't have that kind of money, either."

"Hunter Price invested in your company. He's a wealthy man. Surely he gave you something to put away."

It truly terrified her that this man knew these details of her life. Her agreement with Hunter had been nothing but discreet. Yes, he had invested in Limitless, but those funds had gone right into the business, for office space, staffing and outfitting the entire operation. "I don't have seven million dollars."

"Then come up with it."

"How, exactly?"

"Not my problem. Just keep in mind that Joshua is running out of time."

"Don't you dare hurt him."

The man laughed, a sickening sound that told her he was no stranger to harming people. Teresa couldn't believe this nightmare was happening again. A cocktail of anger and guilt mixed inside her. She'd always been Joshua's protector. She'd practically been his mother. Their own mother, Talisa, was scattered and overwhelmed by the world, although it was hard even now to blame her. She'd done her best as a single mom. Nothing had been right after Teresa and Joshua's father, Nigel, died.

"I'm a reasonable man. I won't hurt him right away," the man continued. "First, I air Joshua's dirty laundry. See how badly that hurts your business. You work with some very wealthy, important people. I'm sure they'd love to learn what your little brother did in Vegas. Your brother that you practically raised. The brother you're supposed to be guiding through life."

Teresa swallowed hard. Her eyes darted to the window, but the sight of the millions of gallons of water rushing over the rocky drop of Centennial Falls was no longer beautiful. It made her even queasier. None of this was fair. She'd worked hard to help Joshua on track. She'd only needed to see him in jail once before she'd become fully committed to keeping him out.

But the truth was that since she'd started Limitless and moved back to Seattle, she'd been laser-focused on her career. She hadn't been keeping close tabs on Joshua.

Every time they'd spoken, Joshua assured her he was doing fine. Now she knew he wasn't exactly keeping his nose clean. She should've been paying closer attention.

"I'm sure your clients will be especially surprised to find out what his big sister did to make it go away."

Teresa's pulse pounded. She quickly glanced at the meeting-room door. No sign of Matt Richmond and that was a good thing. Still, she did not want to risk him walking in while she was having this conversation. Her nerves were too frayed. "Look. I'm going to need time to figure this out. I don't have that kind of cash available." If nothing else, she needed to verify that this was actually true. A big part of her wanted to give Joshua the benefit of the doubt. "I need your number so I can get back to you. The call came through as 'unknown.'"

"That's not how this works. You should know that by now. I'll be in touch." The line went dead.

A tall, broad figure stepped into her peripheral vision. *Oh, God. Matt Richmond.* She took a deep breath, smiled and rose from her seat, only to be confronted by an image plucked from her past, a man she'd only dreamed of running into. Liam Christopher.

For a moment, she and Liam stared at each other. He was even easier on the eyes now than the last time she'd seen him. Six years ago? Seven? His square jaw and the dark scruff along it suited him so well. His green eyes were as piercing as ever. Right now, they were almost too intense.

"What are you doing here?" His voice boomed in the small space.

He must not recognize her. That was the only reason his voice would be dripping with contempt. She stepped closer and offered her hand. "Liam. Hi. Teresa

St. Claire. We've met a few times. Your father was my mentor when I was in business school."

He looked at her hand as if he couldn't be any more repulsed by the idea of touching her. "You think I don't know who you are? As if I could forget. Tell me what you're doing here."

She didn't understand the anger in his voice, but her first instinct was to tell him everything he wanted to know. Perhaps that would calm him down so she could figure out why he was so agitated. "I'm waiting for Matt Richmond. He and I have a meeting scheduled to take place in this room. I'm surprised to see you, but you two are close friends, aren't you?"

"What do you want with Matt?"

Now her patience was wearing thin. There were too many unpleasant things coming out of Liam's stunning mouth. "I'm sorry, but did I miss something? I haven't seen you in six years? Seven? And you march into my meeting all angry?"

"*Your* meeting? I have a meeting with Matt. And I can guarantee you that whatever it is that you think you're going to be talking to him about, I'll be putting a quick end to it."

Nobody messed with her and her business. She was not going to lose this event, especially not when she might have to come up with an exorbitant sum of money to save her brother again. "I don't know why Mr. Richmond double-booked himself, but he's not here, so we're both going to have to wait. Perhaps you can take this time to tell me why you're so upset with me." She pulled back a chair from the conference table and offered it. "Here. Have a seat. Let's talk."

Liam shook his head, his jaw visibly tighter. "Stop playing games."

Teresa felt her own anger about to eclipse Liam's. "Games? I'm playing games? How about you tell me why you're so mad at me."

Liam shook his head again, this time slowly and steadily. It felt as if his eyes might bore a hole right through her. "You know what you did. You ruined my father's life."

Liam Christopher had imagined many times what he might say to Teresa St. Claire if he ever ran into her, but he'd failed to take into account just how badly his temper would flare. He normally played things exceptionally close to the vest, but evidently all bets were off with Teresa.

"Ruined his life? Your father was my mentor." Her pleading tone only made her that much more unlikable. "I've always cared deeply about him. He helped me get my start in business. I have no idea what you're talking about."

"Don't play coy with me. It's insulting." Tension spread across his shoulders and back like a sickness. Although it had been seven years since he last saw Teresa, he would never forget her. Not because she was beautiful, although she was regrettably gorgeous—tall and willowy with long blond hair and striking blue eyes. She was apparently the sort of woman his father had a weakness for. Teresa St. Claire had convinced his father to stray outside his marriage. She was the reason his parents split. She was the reason his mother's heart had been irrevocably shattered.

"I honestly have no idea what you're talking about."

Teresa was either in denial or the type of person who would willingly lie to make herself look good. He had no patience for either. He cleared his throat and stuffed his hands into his pockets. Where was Matt? Liam wanted nothing more than to let his best friend know whom he was about to meet with so he could have Teresa escorted from the building and, hopefully, his life.

"What are you and Mr. Richmond meeting about today?" she asked.

"Not that I owe you an explanation, but we're announcing a partnership during his retreat."

"Maybe that's why Matt double-booked his time. I'm organizing the entire event. Perhaps he wanted us to discuss the details."

This was *not* happening. "You can wager as many guesses as you want, but it's not going to matter. Matt and I have been best friends since college. We are each other's closest confidants. You won't be organizing anything I'm involved with. And I also won't let you take advantage of my best friend."

Teresa visibly winced. A part of him was glad he could get to her like this, but he took no real pleasure in making threats. He only knew that he could not work with Teresa. His partnership with Matt's company on the Sasha artificial-intelligence project had been years and millions of dollars in the making. Plus, he had to let Matt know whom he was dealing with.

"Is there some sort of jealousy here? Are you upset that your father helped me all those years ago? I realize he went above and beyond what most mentors might do, but we were very close. He believed in me."

Jealousy? Teresa had a real talent for twisting things back on other people. "Jealous is the last thing I am.

More like disgusted." Liam turned his back to Teresa and spotted Matt making his way down the hall. Liam met him at the doorway. "We have to talk about her."

"Mr. Richmond, whatever he's about to say, I can explain." Teresa was right behind Liam, craning her neck over his shoulder to get a glimpse of Matt. The desperation in her voice reeked of false drama. There was no explaining away what she'd done, and she knew it.

"Matt, you trust me, right?" Liam asked.

"Of course." Matt looked beyond bewildered, which wasn't an expression Liam had seen many times on his friend's face. Matt was the calm and collected guy with his finger on the pulse of everything. It was impossible to catch him by surprise, which was part of the reason Matt and Liam had hit it off the very first day they met. They both prided themselves on being unflappable. They simply pulled it off in very different ways.

Liam glanced over at Teresa. Her vivid blue eyes were wide, darting back and forth between Matt and him. It would have been so easy to cut her off at the knees, but Liam wasn't going to let her off the hook so easy. She could try to explain herself to Matt. "Whatever you've hired her to do, whatever business arrangement you two have, you'll do yourself a favor if you end it right here. She can't be trusted."

"Mr. Richmond, I have no earthly idea what Liam is talking about. And whatever he may think of me, I assure you that has no bearing on my abilities as an event planner."

Matt shook his head, still seeming confused. He turned to Liam. "Do you want to tell me what's going on?"

"She and I have a history. Or more specifically, she

and my father. But I think you should have her explain it." *Every dirty detail.*

Matt sighed and pulled Liam aside. "Look, she and I are weeks into planning the retreat. I'd rather not throw all of that work away. This event is already taking on a life of its own. Give me a chance to meet with her and I'll catch up with you later, okay?"

Liam knew Matt had a point. Letting business and personal matters intermingle was never a good idea. Matt was a stickler for keeping the two things separate. Liam was as well, but he was apparently having a weak moment. Maybe he simply needed to go outside and clear his head. "Yeah. Of course." Liam turned to look at Teresa one more time. He expected to see her gloating, but she looked worried. Good. Let her suffer at least a few repercussions. With nothing left to say, he stalked out into the hall.

He headed for the bar just beyond the lobby. It had a large balcony overlooking the falls. He looked forward to a shot of autumn air to clear his head, but every step away from his altercation with Teresa left him feeling more foolish, and that in turn only made him more angry. He knew he shouldn't let his emotions get to him, but the matter of Teresa was a complicated one.

The night Liam had first met Teresa, he couldn't have been any more entranced and enchanted. His father had asked him to dinner at the house, the Christopher family estate on the west side of Mercer Island. His father hadn't made note of the occasion, only saying that he had a promising student in the class he was teaching at the University of Washington, his alma mater. Liam hadn't wanted to attend the dinner. He was twenty-five by then, fully independent and making a name for himself within the family company. Plus, he knew exactly what was going to happen at dinner that night. His father would start to drink too much and would begin regaling their esteemed guest with tales of business conquests and billions made. Liam and his mother, Catherine, would exchange pained smiles and endure it. Liam didn't begrudge his father his success. He only disliked his obsession with it. Nothing was ever enough.

Much to Liam's surprise, that night's dinner guest was a breath of fresh air. Yes, his father was being a bit of a boastful blowhard during the meal. But Teresa St. Claire was as charming and beautiful a woman as Liam had ever seen. She was smart as a whip, with a wit that made him laugh more than once. She had a broad range of interests, was keenly focused on business and was nothing but eager to take on the world. No wonder his father was so enamored of her. Liam was as well. In fact, he'd never encountered a woman quite like her—an unparalleled beauty, sexy and enticing, but wholly enthralled with the business world. By the time dessert was served, Liam was convinced that meeting Teresa was fate. She was his perfect woman. At the end of the night, he walked her out to her car and made his move.

"It was so nice to meet you," she'd said, offering her hand.

Liam could hardly think straight when her skin touched his—there was an unmistakable zap of electricity between them. He'd gazed down into her deep blue eyes, made even more complex and intriguing in the soft evening light. "I really enjoyed meeting you. I'd love to see you again. Would you like to have dinner next week? Just the two of us? There's an amazing new seafood place downtown. The St. James?"

Surprise crossed Teresa's face. "Oh. Wow. That does sound nice." She'd looked away, untucking her hair from behind her ear, almost as if she was trying to hide from him. "But my life is crazy right now. I'm working two jobs and going to school. I'm surprised I even had time to come tonight." Her eyes fell on the house and her expression changed to one of longing. Liam had never regarded his childhood home with the awe and wonder she did in that moment. In many ways, the house had seemed like a prison when he was growing up. But Teresa saw it differently. He could see it on her face—she aspired to a life like the one his family had. She thought it was perfect. If only she knew the truth. "Your father has been so generous with his time and advice. I'm so thankful for his help." She turned back to him. "And I'm so glad we had a chance to meet. Perhaps we can get a drink sometime. When my life has calmed down a bit."

Liam hadn't needed more explanation than that. He'd been turned down very few times, but he knew the brush-off when he heard it. "Of course. I understand." Liam had his own craziness, working for the Christopher Corporation and trying to carve out a place for himself while living in the shadow of his dad. It would have been nice to have had a distraction as beautiful as Teresa St. Claire. Maybe even a relationship. There was a huge part of Liam that longed for a connection with a woman, in the same way Teresa seemed to long for a big, fancy house. Apparently she was *not* his dream woman. "Have a good night."

During the weeks that followed, Teresa regularly disproved her assertion that her life was too crazy for something as trivial as a dinner out. His mother had reported Teresa's regular visits to the house. She and his father were often shuttered away in his home study, and his mother, who was deeply suspicious of most people, would spend endless amounts of time speculating about what they were doing. "It's been hours, Liam. What could possibly be so important?"

If only his mother had known what torture it was for him to hear these things. He wanted Teresa, badly, and she only had time for the one man who'd never had time for him—his father. "Mom, I don't know. I'm sure it has something to do with the class she's taking."

"I think there's something else going on. I think he's having an affair with her."

That leap had made Liam sick to his stomach. His father had many personal shortcomings, but to Liam's knowledge, he'd never cheated on his mother. She'd clearly never suspected it. If she had, Liam would have heard about it. His mother told him everything. "I'm sure that's not what's going on. I'm sure it's all perfectly innocent." Only Liam wasn't so sure anymore, either. This all seemed so peculiar.

Then one night, his mother had called, frantic. "She's here again. I can't take it, darling. I just can't do it. Your father is throwing this affair in my face."

"Mom, he's not having an affair." Liam had said it with zero conviction.

"Please come to the house. I want you to see them together. I need to know that you really believe that. If you tell me there's nothing going on, I'll believe you. You're so good at reading people. Much better than me."

The idea of seeing Teresa again brought up a complicated mix of emotions. Liam was still hurt by her declining his dinner invitation. His ego wouldn't have been so bruised if she wasn't spending a great deal of time with his dad. "It's late and I have a big day tomorrow."

"Exactly, Liam. It's late. Why would she still be here? Please come over and tell me I'm not crazy. I can hear music and laughing."

Liam's heart was filled with dread, but he couldn't say no to his mother. Her paranoid tendencies were purely a product of his father's detachment. "Okay. I can be there in thirty minutes." He'd hopped in the car and raced over, hoping to hell Teresa would just be gone by the time he arrived. Unfortunately, he was not so lucky.

"They're still in the study," his mother muttered when Liam reached the door. Her breath smelled of vodka. "The door is open a tiny bit. Will you look and see what they're doing?"

Liam had no patience for this cloak-and-dagger routine. If the door was cracked, nothing was going on. His dad might be foolish, but he wasn't stupid. "I'm putting an end to this right now." Liam marched down the hall and raised his hand to knock on the door frame. But then he caught a glimpse of Teresa through the narrow sliver of open door. She was sitting on the edge of his father's desk, her legs crossed, a tight black skirt riding up to nearly midthigh. His father brought her a drink. Teresa toasted his father, saying she was so glad she'd found him. They smiled at each other with such adoration that Liam felt sick. They clinked their glasses and each took a sip, then Teresa hopped off the desk, gripped Linus's shoulders and kissed him tenderly on the cheek.

Liam couldn't watch anymore. He slunk away without saying a thing.

"Well?" his mother asked, waiting in the foyer.

"It's nothing." Liam hated to lie to his mother, but

he needed time to think. He knew how she would react if he confirmed her suspicions. There would be chaos. And Liam couldn't afford that with his dad at that time. He was about to propose the company undertake a risky project that would eventually become the Sasha technology. He needed his dad on his side. "They're talking about stuff for his class. She must need some extra help."

"You're sure?"

Liam nodded, telling himself that he would find a way to confront his dad about Teresa. As soon as the Sasha project was approved. "I'm sure." He'd leaned down and kissed his mom on the cheek. "Get some sleep. I'll talk to you soon."

Seven years later, that night was still so vivid in Liam's memory, and having seen Teresa only brought up the disappointment he'd had with himself over not telling his mom the truth. He walked up to The Opulence's bar and flagged the bartender. Early afternoon, and it was quiet, with just a couple sitting at one of the tables. "Club soda with lime, please." He craved something harder, but that would have to wait. He and Matt needed to have a long talk about Teresa.

"Coming up," the bartender said.

Liam took a seat at the bar. Dark thoughts and questions continued to tumble around in his head. And then it dawned on him—if Matt was so eager to give Teresa St. Claire a free pass simply because she'd worked for weeks on planning the retreat, maybe Liam needed to do some digging into her life. After all, Liam knew very little about her, and where there was one misdeed, there were often many. Maybe Liam needed to give Matt more reason to fire her.

Three

Teresa took solace in one fact—today could not get any worse. Between the threatening phone call about Joshua and running into an inexplicably irate Liam Christopher, she couldn't have imagined a more miserable beginning to her twenty-four hours at The Opulence.

"Let's get started." Matt clapped his hands. "I have a million things to get to today." He took a seat at the conference table, leaning back in the black leather chair. Despite being one of the most powerful and wealthiest men in the business world, Matt wore dark jeans and a charcoal-gray dress shirt with the sleeves rolled up. He was famous for rarely wearing a suit.

"Yes. Let's." Teresa sat opposite Matt. She pulled out her binder, already bulging with papers and notes. Matt had brought nothing but himself to the meeting, but she was used to that by now. Matt Richmond kept everything in his head. "Shall we start from the top? The guest arrival on Friday afternoon?"

Matt's blue eyes lit up. This event clearly meant a lot to him and he was excited by the prospect of knocking people's socks off. "Yes. Perfect."

Teresa began to brief Matt on the latest details. She showed off artist's renderings of the decor for The Opulence's lobby and samples of the custom room keys being printed for the weekend. She went over each item in the goody bags guests would receive, which included complimentary personalized luxury skin-care products, a $12,000 Tiffany & Co. watch with a custom cobalt blue face, and a seven-day stay at the all-new Kapalua Lanai Resort in Hawaii, the latest in Richmond Industries' hotel-management portfolio.

Matt was sparing no expense since it was his company's fifth anniversary, nor was he holding back his opinions. His reactions were mostly enthusiastic, but even the elements he was wowed by still required changes to please him. Teresa nodded and made endless notes, realizing it would be a miracle if she got any sleep at all before the retreat. There was a lot to be settled and Matt expected nothing short of perfection, and that meant she had to be perfect, too. But there were outside forces in the mix—the mystery man, the Joshua problem and Liam. If any of them blew up in her face before the retreat, she was sunk.

"I'd like you to go over the Saturday night gala menu with Nadia and Aspen. Nadia knows the dietary restrictions of our VIP guests and Aspen should be apprised of all catering decisions." Aspen Wright was the events manager for The Opulence, but Matt had pushed her aside in favor of Teresa. This had already created friction.

"Nadia and I have a meeting scheduled for 3:00 p.m. Aspen is away from the hotel today, but I'll make sure she knows everything." Teresa had met Nadia a few times, and they'd communicated about the retreat, but their working relationship would intensify over the coming weeks. Teresa hoped it could be a good one.

"Great. You two can have your meeting while Liam and I go over the details of Saturday morning. As soon as we've decided on everything, I'll bring you in." When Matt had first hired Teresa, he'd asked her to block out one hour of the retreat schedule Saturday morning for an undisclosed event.

"Liam is involved with the top-secret project?"

Matt nodded. "Something we've been working on for years. We're keeping a very tight lid on it. He'll be running the presentation, but I won't be able to give you details until a day or two before the retreat. Sorry. It's just the way it has to be."

"Of course." This made Teresa all kinds of nervous, not only because she needed to know her role in this mysterious announcement, but also because the topic of her would invariably come up in Matt's meeting with Liam. She had to speak to Liam today, privately, to find out what he'd meant when he said that she ruined his father's life. Linus had been nothing but a fabulous mentor to her and she'd always shown her deep appreciation. He was the reason she got her start in event planning at MSM. He'd made the call to get her the interview with Mariella Santiago-Marshall. That was a professional leap that would have taken an average person years to make.

It wouldn't have been possible without Linus Christopher's help.

"Are you okay?" Matt asked. "You seem distracted."

Teresa was mortified that she'd let her mind wander. "I'm perfectly fine."

Matt sat forward and smoothed his hand over the glossy wood table. "Do you want to tell me how you know Liam?"

"We met a long time ago. His father was one of my professors. It doesn't go beyond that."

"Liam seems to think it does."

Teresa drew a cleansing breath in through her nose. "I honestly have no idea what he was alluding to. Whatever it is has no bearing on my ability to plan your party."

Matt leaned back again and folded his hands over his stomach. "It seems to be affecting your concentration."

"Not at all. If I seem deep in thought, it's only because your comments gave me some ideas I'm eager to start on."

"I can't afford a single misstep, Ms. St. Claire. One whiff of trouble and I'll bring Aspen in to coordinate. She was unhappy with me for giving you the job."

"There won't be any problems. I can promise you that." She was used to demanding clients by now. She'd dealt with tons of them while working for MSM. The betrothal of Delilah Rhode and Alex Dane certainly stood out as a bad one. Between the happy couple's parents warring over glitz and over-the-top decadence vs. understated elegance, and the pre-wedding party that ended with the mother of the bride duking it out with Mariella Santiago-Marshall's sister over a handbag, Teresa had seen it all on that one day alone.

She'd thought coming back to Seattle would be easier, or at the very least, calmer. But now she had two very different ghosts from her past staring her down. Either could be her undoing. "Is there anything else, Mr. Richmond?"

"I think it's all well in hand for now. Liam should be heading in any minute. What do I say when he asks me what you said about your past?"

Teresa hated that this was still being discussed and she was eager to put an end to it. "I'm happy to stay for that part of the conversation. As I said earlier, I have no idea what he's talking about."

Matt shook his head. "It's okay. I'd rather skip any fireworks today. I have enough of that going on already. Let's just make sure you and Liam are ready to play nice by the time this retreat comes along."

The notion of playing nice with Liam nearly made her laugh. Oh, she'd like to play with Liam if he could drop the attitude and get back to being the sexy, brooding guy she quite enjoyed looking at. Unfortunately, she was certain he had no interest in her. "I'm always ready to play nice. As for Liam, I'm not quite sure what it will take to make him happy."

Liam filed into the meeting room minutes after Teresa left, but as near as Matt could tell, those two had not had a run-in. Liam seemed remarkably calm as he closed the door behind him. "I saw the *TBG* story." He rounded to the other side of the conference table and took a seat. "I don't want to be a jerk, but what in the hell are you doing? Sleeping with your assistant?"

A frustrated grumble left Matt's throat. He wasn't sure what to be more angry about—the fact that he'd made a mistake, the fact that the entire world knew about it or the fact that Shayla, a woman he paid an exorbitant amount of money to, had failed to do her job and get the story taken down from the site. "It just happened. We were at the hospital fund-raiser I'd had a brutal day at work, the champagne was going down a little too easy, and Nadia…"

Matt was struck with a powerful image of Nadia in the dress she'd worn—it hugged her full hips and dipped low in the front, the gentle swell of her breasts driving him crazy. Every man in the room had noticed—a normal occurrence, as Nadia was a singular beauty—but last night it was like she was lit from within. She could have gone home with any number of men—at least a dozen asked her to dance. But she dismissed them all and stayed by Matt's side, making him laugh more than once and charming him with every flash of her eyes. Sure, he was her boss, but this had been a social affair. She wasn't obligated to do anything but have fun. It had taken only one trip around the dance floor, his hand settled on the small of her back and hers on his shoulder, their bodies pressed together, before she asked the question, "Do you want to get out of here?"

Liam waved his hand in front of Matt's face. "You were saying? Nadia?"

Matt needed to get his head out of the clouds. It wasn't like him to let a woman have this kind of effect on him. "Nadia just has this way of picking up on what I'm thinking. She got me out of my bad mood." Had she ever, although a few orgasms would do that to a guy. "Nobody else seems to care."

"I care. I just don't need to sleep with you to prove it."

"Very funny."

"I hope you're being careful. You don't have the best track record with women."

Liam wasn't wrong. Matt had a bad knack for short-lived relationships and sleeping with women with hidden agendas. His business, his personal fortune and his family made everything more complicated. His parents were always expressing their disapproval of his romantic life. "Just settle down" was a familiar refrain. "I know. I know."

"Don't dismiss it like that. This retreat means as much to me as it does to you. I need the Sasha project to be a slam dunk. Is this really a good time for you to be in the tabloids?"

"Look. I'm on it. Shayla is killing the story."

"It doesn't matter. It's already out there."

Matt's appreciation of Liam's honesty was losing its luster. "What about you and Teresa? Is your issue with her going to become a problem? I can't pull another talented event planner out of my back pocket."

Liam's nostrils flared. That was never a good sign. Matt knew Liam well enough to recognize just how angry he was. "Did she tell you what she did? Did she own up to it?"

"No. She has no idea why you're so angry with her. And frankly, it has me wondering what is going on with you." Was the stress of Sasha getting to his best friend? Was it clouding his judgment?

"She had an affair with my dad when she was his student. That was the final straw for my mom. Teresa St. Claire is the reason she and my dad got a divorce."

"What? Seriously?"

Liam nodded solemnly. His relationship with his parents was complicated. His mother was a ball of anxiety and his father was notoriously detached. Like so many type A moguls, Linus Christopher was so focused on the bottom line that his family was of little consequence. "We both know my dad can be an idiot when it comes to interpersonal relationships, but as far as I know, he'd never cheated on my mom until Teresa came along. The fact that she's pretending as if it doesn't exist makes it so much worse."

"Are you positive they had an affair? Are you sure this isn't a case of your mom overreacting?"

"I know what you're saying, but I saw it with my own two eyes. They were in each other's arms in his office."

Matt could hardly believe what he was hearing. He didn't know Teresa particularly well, but nothing about her suggested she'd behave in such a manner. "You two need to talk this out. It was a long time ago and maybe it's time to bury the hatchet. Neither you nor I want a single thing to go wrong with this retreat. The Sasha announcement is hugely important to us both. Teresa does a top-notch job and more than anything, there's no time to find someone else. I really think you need to hash this out."

Liam pressed his lips together firmly. His mind was always going. It was one of the things Matt really admired about his best friend. No stone went unturned. But he also knew it was Liam's undoing. Overthinking never helped anything. "Fine. I'll talk to her. But I'm not promising a thing."

Four

Teresa was relieved she'd made it out of her meeting with Matt without running into Liam, but she didn't like the idea of so many loose ends. She needed to get a handle on what his problem was and smooth his ruffled feathers. She could not afford to have Matt Richmond think anything less of her. But first, she needed to reach out to Joshua and figure out what in the hell was going on. The bar was quiet, so she ducked into one of the secluded nooks, opposite a modern two-sided fireplace. She dropped down into one of the sleek chocolate-brown leather chairs and dialed the number for her brother.

The phone began to ring and she sat back, crossing her legs and gnawing on the thumbnail of her free hand. She hated feeling this anxious about Joshua. She hated worrying about him so much.

"This is Josh. Leave a message."

"Hey, Josh. It's your sister calling." She debated whether she should divulge the details of the phone call from the mystery man, but she thought better of it. She didn't want to spook her brother. "I had a spare minute between a few meetings. Thought I'd check in and see how you're doing. I hope everything is good. I miss you. I love you. Call me back when you have a chance."

She ended the call and looked at her phone for a minute, willing it to ring. *Please call back. Please call back.* It didn't happen. She took note of the time. Ten minutes before she was supposed to meet with Nadia about catering and menus. She had enough time to call The Fixer, and although she didn't look forward to it, she knew she'd feel better once she'd gotten it out of the way.

An attractive man wandered over and sat down a few yards away from her, near the tall windows that showed off the wooded vista and the falls. So much for her sliver of privacy in this part of the bar. She'd have to go outside to finish her errand.

But first a stop for a shot of liquid courage. "Bourbon. Up. Please."

The bartender nodded, flipped a glass over in one swift motion, slid it onto the bar and poured her drink. "Would you like to put this on your room?"

"Yes. I don't know the number yet, though. I arrived and walked right into a meeting."

"Don't worry. I'll find it."

Teresa took the glass in her hand and swirled the bourbon. It wasn't like her to drink during the day. It certainly was out of character with a meeting a few minutes away. But today had already been harrowing and she wasn't sure she'd make it if she didn't find a way to unwind. She tossed back the bourbon, the rush burning all the way down, followed quickly by a wave of warmth. "Thank you," she said to the bartender. She hustled back through the lobby and outside near the valet stand. She would've gone onto the patio off the bar, but the roar of the falls would've been too much. She fished her phone out of her pocket and looked up the number for The Fixer, which she didn't dare keep in her main directory. This was in a password-protected file. Her fingers trembled as she pressed the green button to make the call.

"Ms. St. Claire," The Fixer answered, his voice rich and calm. Teresa had never understood how the man could stay on such an even keel. He did terrible things, mopping up scandals and covering up lies. He made people disappear if necessary. "I wasn't expecting to hear from you."

"It's my brother. Joshua. I got a call from a man today saying Josh is in trouble again and owes seven million dollars."

"I see. And what would you like me to do about it?"

She nearly asked if the line had broken up while she was talking. Seven million dollars and he hadn't missed a beat. "I'd like you to check on him and see if he's okay. I left him a message, but he hasn't called me back yet."

"I'm not a babysitter, Ms. St. Claire."

"I realize that. I… You know I can't be there. I'm in Seattle. I can't just hop on a plane to the east coast. My job won't allow it. Don't you have someone who can do it for me?"

"Always. I do want to remind you that I'm not a charitable organization. I do work for a fee."

However much The Fixer wanted, she was sure it would be less than seven million dollars. "Yes. Of course. Whatever you want."

"You're working for Matt Richmond right now, aren't you?"

The Fixer's ability to know everything about everyone was uncanny. And a bit terrifying. "I am."

"Keep those ties in good shape. I might need a favor."

Teresa had no idea what that could possibly mean, and the thought of owing this man anything was unsettling at best, but she wasn't about to argue. She'd worry about that down the road. "Sure. Yes."

"Okay, then. I'll have one of my associates check on Joshua's safety and look into exactly what sort of trouble he's gotten himself into."

Teresa felt so relieved, it was as if someone had removed lead weights from her shoulders. "Thank you."

"You're welcome. I do want to point out one thing, though."

"What's that?"

"Your brother is the sort of person I'm usually hired to get rid of."

A chill charged down Teresa's spine. "Excuse me?"

"He's a liability. Someone who could make a publicity nightmare. Let's be honest. That's the real reason you're calling. You don't want word to get out about your little brother. It could get you fired from working for Richmond."

How dare he make such assumptions? She might doubt herself now and then, but one thing she didn't question was whether her heart was in the right place. "You couldn't be more off base if you tried. I love him. More than anything. Just please keep him alive and out of jail."

"There's no need to get upset. I was merely connecting a few dots. I will have someone check on Joshua and I'll get back to you as soon as I can."

"Hurry. Please." Teresa hung up the phone, unable to ignore the way her heart was threatening to pound its way out of her chest. She straightened her jacket and turned, only to see Nadia, Matt's assistant, less than ten feet away, chatting with one of the doormen. Teresa stopped in place, her mind scrambled as she tried to remember the exact words she'd said to The Fixer. Had Nadia heard the conversation? So many thoughts had been zipping through Teresa's brain, it was hard to know the difference between the things she'd said and the things she'd kept to herself.

She approached Nadia. "Hey there. Are you ready to sit down and have our meeting?" Teresa clung to her forced composure. Her future and the success of her company depended on it. She'd never be able to truly help Joshua if she got fired from the biggest job of her life.

Nadia didn't let on that she'd heard every minute of Teresa's side of the phone call she'd made. "Is it okay if I pull you into an impromptu meeting with Shane Adams and Isabel Withers? Shane is the president of the Richmond Hotel Group. Isabel is The Opulence's concierge. She has some ideas for couples' activities during the retreat."

"Ooh. Couples' activities? I'm intrigued." She laughed quietly. If Teresa was in any way upset by her call, she didn't let it show.

Nadia waved her inside. "Come on. I'll introduce you. Shane is only here for a few more minutes, and I need to catch him. He's one of those people who's so busy it's impossible to schedule a meeting." The two strode back into the lobby. Ahead, Isabel was sitting at her desk near check-in while Shane was standing a few feet away, his nose in his phone. "Hi, guys. I just need to grab a few minutes of your time."

"Good." Shane darkened the screen on his phone but held on it to like it was his lifeline. "I have a crazy schedule today."

Nadia didn't bother acknowledging his statement. Shane was a workaholic. Everyone knew it and there was no use telling the guy to slow down and breathe. "I wanted to see how we can bring Isabel in on the retreat. Since she's started working here, the resort has really gained a reputation as a romantic destination."

Isabel smiled and stood proud. Her red hair was up in a polished twist, but a few strands framing her face softened her usually austere styling. "Actually, I like to refer to myself as a romance—"

Shane's phone rang loudly. He glanced at the screen and muted it. "Sorry. I'll call them back in a minute."

Isabel cleared her throat and tried again. "Well, let's just say that I like to play up our more romantic amenities, and Nadia had mentioned that so many of the guests are coming with a spouse or significant other. The spa is available for couples' massages. We can have House-keeping put out candles at night and turn down the bed with rose petals. There are romantic dinners, of course, and couples' yoga. Really whatever people want."

"Perhaps it would be best if we present our guests with a menu of services prior to their arrival," Teresa offered.

"I can call them a week before the retreat and find out exactly what they want," Isabel said.

"That sounds great," Nadia said.

Shane looked a bit lost. "I guess my only concern is whether we have enough staff to handle these requests."

"I have a list of massage therapists and other local vendors if we need to bring in additional help," Isabel said. "I think it could be a real boon if we get some celebrities and A-listers talking about what we offer here."

"Yes. The feedback we've received on your job performance has been quite positive," Shane said.

Isabel's face flushed bright pink. "Thank you," she said.

Nadia couldn't help but notice the whiff of romance in the air and not just because Isabel was focused on creating it. The way she looked at Shane, with both adoration and longing, made Nadia wonder if that was her expression when her gaze fell on Matt. Perhaps she'd been too hard on him earlier. Of course, they had to stop this runaway train, but she should probably stop throwing around words like *mistake*. "It sounds like we're all on the same page. Teresa and Isabel, if you can coordinate and let me know if you need any help, that would be great."

"Are we done?" Shane asked. "Sorry, I really need to go."

Isabel's face fell, telling Nadia her suspicions were correct. There was a major crush happening here and it was all traveling in one direction.

"Yes. Thanks." Nadia turned to Teresa. "Is it all right if we go upstairs and meet in Matt's suite? My laptop is up there."

"Sure," Teresa said.

The two women made their way upstairs, settling in the most suitable work area in Matt's room, at the dining table near the writing desk. They went over the menus for the entire weekend and came up with a long list of questions for Aspen. Accommodating each guest's dietary guidelines would be a challenge, but Nadia felt as though she'd successfully handed the baton to Teresa.

"Any other questions?" Nadia asked.

Teresa shook her head. "I don't think so."

"Everything else is going well? No bumps in the road?" Nadia stopped short of asking about Tercsa's phone conversation. She hoped she might explain it on her own. If she didn't, Nadia had to mention it to Matt.

"I need to sort out a few things with Liam Christopher, but otherwise, no."

"I could see how there might be issues. The Sasha announcement is going to be big. Both Matt and Liam are pretty anxious about it. Liam's been working on this technology for years."

Teresa cocked her head as if Nadia had taken her by surprise. "So that's what it's called? Sasha?"

Nadia felt the blood drain from her face. "Did Matt not tell you in your meeting? I thought he was telling you today."

She shook her head. "He said he wanted to keep a lid on it a little longer. I guess Liam is paranoid about the news getting out."

Nadia closed her eyes and pinched the bridge of her nose. "You can't breathe a word of this to anyone. I need you to promise me you won't. Matt and Liam will never forgive me."

"Of course." Teresa raised a finger to her lips. "Your secret's safe with me."

Nadia wasn't sure she could trust Teresa. She needed to give herself a little insurance. And the only ammunition she had was the information she'd gained an hour ago. "I hope your phone call downstairs wasn't anything too important. I'm sorry, but I couldn't help but overhear."

Teresa blanched, her skin pale as a ghost. "That was personal and I'd like to keep it that way. Surely you understand. Just like you wouldn't want me talking about the *TBG* story."

Nadia swallowed hard. Teresa was not afraid to throw a punch when needed. "That was taken down from the website right before our meeting. There's nothing to talk about anymore."

Teresa gathered her things. "Here's some free advice. Women are judged for these things far more harshly than men. The world is changing, but we aren't there yet. You need to protect yourself. Put your own interests first. You know Matt Richmond won't hesitate to do the same."

Nadia knew Teresa was right. Nadia had given herself virtually that exact speech in the car on her way up to The Opulence. "I hope I can trust you to keep the story to yourself."

"Of course. Bad tabloid news is the last thing I want interfering with this event." Teresa got up from the table while Nadia tried to ignore the way her statement made her stomach sour. "I'm going to my room to get freshened up before I head into my last meeting today."

Nadia showed Teresa to the door. When she glanced down the hall, she saw Matt striding toward them. Her heart made its presence known, thumping wildly.

"Mr. Richmond," Teresa said.

Matt's sights flashed to Nadia for an instant, making heat rush through her. "Please. Call me Matt. The next month and a half is going to be crazy. We might as well get to a first-name basis now."

"Great. Thank you very much for today. And don't hesitate to reach out any time, day or night, if you need anything at all." She started to walk away, but Matt stopped her.

"You can start by making peace with Liam. You two have some things to work out and I'd like it taken care of before you head back to Seattle tomorrow morning."

"Certainly. I'll track him down," she responded, then continued down the hall.

Nadia couldn't help but wonder what that exchange had been about, but she needed to focus on controlling herself. Her desire to take off Matt's shirt right now was overwhelming. She couldn't stop looking at the buttons of his shirt, her fingers twitching at the thought. "I heard the *TBG* story went away," she said quietly.

He nodded and placed his hand on her back, sending waves of warmth though her. "Come inside. This isn't a conversation for the hallway."

Nadia froze for a moment, knowing exactly how she was going to feel the minute they were alone.

"It's okay, Nadia. I won't bite."

She blew out a frustrated breath and breezed past him. "I know that."

As soon as the door was closed, he took her hand. "That is unless you want me to."

Five

Here they were, all alone, no one to bother them. "Matt, I'm sorry about what I said earlier. I could have found a nicer way to say what I did. I don't want you to think I regret last night."

"You sure? I'd rather you just be honest with me if you're really feeling that way. I'm big on honesty. You should know that by now." His voice was a low, sexy rumble that shook Nadia to her core.

"I do not regret it. Scout's honor."

"Good. I would hate that." He stretched his arms above his head and yawned, his biceps straining against his shirtsleeves. It was one of the sexiest things a man had ever done in her presence.

"You tired?" she asked.

"Exhausted. Somebody kept me up until four thirty in the morning." His eyebrows bobbed up and down.

"And it nearly ended up being an international incident."

He shrugged. "I've seen worse. And even better, it's gone now. No one from the office has said anything to you, have they?"

Teresa wasn't really a coworker, so she let it go and shook her head. "No. Crisis averted, I guess."

"So that's that, then. We go back to the way things were before. We don't say anything about it. We pretend like it doesn't exist?"

All she could think about was that she didn't want to go back to the way things were before. She didn't want to pretend like it hadn't happened, even when she knew that was the sensible thing to do. "I'm worried I haven't fully gotten you out of my system."

He grinned and walked across the room, then poured them each a drink. "You already know I haven't gotten you out of mine. I told you as much earlier." He turned and handed her a glass, clinking his with hers. "Here's to a woman with all the power."

Nadia took a sip for courage, wondering if that was really true. Could she have a man like Matt at her beck and call? Was it as simple as telling him she wanted him? Her heart was beating so fiercely at the prospect that it was threatening to march its way outside of her body. "So I'm calling the shots here?"

"Whatever you want." He took a sip of his drink, but he didn't take his eyes off her. When he set his glass back on the table, he stepped closer. "We're all alone."

Everything about him was so overwhelming—his woodsy cologne, his hair begging to be touched and her knowledge of what his chest looked like out of that shirt.

"I do like that thing you do with your mouth." She bit her lower lip as soon as she'd said it. She'd never uttered anything so bold to a man, but it was freeing to be honest.

"This?" He placed the softest tease of a kiss on her lips, making her light-headed.

"That's a good start."

"Or maybe I should kiss you somewhere else." He popped the buttons of her blouse free, one by one. His determined fingers traveled lower, while want and need were the strongest forces at work in her body. He peeled back her blouse and slipped her bra strap from her shoulder. Pulling the lacy cup down from her breast, he lowered his head and drew her nipple into his mouth, gripping her rib cage with both of his firm hands.

Nadia gasped. He swirled his tongue. Her skin puckered and drew tight. She dug her fingers into his thick hair. "Both. Please. Now."

"Wait. One more."

A clever and slightly devious smile crossed his lips. He dragged his hands down her waist to her hips, dropping to his knees. He slipped his fingers under the hem of her skirt and pushed up the fabric, gathering it as he went, palms flat against her thighs. Nadia could hardly believe what was happening—one of the most brilliant and powerful men in the world was about to pleasure her. His eyes swirled darker and he tugged her black lace panties to one side, leaving her bare to him. He nestled his face between her legs, his tongue finding her apex. A jolt of electricity hit her so hard her legs nearly buckled. She reached for the back of the chair behind her, but that only gave him better access. He had her at his mercy. She would give him anything he wanted.

"Matt, please. I want it all. I want you." Even in the

moment, wrapped up in the urgency of wanting him naked and the heat that was coursing between her legs, she couldn't escape the weight of her words. She wanted it all—this magnificent man *and* the amazing job that went along with him.

"Good." He rose to standing and took her hand, leading her to the bedroom while he used his free hand to untuck his shirt. They stepped inside the gloriously appointed room and Nadia took charge, turning him around with a tug on his hand. They smashed their bodies and mouths against each other. Tongues swirling. Hot and wet. Her fingers scrambled through the buttons of his shirt and she pushed the garment off his shoulders, never letting the contact of their lips break. Next were his pants, which fell to the floor. Matt stepped out and pulled on her elbows, walking backward to the bed. He sat on the corner of the mattress.

"Why are you still wearing so many clothes?"

She laughed quietly. "Because someone hasn't taken them off yet."

"It's impossible to get good help these days. Let me start with that skirt." With a twirl of his finger, he invited her to turn her back to him. He drew down the zipper, then the skirt and finally her panties, all the way to her ankles. A groan escaped his lips. She loved hearing that noise, knowing that he wanted her. "The shoes stay on," he said.

She looked back at Matt over her shoulder. His normally bright eyes were dark with desire. "Yes, sir." She bent over and carefully stepped out of the panties while Matt cupped her bottom with his hands and got an eyeful in the process. She straightened and turned in his arms, wearing only her bra and black stilettos.

Still sitting, Matt wrapped one arm around her waist and pressed soft open-mouth kisses against her belly while dragging his fingers up the inside of her thighs. Everything she had been feeling that morning was ten-fold now. Her thighs weren't merely on fire. They felt like they would never cool down. He spread her folds with his fingers and pressed his thumb against her center, working in circles and making her dizzy. She reached behind and unhooked her bra, casting it aside. She raised one leg to give him better access, planting her foot on the bed. She'd never felt so sexy in her entire life. Matt slid a finger inside her, his thumb still applying the perfect amount of pressure.

"I love how wet you get for me." Matt slipped a second finger inside, slowly gliding deeper.

"Honestly? Just being around you makes me wet." It was so liberating to let go of these things she normally held so tightly in her head. She dug one hand into his hair and with the other cupped her own breast, rolling her nipple between her fingertips. The pleasure coiled between her legs. Matt had her so close.

Matt groaned again. "Seeing you touch yourself is so hot."

The pressure was becoming too much. She was having a hard time keeping her eyes open. "I'm going to come if you aren't careful."

"Just let go. I want to watch you unravel. Then I'll do it to you again."

That was all she needed. She sucked in a breath and the orgasm rolled through her, her muscles drawing tight and releasing. Again. And again. She looked down at Matt and their gazes connected, hot and intense, as the waves of pleasure continued. She lowered her head and kissed him slowly and deeply, telling him just how incredible that had been. "Your fingers are amazing, but I want to feel you inside me," she muttered against his lips. "I want you holding me down against the bed."

"That's what I want, too. I'll get a condom." Matt sprang up from the bed and Nadia tugged back the fluffy white duvet, then took her few seconds of alone time to arrange herself seductively on the bed, lying on her side, black heels a sexy contrast to the bright white of the bedding.

When Matt reappeared, he was a vision, and a naked one at that—long legs, firm muscles and abs she wanted to outline with her tongue. He tossed her the foil packet and she tore it open as he set a knee on the mattress. She reached out and wrapped her hand around his rock-hard erection, stroking firmly and rolling her thumb over the swollen tip. Matt closed his eyes and placed his hands on his hips, jutting them forward. Nadia scooted closer on the bed and took him in her mouth, her tongue pressing against the underside of his length. She felt the tension in his pelvis. She wanted every ounce of energy he was holding back. The need was centered between her legs, but she needed him on an even more primal level, like she was hardwired to want him. Unable to wait any longer, she gently let go and rolled on the condom.

She rolled to her back and spread her legs wide for him. Matt climbed onto the bed and positioned himself between her knees. He took his length in hand and lowered himself, slowly driving inside. Inch by inch she learned all over again how perfect a fit he was. This was even more sublime than it had been last night. She was no longer wrapped up in surprise. She could enjoy it, and she did, relishing every artful rotation of his hips. She wrapped her legs around him, pulling him in closer, feeling at one with him. His strokes were deep and strong, already aiming her straight for her peak. She was so torn. She loved to look at him, but it took so much strength to keep her eyes open. She pivoted her hips to let him go even deeper. Closer. But that's when the pressure started to become too much to take. She sucked in a sharp breath and Matt's breathing grew choppy and short. He dropped to his elbows, planted them above her shoulders and burrowed his face in her neck. He kissed the sensitive skin beneath her ear, licking then nipping at her lobe. Meanwhile, he employed the most glorious rocking of his hips, which doubled the hot friction against her center. Every pass had her a little bit closer, but she wanted to wait for him. She wanted them to reach this point together.

"Are you close?" she asked.

"Mmm-hmm," he groaned. "Very."

Nadia focused on holding on, but after a few more strokes, it became too much and she gave way. That was apparently enough for Matt. He followed right behind, pulsing inside her as she felt her own body grab on to his. Everything had fallen into rhythm—breaths and heartbeats, kisses and moans. Matt pulled back his head and smoothed her hair from her face. He kissed her deeply as the final delicious swells of satisfaction rolled through her. She knew then that this was way more than sex or a mind-blowing orgasm. It was like she was rolling around on a cloud, floating up in space, light as air.

"You're amazing." He dotted her collarbone with dozens of kisses, then rolled to her side.

"You're the amazing one." She curled into him, pressing her lips against his chest and drawing in his perfectly masculine smell. She knew she shouldn't feel so content in his arms. So happy.

"I want you to stay the night. No one will have to see you sneaking out. We can be together. All night. Until morning."

She smiled, but on the inside her heart was breaking. She knew this wasn't right. They couldn't continue like this. Their day away from the office was a fantasy. As soon as reality crept back in, this connection she had with Matt would go up in smoke. "Until morning. Sounds perfect."

Matt had asked Liam to experience as much of The Opulence as he could during his brief overnight stay. Liam was nothing but a good friend, so he'd holed up in the bar, enjoying a manhattan and taking note of the ambience and amenities. There were several dozen people around, mostly couples enjoying the multitude of fireplaces and cozy places to sit, while off in the dark, Centennial Falls continued its endless churn.

Liam had found a quiet corner booth in the bartender's direct line of vision so he could signal for a refill. At the table next to his, a man and woman were kissing. Liam had never understood public displays of affection. He didn't believe in putting on a show. Still, he felt a pang of jealousy. He wished he could tune out the rest of the world like that. Get lost in a woman. Take a break from the endless cycle of work, work and more work.

He finished his drink and decided he couldn't stomach any more time spent alone while things were heating up at the next table. He was about to slide out of the booth when in walked Teresa St. Claire. He froze, unsure whether he should try to sneak out or stay put and hope she wandered off elsewhere.

And then there was a third option—sit back and admire her. She still hadn't spotted him and he would've been lying if he'd said he wasn't enjoying watching her. She'd changed clothes and was now wearing a showstopper of a dress—black, off both shoulders and hugging every curve. Her blond hair was up in a high ponytail and he could imagine how much fun it might be to tug on it. He still wasn't sure what to make of her. The few times he'd had his investigator look into someone, he'd gotten at least an initial report lightning-fast. Usually within an hour. Not with Teresa. Everything discovered so far was the stuff he already knew. *Dig deeper*, he'd told his investigator. Everyone had dirt. Everyone.

Teresa turned in his direction and caught sight of him. She wasted no time and sauntered toward him, hips in full sway. "There you are." She looked down at him, perfect eyebrows arched high, crimson lips pursed.

Liam struggled to find an appropriate response. Matt had told him to make peace. "You found me out. I'm in the bar, drinking too much."

She set her clutch handbag on the table. "Scoot over, okay?"

He did as she asked and she slid into the bench seat right next to him. Her perfume hit him first, something he hadn't noticed earlier when he'd been so angry. It was sweet and soft, everything he wasn't. "Can I get you a drink?" he asked.

"What are you having? Or I guess I should say what *were* you having?" She picked up his empty glass and rattled the ice.

"A manhattan."

"How very stodgy and old-fashioned of you." She smiled, letting him know she was only having fun.

"It's a classic."

"Fine. I'll have one, too."

Liam flagged the bartender, flashed him two fingers and pointed at his empty glass. "To what do I owe this visit? Were you seriously looking for me?"

"Matt wants us to iron out our differences and I do everything Matt says. This job is very important to me."

Just when he was starting to relax, the reality of the job before them hit hard. "He expressed the same sentiments to me. He'd like us to at least make peace." Liam still wasn't sure how he felt about the idea. He'd been holding on to ill feelings toward her for years. Her physical presence was certainly helping to soften his opinion of her, though. He could admit that much.

The waiter brought the drinks from the bar, removed Liam's empty and then moved away to give them privacy.

Teresa held up her glass to toast. "To peacemaking."

Liam wasn't convinced it was possible, but this was his third drink so he was certainly more optimistic than he'd been an hour or two ago.

Teresa stirred her drink, stabbing at the ice cubes, then sat back and looked at Liam. They were shoulder to shoulder, arms touching. He admired the exposed contours of her collarbone, the shimmer of her skin. She was stunning. On any other day, with any other woman who looked like her, Liam would have been making a concerted effort to seduce her. Not Teresa. He might be tempted but he wasn't stupid.

"So. Tell me why you hate me," she said.

"That's a question straight out of high school if ever I heard one."

"It wasn't a question, it was a directive, and I'm sorry if my getting to the point bothers you, but I'd just like to know what the hell happened today."

He pressed his lips together tightly, choking back the grumble in his throat. He needed to come out with it and find a way to get past it, at least temporarily. "Your relationship with my father was the beginning of the end of my parents' marriage. Now neither of them is happy, especially not my dad, who had to move out of the house and is now even more of a workaholic than he used to be."

"My relationship with your dad was a two-way street. I never forced him to take me under his wing. And he approached me. I was too intimidated by him to say a thing." She took another sip. "And almost no one intimidates me."

"Take you under his wing? Is that what we're calling it? I'm not a fan of that particular spin, honestly. Let's call it what it was. An affair."

Teresa clunked her glass down on the table and shot him a look that was equal parts insulted and astonished. "An affair?" she asked, a little too loudly.

"Hold your voice. People are looking." Liam shifted in his seat. "I can't afford to have an argument with a beautiful woman in a public place. Some idiot with a camera phone will make my life a living nightmare."

"I did not have an affair with your father. That's a lie. I don't know who told you that, but it's not true."

"Nobody needed to tell me. I saw it with my own eyes." Liam took a long slug of his drink to ward off the mental images of that night, but they were coming right at him, one after another. "You two in his study. Drinking. Laughing. Toasting. Your skirt up to the middle of your thighs. And then you hop off his desk and kiss him. I can't believe you would do that, especially in the house he shared with my mother. She welcomed you into her home and that's how you treat our family?"

For a moment, Teresa did nothing more than nod and look him square in the eye. It was almost as if Liam could see the cogs turning. "Laughing and toasting? I kissed him?"

"Yes."

She shook her head emphatically. "No. That was the day I got the job with MSM Event Planning in Santa Barbara. Your dad arranged the interview with Mariella Santiago-Marshall, which was an impossible ticket to get. Every future event planner in the world wants to train with her. That's why we were toasting. That's why I kissed him. On the cheek, I might mention. I never, ever kissed your father on the mouth. It would be rude. And strange. He was my mentor."

Liam wasn't sure he should believe her. Teresa was clearly a fast thinker and, of course, anyone who was trying to save their current job could fabricate a story to explain their past misdeeds. "You realize I don't have any reason to believe you. I saw what I saw."

"No, you saw something that was purely innocent. I swear. Me being mystified at your attitude toward me earlier today was genuine. Now you know why I had no idea why you were angry. Honestly, I thought it was because I turned you down, which seemed a little absurd since it was seven years ago and…" She turned and eyed him up and down. "Look at you. You can have any woman you want."

Liam could admit that he had been hurt by the way she'd dismissed him all those years ago, but perhaps that was because she was the only woman who'd captured his imagination in no time at all. "Now you're trying to deflect."

"I'm not. You're easily one of Seattle's top five most eligible bachelors. I'm sure your bed is plenty busy."

"That's an awfully big assumption."

"No, it's not. I know men. When anything is theirs for the taking, they take."

If only it was that easy. Liam had never had a relationship that lasted longer than a few weeks. It was simply too difficult for him to be at ease with someone. To trust. He found himself questioning everything and everyone. "My tastes are discerning. I won't fall for just a pretty face."

"Of course not. I'm sure you want the whole package. Long legs, great boobs, beautiful hair."

Like you, Liam nearly said. "I'm not opposed if that's what you're asking."

Teresa knocked her knee into his leg. "I'll keep that in mind. This single girl doesn't want to stay that way forever. For now, I want us to get along. Frankly, I need us to get along if I'm going to be helping you with the announcement of this big secret project of yours."

Liam drew in a deep breath. Perhaps Teresa was right. Perhaps Matt was, too. With his private investigator on the case, Liam would discover the dirt on Teresa St. Claire. He didn't have to take her word for it. And in the meantime, that one-hour time slot on Saturday morning during the retreat was immensely important to him. He needed to wave the white flag of surrender, at least for the moment. "Fine. We will declare a cease-fire."

"Not a truce?"

He shook his head. "I'm not sure I trust you enough for that."

Teresa stirred her drink again then looked over at him, their gazes connecting. Liam felt as though she was drawing electricity from thin air and sending it right through him. "Then we're even. Because I don't trust you, either."

Six

Nadia had been back in the office for a little more than a day after her tryst with Matt at The Opulence. It had been a lonely return, and not just because it was the inevitable crash back to reality. Matt had a business emergency in Miami and had left straight from the resort that next morning. They'd made love before he left, just a quickie, but it had been truly bittersweet. She'd had no choice but to remind him afterward that it couldn't happen again. He'd only said that he understood before leaving her with a parting kiss that lingered on her lips for hours.

Matt was set to return today and that left Nadia a jumble of emotions. She was always excited to see him, but she was also quite certain that people in the office were talking about them. Those not-so-discreet whispers would likely become harder to detect when he was back, but Nadia was certain they'd continue until she and Matt gave the office busybodies something else to talk about.

She was finishing up an email when her phone beeped with a text. She turned and glanced at the screen, seeing a name she hadn't thought about in quite some time— Hideo Silva. She and Hideo had been close friends in high school but hadn't seen or spoken to each other in at least four years.

In Seattle today for a photo shoot. Would love to grab a drink. I miss you!

Hideo was a top-tier male model, traveling the world, appearing in countless magazines and regularly dating Hollywood starlets. It was part of the reason he and Nadia rarely spoke. He was off living a jet-set life she couldn't keep up with. I have a party to go to for work. Do you want to come with me? I miss you, too!

I would love it. Can't wait to catch up. I'll call at 6 and we'll make a plan for me to pick you up?

Perfect. See you then!

Nadia returned her phone to her desk, wondering how Matt would react to this development. There was nothing romantic between herself and Hideo, and there never would be. But he was devastatingly handsome and most men did not react well to being around him. Nadia had witnessed it dozens of times in high school. But perhaps the timing of Hideo's visit was perfect. She and Matt needed to get back on a more professional track. As amazing as their night at The Opulence had been, it

was a startling example of how little self-control she had
when it came to him. She'd gone there determined to end
it and she'd done exactly the opposite. Even worse, her
resolve had lasted only a few hours before they ended up
in bed together again. She'd told herself "one more time,"
but that wasn't the way it had happened at all. They'd
spent all night making love. They ordered dinner in.
Nadia hadn't spent more than a minute in her own room.

Out of the corner of her eye, Nadia spotted Shayla,
the head of PR, marching down the wide corridor outside Matt's office. On the surface, Shayla was drop-
dead gorgeous, with long silky black hair and a flawless
complexion. Her tastes were discerning and expensive.
Only the finest designer clothing, shoes and accessories
would do. But once you knew the real Shayla, it cast
her assets in a distinctly different light. She was ruth-
less. She scared the crap out of the interns in the office,
and most of the admins for that matter. With a single
pointed glare, she could send a person running to the
bathroom in tears. But Shayla was excellent at her job,
one of the best in the world. She was also one of Matt's
original employees, and thus afforded herself all of the
snobbery that she could claim from having been around
longer than anyone else.

"If it isn't the beauty queen," Shayla quipped.

"Please don't call me that. I know you don't mean it
as a compliment."

"Fine then, Ms. Gonzalez. We need to have a chat
about a few things." Shayla wrinkled her nose. "Things
I'd rather not bring up with HR."

Nadia felt like the bottom of her stomach fell out.
She fought back her inclination to bark at Shayla that
HR ultimately took orders from Matt, and Matt was not

going to let Nadia get in trouble. But she wasn't entirely sure that was true. She'd only known Matt for fourteen months and she'd spent every minute of that time with a monster crush on him. She'd seen sweet, affable Matt Richmond throw very good people under the bus. "Okay. Shoot."

Shayla perched herself on the edge of Nadia's desk and took a long gander in both directions before speaking. Shayla never wanted anyone to catch her saying something horrible, and she'd said plenty of ugly things to Nadia. "I'd like to get the lay of the land here, just so I can be prepared to deal with it if the press comes to me. Did you start sleeping with our boss right away or did you spend a few months wagging that curvy bum of yours in his face before he had a weak moment?" Shayla admired her manicure as if she'd asked Nadia the most innocuous of questions.

Nadia felt her whole body get cold. "This was a recent thing."

Shayla nodded, but there was so much snide skepticism on her face Nadia wondered how she could hold her head up straight. "Recent like a month ago? Right before he gave you that new car as a bonus?"

Nadia was horrified at Shayla's suggestion, but she knew very well that it could be misconstrued that way. "That was for a job well done. I worked hard for that car."

Shayla raised an eyebrow. "I bet."

Nadia wasn't going to have this conversation. Shayla had shown her cards too soon. "Can I help you with something? I have work to do."

"No. Just wanted to let you know that I don't appreciate having to clean up your messes. Or even worse, having to take the heat for it. If you're going to carry on like this, at least take the time to be discreet. You didn't bother to stay in your own room at The Opulence? How obvious can you be?"

"That's not true. I had my own room."

"Nobody slept in your bed."

"You don't know that."

"Oh, but I do. I have connections everywhere in this company. From the highest executives all the way down to Housekeeping at our management properties."

Nadia was really going to have to watch her back. There was no telling how much gossiping Shayla might do. She was tight with a lot of people in the company. "I'd prefer it if you didn't devote so much time to digging up dirt on me."

"Don't tell me what to do with my time. You are on very thin ice here. You're already past your expiration date with Matt."

"Expiration date?"

"You've worked here for fourteen months. He's never kept an admin for longer than a year. I think he gets tired of the scenery. Wants a change of pace."

"He's not like that."

"Oh, no? Matt is an unimaginably wealthy, powerful and handsome guy. He can have any woman in the world. You think you're so special because you won a beauty pageant when you were a teenager? That was a long time ago."

"I have my job because I'm good at it. And that's the reason I've kept it, too."

"Then I suggest you focus on that. You can start with that party Gideon Johns is hosting tonight. I know you and Matt are both going to be there. Maybe try not to play footsie with Mr. Richmond while you're there."

"For your information, I'm bringing a date."

From down the hall Nadia could hear a chorus of voices saying, "Good morning, Mr. Richmond."

Shayla hopped off Nadia's desk. "We didn't have this conversation."

Nadia didn't bother to reply. Anything she said would be turned against her.

Matt strolled up to them, all smiles. As serious and hard-nosed as he could be, Matt was always warm and pleasant with her. He made her heart melt a little bit every time she saw him. "Ladies," he said. "Are we having a meeting of the minds this morning?"

"Nadia and I were talking about Gideon Johns's party tonight. Should be fun."

"Oh. Right. I forgot about that."

"I'll see you both later this evening," Shayla said, slinking back into whatever hole she'd climbed out of.

Nadia rose from her desk and took Matt's jacket from him. "Party starts at seven. No dinner, just heavy hors d'oeuvres. Mr. Johns booked one of his favorite bands."

"Of course he did. The guy is a music junkie." Matt took several strides into his office, but stopped and turned back. "You coming?"

Nadia was stuck, frozen, unsure what to do. This was the first time they'd been together in the office since sleeping together. She normally wouldn't think twice about following him into his office. Now she was worried about who was watching and what sorts of signals she might be putting off. The fact that the walls of his office were entirely made of glass wasn't helping the situation. The instant someone lowered the privacy shades, everyone would start to gossip. She knew very well how the rumor mill worked. "Of course." She crossed the threshold and closed the door behind them. People might be able to see, but she didn't want them to be able to hear.

Matt got situated behind his desk, taking out his laptop and plugging in his phone to charge. "Have you heard from Liam by any chance? I've been trying to reach him, but I just get his voice mail. I want him to rethink coming to Gideon's party tonight. I think he'd have fun."

"I'm not sure, but I can certainly try to get him on the phone."

"Thanks."

Nadia took a step closer to his desk, feeling awkward and intimidated. "Matt, I hate to bring up personal stuff at work, but I just want to make sure we're both on the same page with what happened at The Opulence."

He nodded, sat back in his chair and folded his hands across his stomach, bringing to mind the feel of his muscled abs beneath her hands. Damn, she was going to miss that. "We agreed it was the last time, right? I mean it's a real shame, but I get it. We should just be glad that tabloid story didn't blow up in our faces."

"That's what I wanted to talk about. It sort of has. At least for me. People are whispering when I walk by and one person actually said something to me about it."

Matt raised both eyebrows, creating those adorable crinkles in his forehead. "What happened?"

Nadia didn't want to get too specific. There was no divulging Shayla as the source without it later coming back to haunt her. "Let's just say that I got a few snide comments about sleeping with the boss. And an assumption that it might be tied to the car you gave me as a bonus."

He shook his head. "No. You earned that car. Fair

and square. That was a good month before anything happened."

"I know that. You know that. But you can also imagine how it looks. I can't afford for anyone at work to see me in a light that's less than professional. I need this job. It's important to me."

"I'm not going to fire you. You're the best admin I've ever had, by far."

"And you know that it isn't just your decision. All sorts of outside forces can come into play if a particularly bad story gets out. The board of directors. Stockholders. You have to answer to people, Matt. You aren't an autonomous ruler."

His lips pressed into a thin line. She hated that look of concern on his face. It didn't suit him. "Don't remind me."

"I'm just saying that for both of our sakes, we should agree that we had fun together, but now we're back to the way things were before."

He blew out a breath and took a glance out the window. "Agreed. I don't like it, but I agree."

She wasn't sure what about it he didn't like—the idea of not getting to have sex with her anymore? But she wasn't going to press for additional information. She had what she wanted. "Great. I'm glad we agree."

He turned back in his chair. "When you say you need this job, do you mean you really need it? Like things would get bad if you lost it?"

Nadia nearly laughed. Matt was very down-to-earth, but he'd grown up with extraordinary wealth. The man had never wanted for anything. "Yes. Things would get bad. I need to earn a living, Matt. Just like almost everyone."

"What kind of bad? Because if we aren't paying you enough, I can fix that."

"This is not the time to give me a raise."

"You didn't answer my question, though. What kind of bad?"

Nadia didn't like to talk about her personal life at work, but she couldn't deny that she and Matt had a strong connection. He was sweet and caring. He was interested in people's lives. "My parents rely on me to help make ends meet. My mom got sick right before I came to work here. Breast cancer. She's okay, but my parents didn't have great insurance. My mom is a teacher and my dad owns a coffee-roasting business and a handful of coffee shops. Money was always tight. So, I stepped in to help, just so they wouldn't have to risk losing their home. That house is a big piece of their retirement. I wasn't willing to let them lose that."

"I had no idea. Why didn't you tell me this before?"

Nadia shrugged, feeling a bit embarrassed. "Because it had nothing to do with my job. I mean, lots of people have burdens. I'm helping my parents pay off some medical bills. I'm helping with my sister's college tuition. It's not a big deal. I have a budget and I stick to it and it's not a problem. I'm not wanting for anything."

"But if you lost your job, all of that would fall apart."

"Well, yeah."

He nodded solemnly. "Okay. I get it. We can't allow ourselves to get into a situation where any doubt could be cast on your abilities. We'll focus on work and leave what happened in the past."

Matt had just said everything she'd wanted him to say. This was the smart course and Nadia prided herself on being sensible. So why was she feeling so profoundly sad? "Just a memory."

"An incredibly hot one."

Nadia shook her head. Matt was going to be the death of her. "Do you need anything right now? If not, I'm going to get back to my desk."

"No. I'm good."

Nadia headed for the door.

"Oh, uh, Nadia. You're coming to Gideon's party tonight, right? Do you need a ride? I can have my car come by and scoop you up."

She smiled sweetly while digging her fingernails into the heels of her hands. "I am going, but I don't need a ride. I'm actually bringing a date." The instant the words left her lips, she felt a deep urge to explain herself. She didn't want to hurt Matt, no matter what. But she also had to be strong for once. If she had a means of putting up walls with him, she should do it. It would be better for both of them in the long run.

"I see. Someone special?"

"An old friend. Hideo Silva. He lives in New York, but he's in town for work."

"What does he do for a living?"

"He's a male model."

Matt averted his eyes and gathered some papers on his desk. "Excellent. Well, have fun."

"It's not a big deal. We're just friends." The words came out a bit desperate and Nadia hated that she'd bothered to divulge this information.

He popped his eyebrows at her and nodded. "It's a free country, Nadia. I have no control over you."

"I didn't want you to think…"

"What? That you'd moved on? We had our fun, Nadia. You made it clear that it's not going to happen again."

Nadia nodded solemnly, but all the while her stomach soured and her heart felt as though it was crumbling. "I guess I'd better get back to my desk."

"Yes. I think that's for the best."

Teresa was glad she had Gideon Johns's party tonight to distract her. Not that she wasn't incredibly busy. She'd never worked harder or slept less, but she had it under control, and most important, Teresa always worked best under pressure. Plus, all of this preoccupation was keeping her mind off Liam.

She couldn't get that conversation in the bar off her mind. He had looked good enough to kiss, and under any other circumstance, she would have tried her hardest to persuade him that was a great idea. She would have done everything in her power to take Liam upstairs to her room at The Opulence. But because of what he thought of her—that she'd had an affair with his father and ruined his parents' marriage—well, she couldn't risk him thinking she was a woman with a big arsenal of feminine wiles. She certainly couldn't flirt. Liam was hands-off. At least until the retreat was over.

Luckily, although Liam had been invited to this A-list party, he'd RSVP'd no. That would make the evening much easier to navigate. She'd make Mr. Johns a happy client and, most important, demonstrate to Matt Richmond that he'd unquestionably made the best choice in hiring her as an event planner. Everything on the professional front was coming together nicely.

On the personal front, she'd finally heard from Joshua. He'd called while she was in the shower that morning, although when she'd tried to call him back, she only got voice mail. He'd assured her everything was fine. He had it "under control." The Fixer had contacted her as well, saying that it appeared Joshua had some gambling debts, but that he was paying them off and wherever the seven-million-dollar sum came from, it didn't seem to be real. The whole thing sounded a bit suspicious to Teresa, especially since the man never called back. He'd said he'd be in touch, but had done no such thing. In her limited experience, people like that follow through on their promises. For now, she had to trust Joshua to handle his own affairs. She loved him, but she couldn't be his perpetual babysitter.

Teresa's assistant, Corinne, ducked into her office and placed a coffee cup on her desk. "Here's your two-o'clock latte and your mail." Corinne pushed aside a pile of notes and papers from The Opulence event. "Also, you will not believe what's on TV right now."

"Please tell me it doesn't have to do with the retreat." This event had become so complicated it was like trying to fight off a dragon with three heads. Just when she got one thing under control, something else went off the rails.

Corinne's blazing red corkscrew curls bobbed up and down when she shrugged. "Sorry, but it has to do exactly with that. Come and see. It's best if you know now."

Teresa planted both hands on her desk and pushed herself to standing. Her lower back was stiff from sitting for too long. She really needed to go to the gym and get a massage and take a minute to breathe. Sex might not hurt, either. She could certainly stand to blow off some steam.

She wandered out into the main Limitless Events office. Normally the large and open loft space was abuzz with activity, but right now, everyone was in the far corner, looking up at one of the flat-screen TVs mounted to the exposed brick wall. Teresa hurried over. Sure enough, her biggest nightmare was playing out before her eyes.

The crawl at the bottom of the screen read: *Peter Bell, lead singer of rock band London Town, arrested for felony battery after altercation with fan.*

Teresa closed her eyes and pinched her nose in an effort to ward off the headache that was about to ravage her head. London Town was not only her headliner for the Saturday evening gala during the Richmond retreat, but it had also been a real coup to get them in the first place. They did not like to perform at private events, especially ones hosted by the rich and famous. She didn't even need to know Mr. Bell's legal fate to know that there was no way his band could perform now. Even if the charges were dismissed or he was released on bail, the media backlash would be too much. Matt wanted no problems and this was officially a big one. Teresa had to find a top notch, A-list performer who just happened to be available on a Saturday night in a month. *Great.*

With no time to lose, Teresa hustled back to her desk to go through her original planning notes and brainstorm. She might need to call Gideon Johns, since he had his finger on the pulse of all things music-related. But as she stepped inside her office, she realized she didn't need to think long. On top of the stack of mail Corinne had delivered was the latest issue of *Hundred Proof* magazine with gorgeous Jessie Humphrey on the cover. Jessie's voice was powerful, but like velvet, and she was one of the most in-demand performers around.

Teresa had no idea if she was on tour or even in the country, but she had to at least look into it.

With a quick internet search, she found the number for Ms. Humphrey's management, who in turn referred Teresa to her booking agent's office. Teresa explained her predicament as succinctly as possible. "I realize it's incredibly short notice, but this is for a private retreat for Matt Richmond. No expense will be spared. Ms. Humphrey will have the most luxurious accommodations, we'll cover all of her travel and we'll have the finest production. Anything she needs, she'll have it."

"Send the offer in writing and we'll take it to her team. No promises. She is available that weekend, but that is highly unusual and she would typically be spending that time resting."

Teresa thought back to her conversation with Nadia and Isabel at The Opulence. "The resort has a high-end spa. We can book her any treatments she wants. And I can personally attest to just how relaxing an atmosphere it is."

"Like I said, send over the offer and we'll look at it."

Teresa sweetly said goodbye, then grumbled as soon as she hung up the phone. If she wasn't able to book Jessie on her own, she might ask Gideon Johns if he had any connections that might come in handy. But she'd wait to see if she could manage it. She hated asking anyone for a favor, especially a billionaire client like Mr. Johns. She needed him thinking she could move mountains if necessary. Speaking of which, she'd better knock out a few more hours of work before heading home to get dressed for Mr. Johns's party.

Seven

Liam had hoped to skip the Gideon Johns party, but Matt had talked him into it.

"Hey, stranger. What's up? We hardly spent any time together at The Opulence," Matt said when Liam climbed into his gleaming black Aston Martin Valkyrie. Matt had an extensive collection of cars and on a night like tonight, when it was just the two of them out on the town, they both agreed this was more fun than having a driver take them.

"I'm not the one who disappeared." Liam shot a pointed glance at his best friend.

"I didn't plan for things to happen the way they did." Matt kept his eyes trained on the road, but he shifted in his seat.

"Let me guess. You and Nadia." Liam caught Matt fighting back a smile. "You are playing with fire, my friend. I'm serious. There's no way this ends well for you."

The trace of happiness on his face vanished. "I know. I know. There's just something about her. She makes me happy. And the minute we're alone, we can't keep our hands off each other."

Liam had experienced that last part with plenty of women, but the part about someone making him happy? It had never happened. No woman had come close to making his life better. "Just remember that there's a person on the other side of this equation. If you hurt her, you're going to lose someone you obviously care about and the best assistant you've ever had."

"Got it. New subject, please. You and Teresa. Have you two at least reached a stalemate?"

"I suppose. She denies the affair with my father, but I'm not sure I believe her. I know I don't trust her."

Matt let out a deep exhale. "I'm a little worried about that, too, to be honest."

"You are? Why?" Matt was the guy who worried about too little. He was the one who had dismissed Liam's concerns about Teresa in the first place.

"Nadia overheard Teresa on the phone that day at The Opulence. She was outside, clearly trying to get some privacy. She said something about how she loved some guy and didn't want him to go to jail."

Liam knew he should have gone with his gut. Teresa was not to be trusted. She'd specifically told him that night at the bar that she was unattached. She'd even used the word *single*. And jail? What was she wrapped up in? "I had my investigator look into her. He's found nothing. And I told him to dig deep."

"That's weird. There's always dirt."

"Precisely why I'm sure that something is up."

"Maybe we need to take things into our own hands,"

Matt said, stopping at a red light. "And by we, I mean you."

"What? When?"

"Tonight. At this party. You're the one who has a past with her. I hardly know her and she's in my employ right now. You're the obvious person to try and get her to slip up and say something she doesn't want to."

Liam grumbled and looked out the window as Matt took the corner and pulled up to the valet stand outside the Chihuly Garden and Glass exhibit at the base of the Seattle Space Needle. "I was hoping to give her a wide berth this evening."

Matt put the car in Park and turned, clapping Liam on the back. "Sorry, buddy, but I need you to do this for me. If I'm going to have to cut her loose, I need to do it now."

"Fine. But you're buying the drinks tonight."

Matt laughed quietly. "Are you kidding me? It's a Gideon Johns party. It's open bar."

The two men climbed out of the car and began their walk up the red carpet that led up to the museum entrance. The all-glass structure was a sight, a modern cathedral ablaze with light set against the backdrop of the night sky. Up ahead, Liam spotted Teresa, looking like a million bucks in a slinky but tasteful black dress. She appeared to be overseeing two women with clipboards who were likely the custodians of the guest list. She was abuzz with activity, smiling and chatting, giving directions and gracefully gathering guests to stand for photographs before entering the party. It might take some doing to get her alone tonight, but he had no choice. Matt was his best friend and he would not let him down.

Matt tugged on Liam's jacket and leaned closer. "Nadia's here. With her date." With a toss of his head, he indicated they were standing behind them.

"A date? Did you know this was going to happen?" Liam carefully craned his neck, spotting Nadia and her date several people back. The guy had his arm around Nadia and they were eagerly talking to each other.

"I knew. She told me in the office earlier. She said he's an old friend. In town for the night."

"Maybe this is a good thing," Liam said out of the corner of his mouth. "Maybe this will remind you that you need to move on. Nothing good comes of a relationship with Nadia that's anything beyond professional."

Just then Liam felt a hand on his shoulder.

"Look who we have here. Two of the most handsome men in all of Seattle." Matt's head of PR, Shayla, had inserted herself between Matt and him. It was so like her. She was beyond pushy.

"Hi, Shayla."

She unsubtly smoothed her hand over Liam's shoulder. "Hello, Liam. Looking dashing this evening."

"You as well," Liam said, not necessarily meaning it, but feeling that it was something he had to say.

"I see that Nadia brought a date. What a hottie he is." Shayla practically purred it into Matt's ear.

Matt shrugged his shoulder. "Shayla, do you mind? Liam and I were in the middle of a personal conversation."

She shook it off. "Oh. Yes. Of course. I'll catch up with you two later."

"The date thing really bugging you that much?" Liam asked.

"No," Matt said, with a tone that distinctly suggested he was nothing if not completely annoyed. "I just don't like it when Shayla sticks her nose in everything."

* * *

Teresa continued her work as guest-list spotter, identifying each guest before they reached her assistants, then slyly feeding them the name with a whisper. Teresa knew VIPs and they took great offense when someone didn't recognize them. No one wanted to give their name. Of course, that meant Teresa had spent hours memorizing names and faces, since she hadn't been back in Seattle long enough to truly know the current landscape of the wealthy and fabulous in the city.

Out of the corner of her eye, she spotted Liam and Matt. "Matt Richmond and Liam Christopher are next," she quickly muttered to one of her helpers, before turning her attention to the two men. "Welcome, gentlemen." She hugged Matt, then regarded Liam with a penetrating glance. He unsubtly eyed her from the top of her head all the way down to her perfectly pedicured toes. She felt naked. Exposed. In a dangerous, but delicious, way. "Mr. Christopher. I thought you weren't joining us this evening."

He shrugged. "What can I say? My best friend convinced me it might be fun."

"I assure you it will be exactly that. Please. Come in. The bars are right inside the doors, servers are bringing around small bites, and the band should be starting any minute now."

"Speaking of band," Matt said, "I heard there's a problem with London Town."

Teresa shook her head. "Already handled. I'm this close to booking Jessie Humphrey." That was a stretch, but she could afford to do nothing less than wow Matt Richmond right now.

"You got it fixed that quickly? Excellent. I'm impressed."

"All in a day's work." She dismissed it with a ready smile, knowing it would take more like an entire week's worth of phone calls, begging and logistics.

Matt and Liam stepped into the party, but Liam turned back to her, taking her hand. It was only the tips of her fingers, but to Teresa's surprise, it sent a verifiable jolt through her. "I'm hoping you'll save a dance for me."

"You are? Is this part of waving your white flag?" The words spilled from her lips before she had a chance to really think about how rude they might sound.

"I try never to surrender, but I might be willing to give up some ground." He cocked one thick eyebrow for effect.

Teresa had to try very hard not to fixate on the curve of his lips or the appealing shadow of his facial scruff. Liam was so her type it was ridiculous. "Color me intrigued." She didn't offer more, and turned back to focus again on the guest list, but her heart was beating hundreds of miles an hour, like a jackrabbit with a bad coffee habit. What did Liam mean by that? Was he up to something? Or was he actually softening his approach? The latter, although a nice idea, seemed unlikely.

She helped with the next fifty or so guests, including Nadia Gonzalez and her unbelievably hot date, whom Teresa was sure she'd recently seen in a men's magazine. She couldn't help but wonder how Matt might be handling that particular development, although knowing the world of corporate PR, someone had probably arranged the pairing to give the illusion that Matt and Nadia were not a thing.

Teresa filtered through the party, stopping to make sure guests had everything they wanted and were having a good time. The band had started playing, but as was par for the course with most of these occasions, people were crowding the perimeters of the dance floor and not actually paying attention to the entertainment.

Teresa smiled and stood straighter when she saw Gideon Johns heading for her. Even in a crowd of fabulously beautiful people, Gideon stood out. He had a tall, broad frame, dark, warm eyes and a killer smile. He was the epitome of a truly dashing gentleman, the kind of man most women hoped would sweep them off their feet. He grasped her elbow and they exchanged kisses on both cheeks. "The party is amazing, Teresa. You've done a wonderful job."

Teresa saw a twinge of uncertainty on his handsome face. "But nobody is dancing and that has you worried people aren't having a good time." One of the first things Mariella Santiago-Marshall taught her in event planning was to acknowledge and address problems before the client had a chance to.

Gideon's straight shoulders relaxed. "Yes. What can we do about it?"

Teresa spotted Liam over by one of the bars, chatting with Matt. "I'll get it going. Don't you worry about that. Just, please, enjoy yourself." Before she had a chance to let her pride get in the way, she buzzed through the crowd and approached Liam. "I'm here to claim that dance you asked for."

Liam swirled the ice in his glass, looking down at her with his trademark steely expression. "We'd be the first ones out there. It's not really my style."

Of course, he had to put up a fight. Nothing about this

could be easy. "I doubt that very seriously. I'm guessing you don't like to do anything that other people are doing. Come on." She plucked his glass out of his hand and set it on the bar. "Can you babysit his drink?" she asked Matt.

"Of course."

With Liam in tow, Teresa wound her way through the crowd. When she spotted Nadia and her boy toy standing near the dance floor, she saw an opportunity to help things get started a little quicker. "Come on. You two should dance."

Nadia looked at her date and he didn't hesitate to take her hand and follow along.

Teresa might have been in charge of their route, but when they reached their destination, Liam took control, coming to a stop and pulling on Teresa's hand and twirling her into his arms. He placed his hand on her back and drew her close with a definitive tug. His cologne filled her nose, and the feeling of his form pressed against hers made every nerve ending in her body come alive. She'd forgotten what it was like to be in a handsome, sexy man's arms. It had been far too long. He started their rhythmic sway and Teresa did her best to relinquish control and let him lead. It was very, very difficult for her to let someone else be in charge, even a man as commanding as Liam.

"You're a surprisingly good dancer," she said, raising her chin and speaking right into his ear.

"Why is it surprising?" He kept the side of his face close to hers. That stubble she'd been admiring scratched her cheek, and she enjoyed it a little too much. "Years of cotillion at my mother's insistence. She's very big on social skills and propriety."

"You just seem a bit buttoned-up, that's all. In my experience, men like you have a hard time letting go when it comes to anything that involves their body."

Liam cleared his throat and pressed even more firmly on her lower back. "Trust me. I have zero problem in that department."

A steady stream of warmth encircled her, like someone had drizzled hot honey all over her body. She felt her shoulders loosen. The skin of her chest and neck plumed with heat. "I'll have to take your word for it."

"You never know. Stranger things have happened."

Teresa wasn't sure what he meant by that and was honestly a bit scared to ask. If ever anyone needed proof that she was in over her head, that was it. She was scared of very little. "Why do I have the feeling you're trying to get something out of me?" she asked.

He spun her to the middle of the dance floor, and much to Teresa's delight, five or six other couples joined them. Off in the distance, she could see Gideon smiling. Her plan had worked. Which meant she could focus on Liam.

"Well, I do have a question for you," he said.

She really hoped this wasn't going to be more about his dad. She'd been clear with him that nothing had happened and the idea of rehashing it was tiresome. "Go for it."

"You specifically told me at The Opulence the other day that you're single, but I've heard that's not true. Why lie about it?"

"Heard from where?" Teresa attempted to make eye contact, but Liam's eyes were cast off to the side. She placed her fingers against his cheek and her thumb on the tip of his jaw, forcing him to look at her.

"People talk."

Likely story. "Well, I don't know who's gossiping about me, but I am as single as they come. I have no reason to lie about that."

"You sure? No special guy in your life? Someone you love?"

What exactly was he getting at? "Definitely not."

"I don't think I know you well enough to know if you're telling the truth." He no longer had any hesitation about confronting her with his gaze, his expression both dark and daring. It made her want to do dangerous, foolish things.

"We're in the middle of a dance floor in front of hundreds of people. Everyone is watching us and how close we're dancing." Their hips were already pressed against each other, but Teresa wanted to make her point. She angled her hip and rubbed up against the front of his pants. There was a distinct stiffening between his legs, which filled her with some feminine pride. "Do you think I would dance with you like this if I was taken?"

"That doesn't prove a thing." Liam made the mistake of pursing his lips and Teresa was stuck for a moment, staring at them, struck with a curiosity she had to quench. They were so perfect. Full. Firm-looking. And then there was the man behind them. What kind of kisser would Liam be? Reckless? Careful? Determined?

"Then this will." Teresa raised her hand again, this time to the side of his neck. She cupped her fingers around his nape and pulled him closer, allowing her eyes to flutter shut while she let pure instinct take over. She laid the softest, sexiest kiss on his lips she could muster. The sort of maddening kiss that kept a man coming back for more.

It was perfect. But she hadn't taken the time to calculate his response. His hand pressed against her lower back, making the move she'd made with her hips look like child's play. He tilted his head and urged her lips apart with his tongue, taking the kiss deep. So very deep. Teresa bowed into him. It was the only thing that made sense, especially when white-hot heat began zipping up her thighs and making everything between her legs ache for more.

She wanted him.

More than she'd wanted any man in a long time.

And that scared her. She wrenched her lips away from his and was jolted back into the present—where hundreds of people she should be entertaining and impressing were likely watching. What was she doing? Had she lost her mind?

"We can't do this…" she muttered.

"You kissed me, Teresa."

She stepped back, if only to gain some composure. "I know that. And now I'm not kissing you." She made only a cursory glance at his face, but she could see that it was colored with confusion. Of course he was confused. She was, too. She had to get to the ladies room and get her act together, ASAP. "I have to go." She turned and wasted no time hustling off the dance floor, leaving Liam behind to fend for himself. She greeted guests along the way, but only in the most superficial of ways, saying hello and breezing past. She felt like her heart was going to burst out of her chest.

Finally she reached the ladies room and ducked inside. Meanwhile, only one thought was running through her head. *I kissed Liam Christopher.* Unfortunately, the possible repercussions quickly followed. Liam and Matt Richmond were best friends. They'd come to this party together and Teresa had not only laid a serious kiss on Liam's lips, but she'd also just abandoned him on the dance floor. What was Liam's only logical action at that point? To walk back, alone, and join his friend, at which point he would most likely tell him exactly what had happened. She was quite certain that the question of her sanity would be raised.

How stupid could she possibly be?

She first peeked under the stalls to make sure she was alone, then wandered over to the sink and peered at her reflection in the mirror, muttering to herself. "You have got to get your act together. You have to." If anyone asked her why she'd kissed Liam, she would have to say that it was his fault. He'd practically dared her to do it. He was the one who didn't believe she was single. Speaking of which, who had told him that? And why was he interested at all in her personal life? She already knew that he didn't trust her, and she was well aware of his loyalty to Matt.

The bathroom door swung open and in walked Nadia. Teresa straightened, but something about seeing Matt's assistant made a tear roll down her cheek. Had she just thrown away all of her hard work over one moment of weakness for a man?

Nadia smiled at Teresa, but it quickly fell. "Oh, my gosh. Teresa. Are you okay?"

Teresa nodded and bit down on her lip, trying to force herself back onto stable mental ground. "I'm fine. It's just stress. A lot happened today. The party. Finding a replacement band for the Saturday night gala during the retreat."

Nadia joined her at the vanity. "And then you topped it all off with kissing Liam."

"You saw that?" The more hopeful parts of Teresa's brain had thought there was a chance she and Liam had been tucked away in the darkest recesses of the dance floor. Apparently not.

Nadia nodded. "Afraid so. A lot of people did."

"Including Matt?"

"I'm not sure. I haven't talked to him. But I can tell you one thing. There are zero secrets between Liam and him."

Eight

Nadia would've been lying if she'd said she hadn't been shocked when she'd looked over to see Teresa and Liam kissing in the middle of a room packed with Seattle's wealthiest, most influential people. Neither seemed the type to let loose with such a public display, and what a display it had been—hands in hair, open mouths and, without question, there had been tongue.

"What do you think Matt will say?" Teresa asked, seeming a bit desperate.

"He probably won't say anything to you, but that doesn't mean he won't have an opinion about it. You might want to stay away from Liam as much as possible, at least for a little while. Now would not be the time to slip up."

Teresa snatched a tissue from the dispenser on the countertop and dabbed at her cheek. She'd stopped crying, thank goodness. "I think I'm being sabotaged. Liam thinks I lied about being single. He asked if I had a special guy in my life, and he hinted that someone is talking about me. I don't know who it could be or how that would even come up in the first place."

Nadia debated whether she should fess up to her misdeeds. Perhaps it was best to just let Teresa know that eyes were on her and she needed to be a lot more careful. "It was me."

Teresa blinked several times. "Excuse me?"

"I overheard your conversation in front of The Opulence. I heard you say, 'I love him. I don't want him to end up in jail.' I'm sorry, but I had to say something to Matt. This is his first time working with you and the anniversary retreat is immensely important to him."

Teresa folded her arms across her chest, pursed her lips and sucked in her cheeks. For a moment, Nadia wondered if Teresa was tempted to deck her. Nadia was not a cat-fight-in-the-ladies'-room sort of girl. "Can you keep a secret? Between us. I mean, you can't even tell your boss."

Nadia had to think about that for a minute. "You have to understand that my first loyalty is to Matt. If you're about to tell me something that could hurt him, I can't promise to keep it to myself."

Teresa nodded slowly as if she was taking it all in. "Okay. I get that. Just know that the man I was talking about on that phone call was not a romantic interest. I was talking about my brother. He has a habit of getting in trouble and I'm afraid he's done it again. I'm really his only safety net." Teresa's normally strong voice began to shake. "My mother just isn't able to deal with stressful situations like this and so it all falls on me. I'm all he has."

Nadia and Teresa weren't close at all. In fact, they'd already had moments in their short working relationship that had been downright adversarial. But if Nadia understood anything, it was the pull of family, the deep need to do anything to keep them safe and okay at all costs. She stepped closer to Teresa and wrapped her arms around her. Teresa immediately lowered her head on to Nadia's shoulder. "It's okay. I promise. I won't say a word." She rubbed Teresa's back softly. "Is there anything I can do to help?"

Teresa stepped back and wiped a tear from her cheek. "Not right now. I have someone watching out for him and we'll see how it goes. The big thing I could use right now is knowing that I can lean on you when it comes to the retreat. I can't afford for anything to go wrong and I know you feel the same way. Can we help each other? Will you be my ally?"

Nadia nodded eagerly. "Yes. Absolutely. Anything you need, please don't hesitate to let me know. We both want the same thing. For Matt to be happy. Liam, too, I suppose."

"Yes. Their big announcement."

A woman walked into the ladies' room and Nadia smiled, but she knew she had to shut her mouth. Nobody could find out about the Sasha project. "Is that going to make it difficult for you to stay away from Liam?"

Teresa shook her head. "We're supposed to have one planning meeting about the presentation, but that's it. Otherwise, I'm going to stay as far away from him as I can. Apparently I lose all good judgment when I'm around him."

The woman who'd joined them in the bathroom emerged from a stall and came over to wash her hands.

Nadia and Teresa took their chance to step into the adjoining lounge.

"So, who's the hottie you're with tonight?" Teresa asked.

Nadia chuckled. Women had been asking her that all night, any time Hideo went to the bar to get them a drink. "Old high-school friend. We were never a couple. Just good friends. From the chess club if you can believe that. We also did the mock UN together."

"So the beauty queen was also a brain?"

Nadia cringed at the label. "I don't know about being a brain, but school and hard work were always important to me. The pageantry was to make my mom happy."

Teresa nodded. "You and I have a lot in common. Most things I've done in my life have been to please my mom. Or to just help her get by. My dad died when my brother and I were young and I don't think she ever recovered from it."

Nadia had to admit she was getting a bit wistful thinking about her family. "My mother is an incredibly strong person, but the pageants were one of those things she had always wanted to do herself but never had the chance. I think she lived vicariously through me. It was fine, but it's just not how I want to be defined. Beauty fades. And I know I'm a lot more than some makeup and good hair."

Teresa dropped her chin. "Honey. You are way more than that. You are the total package. Brains and beauty."

Nadia smiled. "You, too. Friends of a feather flock together."

After the things Matt had just witnessed from his vantage point near the dance floor, he needed a drink.

He wound his way back to the bar, holding his phone to his ear. He wasn't placing a call. He simply didn't want to be stopped by one of the many guests, any of whom could ask him a potentially uncomfortable question. *Is it true you're sleeping with your assistant? Or is she with the ridiculously handsome guy she brought to the party? Who is that woman Liam was kissing out on the dance floor?*

"A shot of Don Julio, please." Luckily, Gideon spared no expense at his parties, which meant Matt's favorite top-shelf tequila was available. He stuffed his phone back into his pocket and fished a hundred-dollar bill out of his wallet, tucking it into the tip jar.

"Wow. Thank you, sir," the bartender said.

"No. Believe me. Thank you." Don Julio was for sipping, but Matt knocked back the drink and shook his head. It was a jolt of warmth he needed, and smoothed his unusually ragged edges. Matt prided himself on rarely getting rattled, but watching Nadia slow-dance with her "old friend" had done something to him. The guy's hand had settled far too easily on the small of Nadia's back as he'd snuggled her close. They'd talked and laughed, every second of it an excruciating test of Matt's patience. He wasn't sure he'd ever had such a purely irrational and visceral reaction to anything. Even now, just thinking about it, made his pulse race and the blood course through his body like a raging river. All he'd wanted to do was march out onto that dance floor and claim what he wanted—Nadia.

But she was not his. She'd been very clear about that. Crystal clear. But even knowing that, he'd still had to force himself to turn away. He'd had to talk himself through not making a scene. Was he losing it?

He turned and ran right into Shayla.

"Great party," she said.

"Fantastic. Teresa does an incredible job."

"She did quite a job on your best friend a few minutes ago. What's up with that?"

Matt had really hoped he'd been one of the only people to notice, but, of course, Shayla had seen it—she had a knack for catching people at their weakest. Or most embarrassing. "I do not know. And frankly, it's none of my business." Although it really was his business. Teresa was working for him. He needed her focused on the job at hand. And as for Liam, well, Matt had never seen him so much as hold hands with a woman in public, so seeing him kiss Teresa had been a true shock to the system. Liam had offered no explanation, either, and had simply told Matt that he was calling his driver and heading home. Matt would've gone after him if Liam hadn't made it clear that he needed to be alone.

"Nadia seems to be having a great night with that male model," Shayla said, her voice dripping with innuendo.

Matt was not about to take the bait. "How could she not? The band is really good."

"Hideo Silva is even hotter in person than he is in pictures."

Shayla could be frustratingly transparent when she was trying to get in her digs. "That's not really my call." Of course, the mention of it had brought the vision right back into his head—Hideo lowering his head and speaking into Nadia's ear, holding her close. In his mind, Matt could see her laughing, tossing back her mane of thick blond hair, the one he loved running his fingers through. He recalled every lovely inch of the stretch of her neck. Kissing her buttery soft skin was one of the most sublime experiences he'd ever had. Matt was not the jealous type. He had no reason to be envious of anyone. He had the world at his feet. But in that moment, he had been certain that if the world hadn't been watching, he would have lumbered right over to Nadia, taken her hand and led her far away from the handsome guy she was dancing with.

Across the room, Matt spotted Nadia, making her way from the ladies' room back to Hideo, who was standing at the one of the high cocktail tables, staring at his phone.

"You'll have to excuse me," Matt said to Shayla, not offering any further explanation. He walked double-time, not bothering with the charade of his phone. He had to talk to her before she reached her date. "Nadia." He grasped her arm, but quickly let go, even though he didn't want to.

"Matt. Hi." Nadia's gaze flew to Hideo, then returned to Matt. She frantically scanned the room, obviously trying to take note of who saw them together. She kept her distance from him, which made part of him die on the inside. All he wanted to do was touch her. Kiss her. Hold her in his arms. He was in trouble. He knew he shouldn't be feeling this way.

"How's your night with Hideo? Shayla thinks he's hot."

"Shayla thinks everything with a penis is hot."

Matt laughed, which at least lightened his mood. "Very funny."

"It's true. I'm sure she has the hots for at least five or six guys at work. I'm positive she has the hots for you, although every woman at work has some sort of thing for you."

Was she trying to deflect to make him feel better? Was she trying to make a point that if he couldn't have her, there were plenty of other women he could have? "Shayla used to date my brother, Zach. If that's true, I don't notice it."

"Of course you don't." Nadia sighed and looked away for a minute. "I should probably get back to Hideo."

Once again, Matt was saddled with disappointment. "Don't go. Stay for a minute. Talk to me."

Nadia cast him a look that made him feel foolish. "Matt. What kind of person would I be if I just stranded him? He's here from out of town. He doesn't know anyone."

She was right. Matt needed to get a grip. But he also had to get these feelings off his chest. It felt like he was being crushed by them. He made sure no one was looking and took her hand, leading her to a corner. "I need to tell you one thing. I felt sick when you were dancing with him. I couldn't handle it. I can't handle it."

She narrowed her eyes on him and cocked her head to one side, her beautiful blond hair cascading down her shoulder. "Seriously?"

"Honestly? I was surprised how much it bothered me."

"You don't strike me as the jealous type."

"I'm not. But apparently all bets are off with you." He dared to step closer, hoping the darkness of this corner of the room afforded them at least a little privacy. "I saw his hand on your back and all I could think was that my hand is the only one that belongs there."

"Matt, we talked about this. I like you a lot, but we both know this won't work. I can't lose my job and you're not the kind of guy who gets serious, anyway. I'm a one-man woman and I don't do well with casual. It's just not in my DNA."

Matt swallowed hard, his mind racing. She had such

a talent for pointing out every obstacle between them. "What if it was more than casual?"

"What? That's crazy? Like announce it to the company? You do not want to do that."

No. He wasn't ready for that. It would be reckless and premature. But he might be ready for something else—anything to prove to her that he really was serious about his feelings for her, even when he couldn't see a way to make it work between them. "I'm not talking about that. I'm talking about you and me taking a step forward behind the scenes. Away from the public eye."

"Like what?"

"Meet my parents. Come have dinner at their house."

Nadia didn't speak for several moments, just blinked like crazy. She turned away for an instant and when she turned back, she looked scared. "Shayla was right around the corner. What if she heard us?"

"I doubt she heard a thing. The music is loud. Just tell me if you don't want to do it and I'll never mention it again." Moments like this were the real reason he never put his heart on the line. He couldn't stand the thought of rejection.

"No. I mean, I'm not sure. Let me think about it, okay? I'll call you tomorrow?"

"Please. Think about it. I'm serious about the invitation."

"Okay." She stepped closer and kissed him on the cheek. "Try to have a good night, okay?"

"I will," he said, then watched her disappear into the crowd. Of course, that was a lie. Matt wouldn't have a moment of fun while Nadia was with another man in the same room.

Nine

The morning after Gideon Johns's party, Nadia woke to a text from Shayla.

Matt is going to freak out. I need Teresa St. Claire's phone number so I can get control of this mess. Call me.

"Good morning to you, too," Nadia mumbled to herself, sitting up in bed and leaning back against her upholstered headboard.

Following Shayla's unpleasant but completely in-character message, was a link to an online business journal article filed in the wee morning hours. The headline made Nadia's stomach lurch:

Liam Christopher to Unveil Sasha Project at Richmond Industries Exclusive Retreat

She quickly scanned the article, which was mostly direct quotes from Teresa. Apparently she had spoken to the reporter at the party and they had been digging for details of the retreat. It was becoming a source of gossip since so no one knew exactly what was set to happen at it, only that an invitation was highly coveted and impossible to get. The problem was that Nadia knew very well that she'd been the person to spill the secret of Sasha to Teresa. If this was anyone's fault, it was hers.

Nadia had to get out in front of this and she needed to start with Teresa. It was still early in the day. There was a very good chance Matt didn't know about this yet. Unlike a lot of CEOs, he made a habit of keeping his phone in his home office while he was asleep. The man suffered enough interruptions in his life. He needed to get sleep.

She hopped out of bed, wrapped herself in her robe and padded into her cute but modest kitchen to make coffee. As soon as it began to drip into the carafe, she dialed Teresa's number.

Teresa answered before there was a single ring. "Nadia, I swear I didn't say a thing. You have to believe me. I would have called you earlier but I didn't want to wake you."

"If you didn't say anything, then how do you explain what it says in the article?"

"I don't know what to tell you. You're going to have to believe me. I didn't say a thing. I *wouldn't* say a thing. We talked about this last night. I can't afford for a single thing to go wrong with the retreat."

"Did you do the interview?"

"I talked to that reporter for less than two minutes. He was lurking at the end of the party so I introduced myself, and when he realized who I was, he asked about the retreat. All I said was that it was going to be fabulous and people would be talking about it for years to come. I swear that was all I said. The word *Sasha* did not cross my lips. I have no idea where he got that other information."

Nadia sucked in a deep breath. The Richmond Industries main office was occasionally a leaky ship, and the information could have come from any number of people. For that matter, Nadia had no idea how tightly the information was controlled at Liam's company, Christopher Corporation. Still, there were a few indisputable facts staring her in the face. First, the article had only mentioned the name *Sasha*, and not the nature of the project. That much was good. The damage was contained. Second, Teresa had no real reason to sabotage the retreat or Sasha, so what she was saying had to be true. And third, regardless of those details, Nadia had slipped in front of Teresa and she had to come clean with Matt.

"Okay." Nadia pulled a coffee mug out of the cabinet. "I'll smooth things over with Matt, but I can't promise he'll be able to do the same with Liam. You might have to do that much yourself."

"I thought I was staying away from Liam. Remember? Giving Matt's best friend a wide berth so as not to look unprofessional?"

Nadia took a long sip of her coffee. "At this point, our first concern is keeping him from blowing his top, especially to Matt. I don't think smoothing feathers is an unreasonable idea."

"All right then. I'm on it. I'll need you to text me his address. It's Saturday. I'm going to have to track him down at home."

"I'll send it as soon as we get off the phone. Let me know how it goes, okay? I'd like to know where we stand."

"I will. And Nadia?"

"Yes?"

"I owe you one."

"Don't worry. I'm not a person who keeps score." Nadia hung up and glanced at the clock. It was only a little after seven thirty. She knew Matt's Saturday schedule well. He typically slept until seven, then did an hour-long workout, staying away from his phone and the news. It was his detox time. Which meant Nadia had about twenty minutes to get cleaned up, get to his house and convince him that Teresa had not sunk the ship. At least not on purpose.

She had no interest in talking to Shayla, nor did she want Shayla to think she was ever going to adopt the habit of taking orders from her, so she sent her a text.

I have everything under control. Consider yourself out of it.

Teresa tried Liam by phone as soon as she got off her call with Nadia, but he didn't answer. She wasn't surprised after the way she'd acted last night, kissing him on the dance floor. Seeing her name on the caller ID was probably enough to make him turn his ringer to mute and block her number. He might even chuck his phone into Puget Sound. Which meant that she was going to have to track him down in person. She was going to have to swallow her pride, twice, up close and personal.

For that reason, she knew she needed to put her best self forward. That meant striking a balance between business polish and weekend casual—form-fitting jeans, her favorite Jimmy Choo black boots and a sleek black cardigan that showed off just enough of her assets to hopefully keep Liam off-kilter enough to accept her apology. Or more accurately, apologies, plural.

Coffee in hand, she raced over to Liam's through driving rain. She was still angry with herself for the way she'd acted at Gideon's party, although now that the fog had cleared and she had the perspective of a new day, she knew the reason she'd done it. She'd regretted *not* kissing Liam one other time in her life—the night they met. Regrets did nothing but hold you back as far as Teresa was concerned, and she did her best to avoid them by not being afraid to go for it. Trying and falling flat on your face was preferable to being left with questions. Teresa did not do well with the unknown or chances not taken. She always wanted to know what she was up against or what was out there in the world for the taking.

Liam's house was in Leschi, which was situated on Lake Washington. It was one of the most affluent areas of Seattle, like West Mercer, where his childhood home was. But Leschi was more diverse, more new money than old. Teresa had to wonder if this had been a conscious decision for Liam, in an attempt to distance himself from his father. Yes, Liam was a formidable businessman, but he was still working for his dad, still living in his shadow. Perhaps that was part of the reason he was so protective of the Sasha project.

Much like the man himself, Liam's house was an elegant fortress, with tall stone walls and a modern wrought-iron gate. She rolled down her window, heavy rain still falling, and jabbed the button for the intercom, then quickly pulled her arm back inside the car. The sleeve of her sweater was already soaked.

"Yes?" a woman's voice said through the speaker.

"Teresa St. Claire to see Liam," she called loudly, to avoid having to stick her entire head out the window. Several moments ticked by, the rainwater rolling into her car and dripping onto her pants leg. It would be just like Liam to send her away or make her sit there while she got waterlogged. But instead, the gate rumbled and swung open. Teresa rolled up her window and pulled up in front of the house. She turned and looked in the back seat for her umbrella, but it wasn't there. She hadn't been smart enough to bring a rain jacket, either, which meant she was about to arrive on Liam's doorstep decidedly less polished and put-together than she would have liked.

She sprinted to the heavy double doors, trying to dodge the rain. Luckily, the entrance was covered, but Teresa didn't have a second to compose herself. Liam was standing in the doorway, filling it up with his broad shoulders and formidable stature.

"What do you want?" Even through the deafening rain, Liam's voice boomed. As jarring as the noise was, Teresa couldn't help but be drawn to it.

"We need to talk and you didn't answer your phone." Still winded from her sprint from the car, she smoothed her wet hair back from her face.

"We have nothing to say to each other, especially after that stunt you pulled last night. Or should I say two stunts, after that interview you did? Are you trying to get Matt to fire you? Or is sabotaging me your primary goal?"

A droplet of water fell from the end of her nose. "Are you seriously going to send me away when I'm standing on your doorstep like a drowned rat? Can I at least have a towel and borrow an umbrella?"

His lips pressed into a thin line. The man wore his displeasure the way most guys wore clothes—out in the open for anyone to see. This was not the Liam she'd met that night at his parents' house. He'd changed over the last few years. He was harder, and not in a good way.

Finally, he stepped back. "Fine. But you're only staying for a few minutes."

Teresa ducked inside, but stopped on the area rug on the other side of the threshold. Liam disappeared into what appeared to be the living room, but she didn't follow. She didn't want to drip water all over the pristine dark hardwood floors in the foyer, or on the expensive leather club chairs visible from her vantage point. Beyond, a fire crackled in the fireplace and all she wanted to do in that moment was sit in front of it and have a polite conversation with Liam, but she now knew that wasn't going to happen.

He stalked back into the foyer with a fluffy white towel and handed it to her, then stood back, arms folded across his chest. Teresa gathered her hair in a bundle and squeezed it with the towel, unable to keep from admiring Liam, who was wearing a fine charcoal cashmere sweater and dark jeans. In terms of things she wanted to curl up with, Liam was now at the top of the list.

"I take it you read the interview," she said.

"You just torpedoed years of hard work."

She shook her head. "But I didn't. The word *Sasha* did not cross my lips. I swear."

"But you know about it. So why should I believe you?"

"Because believe it or not, Liam, I want you to be successful with your endeavor. I want Matt to be, as well. I need you both to walk out of the retreat weekend being nothing but impressed with me."

A grumble escaped his throat. "Kissing me on the dance floor isn't a great way to impress the man who hired you."

Now they were on to the *second* thing she was going to have to apologize for. How quickly this conversation was going from bad to worse. "So you talked to Matt about it?"

"I didn't have to. He saw it. Everyone saw it, Teresa. What were you thinking?"

Teresa looked up at Liam and those fierce eyes of his. Would she see a softer side of him ever again? Or was she doomed to get nothing but his steely exterior? The only way to find out was to put a chink in his armor, and her best weapon was the truth. "You want to know what I was thinking? I was thinking that you're one of the sexiest, most mysterious and interesting men I've ever met. And that the night I met you and you asked me out, the thing I regret most, aside from turning down your invitation, is not kissing you."

The instant she was done making her confession, Teresa realized she'd hardly taken a breath. Her heart was pounding as she waited for Liam to answer. React. Something. There was an edge of surprise on his face, but there was something else going on behind the shield of his eyes. He was thinking about what she'd just said. Thinking hard. And since no words were coming from his lips, she had no choice but to assume the worst.

"I don't know what's going through your head right now, but it's the truth, okay?" She took the towel and placed it gently on a console table next to the front door.

"I came here today to explain myself. I swear I did not tell that reporter about Sasha. And I came to apologize. I'm sorry I kissed you, Liam Christopher. I'm sorry you're so appalled by the fact that it happened." She turned and reached for the doorknob, yanking the door open. The rain was falling even harder now, but Teresa didn't care, and rushed out onto the landing.

"Stop," Liam said. "Wait."

Teresa did as he asked, looking back over her shoulder at him. "What? Do you have something else horrible you need to say to me?"

He shook his head. "I wanted to say that I'm sorry."

"You're sorry?"

"For thinking the worst of you. I had no idea you felt that way about the night we met."

She turned and shook her head at him. "So now that you know that I wanted you, you're willing to forgive me? I had no idea you had such a fragile ego."

"I don't. But at least I know now that you didn't kiss me for some ulterior motive. And I know now that I'm not crazy."

"Crazy about what?"

"For thinking we had a connection that night we met. All these years later and I was still doubting myself."

For some reason, Teresa had an awfully hard time buying the notion of Liam being anything less than supremely confident. It would take some time to get her head wrapped around it. Time away from here. Away from Liam. "Well, now you know what it's like for the rest of us."

Nadia made it to Matt's house five minutes later than she wanted to arrive. His security detail buzzed her through the gate and she pulled up in front of his palatial home. The last time she'd been here was the morning after the hospital fund-raiser, when everything between them had started to change. She'd once thought that going to bed with Matt would be like a dream, and although the actual event was even better than she'd ever dared to imagine, everything else had become more complicated.

She grabbed her umbrella, then climbed the stairs double-time, rang the bell and straightened her sweater. She'd gone with a cobalt blue cashmere V-neck and she could admit to herself that she'd chosen the garment for very specific reasons. Matt always complimented her when she was wearing blue and she knew he liked to admire her cleavage. He'd told her as much when they were at The Opulence. She needed to distract him while she figured out whether it was worth risking her professional future to wade into deeper waters with him personally. He was expecting an answer about what had once been unthinkable—dinner with his parents.

Carla, one of Matt's housekeepers, answered the door. His staff had once been kind to her, but there was now a distinct air of cold disdain. The only thing that had changed was that she and Matt had slept together and everyone knew it. Apparently they did not approve.

"Mr. Richmond is downstairs in the home gym."

"I'm going to go speak to him now if that's all right. This is a rather urgent matter."

"Mr. Richmond has instructed us to let you do whatever you need to, Ms. Gonzalez."

Somehow that was not reassuring in the least. "Great. Thank you. I know the way." Nadia left the umbrella by the door, then hustled down the wide central hall, past the great room, library and kitchen, to a back staircase that led to the bottom floor of the home. Matt's house was built into a hillside and he had turned this lower level into a bachelor's paradise, featuring a theater with a fully stocked concession stand and seating for at least twenty. It also had a rec room that rivaled the most extravagant man cave, with pool tables, arcade games, a full bar and a bank of flat-screen televisions for watching every game imaginable, all at the same time. At the very back of the house was an expanse of glass doors overlooking the pool and spa.

She admired the view for a moment before venturing farther in search of Matt. The tall trees and perfect landscaping were only barely visible on this rainy, foggy morning, but she still appreciated it. Her apartment had a decidedly less glamorous view of a busy parking lot, while this vista was peaceful and serene. It hinted at a life where there were no worries, but she knew that wasn't reality. Would this kind of life ever be for her? Not only did it seem impossible, but it also didn't even seem likely. She knew she didn't need any of it, and she also wasn't sure she wanted it. Rich people seemed to have problems that were infinitely more complicated than hers.

For now, she had to hunt down Matt. She was not looking forward to breaking this news, but she had to. Around the corner, she found him in his gym on an incline bench, doing chest presses with a barbell. He had his earbuds in, and she didn't enter the room, but simply stood in the doorway and admired him. His muscles strained against the sleeves of his black T-shirt as sweat rolled past his temples. His normally disheveled hair was pushed back from his face and that look of earnestness and concentration while he focused on his workout made her smile. For a man who had been given every imaginable advantage in life, he still worked hard. He always wanted to be his best. She could hardly believe he'd spent even a minute being jealous last night. Hideo was a sweet guy, a good friend and admittedly easy on the eyes, but he was no Matt, a man who was uncommonly brilliant and kind, handsome but not consumed by it. Matt had absolutely nothing to be jealous of.

Matt rested the barbell on the rack and sat up on the bench, dabbing at his forehead with a towel. He pulled out one of his earbuds and that was when he noticed Nadia. "Hey. Isn't this a pleasant surprise?" His heartbreaker of a smile crossed his lips. The way his eyes lit up made her breath catch in her chest and her knees come close to buckling.

"I wish this was a social call, and I hate interrupting your downtime on Saturday, but we have a situation." She walked into the room, every step closer making his pull on her a little more impossible to ignore. "I wanted to tell you about it personally."

He swung a leg over the bench, then got up and walked to her, taking a long drink from his water bottle. His shirt lifted, revealing an innocent sliver of his stomach, but it gave Nadia all sorts of ideas that were anything but pure. She wanted to thread her hands under that T-shirt and peel it right off his body. Then do the same with his shorts. Perhaps this should have been a phone call. "What's up?" he asked.

"Teresa talked to a business journal reporter at the end of the party last night. He asked about the retreat and somehow ended up writing a story with the name *Sasha* in the headline."

Deep creases appeared in his forehead. "How did that happen?"

"She swears she didn't say a thing about it, and of course I have no way of verifying that, but she really has zero reason to talk about Sasha. But I do need you to know that the reason she knows about Sasha at all is because of me. I slipped in front of her when she and I had our meeting at The Opulence. We wouldn't have to even ask ourselves this question if I hadn't messed up."

"Are you covering for her?"

Nadia shook her head. "No. It's my fault."

"And what were the details revealed? I need to know how bad things are going to get with Liam."

"No details. Just the name. There isn't even any mention of it being a technology-based project. But I realize it's less than ideal. It's not what you and Liam wanted. And I'm really sorry. I messed up. I understand if you're upset."

A breathy laugh left his lips. "You're amazing. You won't let the blame fall on someone else, will you?"

"I own up to my mistakes."

"In a business where almost no one does that."

Nadia shrugged. "Don't put me on a pedestal for doing what's right. I really should have told you when we were at The Opulence." Heat flushed her cheeks as she thought about the things they'd done to each other that afternoon. And that night. And the next morning. That moment when he'd dropped to his knees in front of her and lifted up her skirt? She'd revisited it in her mind dozens of times since it had happened. It still made her dizzy. "I guess I was too distracted. By you."

"And do you still find me distracting?"

It would be so easy to lie and say no and walk away.

But it went against everything in her nature to hurt Matt or to be dishonest. "Ridiculously distracting."

"And what about Hideo?"

Nadia shook her head. "He's an old friend. Nothing else. Don't let your jealousy show, Matt. You don't need it. You have everything."

"I don't have you."

Yes, you do. The words were sitting right on her lips, even when it was the most damning detail in her life. She could spend her entire day questioning what she was doing with Matt, but she knew at her core that her desire for him ran deep. "Things are complicated. We didn't think that part through."

He agreed with a subtle nod. "I know. But I'm ready to make things even more complicated. I was serious about you meeting my parents. I want it to happen. This week, if possible."

Nadia's heart cartwheeled and did a backflip. She couldn't help it. It meant a lot to her that Matt wanted to pull her into the personal side of his life, even when it could make things even messier between them. She craved messy right now. She craved Matt. "Okay. If you think it's a good idea, then yes."

"Good." A sly smile crossed his lips. "You know what's distracting? That sweater. You look unbelievable in it." He grinned and stepped closer until they were nearly toe-to-toe.

"I thought you might like it."

He slipped his fingers under the hem of her sweater and ran his fingers back and forth against the fabric, his knuckles grazing her bare stomach. "I'd love to kiss you right now, but I'm all sweaty."

Nadia put her hands behind her back, rose to her tiptoes and pecked him on the lips. "Maybe we need to get you into the shower and distract each other."

"You have the best ideas." He grabbed her hand and began walking to the back of the gym.

Nadia stumbled along. "Wait. In here? Really?"

"Yes, really. The best shower in the whole house is back here."

Sure enough, back behind the water cooler was a door into a bathroom that rivaled any fancy hotel Nadia had ever been in. With cool gray slate tile, a long vanity topped with Carrara marble and a glass shower enclosure built for two, she was in awe of how beautiful this room was. And that she and Matt had it all to themselves. So much better than a phone call.

Matt wasted no time while Nadia put her purse on the vanity. He kicked off his shoes and stripped off the rest of his clothes. He was already hard, making Nadia wonder what she'd ever done to be so lucky. He reached into the shower and cranked the water, then turned his focus to her, starting with her sweater, which he didn't toss on the floor but rather folded neatly and placed on the vanity. Nadia adored the attention, and the way the color in his eyes darkened when he looked at her as he removed each item of clothing. Her boots and socks. Jeans. Bra. And finally, her panties. She stood before him completely naked, feeling as admired as a woman could feel, and that was a feat on its own. He'd hardly touched her.

He opened the shower door and she stepped into the warm spray, her muscles immediately relaxing. Matt stood behind her, pressing his erection against her bottom. He placed his hands on her hips and began kissing her neck, using the gentlest touch, all while the steam began to swirl around them. "You are a goddess. You know that, right?"

She didn't really know that, but it was an awfully nice thing to hear. "You're so sweet to me." *You make me want to give you everything.*

He reached past her for a bar of soap and rolled it in his hands, his arms threaded under hers. He spread the creamy lather up her stomach, then over her breasts, his hands working in deft circles, stopping every few passes to pluck at her nipples with his fingers. Nadia reached above her head and wrapped her hands around his neck, giving him unimpeded access to her entire torso. She pressed her bottom harder against his length, rocking her hips back and forth. Matt groaned into her neck then rinsed off one of his hands. Moments later his fingers were spreading her folds, rubbing her apex in perfect circles. His other hand cupped her breast, pinching her nipple and making her skin impossibly taut. The heat in the shower was building and so was the pressure between her legs. Tighter. Coiling. Zipping from her nipple to her clit and back again. Over and over until the pressure won. She knocked her head back into Matt's shoulder and called out. He slowed the motions of his hand between her legs, but he didn't stop. He seemed to be reading her gasps. Her breaths. And reacting to every sound.

She turned in his arms and kissed him deeply, the waves of pleasure still lapping at her muscles. "That was incredible."

"I love the noises you make when you come. I want to make it happen again. And again." His hands were all over her hips and butt, his eyes still raking over her body.

"I want you inside me." Nadia smiled and handed him the soap. "But somebody needs to clean up."

"I'll be fast."

It was Nadia's turn to soap him up, spreading the silky bubbles over his glorious chest while his hands were working the shampoo through this thick hair. Even after that mind-blowing orgasm, she still hadn't had enough of him. She wanted it all. He rinsed off and turned off the water. They didn't bother with towels, just stepped onto the bath mat and immediately fell back into each other's arms. The slick, wet skin of her breasts met his dripping chest and they spun their way to the vanity, hands grabbing and pulling, water going all over the floor.

Nadia reached back for the countertop and Matt followed her lead, digging his hands into her bottom and lifting her. The cool marble was a delicious contrast against her skin. She wrapped her legs around his waist and dug her hands into his thick hair, kissing him, their tongues winding as water dripped everywhere. Her hands followed the muscled contours of his back. All she wanted was this closeness with him. "I have a condom in my bag," she said, reaching inside and pulling it out.

Matt kissed her shoulder while she tore open the packet. Then he stood back and watched as she rolled it onto his erection. He got even harder in her hand and that made her ridiculously impatient. Matt again grabbed her hips, this time pulling her to the edge then guiding himself inside her once she was in the perfect spot.

His first strokes were slow and deep, and Nadia wrapped her legs back around him. But she could tell that he was already close—his eyes were shut, and his mouth slack. She pushed back against him harder, encouraging him to go faster. He didn't need to be gentle. And he read her cues, driving into her, sending her back toward her peak.

Nadia planted her hands on the counter back behind her and had to smile when she saw the way Matt was mesmerized by the way her breasts bounced with every forceful thrust. He was going even faster now and Nadia was right at the brink when she grabbed his hand from her hip and placed his thumb against her apex. He needed no further instruction. Two passes and she was jerking forward, calling out again, Matt following, his breaths heavy and ragged as he pulled her body against his and they rode out the waves together.

Several moments of pure silence passed between them and all Nadia could feel was the warmth and security of his embrace and the way her heart beat so fiercely in her chest. It was like her own body was telling her everything she already knew on some level. *Hold on. You're falling for him. Hard.*

Ten

Nadia knew it was dangerous to allow herself to get excited by the prospect of dinner with Matt's family. Her heart and brain were at war right now, and she worried that this was yet another case of Matt being incredibly optimistic and Nadia ignoring the reality of their situation. She was not from his world. She was his assistant. It would be a monumental task to get his family to see her as anything more than a temporary, and quite possibly foolish, distraction.

Matt reached across the center console of his car and took her hand. "I don't want you to be nervous. It'll be fine. They're very nice people."

"Okay." Nadia didn't want to feel so on edge, but she did. She'd changed clothes six or seven times before Matt came to get her, eventually deciding on a demure knee-length navy blue dress with a matching cardigan and pearls. Nadia didn't consider herself a flashy dresser, but this outfit was going for superconservative status and she didn't like it at all.

"You look beautiful tonight," Matt said. "I don't think I've ever seen you wear that before."

"The last time I wore it was to my uncle's funeral. I figured this was safe. I didn't want your family to judge me by my appearance. You know how I feel about that."

"I know," Matt said. "Just don't overthink this whole thing. It's dinner. Nothing more."

Nadia shook her head. "But it's big. This is a step forward."

"Think of it as the start of us being closer."

"Is that really what you want, Matt?"

"It is if that's what you want."

Her heart sank. She didn't want to be demanding or have to ask for things. She wanted this to be a mutual agreement, a conclusion they reached together. "That's not an answer."

"I feel like anything I say will be the wrong thing. The truth is that I get involved with a woman and I just see where it goes. I don't think about the destination." He squeezed her hand. "I just enjoy the ride."

Nadia let out an unflattering snort. "I bet."

"That's not what I meant and you know it. I'm doing this because you told me that you needed more. This is me giving more."

She did appreciate that this was difficult for him. He wasn't the only one putting a lot on the line. "I know. And I appreciate your willingness to try." She only hoped it didn't blow up in their faces.

"That's all that matters." Matt took a turn into a

neighborhood and the houses began to get decidedly larger, and were farther apart and much more stately.

"This is where you grew up?"

"Yep. My parents inherited the house from my mom's parents. My grandma and grandpa retired in Miami and left us to deal with the rain."

Nadia could only think about her childhood neighborhood, which would be best described as quaint. The yards were tidy and kids ran around everywhere, but it wasn't the land of fancy cars or swimming pools. It was a working-class area with grocery stores and strip malls and people doing their best to provide. She'd loved it because it had always felt very real. The world of Matt's parents was so polished, which she struggled with. He wasn't like that. He was genuine, honest and affable. Hopefully that meant he was a product of his upbringing rather than the mansion they were pulling up in front of, with its towering columns, countless sharp-peaked dormers with white wood shakes, hulking trees artfully lit up and a garage with five bays.

"Wow. It's beautiful," Nadia said, climbing out of the Aston Martin. Matt was immediately at her side, holding her hand.

"Thanks. Now let's go meet my family." He led her up the stairs to a pair of tall glossy black doors. He turned the knob and they stepped inside a foyer so big it was like a ballroom. From the sky-high ceilings to the untold number of oil paintings on the walls, from the grand piano in front of the two-story windows to the endless stretch of shiny wood floors topped with Persian rugs, everything was pure luxury and elegance. "Hello? Mom? Dad?"

From around a corner, a man with a striking resemblance to Matt appeared, a cocktail in one hand. Nadia had seen pictures of Matt's father before. This was *not* Matt's dad. "Hello, Matthew. How are you?"

Matt dropped Nadia's hand and took a single step forward. "Zach. What are you doing here? I didn't know you were coming to town." Nadia had been right—this was Matt's brother.

Zach put his drink on a glass coffee table and held out his arms wide, but he struggled to stand up straight. He'd clearly been drinking. "Don't I get a hug? And an introduction?" He directed his gaze at Nadia and smiled, but there was something creepy about it. A chill ran down Nadia's spine.

"Yes. Of course. Sorry." Matt embraced his brother, but it was quick and there was nothing warm about it. Matt rarely talked about Zach, but Nadia knew some of the backstory. Zach had been a part of the original formation of Richmond Industries, but had left under suspicious circumstances after only a year. "This is Nadia."

Zach reached for Nadia's hand and kissed it. She couldn't get it back fast enough. "Oh, I know all about Nadia. I read *TBG*." He looked back and forth between Matt and Nadia and wagged his finger. "You two should really be more careful. You never know who's around with a camera."

Nadia pressed her lips together tightly. If this was how tonight was going to go, it did not bode well.

Zach tossed back his head and laughed. "I'm just giving you two a hard time. Come on. Let's have a drink." He waved them over to an adjoining room with a wide-arched entrance and a beautiful mahogany bar at one end, lined with tall upholstered bar stools. "I'm having a gin-and-tonic. I hope that's okay with you both."

Nadia took Matt's hand and followed him into the room, which was almost like a cigar lounge, with dark oversized furniture and a coffered ceiling. She climbed up onto the stool next to Matt, still trying to figure out what in the world was going on.

"I'm just so surprised to see you," Matt said as his brother mixed a drink. "How long are you here?"

"As long as it takes to keep you from destroying your company and making an embarrassment of the Richmond name by running around town with your assistant."

Nadia wasn't even sure she'd heard what Zach had said correctly. Luckily, Matt had the courage to ask the question that had to be asked.

"Excuse me? What did you just say?"

Zach set the two drinks on the bar and leaned against the counter lining the wall. "You heard me. I can't believe you thought you could be the one CEO who could pull this off. The board is going to skewer you if you keep this up." He then set his sights on Nadia. "I heard you were bringing her to dinner with Mom and Dad and I had to step in. You know that they have a very hard time saying no to you, so I figured I would do it for them."

"Wait a minute. Where are they?"

"They're in Portland for the night. I convinced them it was best for me to do the dirty work and for them to stay as far away as possible." He turned back to Nadia. "I hope you don't mind having dinner with the Richmond family B team. My parents thought this was a safer move. Just, you know, considering all of the tabloid stuff. It really bothers our mother. And our dad, well, he's on Matt's board and he really doesn't want to have to answer questions about his son's womanizing ways."

Nadia felt queasy, and not just because she'd barely eaten anything all day. "Maybe I should go sit in the car."

Matt turned to her. "No. Stay. You need to understand a few things about Zach. If you look up 'black sheep' in the dictionary, you'll see his picture. He is not an accurate representation of the feelings of anyone in this family, including my parents."

Zach scoffed. "Am I the golden boy? No. That's only because I never had any interest in falling in line. That's only because I refused to be the number-two guy at Richmond Industries."

"You were caught doing drugs at work. You hardly ever showed up and when you did, you were drunk. You stole money from the company. From me. I had no choice but to fire your ass. You're lucky I didn't make a big spectacle of it," Matt said, his voice uncharacteristically bitter. "Why don't you tell Nadia what your current status in Mom and Dad's will is."

"This really isn't any of my business…" Nadia said, getting off her bar stool and leaving her drink untouched. "I'm not comfortable with this conversation. I need to go outside. At least for some air." What Nadia really wanted to do was shrink until she was nothing. Until she disappeared.

"Hold on a second, Nadia. At least let me walk you to the car so I can make sure you're okay." Matt turned to Zach. "And you. Don't go anywhere. We are not finished here."

Nadia led the way, walking several paces ahead of Matt. She knew she never should have let herself think this was a good idea. At every turn in her brief relationship with Matt, she'd known it wouldn't work, and yet she kept pushing. She needed to resign herself to the fact that they were doomed. This was not going to magically fix itself. There were too many forces against them.

She flung open the door and rushed down the stairs to Matt's car. The headlights flickered and the horn chirped when he pushed the button on his fob. Nadia climbed in on the passenger side and wrapped her arms around herself.

Matt crouched down next to her. "I am so sorry, but I promise you that my brother is a psycho. There's a reason why we have no relationship. My parents even wrote him out of a decent chunk of his inheritance last year."

"So then why did they listen to him? Why aren't they here tonight?"

Matt took Nadia's hand. "I think this happens a lot with families when there's substance abuse. Nobody wants to believe their child is a bad person. Nobody wants to believe their child can't change. My parents might get upset with him, but they love him a lot. And they continue to give him the benefit of the doubt, even when he's burned them many times." Matt turned his head and glanced up at the house, then looked back at Nadia. "You'll probably find this hard to believe, but he can be very charming. Just ask Shayla. Those two dated for nearly two years."

Nadia didn't normally roll her eyes, but she couldn't help herself. "Yeah, well, as near as I can tell, they deserve each other."

"I'm going to go back in and talk to him, but just for a few minutes. He's too drunk for a real conversation, anyway. Will you be okay out here by yourself?"

She nodded. "Yes. But don't be long. I want to go

home." She hated the way her voice wobbled, but she couldn't help it. She was upset.

"I know this was a lot, but I promise I'll make it up to you. And I'll fix things with my parents, too. You'll see—everything will be fine." He leaned into the car and kissed her cheek. "Be back in a few."

With that, Matt made his way back up to the house and Nadia closed the car door. She pressed her hand against the spot where Matt had kissed her, wondering why life had to be so unfair. How could two people possibly have so much standing in their way?

Matt stormed up the stairs of his parents' home. He could not believe how upside down this night had gone. His parents had been guilty of putting the blinders on many times when it came to Zach, but he couldn't understand how he'd convinced them that his desire for them to meet Nadia could be so awful. Yes, she was his assistant. But she was a wonderful woman.

Matt walked back inside and stopped short of slamming the door behind him. "I don't understand what you want from me, Zach. Just tell me."

Zach was now sitting on one of the sofas in the living room. He'd put his cocktail glass on the wood end table without a coaster. If Matt's mother had been there right now, she would have been having a fit. "I want you to take me back at the company. I want back in on the Sasha project. I was there when you first started talking to Liam about it. I want everything you promised me when we started the company. Notice I said we, not you. We started Richmond Industries together and you cut me out. You think I don't see how much money you're making? It's obscene. Flying around in your corporate jets and spending a fortune on parties for your famous friends."

And now Matt felt as though a light switch had been flipped. He could see everything. "You leaked the Sasha story. That was you, wasn't it?"

Zach knocked his head to one side. "It was hardly a leak. I only divulged the name. And it was just to get your attention. Unfortunately, you left me sitting by the phone waiting for a call. I'm surprised it took you this long to figure it out, but you never were the smart one."

"I'm not taking you back at the company. You know what you did and I'm not letting you back in. I don't care what kind of story you told Mom and Dad, but I'm not falling for anything you have to say to me. I'm just sorry you had to go and tamper with my relationship. What Nadia and I have is special and tonight was supposed to be a step forward and you've ruined everything. How can that possibly make you feel good?"

"It's all quid pro quo, brother. If you hadn't fired me, Shayla never would have dumped me. We were in love. We were going to get married."

Matt could hardly fathom the way he and his brother remembered things in such radically different ways. "Shayla never loved you. She saved her own skin so she could keep her career on the right track. She knew where the company was going and she wanted to be there for the ride. And it's paid off for her. Very well, I might add."

Zach got up from the couch and walked back over to pour himself another drink. "I heard you had her pull the *TBG* story about you and Nadia. Making her do all of your dirty work these days?"

"How do you know about that? Were you involved

with that, too?" Just when Matt wrapped his head around one bizarre fact, another one came down the pike.

Zach shrugged and knocked back his drink. "Have you figured out who owns *TBG* now? Bo Wilson, my dear and loyal fraternity brother. Honestly, Bo has been more of a brother to me than you ever have."

Matt's headache just got a whole lot bigger. And he could no longer stand the sight of Zach. "I'm leaving now. I'm going to take Nadia home and I'm going to call Mom and Dad and try to unravel whatever web of lies you managed to spin tonight."

"You didn't give me an answer on the job. We don't have to actually work together, if that's your problem. Put me in Los Angeles or New York. We can stay out of each other's way."

Matt had to let out a breathy laugh, if only to alleviate some of the stress of the situation. "I can't think of anything scarier than you working for Richmond Industries without oversight from me. Neither one of those scenarios is going to happen. You're lucky I'm still willing to be cordial to you at Christmas. That's all you're ever getting from me." Matt marched to the front door. He'd had enough.

"I'll be sure to let Bo know that you liked that first story he ran about you and Nadia," Zach called just as Matt was opening the door.

"What does that mean?"

Zach shrugged, his trademark move. He always did everything he could to appear innocent and clueless when he was anything but. "I'm just saying you never know when Bo might run another story. Nadia is so pretty. She really should have her face all over the *TBG* website so people can admire it."

"Stay away from Nadia."

"I don't have to be near her to hurt her. Or hurt you, for that matter."

Matt took one more step back toward Zach. His heart was pounding in his chest. He clenched his fists tight. If he was the type of guy to throw a punch, he would have done it right then and there, if only to knock that smug look off Zach's face. "Do not threaten me."

"I guess we'll have to see what happens. You know where to find me if you change your mind."

At that, Matt turned and made his real departure, this time slamming the door, not that it likely mattered to Zach. His mind was racing, but he knew one thing. He could not tell Nadia about what his brother had said. It would only hurt her. It would only hurt *them*. Things were still so new and tenuous between them. He wanted the chance to keep going, even when the world was throwing roadblocks in their way.

Matt climbed into the car. Nadia was in the same position, arms wrapped tightly around herself. He started up the engine and sped out of the driveway. "I'm so sorry about tonight, and my brother. That did not go the way I planned it to. Obviously. You need to know that he really is a big liar. Nothing he said tonight was right."

"Is that really true, Matt? I mean, he's said things that you and I have both thought. I'm sure your parents wanted no part of having me over to the house. I'm sure they're hoping that I'll end up being a passing fancy. That you'll move on to a different assistant and I won't be in your life anymore. That doesn't speak well for us having a future, Matt. It's sweet that you're all caught up in this idea, but I don't think it's going to work."

Matt had to wonder whose side Nadia was on. He

wasn't about to give up so easily. If nothing else, he had to do it on principle. He and Nadia had done nothing wrong. Their relationship was built on mutual respect, admiration and consent. Yes, she wanted a lot more than he normally gave, but he wasn't ready to quit. Not yet. "I'm serious about Zach. He is a weasel. And he can say whatever he wants, but it's not going to change what's between us. It doesn't matter."

"But it does matter. Family is hugely important to me, Matt. I'm not only not off to a great start with yours, but tonight also felt like the universe trying to send a message that we can't have a real future together."

Matt had never been so frustrated in all his life. He pulled up to a red light and turned to Nadia. "I care about you. A lot. I'm not ready to give up on you, as long as you aren't ready to give up on me. Have you lost all faith in me? Just because of one conversation with my horrible brother?"

Nadia smiled and looked down at her lap. "I'm not ready to give up on you."

"Even after tonight?"

She sucked in a deep breath and looked out the window. "I guess not even after tonight. But I do want you to talk to your parents. If they aren't on board, we need to have a serious conversation."

The light turned green and Matt whizzed through the intersection. "Absolutely. My sentiments exactly. Tomorrow I will clear the air with them, we'll get it all straightened out and we can just pretend that tonight did not happen." *I know that I'd certainly like to forget it.*

"If you say so."

Matt was coming up on the turnoff to drop Nadia back at her place, but he didn't want to say goodbye.

Not like this. Not after the night they'd had. Plus, they hadn't eaten, and he was starving. "Want to grab some takeout and bring it back to my place?"

"I *am* hungry. You promised me dinner."

Matt grinned and reached over for Nadia's hand. "Awesome. Chinese or Thai?"

"Thai. Definitely."

"And I want you to stay over. The whole night. No sneaking out in the dark."

"What about when your staff arrives in the morning? They all give me the evil eye when I'm there. Nobody thinks we're right together."

"But I think we're right together. And I think you think that, too. That's all that matters. I don't care about anything else."

Eleven

Liam could not get Teresa off his mind—probably because there was so much to think about. If she hadn't come to visit him last weekend, he would mostly have their kiss to ponder. What a kiss it had been, like the entire world opening up, her beautiful body bowing into his, soft and luscious and wanting more. Just as quick, she'd pulled away, shocked and surprised, darting across the dance floor and disappearing into the dark recesses of the party.

But the next day she'd given him an entirely new revelation, a new lens for viewing that kiss. She'd said that she regretted not kissing him the night they first met. He'd truly wondered many times if his attraction to her had been one-sided and, of course, he'd banished all thoughts of it when he thought she'd had an affair with his father. But she'd vehemently denied it, she had a plausible explanation, and most salient was the fact that his investigator had failed to dig up any dirt on Teresa St. Claire. If she had ever done anything wrong, he couldn't find it. Was it possible that she was exactly what she seemed to be—a driven and determined, but equally gorgeous and sexy woman? Or was something else going on behind that beguiling facade?

This was not a good time to be asking himself these questions. It was past 7:00 p.m. on a Tuesday and he'd just obtained a security pass to gain access to the waterfront warehouse near Pike Place Market, where Teresa's office was. They were set to go over the precise order of events for the Sasha announcement at the retreat. Then Teresa and her team could arrange the technical side—lighting, music, visuals.

Liam took the stairs up to the second floor, emerging in the office for Limitless Events. It was an impressive loft space with twenty-foot ceilings, arched windows lining the exposed brick walls and original hardwood floors. A dozen desks or so were neatly arranged in clusters. Teresa had quite a setup here. Liam could only imagine how bustling it must be during the day. For now, it was dead quiet, aside from a young man sitting at a desk at the far side of the room, the blue light from a computer screen illuminating his face.

"Hello?" Liam asked, his voice practically echoing in the open space.

The man looked up from his keyboard. "Can I help you?"

"I'm here to meet Teresa. She said she'd be waiting for me."

"In her office." He pointed to a glass-walled room with white shades pulled and the door closed. A soft glow came from inside. Someone was definitely in there. "I'd knock first if I were you."

"Of course." Liam strode over and tapped the glass door with his knuckle.

Teresa arrived seconds later, but she didn't open the door all the way. "We have to reschedule."

"What? Why?"

"Something came up." Her voice did not have its usual confident tone. She was rattled.

"Is something wrong? Can I help?" Liam couldn't help it. When he saw a woman who was upset, he wanted to fix the problem. Make it go away. Perhaps it was a conditioned response. He'd been doing precisely that for his mother since he was a little boy.

Teresa shrank back from the door. "Just go, Liam. Why would you want to help me? You don't even like me."

He took his chance and pressed on the door. Teresa was walking over to the window. Her office was mostly dark, the only light coming from the golden glow of the city and a lamp on her desk. "That's not true. I like you. We just have a lot of history for two people who hardly know each other."

She sniffled. She'd been crying, which was such a stark contrast to her nut-hard exterior. "You don't want to hear my sob story."

"What kind of man would I be if I walked away from someone who is clearly upset?" He ventured closer to her and placed his hand lightly on the center of her back. Just like during their dance, she leaned into him. "Tell me what's going on."

"It's my brother. He got mixed up with some terrible people. Two weeks ago I got a call from someone claiming my brother owed them seven million dollars. Turned out not to be true. Or maybe it was true because I just got a call saying he's been kidnapped and they'd call back with demands soon. It sounded like the same voice, but I'm not sure."

"Is this your brother, Joshua?" The instant the words came out of his mouth, he realized he'd made a huge mistake.

Teresa quickly turned her head and narrowed her sights on him. "How do you know my brother's name? Nobody is supposed to know about him."

Liam cleared his throat. It was time to come clean. "That day at The Opulence. When I first ran into you. I decided to have an investigator in my employ do a bit of digging."

"You did what?"

"I know. I know. It sounds horrible, but you have to understand I believed one thing and you were staunchly denying it. I had to know whether or not I could afford to believe you."

"And you were able to find out about Joshua? That shouldn't happen."

"Only a little bit. Only that you have a brother by that name. There was a record of his graduation from high school, but after that, it's like he disappeared. To be honest, I wondered if something happened to him."

She drew in a deep breath, seeming no less troubled. "It's a long story, but Josh got into trouble in high school, then went to Vegas and got into even more trouble. Drugs. The wrong people. By that time, I was working with Mariella Santiago-Marshall at MSM Event Planning in Santa Barbara. Your dad helped me get that job. I shared my problem with Mariella and she told me about a man her husband worked with. A man called The Fixer."

This was not a shock. The Marshalls were an immensely powerful family of considerable wealth. "I've heard of him. Unfortunately, most people in my world need somebody on their side to make problems go away."

"I was desperate. I had to get Joshua out of jail, out of Vegas, and away from these people. They were very dangerous. He took care of everything. He was supposed to make him invisible."

"Honestly, he did a really good job. My guy took two weeks to find what he did and it wasn't easy."

"The Fixer does a fantastic job. The problem is I want to call him and see what's going on with Joshua, but I don't have the money to pay him and I already owe him a favor that's to be determined. That's a scary proposition in its own right. There's no telling what he's going to ask of me." Teresa began pacing back and forth across the hardwood floors.

Meanwhile, Liam was hard at work thinking of a way out of this. "Let me call my guy. He's not familiar with the situation, but I'm sure you can get him up to speed quickly and you won't need to worry about paying him or owing anyone a favor."

"Not even to you?"

It would have been so easy to take advantage of this situation, but Liam's heart truly went out to Teresa. "Not even to me."

Teresa dropped her head to one side in doubt. "Now why would you do that for me? Two weeks ago, you hated my guts. You tried to get me fired."

Liam swallowed back his pride. He'd messed up. He knew that now. He should have cleared the air with her first before he'd gone to Matt. "So give me a chance to make it right. I'll call him. Let's make sure your brother is okay."

Teresa pressed her lips together, regarding him. She scanned his face like she was searching for something she desperately needed. What was this pull that she had on him? Why was his only desire to gather her up in his arms and see where a kiss could go?

"Okay. Do it."

Liam pulled out his phone and called his guy, who answered right away. "Liam. Nice to hear from you."

"Thanks. I have a friend who's in a real bind and we need your help. She received a phone call saying that her brother has been kidnapped, but she's not sure it's real. We need to find out what the situation is."

"Yeah. Of course. Can you put me on the phone with her so I can find out the details?"

Liam offered his phone. "He wants to talk to you. Get the info on your brother."

She seemed unsure at first then snatched the phone from his hand. "Hello?" She nodded and walked behind her desk. After a minute, she started to rattle off everything she'd said to Liam, along with Joshua's last known address, his cell number, a current photo and the name of a friend he spent time with. "Okay. Thanks." She stared at the phone for an instant, then turned her gaze to Liam. "He's going to call back." There was something so vulnerable in her eyes. She was genuinely petrified. It made him want to protect her from everything. "He said he has a contact where Joshua is. He said it could take anywhere from a few minutes to a day."

Liam nodded, understanding what a delicate situation she was in. Hell, *they* were in. He was involved now, too.

He wanted this to work out okay. "It'll be okay. You just need to find a way to relax."

"I don't think I can do that. Not until I know he's okay." Teresa began pacing and Liam took the chance to remove his jacket and sit on the sleek black leather sofa in her office. The appeal of her form in motion was impossible to ignore—shapely legs that seemed to go on forever, hips that filled out her slim black skirt perfectly and just enough hint of the rest of her figure through a sheer white blouse to make him a little crazy. "What if it really takes a whole day? I won't be able to sleep at all. Not a wink. You don't have siblings, do you?"

Liam shook his head. "Nope. Only child. I always wanted a brother or sister though."

"Careful what you wish for. They can be wonderful, but they can make you crazy. I swear."

Just then, Liam's phone rang. They both jumped. Teresa ran out from behind her desk to Liam. Sure enough, the caller ID told Liam it was his guy. "Is there an update?" Liam answered.

Teresa held on to his arm, her eyes darting back and forth over his face. "What is he saying?"

Liam closed his eyes and tried to concentrate while his guy told him everything. "Okay. Thanks. I'll let her know." He stuffed his phone into his pocket. "He's okay. They tracked his phone's GPS and then got visual confirmation. He was with his friend at some bar. Not sure why he doesn't answer his phone, but I figured you can find that out later."

She dropped to a crouching position, dug her hands into her thick blond hair and began to sob.

Liam dropped to his knees. "What is it? Are you okay?"

No answer came. She was crying so hard that she was gasping for air.

Liam did the only thing he could think to do. He took her in his arms and rubbed her back. "Shh. Shh. It's okay." She sagged against him, crying and trembling. It was as if it was the most natural thing in the world. The only thing that made sense. She held on to him like he was the only thing worth having. He loved the feeling of being there for someone. He always had.

Being in Liam's arms on the floor of her office was the last place Teresa had expected to end her day. But here she was, desperate for air and swallowing back her tears. Liam had been a rock for her. Joshua was okay. She still didn't know what was going on with him, but he was safe. "I'm so sorry. I don't know what came over me. I'm just so relieved. I know we only had to wait a few minutes, but it felt like forever."

"I can only imagine. The important thing is he's safe."

She eased back her head and looked at him. Liam was a puzzle if ever there was one. Who knew there was such a deeply sweet and caring side of him? "Thank you for helping me. I don't know what I would have done if you hadn't been here. I really didn't want to have to call The Fixer. I don't know how I'll ever repay you."

"I don't care about evening the score, Teresa. You can repay me by allowing me to call a real truce. I don't want our relationship to be contentious anymore."

A smile played at the corner of her lips. "Are you saying you want to be friends?" She sat a little straighter and smoothed her hand over the lapel of his jacket, wishing she could explore everything that was underneath it.

"Friends don't kiss each other on the dance floor. Especially not the sort of kiss we had."

"Unless they're friends with benefits," he quipped.

They were both taken aback by his comment, eyes searching, neither speaking. Liam did not let down his guard like this, at least not that Teresa had ever seen. Was he caught up in the moment? Or was there something else going on here? Was this a dream?

"I've never had a friend like that. Tell me how that works."

Liam's eyelids became heavy. He reached over and threaded his fingers between hers then lifted her hand to his lips, leaving behind a tingle that managed to find its way to the most sensitive parts of her body. He didn't take his eyes off her. He merely left their connection to smolder. "I imagine it's like any other friendship. You make each other happy. You blow off steam together." He turned over her hand and kissed her wrist, closing his eyes and savoring the moment as if her skin was the most heavenly thing his mouth had ever touched.

Teresa sucked in a breath, mesmerized by his lips, his dark features, the boundless sexiness of Liam. She did not consider herself a seductress, but damn, she felt sexy, like an entirely different woman when she was around him. Between the intense relief she'd felt at knowing Joshua was okay and knowing that Liam wanted to be friends, that he didn't hate her, she had no reason to leave up her defenses any longer. She could finally follow through on everything she'd started with that kiss.

"I want you, Liam."

"I want you, too." He cupped the side of her face and drew her closer, kissing her. Their tongues found each other, tentatively at first. Gently. Softly.

It was quite possibly even sexier than their first kiss, but it wasn't enough. She wanted more. She wanted to flatten him against the floor and tear off his clothes. She wanted the same from him. She shifted to her knees. He followed, not allowing their kiss to end. They held on to each other, standing for only an instant before collapsing on the couch. Teresa scrambled to straddle his lap, hiking her skirt up to her hips. Liam sat forward and hurried his shoulders out of his charcoal suit coat, tossing it aside. Finally she could get him out of that crisp white shirt, her hands going faster than they ever had before. She tore back the garment, lowered her head and kissed his chest, letting her hands roam his warm skin and firm muscles, twitching with electricity. Liam had both hands on her bottom, bunching her skirt up at her waist and sliding his fingers into the back of her panties. They curled into her flesh, pulling her closer. She spread her knees farther, sinking forward until she could feel his hard erection against her apex.

They began to rock against each other. Just this limited amount of touching left Teresa feeling like she might come. She could only imagine what it was going to be like when she finally had him out of those pants. Breaking their kiss, she sat back and began to unbutton her blouse. Liam's hands shifted to her hips and he slid a little lower on the cushion, letting her put even more of her body weight against his length. The tension between them was such a delicious form of torture, Teresa was caught up in the push and pull of wanting him inside her so badly she couldn't think straight, and wanting to draw this out for as long as it could possibly last.

As soon as her blouse was residing on the floor, she

reached back and unhooked her bra, then let it fall forward, ruffling it from her arms.

Liam shook his head, his eyes admiring. He was pleased. "You are so beautiful. Truly beautiful." He took her breasts in his hands and rolled her nipples between his fingers.

"And you're making me crazy, Liam. I want you. Now." However much it pained her to do it, she climbed off his lap and quickly rid herself of her skirt and panties. She grabbed her purse and pulled a condom out of an inside pocket. Meanwhile, Liam had unbuckled his belt, unzipped his pants and raised his hips to wriggle his remaining clothes to the floor.

He sat, waiting with knees apart, his impressive erection on full display. Even from a few feet away, she could see how hard he was for her and she couldn't wait to have every inch of him. She stepped closer and took him in her hand, stroking firmly from base to tip. Every part of him she touched was hard and hot. She wanted that fire. She needed it. He closed his eyes and knocked his head to one side, drawing a slow breath through his nose.

"Never stop touching me like that," he muttered, his voice coming from the deepest parts of his throat.

"Something tells me you'll like this even better." Teresa had other plans. She tore open the packet, rolled on the condom and straddled his lap, guiding him inside. She sank down onto his body, her mind a riot of thoughts about how good he felt and how unlikely this scenario was. She never thought she and Liam would be having sex in her office. Fantasized, yes, but reality? She would have put money on it never happening.

They began to move together, falling into sync, a perfect rhythm. Teresa knew this wouldn't take long. Liam kissed her neck then angled his head lower, swirling his tongue around her nipple. She curled her fingers into his firm shoulders, rolling her hips against him, over and over again.

"You feel amazing," he said, his breaths already shallow. "But I need you to know something."

"What?"

"As soon as I make you come, we're putting our clothes back on and we're going to my place. I want you in my bed." It wasn't an invitation or a suggestion. Liam was issuing an order. Teresa, despite never wanting to take directives from any man, couldn't have been more turned on.

"We were supposed to get some work done tonight." She kissed him, knowing that work was the absolute last thing she cared about.

Liam laughed quietly against her lips. "You think I care about that? Because I don't. Not when I know I can have you at my mercy all night long."

Twelve

Two days after his run-in with Zach, his brother made good on his not-so-subtle threat to sabotage Matt and Nadia's chances at happiness by planting a story on *TBG*. The headline was so much worse than Matt could have ever imagined: "Beauty and the Boss Part Two: Playing Every Angle."

This time, the story was all about smearing Nadia and her name. Everything was twisted to show her in the most negative light imaginable. It talked about her beauty-pageant days, and how no one would have ever thought a woman like that would end up with so much responsibility and such a high-pressure job. It suggested that she was playing Matt and Hideo against each other and included photos from the night of Gideon's party, showing her in what could be construed as romantic situations with each of them. It mentioned the car Matt had given to Nadia as a bonus, suggesting, exactly as they'd feared, that it was given to her in exchange for sexual favors. It said that Matt was considering Nadia for a huge promotion and bonus, both of which were absolute lies, but he knew now that Zach would do anything to get back at him.

To make matters even worse, the story had gone live at 8:59 a.m., Seattle time, precisely when everyone at Richmond Industries would be sitting down at their desk, most of them checking email and online news before digging into the meat of their day. Matt could already hear the commotion out in the hall. His employees were milling about and talking, unsubtly walking past his corner of the office and glancing over before offering a phony wave and making a quick escape. Nadia had gone to the ladies' room and would likely be back any minute now.

Matt had to act, and quickly. He picked up his office phone and buzzed Shayla's extension. "Let me guess. The *TBG* story. I just finished reading it."

"What the hell, Shayla? How can they run this stuff? Am I going to have to call my lawyer?"

"It's not a bad idea, but you know that they can get away with saying a lot of stuff. And I mean, how much of the story is inaccurate? From where I'm sitting, most of it is pretty well on the mark."

"I am not considering Nadia for a big promotion or raise. That part is completely fabricated."

"Can you prove that you've never talked about it?"

"How do I go about proving that?" Plus, Matt knew the reality. He had discussed a raise with Nadia and she'd said no, wanting to avoid a situation exactly like the one they were in.

"You don't. Which is exactly why they published it."

Matt grumbled, beyond frustrated. "Can you make it go away?"

"I can try. But perhaps you should consider the fact that Nadia has become a liability. That's one way to make the problem go away for good. She's already worked for you longer than any other assistant. Nobody will bat an eye if you hire someone new. *TBG* will move on to the next story."

Matt glanced at his laptop and that's when he saw new email messages start to pop up, all from Richmond Industries board members, all with subject lines pertaining to the *TBG* story. "I'm going to pretend you didn't say that. Just please do your best, okay?"

"I always do. Is there anything else?" Shayla asked.

"No. Thank you." Matt hung up the phone and dared to open one of the emails. It very plainly stated that there was great concern about Matt's assistant and perhaps Matt needed to quietly have HR arrange a severance package so Ms. Gonzalez could move on with her life and stop causing the company undue bad publicity.

Matt didn't even have a chance to look at the rest of the messages before Nadia was in his office. "Did you see?" Just like that day at The Opulence, she had her phone in hand, and thrust it into his line of sight, confronting him with the ugliness of tabloid news. "My sister has already seen it. She said people in her dorm asked her about it. It's only a matter of time before my parents see this. They made me look like a gold digger, Matt. They made me look like a ditzy blonde. I don't know what to do." She sank down into the chair opposite his desk and stared at her phone again, flicking at the screen and shaking her head.

Matt pushed back his chair and rushed over to Nadia, taking her phone from her and placing it facedown on his planner. "Don't look at that anymore. Nothing good comes of it." He perched himself on the edge of his desk.

"This is just going to keep happening. It's not going to stop. It doesn't matter that I work hard or that I'm smart. They can paint me any way they want. They can make me look like an idiot beauty queen with designs on a very wealthy and powerful man and there's nothing I can do to stop it."

"I've already talked to Shayla. I'll call my lawyer if that will make you feel better. Nothing stops something like this better than a lawsuit. These tabloids are cowards, deep down."

"Shayla can't put out every fire there is, Matt. I already promised her she wouldn't have to do this again and now it's happening all over again."

"What do you mean you promised her it wouldn't happen again?"

Nadia sighed deeply and looked up into his eyes. "After The Opulence. That first morning after your emergency trip to Miami? When I told you that one of my coworkers had given me a hard time? That was Shayla."

Matt felt his jaw go so tight it was as if it was wired to his skull. "I'll talk to her. I'll get it straightened out."

"No. Matt." Nadia scooted forward on her chair and placed her hand on his arm. "I don't want you to talk to Shayla. She might not be my favorite person, but she has a hard job and we both know it isn't fair she has to deal with this. She should be concentrating on the good things the company does, like the Sasha project or the retreat. She shouldn't have to spend her days fighting off pulpy stories like this."

"She's my employee. She'll do whatever I ask her to do."

Nadia shook her head. "That's not very fair. She's worked for you for five years. I think she's earned better treatment than this."

"I don't understand what you're saying, Nadia."

"I hate to say it, but this time it might be best for us to stay away from each other, at least for a little bit. Maybe permanently. And I feel like the writing is on the wall. I can't work for you anymore. As much as I hate to say that."

"What do you want to do? I can transfer you into another division."

"You know how that's going to look. Like you're just finding a way to keep your girlfriend around."

Girlfriend. "I've never heard you refer to yourself like that."

A look of panic crossed her face. "Oh, God. I'm sorry. That was presumptive. I know that what we had was just casual. You were very clear about that."

"No. No. I like it. I like the idea of you being my girlfriend."

Just then there was a knock on Matt's door. It was Shayla. Matt waved her in. "Can you and I talk in private for a moment?" she asked.

"Whatever you have to say to me, you can say in front of Nadia."

But Nadia was already getting up from her chair. "No. No. It's okay. I need to get back to my desk, anyway. We'll finish this conversation later." She scrambled out of the room, closing the door behind her.

He turned his attention to Shayla. "Do you have an update on *TBG*? Are they taking down the story?"

"Actually, no. They are refusing to take my call. And I don't know if you've taken a gander at your email, but the board is pretty up in arms over this whole thing and they're all coming to me, demanding an explanation."

"Well? What are you telling them?"

"That it's not my fault a tabloid decided to run a story about one of the wealthiest men in the country having an affair with his beauty-queen assistant. Matt, you pay me the big bucks to keep your company in the best possible light. That means telling you things you don't want to hear. She has to go. It's the only way forward. It's the only way you salvage the company and its future."

Matt didn't even want to think about it. It made him sick to his stomach. "A leave of absence. Paid."

Shayla folded her arms across her chest. "Obviously this is not my call nor my area of expertise, but this isn't really a professional infraction on her part. It's more a case of being a liability. You can't give a liability a leave of absence. You have to get rid of it. Or her, I should say."

Matt felt as if his heart was about to turn in on itself. He couldn't believe those words were coming out of her mouth. He couldn't believe the choices he was being confronted with today. "I'm going to need to talk to HR about a severance package."

"Do what you have to do, but I'd do it quickly if I were you."

Matt looked through his glass wall at Nadia, who was typing away at her computer and talking on the phone at the same time. He wanted to give her more, but he wasn't there yet. She'd been right all along. They'd had their fun. If only he'd listened to her weeks ago when she'd said they had to go back to nothing more than a professional relationship. This was his fault. And he had to fix it. Somehow.

Nadia did her best to keep her nose down and do nothing but work, but every minute of that morning had been painful. She couldn't stand any more accusatory glances from her coworkers. And Shayla? The haughtiness she'd displayed when she'd left Matt's office was unreal. Not that Nadia blamed her. If the roles were reversed, Nadia would've been mad and annoyed, too. This situation had been entirely avoidable—she and Matt knew what they were doing, and they had thrown all caution to the wind and done it anyway. She'd also had to sit there and not say a word when the senior members of the HR team had waltzed into Matt's office and hunkered down with him. They'd even drawn the shades, as if Nadia didn't feel like enough of an outcast.

Nadia's phone rang and she wasn't sure she wanted to answer it, but she saw Teresa's name on the caller ID and realized she really needed someone to talk to. Someone who wasn't afraid to be brutally honest, but who also had at least some of Nadia's best interests at heart.

"Hey," Nadia said, answering. She got up from her desk and wandered down the hall and ducked into one of the small meeting rooms, closing the door behind her.

"I saw the *TBG* story. I'm so sorry. They're such bastards."

"I know. I hate it. It's awful. My younger sister saw it and I'm just bracing for the moment my mom or dad come across it."

Teresa sighed. "I don't want to sound like a broken record, but I really am sorry. Is there anything I can do?"

Nadia didn't know where to start. "I have to quit my job, don't I? There's no way out of this. My reputation at this company is ruined. I will always be the woman who slept with the boss."

"Oh, honey. I wish that wasn't the case, but I don't really see another way through this."

The empathy in Teresa's voice really struck a chord with Nadia, one that brought about more than a few tears. "I worked my butt off. I was on my way. And now I have to start all over again just because I had a crush on my boss and I acted on it."

"You had a crush on Matt?"

"Yes. For all fourteen months I've been here. It's pathetic. I'm just drawn to him, I don't know what else to say. Not that it matters. It's all over now."

"Well, it doesn't have to be the end for you and Matt, does it?"

"Without a job, I'm probably going to have to move back to Los Angeles. Nobody is going to hire me. Not in Seattle at least."

"I'll hire you. Right now. Today."

Nadia managed a smile and swiped a tear from her cheek. "You're sweet. And I know very little about event planning. I'm not artistic. I don't have a vision like someone like you."

"I can teach you."

"I don't want you to feel sorry for me, Teresa. Don't offer me a job because you feel bad."

"Look. I'm not. Just think about it, okay? It's not my place to talk you into it. Only you can decide what's best for you. And that goes both personally and professionally. You're an amazing, strong woman who got mixed up in a crazy situation. It could happen to anyone. The important thing is to come out on the other side of it even stronger and more amazing."

"Wow. Thank you for the pep talk. I appreciate it." She sighed for what felt like the millionth time. "I'd probably better go talk to Matt now. He's most likely done with HR and I just need to do this and get it over with."

"Good luck, hon. Call me if you need anything."

"I will." Nadia hung up and walked back to her office. Indeed, Matt's door was open again and no one sitting in the chairs opposite his desk. She couldn't solve the questions of their relationship today, but she could undo at least some of the damage done to Richmond Industries. She could leave with her head held reasonably high. "Knock, knock." She peered inside his office.

Matt had his chair faced toward the window and was looking outside. When he turned to her and she saw the look on his face, she knew that he was aware of what she was about to do. "Hey."

"Can we talk?"

He nodded. "Of course."

She stood before his desk, much like she had her first morning at work, the first time Matt ran through the things he wanted her to do that day. She could remember the way he made her both nervous and excited. She could remember the way he made her laugh like a teenager, and how the longing for him, something that came from the very center of her chest, sprang to life. "I'm going to go write my letter of resignation. There is no recovering from what happened today. I need to start fresh at another company."

"I'm sorry to hear that, but I understand." It wasn't exactly what Nadia had hoped to hear, but she honestly didn't know what she wanted right now other than to leave the building without crying again. "Do you know what you're going to do for work?"

She shook her head. "I don't. Chances are that I will end up moving back to Los Angeles to regroup and spend some time with my family. I'll figure things out from there."

Matt's face fell. "We have a generous severance package for you. I need you to know that I fought for you in that meeting with HR. You got screwed in this situation and I feel horrible."

"I don't want the severance, Matt. It's only a matter of time before that ends up in the papers, too. It's best if it's just a clean break. It's best for everyone."

"But what about us?"

Nadia closed her eyes. Matt's pull on her was as strong as ever, but right now it felt like it might flatten her. "I'm not made for this world. And you and I knew this wouldn't last. There's too much pressure. Too many eyes scrutinizing us and waiting for us to mess up. I don't want to live like that and I won't. The reality is that this world doesn't operate the way it should. Hard work doesn't account for enough." Nadia felt like she might crumple into a ball. Every word was true and agonizing. "Between what happened today and your brother the other night and me needing to be there for my family, it seems pretty obvious what the answer to that question is, doesn't it?"

He shook his head vehemently. "No. It doesn't seem obvious to me."

"Matt. Please. Don't make this harder for either of us. You and I both know that I will leave here and we'll be sad, but you'll move on. You'll be happy and do amazing things and I'll enjoy watching from a distance." The vision materialized in her head. This was the end of the road for them. And it might kill her. "You're not ready to get serious and I'm probably too serious. I've spent the last fourteen months pining for you and wanting you and wishing you would want me, too. And I got a glimpse of that. We had a few weeks that were amazing. That might be all I get, but I don't regret it."

Slow as could be, Matt rose from his chair and came around to the other side of the desk. "All that time you've been here, you were pining for me?"

Nadia playfully slapped his arm. She was desperate for any way to lighten the mood. "Of course I was. And that should tell you that you, Matt Richmond, will be just fine. You will find an amazing woman and get married and have kids someday."

"No."

"Yes." She grabbed both sides of his face and forced him to nod in agreement. "I know you think you aren't that guy, but you are." She poked a finger in the center of his chest, right in the vicinity of his heart. "You are that guy in here. You just need to let him out."

"Nadia. Don't. Don't leave."

That was when the tears started and all she could think was that she had to get out as fast as she possibly could. "It's okay. I promise it will be okay. I'll come back to get my things some other time when you aren't here. Just so it doesn't have to be weird." She popped up onto her toes and kissed him on the cheek, then turned and rushed out the door, grabbing her purse and making a beeline for the fire stairs. It would be easier to cry her eyes out there rather than in the elevator.

And that was exactly what she did.

Thirteen

Liam was having a crazy busy day, but he couldn't stop looking at his phone, wishing it would ring. He was expecting a call from Teresa and, well, he'd be lying if he said he hadn't been looking forward to hearing from her. Even more so, all he could think about was when he would next get to *see* her. They'd had a whirlwind forty-eight hours after the night they made love in her office, much of it spent in bed together. But then she'd had to go out to The Opulence to work on the retreat, and Liam was left wanting more.

There was a frantic knock at his door. His assistant, Duncan, poked his head inside his office before he could even call him in. "I'm so sorry to interrupt, but it's your father. He collapsed after a meeting in Portland."

Liam hardly had time to absorb the news before he

felt as though he'd been punched in the stomach. "Is he still there?"

"He's almost home. I just got off the phone with his assistant. They flew him back on the corporate jet and they're en route from the airport. He asked that you meet him at his house."

"I don't understand. When did this happen? They're already sending him home? I thought you said he collapsed."

Duncan shrugged. "I'm so sorry. That's all I know right now. I called your driver and he's downstairs waiting for you. I've rescheduled your afternoon meetings. Let me know if you need me to move anything for tomorrow."

Liam collected his phone and stuffed it into his pocket, thankful to have an assistant who was so proactive. "You are amazing. Thank you so much."

"No problem, Mr. Christopher. I just hope your dad is okay."

Liam rushed through the office, trying to ignore the way people popped up from their cubicles with looks of horror or mumbled their condolences as he walked by. It was as if his father had died. Liam couldn't bear to think of that. He had to get to him as quickly as possible.

He hopped into the back of the limo and his driver pulled away from the curb. Liam looked out at the gray day. Parts of the sky were black as coal. He really hoped that wasn't a sign of things to come. His phone rang and he quickly looked to see who it was. *Teresa.* Her name brought a smile to his face, which sadly faded. He had been so looking forward to this moment and now a pall had fallen over it.

"Hello, beautiful," he said, leaning back in the seat and drawing in a deep breath.

"You sound stressed. Is everything okay?"

Old Liam's gut reaction to this would have been to not say a thing, but the truth was that he wanted to tell Teresa. He wanted to tell her everything. "My dad collapsed. I'm on my way to his house."

"Oh, my gosh. Liam. Is it serious?"

"I don't know. I guess it can't be too serious. They're sending him home."

"Call me as soon as you know something. I like hearing your voice. It's the best part of my day."

Liam smiled again, still surprising given the current circumstances. "I like talking to you, too. You're a good listener."

"When you talk. You are a man of few words." Teresa let out a breathy exhale on the line. "I'm glad you're going to see your dad. Please send him my best."

Liam winced at that, and he hated himself for having that reaction. He was convinced that nothing had happened between Teresa and his dad. But there was still this voice in the back of his mind whispering to him that women had lied to him before. "I will let him know. Have you thought at all about when you can come back? Or should I make a trip up to The Opulence?"

"As much as I'd love to see you, things are so hectic right now. I'm hoping I can be back in a week."

An entire week. Liam hated that idea, but he understood. "Perhaps we can go out for a nice dinner when you return."

"Or we could eat in," she said, with a very sexy and leading inflection.

"I love the way your mind works."

Teresa laughed, but there was a commotion on the other line, the sound of voices. "I should go. I have a meeting with Aspen about catering for the retreat. It's only a few weeks away."

"You do what you need to do. I'll call you later."

Liam hung up and put his phone on mute, then took a moment to look out the window, the city flying by in a blur while raindrops battered the glass. Even with the scenery, he couldn't keep visions of his dad out of his head. Most sons probably had memories of playing catch or being taught how to ride a bike, but the closest Liam came to that were the times his dad had taken him out on the family yacht. Otherwise, Liam's remembrances were of his dad coming home well after dinner had been served, too tired to do much more than ruffle his son's hair and maybe ask about school. Liam was duly thankful for the hard work his father had put into growing Christopher Corporation. He only wished the man had taken a moment or two to breathe. Which might have had something to with him collapsing. Liam guessed his dad was suffering from exhaustion. It would likely be his job to tell his father to slow down.

The driver pulled up in front of his father's house, the one he bought after he'd divorced Liam's mother. Dad had left the family home to Mom, which had seemed kind at the time, although his mother managed to put it in a bad light, insisting that he'd only done it to stick her with the bad memories of the things that had led to the deterioration of their marriage. Liam had only been to this house five or six times in the five years since the divorce. How sad was that? Liam needed to change that. Maybe his dad's health scare was a wake-up call.

Liam took the stairs two at a time and ducked under

cover from the rain. His dad's housekeeper answered quickly.

"Liam. He's waiting for you. He's been asking about you." She turned and led the way down the large central hall, up the right side of the circular staircase and down the corridor to the double doors of his father's bedroom at the very end. With every step closer, the gravity of the situation seemed to bear down on him. This might be life or death. And since his father never remarried and Liam was an only child, he was left alone to deal with it.

The housekeeper opened the door and looked at Liam with entirely too much pity for his liking. "Be sure to speak softly. And don't raise the shades. The light bothers his eyes."

Liam was even more confused now. The day was as gray as could be. But he didn't ask. He just wanted to see his dad.

Ahead, his formidable father looked tiny in the elegantly dressed king-size bed. A nurse was there, checking his pulse. She turned and saw Liam and smiled thinly, as if she couldn't bear to share the bad news. As to what that was, Liam had no idea. He stepped closer and saw that his dad's eyes were shut.

"Is he sleeping?" Liam whispered to the nurse.

She shook her head. "Resting. It hurts his eyes right now. I'll be outside if you need me."

"Wait, I'm sorry. I don't understand. Collapsing hurt his eyes?"

"No." His father's voice was fragile. Like it might break. "Sit down, son. I'll explain."

Liam took the chair next to his bedside, reaching out for his hand. As soon as he touched him, his dad's eyes began to open, but he closed them quickly. "Dad. Talk to me. Are you okay?"

A smile slowly spread across his father's face. Liam had never seen him look so old or frail. This was not the strong man Liam knew. "I don't want you to get angry with me, but I've had a health situation for the past few years that's finally catching up with me."

"What kind of situation?"

"Brain cancer."

Liam suddenly felt like he couldn't breathe. "What? When did this happen? Is that why your eyes hurt?"

His father nodded. "It's pressing on the optic nerve. That part started a few days ago. I've been taking pain-killers, but they've stopped working."

"Well, we need to get the best doctors in here right away to see you."

"I've already seen the best doctors. I've been all over the world. Nobody can help me."

Liam was stuck between shock and disbelief. None of this felt real. "Why in the world did you keep this from me? Dad, why didn't you let me know this was going on?"

"I didn't want you to worry, and no father wants to admit to his son that he's not as strong as he's always tried to be. Plus, I didn't want anyone at the company to worry, either. There's nothing like a sick CEO to make everyone panic."

"But I'm your son. Didn't I deserve to know?"

His father nodded and took another peek from under his eyelids. "I thought I could beat it. Nobody likes to feel weak like this. But I have to surrender to it now."

The question was right on Liam's lips but he was ter-rified to ask. "How long do you have?"

"Days, Liam. That's why I sent for you right away. You're the most important person in my life. I need you to know that I believe in you. You are going to do great things. When you receive your copy of the will, you will see that you will be named CEO. Just as we've always discussed. You can steer the ship. I know I gave you a hard time about the Sasha project, but you were right about it. I never should have doubted you."

Liam squeezed his dad's hand, desperate to hold on to him. "It's okay. I like that we butted heads at work. It made things interesting."

His dad smiled, crinkles forming at the corners of his eyes. "I always admired that you weren't one to back down."

Liam sighed, his heart heavy. He could hardly believe this was happening. "Is there anything else I need to know about the succession plan or the company?"

"No. It's all sewn up, exactly like I told you. I want you to take the helm the instant I'm gone. It'll make for the smoothest transition if you're strong with it. Take command. Don't hesitate."

"I will."

"But there is something else. Something more personal I need to say."

"What's that?"

"Don't make the same mistakes I did. Don't live for your work. Will you promise me you'll fall in love and get married and have a whole litter of Christopher children?"

Liam had never discussed such things with his father, not even when Liam was a teenager and first interested in girls. His mother had given him the sex talk, and like most things with her, it had come with a touch of melodrama. "I'll do my best. I promise."

"Is there a lady in your life, Liam?"

Liam nodded. "There is. It's very new, but I like her a lot. It's actually someone you know. Someone who wanted me to send her best. Teresa St. Claire."

His father lifted his chin and an unusual look crossed his face. "Really? How wonderful. She's a lovely girl. So much drive and determination."

"I know. I get the distinct feeling I should stay out of her way."

His father laughed quietly. "She was the smartest student I've ever had. She understood business on a level that was uncanny. It came naturally to her and all she wanted was to learn more."

"And that's why you took her under your wing?" Liam nearly stopped breathing, waiting for the answer.

"That and I saw something special in her. She was going places. You know, your mother was convinced I had an affair with her. That was the beginning of the end of our marriage. She would never believe me that nothing had ever happened." His father's voice held the same conviction that Teresa's did when she spoke of this subject. Plus, his dad was opening himself up to Liam in a way he never had. He was putting it all on the line. There was no saving face today. There was no reason to lie. "Not that you want my opinion, but I approve of Teresa if she ends up being your wife."

Wife. Liam could only imagine such a thing in the vaguest sense of the word, like seeing a ghost or a mirage off in the distance. His parents had such a dysfunctional marriage. Seemingly loveless. Could he get it right? Or was he doomed to make the same mistakes? "That's good to know, Dad. I appreciate it."

The nurse stepped into the room. "Mr. Christopher, it's time for your pain medication."

His dad nodded. "Just one more minute with my son."

Liam took his dad's hand. "I'll come and see you tomorrow, okay? In the morning? We can have breakfast and talk some more." With his dad fading, Liam wanted to get everything he could out of these final days, especially with him being so open and honest. Liam had been waiting for that his entire life.

"I'd like that. Very much."

Liam rose and leaned down to kiss his father on the forehead. "I love you, Dad."

"I love you, too, son."

As he walked out of the room, Liam managed a smile at the nurse. Right before a tear rolled down his cheek.

Fourteen

Matt had been avoiding the office for an entire week, finding any excuse to meet people for lunch or coffee, any reason to hop in his car and drive to Portland or… anywhere other than Richmond Industries headquarters. It was simply too painful to walk past Nadia's desk several times a day and see someone else sitting there. All he could think about was how much better Nadia made his day with her beauty, brains and generous ways. Braydon, the temporary assistant HR had sent over, was competent, and he'd probably work out once he got up to speed, but he was also a stark reminder of who was no longer sitting outside Matt's office.

But he couldn't stay away today. It was Monday morning, which meant the weekly meeting with key staff. He had to steer the ship or at least nudge it in the right direction. The retreat was less than two weeks away. There were a million things to do. He was stressed, too. Liam had called a few days ago to tell him that his father was gravely ill. This had come as a shock to Matt, but Liam had sounded as if he'd been hit by a truck. They'd been talking every day since then. Matt mostly just listened as Liam tried to process what was happening.

Matt's phone rang and he was relieved to see it was Liam. "Hey, buddy. How are you doing? How's your dad?"

"He's gone, Matt. He died. Early this morning. I didn't even get to talk to him again. He was too sick to see me yesterday. I showed up at his house and I just got turned away."

Matt dropped his elbow onto his desk and kneaded his forehead. "Man, I am so sorry. Tell me where you are. I'll come to see you. I don't think you should be alone."

"No. No. It's fine. I'm at work and everyone is freaking out. People are crying. Hell, I had to send half of the accounting department home because they were so upset. I need to stay and keep things together. My dad was very clear about this. Everyone at the company needs to be reminded of the succession plan. They need to know that the transfer of power is instantaneous and seamless. They can't see me be anything but calm and collected."

Matt shook his head and leaned back in his chair. "Liam, your father just passed away. It's okay for you to feel bad or show some emotion right now. Nobody is going to blame you."

The other end of the line was quiet and that made it feel like Matt's heart was being ripped out. "I can't. I have to hold everything together."

This was so true of Liam. His family, the business—

he kept it all together. But who was going to keep Liam together? "That's what you do, isn't it? You keep everything together."

"I don't have a choice."

Matt sighed, resigned to the fact that he would never convince Liam to take a break. Not today. Perhaps it was best for him to soldier through the next eight hours and leave his grieving for home, where he could be alone.

Braydon poked his head into Matt's office. "I'm sorry to interrupt, but Teresa St. Claire is on the line. She says it's urgent."

Matt nodded and held up a finger to let Braydon know he needed a minute. "Hey, Liam. Teresa is on the other line. I think she's out at The Opulence, so I should probably take her call. It's probably about the retreat."

"Yeah. Yeah. Of course. Tell her I say hi."

How things had changed in a few short weeks. "How are things between you two?"

"Good. Fine."

"Is there a love connection there?"

"Love? No. We're friends."

Matt didn't want to press Liam any further. That could wait until later. Plus, Teresa was on the line. "Okay. I'll call you later to check on you." Matt ended the call on his cell and picked up his office line. "Teresa. How can I help you?"

"Can you tell me what your relationship is like with your brother?"

Matt nearly laughed, especially thinking about the horrible things that had transpired at his parents' house. "You have a few hundred hours for me to explain? Let's just say that it's adversarial at best. Why do you ask?"

"He was here at The Opulence over the weekend. He

made a bit of an impression on the staff. Drinking too much in the bar and, honestly, talking trash about you a fair amount. One of the bartenders said he bragged last night that he was behind the *TBG* stories."

Matt wasn't entirely surprised. Zach took any chance he could to embarrass Matt or make him look bad. Of course, he'd chosen one of Richmond Industries' most exclusive properties to smear his name. "Thank you for sharing, but I already knew about it. He threatened me with it the night I thought I was bringing Nadia to meet my parents. My brother basically broke Nadia and I up because of it."

"Well, that's not all your brother said. He was railing on Shayla, calling her a snake and saying that she'd forced him to do it. Something about blackmail and forcing Nadia out."

Matt froze in his seat. He could hardly believe what he was hearing. "Do you trust this bartender?"

"I do. I've spent a lot of time trying to get to know the staff. And it wasn't just the bartender who overheard. Aspen heard him say something, and so did Isabel Withers, the concierge. I wouldn't call you if I wasn't certain there was something to the story."

Matt was struggling to put this all together. "Why in the world would Shayla do that? She's one of my most trusted employees."

"I don't know, Matt. You'll have to ask her yourself. And then I think you need to speak to Nadia."

Oh, God. Nadia. She might kill Shayla with her small but capable hands if it turned out that she was behind the tabloid stories. "Thanks for this info. I really appreciate it."

"No problem. Have you heard from Liam?"

"I have. He told me about his dad."

"It's so sad. He called me early this morning, right after it happened. He's so upset. I'm trying to convince him to come relax for a few days out at The Opulence, but he's all wrapped up in the succession plan and the lawyers and the will." So there *was* a love connection between Liam and Teresa. "I'm hoping to see him tomorrow."

"Great. I'm sure he could use the company. And thank you for calling. I really appreciate it." Matt said goodbye to Teresa and called out to Braydon. "Can you get Shayla in here right away?"

Braydon nodded and picked up his phone, then sprang over to Matt's door. "She's on her way."

Matt got up from his desk and began pacing his office, going over the events of the last few weeks. It all made sense now, except that it didn't. He couldn't imagine what her motive would be. Why would she want to hurt the company she worked for? What could she possibly be blackmailing Zach with?

He didn't need to ask himself these questions for long, though. Shayla turned up in his doorway. "Braydon said you needed me."

Matt just looked at her, shaking his head in disbelief. "I need to ask you something and I need complete honesty."

"Of course. You always get the truth from me."

Matt was starting to think that might not be the case. "Are you behind the *TBG* stories? Are you blackmailing my brother?"

He waited for her to defend herself or blurt out that he was wrong, but she did nothing of the sort. Instead, she wandered over to one of the chairs opposite his desk and sat down. "I guess I'm not completely surprised that you found out, but I was hoping that I'd gotten away with it. Nadia's been gone for an entire week and the office is already a better place."

"What in the hell are you talking about?"

Shayla turned to him. "You weren't yourself when she was here. She was a distraction."

"That is not true. And who put you in charge? It's not your place to pull these kinds of strings behind the scenes."

She shook her head and looked down at her lap. "It's your fault, you know. It's not like I didn't try. Every day, Matt. Working hard. Dressing impeccably. Being at your beck and call. If you'd just noticed me, this never would have happened."

"Noticed you? I notice you all the time. You're a complete pain in my ass, but you're a great employee. What exactly were you wanting from me?"

She turned back to him then slowly rose out of the chair. "You. I wanted you, Matt. All that time I was with Zach, it was just to get closer to you. Why do you think I've stayed all these years?" She approached him like a tiger hiding in the tall grass, stalking her prey. "I've had a million job offers. I've had other companies throw money at me. But no, I stayed, because I kept hoping that you would wake up one day and see me as the woman who loves you."

Matt felt his eyes go wide with surprise. He had *not* seen this coming. "You told Zach that I was bringing Nadia to have dinner with our parents."

She kept approaching and Matt started backing up, wanting to stay away. "I had to do something. I heard that pathetic confession you made to Nadia at Gideon's party. I couldn't let you throw everything away like that. Zach had been calling me for weeks, trying to see if I could help him convince you to bring him back on board with the company. I decided to turn the tables on him and ask for a favor in return. As you know, an old friend of his owns *TBG*. I had to make him do the dirty work."

"What could you possibly blackmail Zach with?"

Shayla laughed. "Let me guess. He told you that he's cleaned up his act. Well, he hasn't. He's just as messed up as ever and has a ton of gambling debts. That's the real reason he's back pulling on the family purse strings. He needs the money."

It all made sense now. Of course Zach hadn't really put himself back together. He'd merely managed to make it look as though he had. The trouble was that he could never seem to do anything without making threats. That had always been one of his biggest downfalls. "Shayla, I'm your boss. I've never had a single romantic thought about you. I don't know why you would think I would. It's not appropriate."

Her jaw tightened. "Oh, you're my boss? Now you care about what's appropriate? You were willing to cross that line for Nadia, but you weren't willing to cross it for me?"

"Nadia was different." As soon as he'd said it and he heard his own words, he knew that Nadia was, indeed, different. He loved her. She was the only woman for him. And if he didn't act quickly, he might lose her forever. "Braydon," he called. "Get Security up here. Now."

Suddenly Shayla was like an animal backed into a corner. "You're calling Security on me? I will take you down, Matt Richmond. Even if I have to use Zach to do it."

"You can't hurt me any more than you already have, Shayla. You made me lose the woman I love."

For the first time during their exchange, Shayla looked truly hurt. "You love her?"

"I do. And now I'm going to beg her to take me back." He marched out of the room just as two members of the security team arrived. He looked back at Shayla, feeling nothing but pity for her. "Get her out of here. She's fired."

Nadia had not done well with her brief unemployment. It was not a break, nor was it a vacation. She tried to sleep in, but she only tossed and turned. She'd tried long walks and marathon trips to the gym, but those didn't help, either, especially when she saw people covering their mouths and whispering about her. It seemed that this time, everyone in Seattle had seen the tabloid dirt. This was what her life had become—she was blacklisted.

Even her family was embarrassed. She'd hoped they wouldn't find out about the tabloid story, but they had, and when they called her on it, some terrible words had come up. Words like *shameful*. Her parents were glad she'd quit Matt's company and begged her to come back to California, where she could get a normal job and live a quiet life. It was the last thing Nadia wanted. She knew there were professional challenges for her in Seattle. But she needed someone to take a chance on her and that person was Teresa. So, on her third day away from Richmond Industries, Nadia called Teresa and asked if she could have a trial employment period with Limitless Events.

She asked for no pay, and although she was willing

to work on the Richmond retreat, she wanted to do it behind the scenes. No one could know what she was doing, or where she was working, which was with Teresa. And that meant at The Opulence. Mostly she didn't want Matt to know.

He hadn't reached out once in the week they'd been apart, which was a good thing, but it had all changed today. In fact, he'd called three times and it was only early afternoon. She missed him terribly, but she was resigned to her fate and she wasn't going to call him back. She wouldn't even listen to the messages. They could be friends someday, but even with all of their work troubles aside, he wasn't prepared to give her what she wanted. He wasn't a man who was looking for the long haul. The sooner she learned to live with that, the better off she'd be.

Nadia was hunkered down in one of The Opulence meeting rooms with seating charts for the various meals to be served during the retreat when Teresa walked in. "Is there something wrong with your phone?" she asked.

Nadia picked it up and looked at it. Another message from Matt. "No. Matt keeps calling, so I haven't been answering it."

"Why? Don't want to talk to him?"

"What is there to say? Even with our work problems aside, he's not a commitment kind of guy, and that's all I've ever wanted. It's best if we stay away from each other for a while."

Teresa blew out a breath. "Well, I'm sorry, but I'm afraid that I outed you. He called me an hour ago and asked if I knew where you were, so I told him."

"You did what?"

Teresa shrugged. "Sorry. He insisted. He said it was life or death. He's on his way here right now."

Nadia got up from the table, now in a panic. She wasn't prepared to see Matt. She was wearing a very plain black skirt and boring white blouse and her hair was so frizzy from being around Centennial Falls all the time. "What do I do?"

"Go out to the lobby, wait for him to arrive and see what he has to say?"

Nadia stormed past Teresa and out into the hall. "That's not super helpful."

"Sorry. I'm no relationship expert. Ask anyone."

"Oh, my God. I can't believe this is happening." Nadia strode down the hall, her heart threatening to pound its way out of her throat. She had to prepare herself for what Matt might say. If he asked to get back together, she was going to have to stay strong and say no. And if he asked her something else, well, she couldn't imagine what that might be, so she'd just have to wing it. It then occurred to her that he might simply need something work-related. But that didn't make sense, either. Why would a guy as busy as Matt drive all the way out to The Opulence to ask her a question?

She was heading for the lobby when she heard a voice behind her.

A voice that made her clamp her eyes shut as a million feelings came roaring back to life. "Nadia. I've been looking for you everywhere."

She turned, and the minute she laid eyes on Matt, the notion of being strong went right out the window. She'd have to fake it. "What are you doing here?" Knowing that if she got any closer to him, she'd only get weaker, she stood her ground.

It was Matt who closed the gap between them. "I left you messages. Shayla was behind everything, not Zach." He looked down at the ground and stuffed his hands into his pockets. "Actually, Zach still played his part, but Shayla blackmailed him. So she could get rid of you."

"What did I ever do to her?" Nadia was still trying to catch up to the things Matt had just said.

"It was my fault. She said she was in love with me and had been for years. I know it sounds crazy, but you were the one who got in the way."

Nadia had to laugh, even though it was a short-lived chuckle. "I told you she had it for you." She took zero solace in being right. "I'm glad you figured out the mystery. At least I know now why I lost my job."

"You could come back if you wanted to."

She shook her head, thankful Teresa had taken a chance on her. It made it easier to say no to Matt. "I'm working for Limitless now. It's on a trial basis, but Teresa and I work well together. I think it's going to be good for me."

"I am so happy to hear that. You're going to do an amazing job." His eyes filled with hope, and that made Nadia's heart sink. She loved Matt. She didn't want him to think there was a chance. "Which brings me to the subject of us and back to the subject of Shayla."

"You know I had to leave for reasons that go way beyond Shayla. Your family, and your willingness to commit. Both huge problems."

Matt was quick to shake his head. He took her hand. "First off, I called my parents right after I talked to Shayla. They can't believe what she and Zach got up to. They feel terrible that he lied to everyone. They feel terrible for you. They want to meet you. For real. Just the four of us. No creepy brothers allowed."

Nadia smiled. This was so sweet, and a few weeks ago this would have been the best news ever. "That's nice to hear, but—"

"No. Wait. Hold on. Let me get the rest of this out. Because the rest of this is all on me. I love you, Nadia Gonzalez. I love you more than words can explain. And I'm sorry that I didn't say that while we were together, but I'm saying it now. I realized it this morning after all of the craziness with Shayla. That's why I've been calling. That's why I left messages and drove all the way up here."

Nadia didn't move. She couldn't speak. Hell, she could hardly blink. "You love me? I love you, too."

A purely happy smile crossed his face. "I love you so much that I can't ever let you go. I can't let you out of my sight. I want you forever." And then Matt Richmond, the man she had once thought could never be for her, knelt and looked up into her eyes, holding her hand tightly and filling her with so much love and optimism that she thought her heart might burst. "Will you stay with me forever? Will you be my wife?"

"Yes. Oh, my God. Yes." She tugged on his hand. "Now get up here and kiss me."

Matt stood and swept her into his arms, holding her so tightly that he lifted her feet off the ground. The kiss was warm and soft and absolutely perfect. He was the man she loved and she had him. Forever.

Somewhere off in the distance, she heard applause, which she was sure was just her heart, but then Matt set her back on the floor and she turned to see the lobby full of people clapping. Isabel, Aspen, Teresa, the guys from the valet stand, the bellhops and guests had seen it all. Nadia couldn't even be embarrassed. She was just too happy.

"Congratulations." Teresa gave them each a hug, then took Nadia's hand. "No ring, Matt?"

Matt's shoulders dropped. "I know, I know. I should have come prepared, but I didn't want to wait." He then turned to Nadia and took her hand, bringing it to his lips. "Plus, you should have the chance to pick out whatever you want. I was thinking Tiffany's. In New York."

Was this really her life now? Wow. "Uh, sure. That sounds amazing. I guess we could go sometime after the retreat."

He shook his head. "I was thinking tomorrow night. I have a few things I need to catch up on, but I want you to have a ring as soon as possible. We'll just go for a day or two."

Nadia turned to Teresa. "Is that going to be okay with you? I just started work."

Teresa smiled. "Of course. Who am I to stand in the way of true love?"

Fifteen

Teresa had to admit that watching Matt profess his love for Nadia had certainly put her in a romantic mood. It had been such a sweet moment, and it was so nice to see things work out for them. Today they would be flying off to New York so Matt could take Nadia to Tiffany & Co. for a ring. Teresa would've been jealous if she didn't have her own prize waiting for her back in Seattle. Her dinner with Liam.

She'd been in the car for about a half hour when he called. "Hello?" she answered over the speakerphone.

"So there's a slight change of plans if that's okay."

"I'm already on my way back."

"We're still having dinner. But not at my place. I was hoping we could take out my boat. It was one of the few things my dad and I used to do together and I thought it would be a good way to honor his memory." Just when she was about to mention that she was not much of a fisherman, he continued. "It's nice. I promise. You'll be comfortable."

Honestly, all she wanted was to see him and pick up where they'd left off. "Okay, great."

"Also, you should know that I have my copy of my dad's will and I'm waiting until tonight to open it."

"Why would you wait?"

"It's going to be emotional and I wanted to be away from the office and my house when I did it. Plus, my dad liked you a lot. That means something."

Teresa sighed. She really enjoyed this softer side of Liam. "That all sounds wonderful. Just tell me where to meet you."

"I'll text you the info. How long will you be?"

"I'm a half hour away now. Do I have time to go home and change?"

"I don't really see the point. You won't be wearing clothes for long."

A smile crossed Teresa lips and she ran her fingers along the stitching on the steering wheel. "You make a compelling case. I'll come straight over."

"Good. I can't wait."

Teresa hung up, but found her phone ringing again right away with an unknown number. She really needed a break, but that would have to come after the retreat. For now, she had to answer. "Hello?"

"Hey, sis."

She sat a little straighter in her seat. "Joshua. How are you? Is everything okay?" She hadn't received any more phone calls after Liam's guy checked on Josh. *Please let nothing be wrong now.*

"Everything is fine. I've got everything worked out. Just stop checking on me all the time, okay?"

"Well, maybe if you'd called me back on a more regular basis, I wouldn't need to do that."

"I'm busy, okay. I'm working. I have to have a job, you know."

"Does this job involve things that are legal?" She couldn't take it if Joshua ended up in jail. She'd worked so hard to keep him out. And, of course, she could only imagine trying to explain it to her mother. Teresa was responsible one way or another, whether she liked it or not.

"Yes. I promise. Everything is fine." He sighed heavily. "Look, I know you've always been there for me, but you're not Mom. I can take care of myself. At some point, you're going to have to trust me to do what's right."

A little piece of Teresa felt like it was dying. She'd cared for her brother for as long as she could remember. Forget responsibility. It was her instinct to do it. "I know. I hope you can appreciate why I want to protect you. I love you." Tears began to well at the corners of her eyes.

"I love you, too. Everything is going to be fine. I promise."

His voice was clear and strong and that made her want to believe that things really would be okay. "Good. I'm glad to hear it."

"Cool. Well, I have stuff to do. I'll try to call more often. Bye."

"Bye." Teresa hung up and was overcome with a feeling she didn't have very often—calm. Things were working out. They were falling into place. Who knew that was even possible? Her phone beeped with the text from Liam. She clicked on the link and it pulled up the navigation for Shilshole Bay Marina.

When she arrived, Teresa parked her car, grabbed her Fendi bag and a jacket and made her way over to the docks. There was a wide array of boats out, but no sign of Liam until she heard him shouting her name. "Teresa! Over here!"

She turned and he was at the far end, standing at the end of a gangplank next to quite possibly the largest yacht she had ever seen. She rushed up to him, nearly running in heels. He was smiling and when he swiped off his sunglasses, his intense gaze met hers. For a moment, the rest of the world faded away. The seabirds overhead, the other people on the docks and the hum of the marina became nothing more than a blurry backdrop. Her entire focus was Liam. She savored the sexy way he refused to let their connection drop. It was a thunderbolt straight to the heart.

"How are you?" he asked, grasping her elbows and placing a soft kiss on her lips.

"I'm great. Also, you are a liar. This is not a boat. This is more like a floating city."

He laughed and put his sunglasses back on. "Just wait until you get on board. Then I'll really blow your mind." His hand settled on the small of her back and he ushered her across the gangplank, where a deckhand stood sentry at the very end.

"Wow," Teresa said when she stepped down onto the main deck. "How big is this thing?"

"It's a sixty-eight-meter BNow. Three upper decks above the main deck, two lower—one for me and guests, one for the staff. There's a hot tub and a table for ten out on the aft deck."

Teresa walked ahead with Liam by her side, the wind in her hair as she admired her surroundings. This was just absolutely stunning, with a glossy wood deck and gleaming chrome. Pure luxury with a large outdoor seating area filled with inviting loungers and colorful pillows. Beyond was the hot tub he'd mentioned, which would afford fabulous sea views. With all of it set against the beautiful backdrop of deep blue sea and the slowly setting sun, it felt nothing short of both lavish and romantic. It was like stepping into an instant vacation. And with an incredibly sexy man, to boot.

"Come inside," he said, taking her hand again. "We have champagne and I have something I want to ask you."

Liam had already surprised her greatly with the yacht. She couldn't imagine what else he had in store. But as he tugged on her hand, urging her to join him, she knew she was prepared for anything this man had to offer. Anything at all.

Just as the boat was leaving the dock, Liam led Teresa into the main living space on the boat, an expansive living room with a sleek modern sectional sofa and a huge television, although there was no point in ever turning it on. The 360-degree view from that room was the real focus. Of course, now Liam was focused on gathering his strength to ask Teresa the question he'd been pondering. But first, champagne.

He unwrapped the foil and popped the cork on a bottle of Krug, then filled two flutes. He offered one to Teresa and held his for a toast. "To my father."

She smiled warmly. "Yes. To your father. He raised an amazing son."

Liam took a sip, appreciating Teresa's sentiment, but unsure he could really live up to a label like amazing.

Losing his dad was making him see everything through a very different lens, but the good side of that was he knew he needed to focus on his life outside work. Hopefully a life that could include Teresa.

"You had a question?" she asked, perching on the back of the sofa.

He took a deep breath. "Yes. But first I want to say that I like you, Teresa. I have launched some terrible accusations at you, and not always been on my best behavior and you weren't afraid to stand up to me."

She arched an eyebrow at him, her blue eyes shifting to a darker shade. "I had to defend myself. And I couldn't live with you believing those things about me."

"Absolutely. As it should be. But when you're a man in my position, not many people challenge you. And I think I need that. So, thank you." He swallowed hard. "And so I wanted to ask if you'd be interested in us staying together during the retreat at The Opulence. We'll both be incredibly busy, but I think we both know we'll have a hard time staying away from each other."

"I'll definitely need to blow off some steam."

He took her hand and raised it to his lips. "Take it all out on me. Please."

She stood and led him over to the sofa, where they sat close. "I like you, too, Liam. A lot. You might be the most complex man I've ever met."

A breathy laugh escaped his lips. "That's a good thing?"

"It makes me want to dig past the layers to find the real you."

Liam's fingers went to her jaw and her eyes met his. "I hope you find what you're looking for." He kissed her softly, relishing the way she nearly melted into him. It made him so eager for more time alone with her.

From across the room, Liam heard someone clear their throat. He and Teresa quickly separated, both a bit startled. It was the chief steward, standing with his hands behind his back. "Mr. Christopher, I'm sorry to interrupt, but dinner will be served in an hour."

"Great. Thank you."

"I guess there's no real privacy on a boat, huh?" Teresa asked, sitting back and sipping more of her champagne.

"There will be. Later." Liam glanced down at the coffee table and the thick envelope waiting for him. He hadn't even peeked inside. Something had told him that it wasn't a good idea to be alone when he read the documents, but Matt was leaving for New York this evening with Nadia, and Teresa had indeed been close to his dad. "I guess I'll take this chance to take a look at my dad's will. Get it over with. It won't take long."

Teresa nodded eagerly. "Yes. Of course. Open it."

Liam sat back and opened the flap, pulling out the thick sheaf of papers. "Just a little light reading," he joked.

"Anything in particular you're looking for?"

He began flipping through the pages. "No. Not really. My dad and I discussed it the day he told me he was sick. So I think I know pretty much everything. Of course, I have to make sure it's all in order."

"Of course. A lot of money on the line."

"And the company." Liam leaned forward and took another drink, then went back to reading. "I hope I'm not boring you with this."

Teresa reached out and rubbed his shoulder affectionately. "It's not boring to me. This is your future. And your past. I'm honored to be a part of it. It makes me feel good to know you wanted to include me."

Liam began looking through the personal assets. The vacation house in Bali. His father's yacht, which was moored in the Cayman Islands. The winery and villa in Tuscany. "There's a lot of property on this list. I'm going to need to hire someone just to deal with all of it."

Teresa's eyes lit up. "Ooh. Like what?"

Liam's sights returned to the document. "Mountain house in Switzerland? How does that strike you?"

She patted his leg. "Sounds lovely. Now which way to the ladies' room?" She got up from her seat and Liam pointed her in the direction the steward had taken.

"Right back there. First door on the right."

"Perfect. I'll be right back."

Liam's phone beeped with a text and he pulled it out of his pocket. It was from Matt, a photo of Nadia and him on Matt's jet. Just like he and Teresa, they were toasting with champagne. The message read:

On our way to the Big Apple. See you in two days.

Liam couldn't help but smile at his phone. It felt so damn good to know that Matt had found happiness. True love, no less. Could Liam have that ahead? Was it possible? One step at a time, of course, but it was hard not to think he was on the right track with Teresa.

He tapped out a reply to Matt.

Have fun. Love you guys.

Liam returned to his reading and the long list of personal effects. His father or his lawyer had been very thorough. There were pages and pages of watches and cars and plots of land all over the world. Impatient, Liam flipped ahead to the sections about the business. He just wanted to make sure that everything was in order, that he'd explained the succession plan accurately and that there were no surprises. The stability of the company, especially in light of the passing of its founder and CEO, was of paramount importance.

But when he reached the section where it was supposed to say that one hundred percent of his father's personal stake of the company went to Liam, there was a single detail he had never, ever imagined. Something that made it feel like his heart had not only stopped, but that it might also not ever beat again.

75% of personal stake in Christopher Corporation to Liam Christopher

And…

25% of personal stake in Christopher Corporation to Teresa St. Claire

Teresa returned from the bathroom, looking refreshed. "What'd I miss?"

Liam felt sick. Truly, truly sick. Everything that had been so perfect a few seconds ago had just gone up in smoke. He closed his eyes and took a deep breath before saying what he had to say. "I can't believe you lied to me."

* * * * *